The Printer and the Strumpet

Black Tie
BOOKS

Praise for
The Printer & The Strumpet

"A sharp, media-centric satire set in a rebellious America, *The Printer and The Strumpet* is a fun and satisfying read."
— KIRKUS REVIEWS

"This isn't your usual historical novel. The result offers a particularly clever view of the nation's first birth pangs, told in a lively, fast-paced style."
— BLUEINK REVIEWS

"Clever…compelling…a pure farce. In the entertaining historical novel, *The Printer and the Strumpet*, the American Revolution is seen from the perspective of a flawed wordsmith."
— FOREWORD CLARION REVIEWS

"Brill's comedic flair and assured writing make for page-turning fun."
— SCOTT SEMEGRAN, AUTHOR OF *THE BENEVOLENT LORDS OF SOMETIMES ISLAND*

"A witty novel that slays the absurd notion left by most historical fiction that we, the founders of this great nation, had no sense of humor. Hilarious."
— BENJAMIN FRANKLIN

More good stuff by Larry Brill

The Patterer
Book #1 in the Misadventures of Leeds Merriweather Trilogy

Live at Five
Life, Death and Laughs in a small town TV newsroom

Déjà vu All Over Again
Award-winning comedy of life's ultimate second chance

Black Tie
B O O K S

Published by Black Tie Books

Austin, Texas

Copyright © 2021 by Larry Brill

Cover design © 2021 Brill Graphic Design, Inc.

The Library of Congress has catalogued the trade paperback edition as follows:

Brill, Larry

The Printer and The Strumpet / by Larry Brill

ISBN: 978-0-9960834-4-7

Printed in the United States of America

First Edition

10 9 8 7 6 5 4 3 2 1

This is a work of fiction. The names, characters, places and incidents mentioned here are either a product of the author's imagination, or, in the case of famous but long-dead forefathers and well-hashed out historical events, used for your enjoyment and may not bear any resemblance to reality. Did we mention this is a work of fiction?

www.larrybrill.com

Lar@larrybrill.com

Chapter One
A Reckless Goat

Boston 1773

It was the best of times, it was the worst of times. It was an age of reason when...

When what? Well, when reasonable men should be reasonable, I suppose.

"Flog the frog!" I cursed.

I looked at the words I had written and felt disgusted. I scratched them through with the ink-armed tip of my quill, cursing the gods above from A to Z—Apollo to Zeus—and every minor deity in between, giving no quarter for whether they represented Team Christian or Team Heathen.

Best of times? Worst of times? Rubbish. No self-respecting author would use words so trite to begin an important piece of literature, yet I was having a dickens of a time coming up with anything better. And yet, they did seem to capture the spirit of our current affairs.

Inside Boston's Reckless Goat Tavern, I sat at my usual table next to the massive oak pillar that was as solid as a sentry at one edge of the bar. The crowd was sizable for a Tuesday, and the tavern at the foot of Long Wharf had a raucous spirit, filled with clusters of sweaty longshoremen, tradesmen, and red-coated soldiers from one of His Majesty's regiments on a quick leave from their garrison on the Commons. The crowd mostly ignored a pair of performers in feathered caps wandering through the room making music with a fiddle and mandolin, which added a pleasant harmony to the hum of conversation. As they passed my table I raised my glass, winked at the fiddler, and tipped him with a shilling I slipped into his waistcoat pocket.

I dipped the tip of my quill into the inkpot, holding it in a grip that was both confident and gentle whilst I waited for my muse.

And waited more.

With my left hand I lifted a glass of modest Portuguese Madeira to my lips, relaxed in the smoky glow of light from a lantern on a peg above my head. I was laboring to author a pamphlet addressing the political fever that had gripped the town. Actually, I had been struggling to write the damned thing for several weeks and had gone to the Reckless Goat that night hoping the liveliness of a public inn and a bottle of wine might provide inspiration to finish the manuscript. Finding the perfect opening sentence befuddled me most.

The title was fine. More than fine, truly. It was rather brilliant, in my humble opinion. I had crafted it in my finest hand across the top of the page, dressing the letters with a flourish, and now I stroked it with a tender finger as one might tickle the fancy spot of a good woman.

Treason or Reason: A Guide to Navigating a Divided Land.

Nice, I thought. I dreamed the pamphlet could have some measure of influence on public opinion, a work that might bridge the chasm tearing Boston apart, so badly needed at that moment in time. It was as if my adopted town had split into two cities. Loyalists to the King of England on one end and aggrieved liberal colonists on the other. No one had yet come out in print to take the middle ground and promote peace, so I could see no one better suited than myself to publish a work encouraging pacifists to rise up and smack the snot out of both.

You see, I am a journalist, a wordsmith with a printing press at my disposal and a modest following for the newspaper I published, the *New England News-Journal.* I relied on the brawn of my back to work the press and the strength of my words to inform the public and frequently shape opinions. I took another sip of wine. A large sip because I needed to quench thirst for two—the muse and myself. I reloaded my weapon, put that quill to paper, and began again.

Now is the time for all good men to come to the aid of their...

Their what? Their fellow fellows?

More rubbish. Damn! I crossed that out too. The mother-flogging muse was playing me for a fool. Since it was Tuesday, I had purchased copies of that morning's editions of the *Boston Gazette* and the *Weekly News-Letter,* and spread them open on the tabletop, along with three copies of my own. I placed the *News-Journal* prominently on the edge of the table with the masthead beckoning attention to anyone who might pass by.

"Buy me," it called to the curious, like a strumpet at Flagg Alley or any other bordello in Boston. "Let me entertain you for a mere two pence-half penny."

I looked again at my feeble attempt to start my pamphlet. I envisioned, after some judicious editing, it would take six small pages. Eight at most. We must not be too wordy. Sadly, politics were not really my cup of tea. No, I didn't do politics well. Give me blood and lust, scandal and misfortune, criminal and marital misdeeds of public figures intertwined in gossip-birth coitus. It sells newspapers and I could write blood and lust like nobody's business. In fact, I had a saying about those kinds of stories that I would prefer to feature front and centered in the *News-Journal.* If it bleeds, it…

"Leeds!"

That's me. The bark of my name exploded in my ear like a musket shot at close range. The hearty slap on the back that followed rocked me as if its ball had hit its mark.

"Leeds Merriweather, you pitiful excrement-producing son of a snake in the pulp," Jacob Addison hollered. He was a solid man, round in shape with beady eyes and a nose that was only slightly less sharp than his wit.

"Mr. Addison," I said. I laid down my quill and hit him with my most withering stare. "If you were not the offspring of a skirt-dropping Tory lover, I would take exception to that remark. As it is, I cannot hold your mother's rogue breeding habits against you."

Jacob Addison was my most cherished friend and confidant. I loved him more than my own brothers, though one of those played a significant role in my being banished from the family estate in England when I was a mere teenager, so I will admit my standards were justifiably low by the time I escaped to America seven years ago.

"Leeds, if I actually believed in hell, I would damn you for eternity. But that would be an utter waste of fire and brimstone." He dropped onto the bench across the table from me, holding one hand on the mouth of his tankard to avoid wasting a single drop of ale.

I smiled. Typical Jacob. He was born into a wealthy, established Boston family. Harvard College provided him with divinity training and a bright future in the clergy, but he failed as a Congregationalist pastor primarily because he severely lacked the ability to accept dogma. For three years he shepherded the flock at a church on White Street, where he avoided the trap of Christian hypocrisy by allowing those who filled its pews to vote democratically on matters of faith. A sound idea if you don't think about it too hard. In practice, however, his followers appeared to change doctrine more often than they changed their knickers.

He scanned the newspapers spread across the table between us and gave only a brief glance at the foolscap of useless scribble that I had been working on.

The *Boston Gazette*, in particular, seized Jacob's attention. He raised it, opened to page two, and smacked it with the back of his meaty hand. "My God! Will you look at this?"

I merely shrugged.

"Did you see this wretched piece?"

"I saw it," I replied.

"The *Gazette* is attacking you. It's dastardly, I must say. You should read it."

"Yes, Jacob. I have. Several times."

The *Boston Gazette and Country Journal* was unquestionably the most influential newspaper in the Massachusetts Bay Province and surrounding colonies. Isaiah Thomas' *Massachusetts Spy* had a greater reach, with thousands of subscriptions all the way down to the Carolinas, but if you were a bleeding heart liberal Whig with fantasies of rubbing King George's nose in rancid Thames River muck, *Gazette* publisher Benjamin Edes and his main contributor, Samuel Adams, published your newspaper of choice.

The latest edition featured a lengthy lynching of Parliament over the Tea Act and Massachusetts Governor Hutchinson's enthusiastic vow to enforce the law at all costs. It was all the normal things you would expect from Sam Adams, unmistakable in style and tone even though he authored it under the pseudonym *F. Muck Raker.*

"It has Samuel Adams written all over it," I said. "Poor syntax, random capitalization, and truth as loose as a goose. No, this is Sam-the-sham's work, for certain. Not that I was paying attention."

"Of course not." Jacob winked at me. He pointed to a paragraph well down in the piece that cut from the bottom of the second column and jumped to the top of the third column.

> The **WEAK-KNEED** publication, New England News-Journal, like many a Tory sympathizer, will **NOT** stand up for the rights of man, **OUR RIGHTS** as Americans, whilst hiding behind a thin veil of what it purports to be common sense and objectivity. It is time for all American publications to **TAKE A STAND**, yet it is clear that--for this failing newspaper--fealty to Governor Hutchinson the **AUTOCRAT TRUMPS** all else.

"Why attack you? Because you refuse to take a strong stance?" He asked and snorted like a horse with a head cold. Then he read a bit more silently. When he looked up again, he asked, "Are you really a mealy-mouth marmot? What did you do? Bed his wife?"

"I don't know. I might have. What does she look like?"

He laughed. I laughed. And yet I fretted. As much as I wanted to shrug off Adams' jab at my newspaper, it was not easy. Two weeks previous I had bashed the bugger in a *News-Journal* piece, suggesting that Adams had a hand in stoking anger amongst the Sons of Liberty that led to various acts of violence disguised as protest. I must have tweaked his nose when I wrote that tar and feathering Tories was excessive mob behavior.

Keep calm and carry on, I proposed.

So as I sat in the Reckless Goat that night, I pondered the masthead of the *Gazette* and wondered if Sam Adams' words might provoke an attack on my business. Last week, the Sons of Liberty ransacked William Baker's luxury import shop after Adams called for boycotting Tory merchants. Would I be next? I took the quill, scratched three exclamation points on the foolscap next to my pamphlet title, and vowed silently to be more wary in public just in case Adams had planted a seed of retribution in the thick skulls of a mob.

Jacob's eyes, red though they were, twinkled behind a haze of inebriation. "Your passion for apathy is an inspiration, Leeds. But that doesn't excuse Mr. Adams to single you out for vicious attacks simply because you choose to remain neutral."

"Honestly, Jacob, it becomes more difficult with each passing day with journals like this." I poked *The Gazette* and judged it with a bit of envy. Four sheets. Three pence. A way with rhetoric that grows an audience daily. Priceless.

I let the next sip of wine rest on my tongue longer than necessary, looking to the far side of the tavern. Hannah, the barmaid, backed spritely away from the groping hands of two red-coated soldiers, part of His Majesty's Twenty-ninth Regiment. A very large, rough-looking bloke at the table next to them jumped to her rescue. Both sides were spoiling for a fight. There was a good deal of profanity and posturing that stopped short of blows. I nodded in that direction. "Do you see that? This town could very well go to war over a mere dispute in the tavern."

That would not be good. I was only recently feeling comfortable with my lot in life, having achieved my lifelong dream to command a printing press and an influential (if limited in sales) newspaper. And I was deeply in debt still for the effort. *The*

News-Journal was my pride and joy but it did not make much income. It was the government contracts, printing official documents, pamphlets, maps, public notices and such that kept me in business. Several Tories close to the governor's circle provided monthly revenues as I printed for them books, business advertisements, and calling cards—and, in the case of Pastor Graham Franklin, selling his wildly popular monthly sermon guaranteed to be your stairway to heaven for a mere two shillings-six per edition. Pastor Franklin was the governor's spiritual advisor and supporter from the pulpit. And so if my flaccid politics had a most practical motivation, it came with being in bed, financially if not literally at least, with the governor and his pals.

Now, all that I worked for could go up in flames unless somebody could tamp out the smoldering resentment building on both sides.

Jacob understood this more than most. It was his father who established the print shop and the *New England News-Journal* thirty years ago. He owned several other businesses but had a fondness for print. I worked for the old man for three years until Spencer Addison's health failed. When Jacob took over the family's holdings, he offered to sell me the print shop and the newspaper in exchange for a mountain of debt. I still owed more than a thousand pounds, to be paid off with interest. It was my dream; what can I say?

I lit my pipe and then exhaled a pleasant stream, adding to the haze of tobacco smoke that shaded the air in the tavern with a ghostly effect. A soft pillow of flesh, bound in a barmaid's shift, pressed gently against the spot behind my ear as Hannah appeared from nowhere, leaned over me to pour ale from her pitcher, and filled Jacob's tankard. The scent of rose petals after a spring rain replaced the smoke in my nostrils. It was more intoxicating than the drinks she served. As she leaned back, I turned and admired the lace rising to her left shoulder, and the lace rising to her right shoulder and lingered on the cleavage in the valley of her neckline between them. She rewarded me with a smile, and placed another bottle of wine on the table.

"I believe she fancies you," Jacob said after Hannah glided away to serve the longshoremen.

I scoffed. "Nonsense."

"No? She nearly tripped in eagerness to service you, planting her bosom, quite deliberately I assume, against your inebriated noggin, while I sit here ignored to the point of death. You can't fool me, Leeds. I have seen the way your eyes follow Hannah as they did after the brush she gave you with her blouse. Not only did you chase her skirt with your eyes, but were I to inspect further, I would find your loins were not far behind."

"You are married, Jacob. And she has a beau, I hear. No, my friend, as much as I appreciate her ability to raise my, uhm, interest, if you will…"

"Are talking carnality?" Jacob interrupted me with a snicker.

"Call it what you will. Nevertheless, I know it is nothing more than an agreeable way to enlarge…"

"Your carnality?"

"Enlarge the gratuities she collects at the end of the night."

I directed his lewd attention to Hannah serving a rowdy group several tables behind him. We watched as Hannah laughed with three men seated there, exchanged tantalizing glances with each one as if he suddenly, for that one moment, became the only man in the universe, and proceeded to serve each one with the same, suggestively innocent physical contact that she had bestowed upon me.

"Ah, just as well, I say." Jacob winked at me. "No woman could ever compete with your true mistress, that alluring printing press of yours. It has always been so for you. Though you are getting on in years. Thirty years is not so far away. I will tell you once more, we need to get you a woman. One of flesh and blood." He laughed. "With maybe a dash of carnality?"

I took the quill and held it like a dagger that I feigned plunging into my heart. He was right, more than I was willing to admit. The work of the print shop had become satisfying, and yet I found myself thinking more often of how my life needed more. My life needed a woman.

"But not just any woman," I told Jacob.

Nearly seven years in America and I had yet to find one to capture my heart with the perfect combination of wit and a zest for life to match her loving soul and feminine charms. Yes, I was lonely.

On that dispiriting note, and after a wistful silence, Jacob said he was off. His regular game of dice was waiting for him. He left me alone with my uninspired muse, though since neither of us could find the words we needed, we surrendered for the evening.

Before leaving I required a trip to the privy in the yard behind the tavern. I had barely exited the little house and started my return to the public room when voices stopped me. Two figures wrestled in the light of a lantern near the tavern wall. My initial embarrassment at stumbling upon what I assumed were passionate lovers gave way to confusion and anger. I recognized Hannah and her most drunken patron. It was clear she wanted none of him, and yet he persisted, tearing at her clothing.

I lunged forward to the rescue, but before I had taken two steps I was knocked to one knee by a soldier who materialized from nowhere. He set upon the drunken beast, pulling him off Hannah who he had pinned to the ground. With ease, the redcoat cast the attacker aside and threatened him with severe violence if he did not retreat immediately. Then the soldier removed his coat and placed it over the girl to protect her bodice-ripped modesty. Her attacker rose up over the soldier. Too late, I climbed to my feet and tried to stop him as he drove a knife into the soldier from behind. I chased the coward out of the yard but tripped on some discarded lumber.

"Mother flogging bugger," I cursed. That hurt. Blood oozed from where a nail had scratched me above my right eye. I wiped it with my sleeve but did little more than smear it along my cheeks and neck.

I turned back. Hannah was gone. The soldier was alive, a small boot knife still buried in his back. I knelt and offered him encouraging words. The wound was not deep, and I removed the knife quickly. Give credit to the young redcoat. He flinched with less agony than I might if I had been on the wrong end of that blade.

I wiped again at the blood on my face. A commotion at the door of the tavern near the corner of the building was a clear signal. The British were coming.

"Thank god. Reinforcements," I said to the soldier with a grin.

I rose to greet them and handed their leader the attacker's knife. Whatever relief I felt was crushed in the confusion of the moment and then panic when, before I realized it, I was pinned against the wall by a burly soldier at each shoulder as the tip of their commander's sword prepared to carve the Adam's apple from my throat.

Chapter Two
News, Views, and Alternative Facts

I thought I was going to die.

Not from the redcoat's blade that night, nor the beating they inflicted whilst hauling me to the Boston Gaol. Not even from the subsequent four days spent in a jail cell with three large, ugly miscreants whose threats, coupled with their imposing physical bulk and bullying attitudes, left me on guard and sleepless for the length of my stay.

No, I thought I was going to die from mortification. That Isaiah Thomas had printed an account of the tussle behind the tavern in *The Massachusetts Spy* before I could publish the story in my own newspaper was an affront to my pride. The fact that he got so much of it wrong only salted my wound.

My friend David Deerfield, proprietor of the Star Coffee House near my print shop in Hanover District, brought a copy of the latest *Spy* with him on Friday, the day of my release. He also advanced me four pounds to bribe the magistrate and secure my freedom a day earlier than schedule.

"That's not justice; that's robbery is what it is," David grumbled as we departed the jail late that afternoon. The sun was low in the sky but the weather pleasant for early November. "Did I not warn you or did I not?"

I sighed. "I never expected I'd find out for myself."

I paused outside the drive in to the courthouse and jail on Queen Street, allowing my eyes to adjust to the afternoon light. Across from us the *Boston Gazette* held down the corner lot at the entrance to Dashett Alley. A Father with a child in hand stood near its door, obviously reading the latest edition tacked upon the wall. I pulled David in that direction, eager to find out if they had reported the Reckless Goat incident as well.

Having to admit David had foresighted my trouble with the law added to the resentment that left me seriously miffed, to put it mildly. David had urged caution the previous spring before I published a criticism of Governor Hutchinson's new tax on criminal behavior. Everyone, regardless of guilt or innocence, would have to pay a daily institutional fee for food and bedding while in lockup. The governor's third cousin on his mother's side, Chief Magistrate Welford Pendergast, was assigned to collect those fees. Did I heed David's warning? Hah! Skunk spittle, I said at the time. The report caused a flap over nepotism and unwarranted taxation, another embarrassment for the administration. And then, sadly, it was that same Judge Pendergast who presided over my hearing.

"That mother-flogging bastard was all set to let me go free," I said after we had crossed the street and leaned in to read *The Gazette* posted on the wall. I slapped David's arm with the back of my hand, using more force than I had intended. "Sorry 'bout that. But damn it, even after Lawyer Paine provided sworn testimony of my innocence from both Hannah and the soldier, Pendergast cited me just the same."

A stray dog came sniffing me and I kicked it, so that the fur ball might experience how I felt about my treatment at the hands of the court. Boot in this case.

"Sorry that," I apologized to the mutt. I like dogs but such was my frame of mind. The father standing between me and the paper on the wall turned, gave me the skunk eye, and pulled his little boy down the street.

The magistrate found me innocent in the soldier's assault, but after noting that I had authored the critical newspaper article last year, he cited me for disorderly public conduct and imposed two additional days in jail along with a fine to be delivered directly to his chambers instead of the court's treasurer.

"I swear," David said. "The governor is putting all his Loyalist cronies in place, taking over all the courts. Justice is a joke in this town."

"Do you see me laughing?" I said. Then I stopped, faced David, and quickly raised my palm. "Yes, friend. You did warn me." I shook his hand. "Thanks for coming to my aid. I will return the favor, I swear."

At that point Benjamin Edes, publisher and owner of *The Gazette*, opened the front door and leaned on its frame. "Hallo, Merriweather. I see they let you out of the gaol. Care to give us a comment for Monday's paper?"

Edes was a ruddy fellow with round cheeks and large nose. On this day he wore a white periwig that had the appearance of a wren's nest with unattended strands of hair straying in all directions. He was also the most influential publisher this side of the Atlantic. No wonder Samuel Adams, his cousin John, and the other liberal Whigs turned to *The Gazette* first to print grievances against the way Parliament and Governor Hutchinson were running things over here. And any citizen with a colonial bent followed them closely.

"Did you see what *The Spy* printed this morning?" I held up the copy David had given me.

"That I did."

"He all but convicted the soldiers of raping that poor girl, and made a hero of the brute who got away," I said. "This is not remotely true."

David indicated Ede's newspaper on the wall with a nod of his head. "You didn't reprint his story, though."

"I thought Thomas wrote a fine piece of rabblerousing, and as much as I wish it were true, I heard he embellished significant parts." Edes crossed his arms at his chest and his legs at his ankles as he leaned against the wooden doorframe. A casual, confident pose. "When I heard you had been arrested, a witness to this nasty affair, I thought I'd wait for you to explain. No need to rush to print. I can wait until Monday's weekly edition. Why not write something for me?"

"I could do that, or you can steal my article after I publish tomorrow. You'd be wise to print the truth and not the hearsay." I gave his hand a shake as David and I prepared to move on. It was not an unfriendly one despite our roles as publishing competitors. Edes was actually a decent fellow despite himself.

"You'll have more readers if you let me publish it," Edes hollered to our backs as we turned up Dashett Alley toward Brattle Square.

True, but it stung just the same.

The Star Coffee House was a large two-story building of green-blue, part brick, and part clapboard siding that stood apart from the nearest row of homes fronting Brattle Street and opposite the district's Congregationalist church and meeting house. The Star has been in his family for three generations under different names. As more Tories with money built and bought large homes along Brattle Street through the years, the Star transformed itself from a tavern with its own beer distillery to a more refined social spot offering coffee and teas to please the well-heeled customers of the neighborhood. For those who wanted a stiff shot of liquor, though, trust me, one could still get it at the Star. The most popular item was the punch, always available in a large bowl near the kitchen entrance. For the price of a special two-shilling admission fee, it was serve yourself all you could drink. I learned early on it only took about two tankards for that strong punch to inebriate many a man to the point where he would be best advised to turn his horse reins over to a third party and avoid the dangers of drunk riding.

As we approached the front entrance I shuddered. Four soldiers were killing time in front of an outbuilding to the coffee house's western edge, and the sight of them was a reminder of the mess I had endured. The off-building had once been David's livery stable, but the army confiscated it like so many others three years past under the Quartering Act to house His Majesty's troops.

David growled, low and mean, whilst smiling and waving to the redcoats who had become lodgers against his wishes. "Bloody bastards," he said through clenched teeth.

I could feel his frustration but what could we do? And I swear they looked at me with a kind of social profiling I had experienced more than once. Common American, they must have thought. And yet I was Brit by birth. A proud graduate of King Edward VI Grammar School in Stratford-upon-Avon, County Warwickshire no less. Many folks are familiar with one of our more notable alumnus, a fellow named Shakespeare. Class of 1576. Or seven. Bloody hell, no one knows for certain. Without really thinking much of it, as I watched the small company in front of David's stable I gingerly touched the bruised and tender spot under my left eye left by one of the arresting soldiers after they marched me from the Reckless Goat to jail and slammed my face against the bars before opening my cell. "Bloody bastards," I echoed David.

The soldiers returned David's phony greeting with stone-faced stares as flat as the coffee house's front. "Damned buggers don't even know why they're here," he said. He opened the front door and waved for me to lead him in. "Seriously," he continued. "I've chatted them up when they come in for food and drink, which I am required to supply at my own cost, mind you. I suppose they're not bad fellows, precisely, but to a man they don't understand what in Jesus' name they're doing here in Boston. What is the point of it all? And ho! Putting troops in every nook and cranny of town, including my livery stable?"

"Anyone short of King George himself who says they have an answer is a fool," I told him.

"You're giving Georgie too much credit," David said. "*He's* the fool. All I know is these blokes are eating me out of house and home and I resent being forced to pay for the privilege." And then he leaned closer and said in a low voice, "And if the king doesn't either quit picking our pockets or give us a say in Parliament, he ain't going to be *our* king much longer, I tell you."

I quickly shooshed him. "Don't say that." Hardly commanding, it came out like a whine.

David exaggerated a stealth look to his left and right, raised a finger to his lips, and winked at me. Then he said his wife was serving up her best ale and mutton stew on the coffee house menu that night and went to fetch me a bowl.

Proprietor Deerfield was a jovial character on any given day, always looking for a laugh. I was convinced that his political stance tilted more to the left with each passing day. I thought of him as a soft, fuzzy Whig at heart, quick with a quip or a wink and a nudge when serving up criticism of the crown, the laws, and the Loyalists with a side of sarcasm.

The lower floor of the coffee house was beginning to fill with late afternoon diners and drinkers. I knew I shouldn't tarry at Deerfield's place and go straight to my print shop instead. I was eager to get there and begin setting the *News-Journal*'s front page with my eyewitness story of the *BARMAID IN FEAR*, the

LOUT and the *SOLDIER*, but the rumbling in my stomach wouldn't be ignored. And after three days in jail my limbs were as weak as my resistance to a stiff drink. I carried a mug of cider from the bar that boxed in one corner of the taproom and up the stairs behind it to the relative quiet of the subscription den. The second floor also had a small chamber with a washbasin and towels where I could attend to the prison filth that clung to my face and neck. David was waiting with a large bowl of Mrs. Deerfield's stew and a half loaf of bread at a table in the corner of the subscription room.

"This is much appreciated, friend," I said as I lowered myself slowly into the chair. I had to brace myself on the armrests of the chair, for my legs wobbled from fatigue and undernourishment. David leaned back and lit his pipe. With a wry grin, he watched me attack the food like a ravenous wolf. At that moment the mutton stew was the most scrumptious meal I had ever tasted. Freedom will do that to a fellow.

"I'm surprised you are not more enraged, given that the magistrate's jail sentence was entirely uncalled for," David said. "I'd be so furious I'd consult with Benjamin Edes' Sons of Liberty friends about some kind of payback."

"Hmm. Yes, tempting," I said. "But no, violence isn't an answer."

He sighed. "I suppose you would know. It's not your first trip to prison." David picked up the bowl and said he would go replenish it.

No, it wasn't my first time behind bars, unfairly held on both accounts. Compared to the six weeks I spent in London's ancient Newgate Prison, this new jail in Boston was a quality inn. The gruel they served once a day here was just as tasteless, but at least it was free of maggots. I wrapped my hands around the mug of cider, squeezing it as if it might prevent me from falling into despair. Or worse. Self-pity.

It happened seven years earlier, when I was barely twenty. I was scratching out a living as a street Patterer, a news performer in public. The sheriff arrested me, had me flogged and tossed into a cell for attacking the reputation of a distant member of the Royal Family. Scandalmonger was I. Slanderer. Except that the Duke of Earl's misdeeds were flagrant and unquestionably illegal.

I was not prosecuted for reporting misdeeds by the duke, but rather for refusing to identify the source of evidence I provided. Ultimately I was released from Newgate prison when the duke dropped the charges with a hefty bribe to the judge in order to avoid further embarrassment.

Now I sat in David Deerfield's coffee house, twice burned by British justice and my anger growing.

"You believe Jacob Addison will be ready for you when you reach the shop?" David asked when he returned.

On the walk to the coffee house I had told him that, before my release, I had enlisted Jacob to write and set the type for all but the front page of the *News-Journal's* next edition. "He really is more responsible than he appears," I said. "I promise, one way or the other, I will write the front page and set it tonight. With a full press run we will have it ready for your postal riders tomorrow afternoon."

He chuckled. "Even a diversion like a few days in the Boston jail would not cause you to miss a deadline, hey?" He laid three pounds silver and change on the table.

Along with owning one of the more popular coffee houses in Boston, Proprietor Deerfield was one of the city's three postmasters. As such he distributed all its newspapers to subscribers in other cities like New York and Philadelphia. Thomas' *Massachusetts Spy* even had paying readers as far south as the Carolina colony.

I protested his payment. "This is too much. You've done enough already. I mean, four pounds already."

"We'll settle up later. Besides, it's an advance. Get me an additional thirty copies for tomorrow's ride to New York. Your version of the story, with a British soldier as a hero instead of a heel, will sell well at the taverns there, what with that city run by conservative Yankee yahoos. In Philadelphia, this will be a burr in their liberal britches but grab them by the eyeballs and give them something to bellyache about."

Chapter Three
The New England News-Journal

The Merriweather & Associates print shop, home of the *New England News-Journal,* was partitioned into two sections. One was large, an open floor with all the ink, paper, a layout bench, cases of metal type, drying lines strung from wall to wall overhead, and spare parts needed to service the printing press.

The narrow side of the shop was a wall full of shelves on the left that ran about halfway from the front door to the back, at which point it opened to the print room. The right side had a line of waist-high shelves under framed displays of maps, paintings, classic pamphlet covers, and Bible pages full of monk art. This was our retail store. Near the front, I built a counter to display pens ranging from cheap turkey feathers to some fine, expensive goose quills kept under glass. There I could conduct sales and take orders.

At the back I had set up my composing desk with type cases, and another desk for writing in the far corner near the rear door. The whoosh and clack of the press working hard on the print floor greeted me, along with the grunting, cursing, and sniping back and forth of my two helpers, the brothers Bert and Ernie.

Jacob Addison sat at my composing desk at the edge of the large double doors into the main printing floor. He was hunting, picking, inspecting, and eventually transferring letters from the type case into a composing stick. Two letters and a sip of whiskey, followed by two more letters and another sip. And so on.

"Leeds, I had forgotten just how much work is required to fill the pages of this rag. This has been a reminder on why I let Father sell the business to you."

"You let him sell because you were too lazy to take over," I said.

"That is exactly the wrong attitude, my friend. Since you purchased this business from dear old dad, you are now paying me for the privilege of doing all this work. That is my genius. You publish and I reap the profits, minus your miserable little percentage."

"Well, if we don't produce a newspaper right now, my percentage will be nil and your profit less so."

I watched his painfully slow progress. "You were faster once. You're out of practice." Jacob had been quite the printer when I hired on to work for his father. Spencer Addison started him when he was still knee high to an ink barrel, and Jacob still worked at the shop while finishing his studies at Harvard Divinity School when I arrived. His father once admitted with a note of disappointment that he hired me knowing Jacob was not long for the backbreaking work of a print shop.

"Out of practice as an indentured servant to Father?" Jacob now snorted. "Thankfully."

After a long pause I asked, "Where are we? Close, I hope?"

Jacob nodded and added another letter to the composing stick. Then he pointed to the print room. "The brothers are nearly finished with interior pages, waiting only for this." He waved a casual, almost dismissive hand, at the wooden frame where he was setting type in the galley for the front page, leaving a large gap in the center column there waiting for my story.

I went into the press room where my apprentice Bert and his younger brother Ernie were preparing for a late start on the day's print run. I sniffed. Ah, linseed oil and lampblack. So much superior to the polluted air of my jail cell. I inhaled slowly, savoring the smell. Short of perfume on the neck of a passionate woman, nothing excites the senses like linseed and lampblack mixed to make ink for the press. Bert was a fourteen-year-old lad, lean, tall, and smart. God love him, he wanted to be a printer himself someday and spent most of his free time with his nose soaking up prose from one of the books in the front of the shop. His brother Ernie was ten years of age and a decent worker when you could distract him from his daydreams.

Four lines of thin rope crossed the room overhead waiting for broadsheets the boys would print and hang there to dry. Three sheets draped like limp bodies over the line nearest the press. Those were the test samples for me to examine before starting the print run. Bert adjusted his spectacles when I walked into the room, then he took the wooden pole and carefully lifted a single page from above and brought it to me.

"It is good to see you, Mr. Merriweather," he said. "I hope this meets with your approval. Mr. Addison allowed me to set the type for much of this page."

"Aye. And a fine job it is, Bertram."

The three columns on what would become the two interior pages were neatly aligned and the spacing appropriate. Beyond that, I had no mind to study. None of the editorial letters on page two seemed offensive, and advertisements made up the remainder of the copy. I was preoccupied with what I would contribute to the front page to perform my editorial duties. Still, I pretended to study it with interest, lest Bert think I was giving him too much freedom.

"Well, boys, what are you looking at me for?" I finally asked. "Get to work. And Mr. Deerfield has requested an additional twenty copies. Hop to it."

Jacob was locking the iron frame loaded with metal type into place around the fourth page, the back page, of the *News-Journal* when I rejoined him at the composing desk.

"Done," he said.

I pulled a tattered page from the inside pocket of my coat. Jacob had provided me with a scrap of paper and one of those imported German graphite sticks on the first day of my confinement. I had most of my report long before my release and would have the front page ready by the time Bert and Ernie were ready to press again.

"Did you hear? Mr. Kuntner lost his wife?" Jacob asked. He pointed to one block on the fourth page.

"Again?"

I leaned in to see that Andries Kuntner had bought an advertisement, which Jacob had set apart from the other items in a box:

> Publick Notice is Hereby Given to all citizens of the province and counties beyond MARY ELIZABETH KUNTNER, wife of home and bed to one ANDRIES KUNTNER has eloped with a gentleman consort formerly of New Haven.

Mr. Kuntner went on to declare that he would not honor any debts accrued by the runaway couple, though a two-dollar remuneration was offered for Mary Elizabeth's return, should she willingly return alone.

"And you wonder why I have yet to marry?" I said. "This is the third time Mary Elizabeth has wandered, and Kuntner pays to bring her home." I shook my head.

"Maybe I should court Mrs. Kuntner," Jacob snickered. "I could use the two dollars."

I nudged him aside, laid the notes of my report on the slanted table, and began plucking letters from the type case. Jacob lit the lantern that hung from a hook in the ceiling over the composing desk. Night was falling but I smiled. I reckoned Bert and Ernie would have three hundred pages done in less than two hours. I stopped and tilted my head, listening for a grunt, a creak, and a clatter from the press room. Yes, they were getting busy. It would take two more hours to print the front side of the newspaper, and I could leave the boys to fold the *News-Journal*, prepare everything for distribution, and I could be at the Reckless Goat for a pint well before closing.

Jacob picked up the page at my left hand and gave it a brief read before setting it down again so I could continue setting it in type. "Quite a different set of facts from the report *The Spy* published this morning."

"I can't say where Thomas got his information, but his sources were hearsay at best. That's why it is imperative that we publish as quickly as possible. Journalistic mitigation, my friend."

Isaiah Thomas had all but accused British soldiers of attacking Hannah behind the Reckless Goat that night, twisting the truth in the opposite direction. I asked Jacob to fetch me David Deerfield's copy of *The Spy* I had discarded on the shop's counter when I arrived. I held it under the lantern light.

According to Thomas:

> **Word has reached this publisher of a HEINOUS ASSAULT** on Tuesday last upon the virtue of a woman in the darkness behind The Reckless Goat Tavern, likely committed by one **BRITISH THUG** of His Majesty's **OCCUPYING FORCE**. It is the latest in a series of similar **MOLESTATIONS** of our city's **INNOCENT WOMEN.**

Thomas went on to suggest it was the quick action of a Boston citizen, a hero, who wounded the soldier and allowed the woman to escape with her bodice ripped but modesty intact.

Damn him. This was only going to validate the anger and sense of victimization that Thomas' readers felt. These days too many readers, like *The Spy's* most loyal followers, subscribed to only the newspaper aligned with the political beliefs they already held. I dumped the two sentences in my composing stick onto the table and started over:

A CONTRARIAN ACCOUNT TO DECEIT in published reports of mayhem.

That headline would grab some eyes, I thought, though I knew I was disadvantaged in that Thomas' report would be embedded in the minds of many readers already. I sighed. News traveled so quickly those days; every newspaper in the colonies would have a copy of *The Spy* in a week at most. A flog-flipping week! Incredible.

"One more reason to get this done immediately," I told Jacob. "We must not miss Mr. Deerfield's postal riders so that subscribers beyond Boston will have both sides of the story." And as I thought about where to take the story next, I knew the point and counterpoint of our reports would actually enhance readers' interest and sell a few more copies.

CLAPTRAP! I added to the composing stick. I needed to be more forceful than usual in order for the truth to be considered fairly.

Jacob took a glass tumbler from a shelf below the table, poured from the bottle he kept close by, and handed me the glass before adding a double shot to his own. Maybe I wouldn't need a trip to the tavern after all. I sipped the whiskey; it was smooth, more so than usual, so I reached for the bottle. "Scotch. You must have paid handsomely."

"Indirectly direct from Old Bushmills in Ireland. I happen to know someone who owed me a tidy sum from a lucky evening of Whist, and he paid me with this." Jacob grinned in a way a fox would foreshadow the jest to come. "He tells me this particular bottle just happened to fall off one of John Hancock's sloops before the entire shipment mysteriously disappeared as the ship approached Boston Harbor."

"Hancock's ships have a way of losing cargo on the way to customs." I winked and saluted Jacob with my glass. It was unnerving to watch how quickly Jacob consumed his drink. It was gone before I had barely swallowed my minimal sip.

"Leeds," he said. "Given that we are near payment day, we could do well to settle this month's accounts while I am here."

Business had been one iota better than average recently so I shrugged off his request even though it was nearly a week early. I did not have enough English pounds in the locked drawer beneath the shop counter to fulfill my month's rent and debt to Jacob, but I did manage to cobble together one coin of gold and enough silver, five Spanish dollars, a German ducat, and a bill of credit that I was certain Proprietor Deerfield would redeem to fill the balance. A quick assessment of what remained in my cash drawer was actually pleasing.

"Are we good?" I asked as I handed him the money.

"Aye," he said, although he held up the German coin and eyed it suspiciously.

I took my accounting ledger from a nook over my desk on the opposite side of the room, made a notation, and dated it. Jacob initialed the entry. Truthfully, the sums in the debt column were still daunting, but as I ran my finger down the page the arithmetic sang to me and the pattern was clear. I had turned a corner and the improving profits were progress. Lord, if I got through just two more years and three months, the business would be mine—lock, stock, and screw press.

Money in hand, Jacob used that as an excuse to depart. "I would continue to arrange the front page for you if you wish, but since I am inebriated it would be best to leave this work in more sober hands. If you find yourself free in a few hours, join us at the Green Dragon. Governor Hutchinson's son may join us and bring with him a few rich pigeons to pluck.

"Thomas Junior is quite the gambler, I hear."

"*I* hear he cheats, though who would risk the wrath of the governor to even accuse him of such a thing let alone prosecute? I will be on my guard."

When he reached the door, Jacob turned and wagged a finger at me. "And you should be wary as well, my friend."

"Me?"

"I know you. And I can see it in your eye. The fact that you have said nothing about the magistrate's sentence is a tell worse than a card gambler's slip. I'd advise you to avoid mentioning your treatment in the newspaper. At least not yet," he said, pointing to the unwritten page at my elbow.

I stared at him with as much a stone face as I could muster. "It never occurred to me," I lied. In fact, it had been gnawing at me since before I was released determined that if a bribe-grubbing judge could use his bench to annoy me, I would certainly tweak him in return with my printing press. I could only pray I would not face him in court again, for we know how *that* turned out.

"Get along, lads," I shouted to Bert and Ernie. "I'll be done shortly. We have a paper to print and a rabble to rouse."

How splendid.

Chapter Four
The Star Coffee House

"When is a wife not the love of your life?

When service to King George does call.

I've heard tell of the stories,

rich fathers, those Tories,

Selling their daughters at a ball.

Their plot is the breeding

For subjects they're needing,

And propagate more loyalists by fall."

I recited that poem and took a bow from a small, foot-high platform in the corner of the subscription room in the Star Coffee House. Then I pointed to the poem in a block centered on the second page of the *New England News-Journal* in my hand for more than a dozen men in the room before me. I spread my arms as I surveyed the room of patrons, beckoning them to respond to my act. One. Two. Five cups raised in salute to my story. A five-cup review. How grand.

"Tell us more," someone called out.

I slapped the page and read two more sentences from the report attached to the poem to add a bit of meat to the bones of my story about flesh-bartering fathers. "The full story is right here, gentlemen. But if you desire more, you'll have to pay two shillings," I laughed. They did as well. "But trust me, fine sirs, it will cost you less than that overpriced mug of coffee for which Mr. Deerfield is picking your pocket this morning and you'll walk away with your curiosity quenched in the process." They responded with good-natured spirit and a bit of jostling as several queued up to drop their silver into a box on the nearby table and take a copy of the newspaper. And that is what I was all about that day, selling newspapers after teasing an audience with just enough information to induce their purchase. It was my routine for publication day each week.

I was now two weeks past reporting my eyewitness account of the Reckless Goat Affair and a smack down of Isaiah Thomas in the process. I called out *The Massachusetts Spy* by name for misinforming the public about the true details, and the true villain, in the attack on Hannah's virtue behind the tavern. It created quite a stir and generated much discussion in public circles.

But, alas. The public's attention span was so short that stories were printed and quickly forgotten. Keeping the public engaged and discussing a story for as little as three weeks was nearly impossible and made for a maddeningly short news cycle. Now, *DAUGHTERS IN FEAR!* was the story everyone wanted to talk about.

I moved across the room to join Benjamin Church and James Asbey, both advertising clients of mine, near a fire crackling in the hearth. Not yet noon, Mother Nature blessed us with an early taste of what I suspected would be a cold winter to come. Rain and a bit of sleet drove merchants and traders inside to take a mid-morning break, and the sub-scription room was busier than usual. As this edition of the *News-Journal* was so fresh from its printing press womb, I wanted to think the latest news was part of the attraction for these readers. I had already that morning performed a reading and sold a fair number of newspapers at British Coffee House near Market Square.

Mr. Church appeared particularly pleased. "Good show, Merriweather," he said. "It appears You have reeled in a num-ber of fish today."

I looked over my shoulder. It felt as if half the crowd was hold-ing copies of the *News-Journal* and chatting with each other about its contents, though one outlier near us held a three-day-old copy of the *Boston Chronicle* open in front of his nose. Poor devil prob-ably couldn't read fast enough to stay current.

"Yes," I said. "It is a good day, Mr. Church. And that means many will see your advertisement. You made a wise choice for front page placement." I turned and grinned at him.

Benjamin Church ran the most successful auction house in Boston. Rarely a week passed when he did not purchase one, and sometimes two, placements in all the papers in town. His eyes roamed the room before finally coming back to meet mine.

Show me the money. We both knew it was on my mind.

"Oh," he huffed. "Yes, I still owe you, don't I?" He reached into a pocket, withdrew several silver pieces, and handed them to me. "I will send someone around on Monday. We will be auctioning off a fine home on Hanover Street and lots from the estate come December. I think three weeks of placement in advance of the auction should turn out quality bidders." Then he handed me another pound, a pledge to secure premier placement in future editions. I placed it in my pocket and fingered the other coins there. If this kept up, I might accelerate my payments to Jacob Addison and be free of the debt in less than two years. What a nice feeling that was.

"That was some doing," James Asbey said as he jerked his head to the step in the corner where I had recited the news in rhyme. He had both hands wrapped around a mug with a mouth so wide it hid his lips and nose like a highwayman's mask when he sipped. Asbey was a watchmaker on Milton Street and purchased advertisements in my newspaper on such a regular basis that I could risk the pun he was a client who showed up like clockwork. "Daughters for sale. It's an entertaining newsbit, and one'd expect we'll be seeing more in short order."

"Has there really been a rush upon justices of the peace and clergy throughout the colony?" Mr. Church inquired.

Yes, I told him. It seems Tory fathers, loyal to the crown yet owning land on this side of the pond, were marrying off their daughters to the first well-connected loyalist or military man who came courting. Some even resorted to running advertisements in English newspapers offering property and "young, handsome and fertile wives" to men who would emigrate to America. The rationale, promoted and secretly incentivized by rebated tax collections from the Hutchinson administration, was to shield their offspring, and more importantly their daughters' dowries, from the hands of brutish, liberal, and independence-minded Americans. A colony full of Tories was not likely to turn against the crown—one would think.

"If I may suggest, Mr. Merriweather, I have a bit of related information you'd be want to print, I think," Asbey said.

"Offer me a letter and I'd be happy to print it," I replied.

Asbey looked at the floor and shook his head. "Nah, I'm no good with words and proper writing and all that shite. Though I like to read, I don't have the brain for composing."

"Then tell me."

"Well, my landlady? She's the widow Mrs. Morgan. She told me two Saturdays past she spent an evening at a gathering up there in Beacon Hill where she witnessed a bit of daughter bartering, and says it was not the first time."

"Yes," I encouraged him.

"It gets worse," Asbey continued. "Seems the good widow Morgan's wealth is attracting quite a bit of attention. Why, she's had three proposals for marriage just this year."

"That's bad?"

"Yes, and it gets worse, she tells me. The governor's been leaning on Mrs. Morgan to marry a man of his choosing who is willing to settle here."

"Governor Hutchinson gets to pick a husband for her?" I asked. This *was* news. Would the widow talk for the press? This confirmed what I could only report as a rumor to that point: Some of the governor's top lieutenants chased the skirts of wealthy widows to breed a new generation of conservative, value-driven subjects to stem the rising tide of radical liberalism in Boston.

"Worse, ever more," Asbey continued. "Not only is the groom he's hawking related to Gov Hutch, but he's the half-brother to a cousin of an Irish duke. Or some rot like that. Claims to be in line for a title. She thinks he's money grubbing for a fortune like hers to acquire it."

"She's putting up some serious resistance, I hope."

"Indeed. Imagine being coerced into coupling with a man like that." The watchmaker shook his head sadly.

"Too greedy?" I asked.

"Too Catholic."

"Worse."

"Indeed."

Not much later I stood at the coffee bar next to Proprietor Deerfield beneath a large corner window. Rain was tapping lightly against the glass, and the heavy clouds prevented much light from getting into the room, which was paneled in oak and walnut on three sides, making it a comfortable, manly lair. His son Daniel poured two large cups of steaming dark roast and then lightened them up with rum. Rum was a happy thing, for I am no fan of coffee's bitterness, and it requires significant doctoring to be palatable. But coffee's popularity had been rising steadily in Boston. For many citizens all the roasting, grinding, brewing, and sweetening that coffee required was worth the trouble in order to stick it to Parliament for refusing to repeal the tea tax. Thumbing their noses at the government, they would refuse tea and drink coffee, like it or not. I did not like it. Blech.

David withdrew a scrap of paper that had been peeking from the pocket of his waistcoat. "Something for you. I received this just today."

It was a letter bearing a Custom House stamp in the upper left corner with shipping schedules for Philadelphia and Boston.

"You might want to note those tea ships everyone has been expecting—*Dartmouth*, *Eleanor*, and two others I don't recall—are expected here next week," David said. His eyebrows arched, and not in a comforting way.

"Uh-oh. Adams, Hancock, Doctor Warren. They will be outrageously miffed," I replied. "Not to understate the problem, but they've been threatening action for some time and this might incite some major miffery."

"I hope someone can convince the governor to turn the ships away," David said. "Short of that, we could be headed for violence. I'm hearing things, like the south side gang will burn the ships if they anchor within a skiff's spit of the docks."

"Pray that it does not happen. Perhaps the town committee meeting that Hancock called for this evening will hatch a plan for negotiation. One can hope, no?" It was more optimistic than

I felt deep down, but I did not want this talk of confrontation to spoil my mood. I had acquired information for three solid stories in just the past hour. My stomach was warm with tea and rum, and my pocket was full of coin. At the coffeehouse door I looked to the skies. The rain was reduced to a drizzle but the day was still as dark as a widow's heart. I buttoned my great coat and marched quickly through the narrow back alleys to my printing shop hoping to avoid the strong winds while, with my head tucked, I held a firm hand on my hat to prevent it from escaping.

I slipped into the office through the entrance in the rear, removed my coat, and paused, tilting my head to one side to capture the sound of unexpected silence. There was no groaning and clacking, the noises I would expect of a press in labor and the birthing of pages from the other side. Bert and Ernie couldn't possibly have finished the new pages of the day's assignment.

Two steps into the press room I saw Jacob Addison prone and lifeless near the far wall. Little Ernie sat next to him in a ball with his head buried in his knees. He looked up with tears on his cheeks.

"Mr. Merriweather...I think he's dead."

Chapter Five
Breaking News

Dead.

Dead drunk.

By the time Bert burst through the front door with Doctor Warren, Jacob was sitting up against the wall with his eyes closed. Drool trickled from the corner of his mouth, and he hugged a bucket of vomit.

Jacob mumbled and weakly tried to beat Doctor Warren away when he knelt to inspect him. It seemed Jacob had performed a miracle, coming back from the dead. As I reached for his hand, he bolted upright and let out a roar. He blinked several times as if trying to recognize me, and then rolled to one side and began retching. It was all I could do to grab the bucket, lift him to his knees, and position him over it. Doctor Warren took no time at all to diagnose Jacob's ailment.

"A bad case of wine flu," he said. "Or Brandy. Beer. Gin. I don't smell rum, but it's difficult to tell. The odor of his regurgitation suggests it could well be all of them and more. Pick your poison—this man is drunk."

My throat clutched and my stomach revolted. The combination of Jacob's puking and stink that now permeated the print office created a queasiness deep inside, and it galloped toward critical mass in my throat. I looked for a relief pail of my own. Lacking that, I stepped away and leaned heavily on the workbench, panting where the smell of turpentine and ink could fill my nostrils and suppress my urge for a sympathy hurl. Some moments were never meant to be shared, even by the closest of friends. This was one.

Bert and I dragged Jacob from the shop and rolled him into Doctor Warren's wagon for the trip across town to the custody of his wife. As we carried him to his bedroom, Jacob came to with a brief spasm of clarity. He took hold of my arm and squeezed it with what little strength he had.

"I'm sorry, Mrrrweatha…" There were tears in his eyes. "I owe you. Debt."

I tried to comfort him with a smile. "We can discuss repaying me later." It was a joke I hoped would help. But that seemed to agitate him into an all-out bawl.

"I owe you," he sobbed. He repeated it several more times, and then, like a chant of an inebriated monk, repeated it in Latin, a throwback to his days in the Congregationalist ministry.

"*Me paenitet. Me paenitet.*"

Loosely translated, because I couldn't spit in Latin let alone speak it, I guessed he was saying, "I really fucked up. Sorry 'bout that."

Suddenly Jacob stopped crying and his eyes opened wide.

"Incoming," I yelled. Bert and I tossed him the last two feet onto his bed and escaped, chased by the sound of prodigious heaving.

Three hours later I was back at the print shop and I learned exactly what Jacob was trying to tell me. My grammar school Latin had long faded from my head and now consisted almost exclusively of lewd, crude jokes and curses that would make a sailor blush. Thinking of that scum Latin-spewing penitent Addison, all I could say was, "That *Filius Bitch*!"

Loosely translated, *Son of a loose-morals, back-stabbing, gonad twister.*

"'I owe you.' My ass," I grumbled. He was saying "I.O.U."

The print shop was quiet, the press room was deserted, and noon was long passed. I had given Bert and Ernie the afternoon off in the wake of Jacob's commotion that morning. The pamphlet with Preacher Graham's latest sermon ready for printing, and the dressmaker's window sign waiting for composition, could hold until tomorrow. I sat at my writing desk in the back corner of the shop, drawing warmth from fire in the stove, and read a story in the Philadelphia newspaper that I would lift and reprint later.

The tiny bell over the front door tinkled the arrival of a tall, lean fellow in fine attire who didn't seem old enough for hair that had gone entirely white. It fell neatly to his collar. He had an Irish pug nose, round, rosy cheeks, and a hint of a brogue. As I greeted him at the counter I noticed the kind of twinkle in his eye that suggested he took nothing in life seriously.

He introduced himself as Frederick J. O'Donnell, attorney at law, and handed me a scented calling card. If he was not a man of money himself, he was most certainly connected to one. I guessed the latter. But either way I anticipated getting a profitable assignment so, naturally, I liked Attorney O'Donnell before he said a word about what had brought him to my shop.

"How may I assist you, sir?" I asked.

And that's when I had my *Filius Bitch!* moment.

"I am here on behalf Mr. Clinton Murdoch," he began.

My curiosity leapt. *The* Clinton Murdoch? The bloody rich fat cat who, more than anyone else in the Massachusetts Bay Colony, had the ear of Governor Hutchinson?

"Gov-Whisperer Clinton Murdoch?"

Tsk. Tsk. O'Donnell said with a laugh, "Yes. Well, my client is not particularly enamored with that colloquial title you in the press have given him."

I had several well-to-do clients like Benjamin Church, Peter Faneuil, and even John Hancock in my stable, but Murdoch would be quite a catch.

O'Donnell had a dour expression that tempered my disposition. "I am here to collect on a note of debt," he said slowly. "It seems one Jacob Addison has signed over ownership of this note. Mr. Murdoch now owns the debt and requests that you make good on the note immediately."

He withdrew a document of several pages and slid it across the countertop to me. "The transfer of debt, as you can see, is clearly signed by Mr. Addison. And here is a certification of its authenticity from the public notary. And here is acceptance of legal enforcement from the justice of the peace."

"But why? Rather, how? Oh, mother-flogging sweet Jesus, what is happening here?"

We stood across from each other at the counter in my office. He rounded it and strolled past me to the print floor behind us, inspecting everything as he walked and talked.

"It seems Mr. Addison has been very unlucky at cards over the course of several weeks. His debt accumulated. Not only to Mr. Murdoch, but several players of a group which meets regularly for games. My client bartered with the others and consolidated all of those notes into a single debt."

My jaw dropped so far and hard that I swear I would have lost my teeth if it had reached the floor. "Wait. You are saying Jacob gambled away this printing business?"

Even Jacob wouldn't be *that* thick-headed, would he?

"Yes, I'm afraid so." O'Donnell stopped to fondle a leather binding waiting to be filled with pages from an unfinished book piling up on the finishing table. He bent to inspect a case full of lead type, and stroked the frame of the press with the back of his finger, the way a suitor might admire his woman. At least he had good taste in mistresses. I couldn't help feeling that his intentions toward her were less than honorable. He addressed me while pulling on the devil's tail, the lever to raise and lower the platen on the press.

"It was quite a sight to see. I was there. Only as a spectator, of course. I can't afford a seat at that table. But those of us attending only for social purposes, the entire coterie of gentlemen at Crown Tavern, stopped to take note. You could hear a pin drop. With so much at risk on one hand of whist, well, Mr. Addison must have believed he could recoup all his previous losses and then some on a single turn of the cards. I admire his nerve."

He gave a mild grunt before guiding the bar back into place to raise the platen, and then he patted it. "Impressive."

"Let me be very clear," I said. "Even if Jacob did lose the lien I owed him, I have a contract and so I still own this." I waved O'Donnell's documents in my hand, torn between anger and desperation, sweeping them across the sight of shelves, the books, the press, and each corner of the shop.

O'Donnell's response was to shake his head with amusement while shrugging his shoulders. *Can you believe that fool?* he seemed to ask.

Actually, yes. I could see him attempting such a daring combination of hubris and risk, especially under the influence of Lady Liquor.

"You own just less than a third. Mr. Murdoch owns two-thirds. He is the majority owner of the business now. In effect, *he* owns all this unless you buy out his portion. If that is not practical within thirty days, you will forfeit the entire note. Mr. Murdoch will lawfully foreclose and sell it all. The call is yours. Legally you have thirty days to settle accounts, but we will begin foreclosure proceedings immediately thereafter."

There was no way I could raise that sum in thirty days short of selling my soul to the devil. At that moment I felt he already owned it, and that bastard was standing right there across from me in my shop. Options. Options raced through my head. My friend and mentor Doctor Franklin had advanced me a small sum as a down payment to Jacob's father to pledge my good faith. I had repaid him for his help, leaving me only Addison's portion, but this was a much greater sum. And anyhow, how could I ask him to reinvest the money yet again? Credit was nearly impossible since the occupation began because Tories controlled most finances and they would be loath to usurp Murdoch. That seemed to rule out my wealthier clients. Though I might ask.

No, I was trapped unless Jacob or his father had some answer I couldn't see. I squeezed my fists, digging nails into my palms. I reasoned Jacob must have had few other options. Yet, at the moment I would have gladly put his head under the platen of my printing press the moment he sobered up and squeeze the life out of him. Jacob lost my shop, my life, and my love…to Clinton-Flipping-Murdoch.

Frederick J. O'Donnell, attorney at law, gathered his things and, in an off-handed way, drove one more dagger into my soul. "With Mr. Murdoch's connections, I'm sure we could arrange to have any protest you may file considered in Magistrate Pendergast's courtroom. I've read you are quite familiar with the judge, though you have printed some rather unflattering things about him recently. I found the opinion you authored the other week recounting the sentence he gave you quite entertaining, though I'm sure Magistrate Pendergast did not see it that way. By the way, how *was* your stay in the gaol?"

It will have been a trifle if Pendergast decided my future was a long term in debtor's prison. Before I could mount any response short of begging, O'Donnell took my hand in a strong grip, not quite shaking it, while placing his other hand on my arm to steer me toward the door. He smiled in what might have been an attempt to charm me if not for the fact that his teeth were yellow and crooked, and his breath reeked of hygiene mismanagement.

"Come, now, Merriweather, do you feel threatened? Good. Then I have done my job," he said. "Actually we mean you no grief. Mr. Murdoch is a man of tremendous leverage in this town. That is what we seek. We want to make a business arrangement that would allow you to stay in this dank and dusty little shop you are so fond of."

My spine went stiff and I simply couldn't allow a flicker of hope to tease me. I had turned completely away from the impression I had when O'Donnell arrived that afternoon. I did not like this man. I did not like him at all.

Balls!

O'Donnell then suggested it would be in my best interest to dine at the Murdoch mansion on Saturday next. "It will all be quite clear. We have several others with interest in our proposal."

"Have I a choice?" I asked.

"This arrangement has the potential for news reporting in the near future, and business beyond. This could be the beginning of a great relationship," he said at the door. "We shall all profit from it mightily—if you play your cards right."

I was left trying not to think too hard about the consequences if I played my cards wrong.

Like Jacob had done.

Chapter Six
Boot Lickers and Buggers

"I will lick your boots. Every day of my life for the rest of my existence." Jacob could hardly grovel more disgustingly than if he actually got down on his knees in the gutter and kissed my backside.

"Not enough," I replied.

We were still a few paces from the walk up to Clinton Murdoch's Beacon Hill residence on Saturday afternoon. I admit I don't tolerate fools but I don't wear anger well and I couldn't help but pity Jacob for drinking himself blind after gambling away the deed to Merriweather & Associates. However, I was not about to show a hint of compassion. Not yet, at least. Remorse, a gluttony of guilt, and despair drove him to an overnight bender unlike anything I have ever witnessed a man survive. I only wish he had chosen a whip instead of whiskey and wine for his self-flagellation.

"We are going in there, and before the night is through, if you have to beg, plead, and pledge every bit of your inheritance as collateral, we are getting that I.O.U. back," I said. "You had no right. *No right*," I repeated with more emphasis. "To gamble away my life. That's what you've done. Now go in there and fix it."

"I told you. I am leveraged in debt for all I own already. I couldn't get a loan in this town to save my soul. I tried," Jacob moaned.

We stopped on the street outside of Murdoch's house and exchanged looks of amazement. Two uniformed sentries stood at attention on the landing outside the front door, staring with stone faces straight ahead. They ignored my wave, but then rotated their bodies to form bookends as Jacob and I squeezed between them. A butler answered my rap with a brass knocker. The soldiers' post at the door was immediately clear when we were ushered into the library.

Governor Thomas Hutchinson stood at the hearth warming the backside of his britches with a crystal glass of punch in his hand. His wig was perfect, his attire elegant and exceedingly expensive. Expensive enough, I thought, that should I mug him for that suit and pawn it, I could settle accounts with Murdoch and have money to spare. Governor Hutchinson's attendance was a complete surprise and suggested Murdoch had an agenda that I now doubted would involve hard negotiations over brandy and cigars. Curiosity surged right down to my very loins for I couldn't fathom what to expect. Jacob and I held back until Clinton Murdoch stepped up to make introductions.

"Governor, these are the gentlemen of which I warned you," he said with a laugh. This elicited a chuckle from the other men in the room. "This good fellow is Jacob Addison. I believe you know his father Spencer Addison, whose business ventures included establishing the *New England News-Journal* newspaper." Murdoch got only a nod of acknowledgement to the statement. "And this gentleman is the current publisher of *The Journal*, Leeds Merriweather, formerly of London though seems to have taken a shine to America in the four years since his arrival here."

Actually it was nearly seven years, but I was not sure enough of my place yet to correct my host. "Governor," I said and nodded respectfully. "We actually had occasion to meet once, crossing paths at Province House, as I was a workman in senior Addison's employment at the time, delivering proofs of your pamphlet *Massachusetts, History and Heresy*. It was a fine piece, if I'm allowed that."

"You are," the governor responded with a charming if somewhat insincere smile.

A soldier stood next to the punch bowl in front of large windows that looked out over the Commons to the shore. His name was Lieutenant Commander Cole. Murdoch said he was attached to the governor's office as head of security and intelligence.

"Intelligence," I asked with mocking innocence. "Not a term one usually associates with the military."

"No offense taken," Cole smirked while the others chuckled. The joke was too old to sting. He was an interesting character, average height with a wee slouch that seemed less than proper military. He had deep eyes black as a raven's, and his face was pocked from what I suspected was a narrow victory over the pox in his youth.

Attorney Frederic J. O'Donnell lingered near a wall of books on one side, while a Mr. Larson, the governor's chief of staff, was the last introduction. He stood a perfect distance from Hutchinson, just enough to be invisible, yet near enough to read his superior's mind and anticipate his every wish.

We mingled, drank hard cider and rum punch, smoked Virginia cigars, and exchanged pleasantries. Every conversation seemed to be tainted by or eventually turned to some shade of politics. Some shades were darker than others, but it was mostly polite and most assuredly Loyalist. I was standing apart from the others with Governor Hutchinson as his aide. Mr. Larson was rambling through a lengthy account of an attempt the previous day by a committee of city leaders to force the resignation of the customs agents handling the tea cargos of three ships due any day now, following the lead of their counterparts in New York and Philadelphia.

"I don't know why the Adams boys and the others would think that would be successful," Larson said. "A fool's errand."

No one could imagine the Massachusetts customs agents would buckle to the pressure of the anti-tea contingent. The man standing at my right, Governor Hutchinson, had put his two sons in customs house jobs as tea consignees specifically to see the tea landed safely and sold in Boston with minimal controversy. And they would line their pockets with commissions in the process. No, they would not surrender all that.

"I expect to publish a report about it next," I nodded. Then I turned to the governor, who had been sternly silent and watching me while Larson talked. "Do you wish to add a comment, Governor? For my article, I mean."

He ignored the question. "How do you feel about this news, Mr. Merriweather, should we bow to the wishes of the town council?"

"That's not for me to say. I'm not above offering thoughts on various topics, but this I will leave to others. I don't have a squirrel in this hunt."

Governor Hutchinson studied me with squinted eyes. It accentuated his round cheeks in an otherwise angular face. Finally, he said, "You are quite the enigma now, aren't you, Mr. Merriweather?"

"How so, sir?"

"I look at you and I see a man of passion. Surely you have opinions, but the lines have been long drawn between the radical newspapers like Samuel Adams and the good men like Richard Draper of the *News-Letter*. And yet, you pretend to be above that, never tipping your hand," the governor said.

"If only my good friend Addison were so adept at cards," I replied. I couldn't resist casting that line, and the reward was quick. The governor said nothing, but he blinked and his eyes twinkled. Yes, he knew what I was referring to. And I wondered what was *his* game.

"I have found opinion, critical and unwarranted, does occasionally escape Mr. Merriweather's office," Larson interjected.

"Nobody's perfect," I smiled.

"Consider his jab the other week comparing one of our most faithful magistrates to a common pickpocket," Larson said.

"But in the same edition he credited the King's finest of gallantry where no other printer would have troubled himself," the governor said. "We need more of that kind of honesty in the province."

His face relaxed, losing its prosecutor's facade, and I relaxed as well. "There is so much talk these days, and opinions in our newspapers, about a possible civil war between our colonies and the crown. It is shamelessly subtle at times but undeniably present. And it is getting louder. I can't help but wonder, Mr. Merriweather, on which side of that war would you come down?"

"Ask me again when the shooting starts," I replied.

"Ha! Another diversion," Larson, the invisible chief of staff, said. I had almost forgotten he was there, so consumed was I with studying the governor and the way he appeared to be measuring me like a tailor with a cheap suit he wished to push.

At that point we were joined by Lieutenant Cole, the governor's security man. He obviously captured the essence of our conversation. "Are you unwilling to support your king? You are, after all, British born and raised," he said. "Warwickshire, if my information is correct. And you even have a brother who is a member of Parliament."

I had no response. It was as true as it was unsettling. My surprise that he would know such detail of my story must have been written all over my face in large, uppercase Caslon bold type, for the lieutenant dismissed it with a wave.

"Pussssh! No need to worry. We routinely peruse the backgrounds of notable characters—nothing too deep. You should be flattered."

That Lieutenant Cole would admit it with such a cavalier attitude troubled me even more. It must have troubled the governor as well because he took Cole by the elbow and led him to a private exchange near a wide arch leading to an antechamber on the far side of the room.

Mr. Larson and I were left to shift our weight uncomfortably, like a pair of suitors scorned by all the belles at the ball. "Merriweather," he said. He wagged a skinny finger at me while gripping a tumbler of applejack cider. "What so few on either side of the pond realize is that the civil war has already begun. *The Spy*, *The Gazette*, even the *Weekly Advertiser* have cast their lots. You have little time left to make a decision."

"A decision?"

"You can be either a loyal soldier to the crown or a casualty with Thomas and Adams and the rest in the inevitable outcome. The battle at the moment is to win the sympathies of the public. Words and poisonous rhetoric are the weapons you and your colleagues with the press fire willy-nilly at the established order. But we, Merriweather. We have powder and ball, cannon and ships."

I shifted uncomfortably. I didn't need a lecture from this humorless and dour diddletwat. Apparently the expression of disdain on my face wasn't obvious enough to detour him, for he continued.

"You are American. You were born here among the farmers and mechanics. What do you know of cannon and ball?" I asked.

"Now, now. Don't be so impertinent, Merriweather," I heard Clinton Murdoch's voice over my shoulder. Jacob was drifting a few feet behind our rotund host.

"And Mr. Larson," he continued. "Remember, our friend Merriweather here is nowhere near as radical as the others. Sam Adams, for example. I have met Sam Adams." He turned to me and said, "And you, sir, are no Sam Adams."

Wonderful. Now I had something to live down to.

"Well, I must say, Mr. Merriweather," Larson conceded. "I enjoyed your reference earlier to your politics, particularly as a publisher. What was that you said? Like a turkey at the chopping block the night before Christmas dinner…"

"I stick my neck out for nobody," I deadpanned.

Mr. Larson slapped my back and then adjusted his powdered wig ever so slightly. It was creeping down his forehead. He put a hand over his glass where cider sloshed and threatened to spill overboard. He had the vacant eyes of a fop who, though happily loyal now, would just as happily abandon the Tory administration if it suited his bureaucratic well-being.

Jacob beckoned me to slither away where he could point out various books on the library's shelves while speaking in a low voice with our backs to the others. He took a bound volume of almanacs and opened it, pretending interest.

"Murdoch, that bastard, apparently has no interest in giving up the print shop," he said. "He wouldn't entertain any suggestion I tried to offer and said we could discuss it in full after we dine."

"Not a hint of cooperation?" I asked.

Jacob had the book resting on his palm and slammed it shut with that single hand. "No." Then he continued in a whisper. "Though what he *did* hint is that he has use for your help on something that will benefit the governor. But whatever that may be, he wants to control the newspaper. That much I can deduce. But I haven't had enough wine yet."

Bugger the badger. Why did I feel I was about to be mugged? I clenched the glass in my hand, reflecting on my future with my print shop and dusty office, cluttered, tired and worn from years of use, and in need of repair. Many days it seemed like a fat, sloppy, middle-aged mistress, with a face overly painted in ink makeup and wearing the cloth of moist paper after a quick copulation in the printing bed. Yet she was the woman I adored and would not trade for anything.

Until I met Mistress Sally Hughes.

Chapter Seven
Of Mice and Men

Jacob and I still had our backs to the room, evaluating our situation in hushed tones when the swishing of silk and taffeta stopped all conversation and yanked me from self-pity. I did not need to look to know petticoats and perfume had joined us in the library. The sound of their youthful laughter was music to my ears. Four well-dressed women and an even more elegantly attired matron stood beneath the arched entrance from the antechamber. I felt woefully underdressed at that sight.

"What ho. The ladies have arrived," Murdoch proclaimed and began a round of introductions.

I recognized the matron, Mrs. Mae Flowers. Of course it was mere jest that she was one of the original settlers well over a century ago. It was a taradiddle, a fib she happily encouraged. The lines on her face and frail appearance might convince you. Well preserved, I thought, and I knew her to have a feisty disposition. She was a well-known figure about Boston who had engaged me two years earlier to publish and bind a keepsake book of her poems.

A tall, handsome woman I only knew by reputation stood to her right. Mrs. Clarissa Abernathy was a widow with a home on a full acre across the Charles River near Harvard College. She had no wealth beyond that. The way each man stepped forward to greet the elder women in turn was nearly comical, as something that seemed to me a formal dance. The three young women clustered to the right and curtseyed at the sound of their name. Two were Mrs. Abernathy's twin daughters, Abigail and Alicia. And then there was the fairest of them all: Madam Flowers' niece, Sally Hughes.

Murdoch introduced me as a "fine gentleman and publisher of our outstanding newspaper, the *New England News-Journal*." I did my turn at the choreographed minuet, addressing each woman as I took her hand and bowed. I had encountered nobility in London, and while I did not feel uncomfortable, this seemed a bit formal for the colonies. I played along if for no other reason than to touch the hand of Mistress Sally Hughes. She intrigued me at my first look.

Mistress Sally Hughes. I had not seen so lovely a sight since the first sunrise after I was released from my short, but horrific stay at London's Newgate Prison, which now felt like a lifetime ago. Natural as nature itself, even the blush of her cheeks seemed more a product of having been kissed by a rose than anything an alchemist could create.

"Miss Hughes," I said in my best impersonation of a gentleman.

"Mr. Printer."

It was scintillating conversation. We were off to a wonderful start.

"Pardon, Mistress Hughes. It's Merriwea..." The look on her face stopped me. I had been played. Well played. "Oh. Yes, of course, I am a printer. A good one."

Her smile was forgiving as one would pardon a child's faux pas. Although not as tiny as her aunt, the mistress needed to stretch to achieve average height. The hoop skirt beneath her gown that pushed the silk away from her waist as it draped to the floor, accentuated just how slim her frame was, like a stick in a butter churn barrel. If only she sported freckles you would think her to be not much more than a girl of fourteen, but her bearing and diminutive lines framing her eyes betrayed the fact she was moving away out of her prime. Not that I was paying attention.

Her aunt, Madam Flowers, was a thrice-widowed woman of sufficient means from those marriages to eschew most social events in Boston unless she was on the arm of a man of wealth and celebrity reputation about town—such as the good governor, who just happened to be attending this little soiree. She played no favorites when it came to her social escorts. Married, widowed, or single, Tory or a Son of Liberty, it made little difference to a woman of her advanced years as long as the gentleman was younger than she, handsome, socially adept, and with enough money of his own that he would have no designs on hers.

She was fond of saying, usually while waving a bony finger at your chest, "I gave birth eleven times. Nursed each one until they sucked me dry. I will not let any man do the same with my money." And then, with deliberate consideration and a twinkle in her eye, she would add, "Then again, my bosom, well, that's a matter best negotiated in private."

Yes, she could be delightfully crude in a way that is admired in the very wealthy and very old.

Madam Flowers took Mrs. Abernathy by one arm and the governor by the other, steering them to the punch bowl. Mr. Larson tried to join them but the twins guided him instead to where Jacob and I engaged Miss Hughes. Alicia and Abigail were identical in looks and mannerisms, distinguishable only by the shade of honey color gowns they wore, and that one had applied a black beauty patch high on her cheek just below the corner of her left eye, while the other applied a patch to her right dimple. They had healthy, well-defined shapes and batted their eyes in an attractive and an extremely suggestive way. Several suggestive ways, actually.

"And how is it that two charming ladies such as yourself have escaped the notice of eligible bachelors in this town?" Jacob asked, teasing them to open the discussion.

The twins looked at each other and laughed. "Mother brought us here at the end of summer," Alicia said. Or maybe she was Abigail. To this point we had all been left to guess which was which. Their age and the timing of their arrival in Boston at the start of the social season, or as many folks referred to as "the hunting season," with a calendar full of dinner parties, dances, and other gatherings, suggested they and their mother were on the prowl for husbands.

"We have been three years before this in Paris," her twin said.

"Oui c'est is true," the first twin nodded.

Which explained the most interesting of their beauty traits, their dark, full, and sculptured eyebrows.

Mouse fur.

I had seen it a few times among wealthy French ladies and, not coincidentally to my mind, in certain establishments where painted ladies are common, the kind of place where one might experience things I would never admit I had *personally* experienced.

Much.

So much plucking and painting with dangerous lead products in ladies' cosmetics had created a shortage of natural brow beauty in certain circles. In fact, reports from France suggested that the practice of mouse fur applied to the bald eyebrow with adhesive was so common there, entire colonies of rodents lived in fear for their survival.

Widow Flowers and Mr. Murdoch led us to the dining room. Mrs. Abernathy accepted the governor's arm while the twins paired off with Mr. Larson and the young lieutenant.

"Shall we?" I asked Mistress Hughes and offered her my hand.

As the dinner progressed I found myself increasingly enchanted with her and increasingly disappointed that she had been assigned the chair next to Lieutenant Cole. Worse, I found myself increasingly agitated by an irrational jealousy that she appeared too interested in the boorish soldier, while

I sat, charming as a prince and worthy of engagement, mostly ignored.

I was plotting ways to steal her attention, and possibly win a smile from her, when Abigail or Alicia—Dimple Patch Twin—diverted the flow of conversation in my direction.

"Mr. Merriweather. Were you truly a news performer in London once upon?" She giggled, raised her hand to her mouth, and then waved at the air before her hand landed, accidentally I'm sure, in the lap of Mr. Larson sitting next to her. Did anyone but me notice how long it lingered there? "You know, I've been told more than once that I could act on the stage if I wanted."

If you keep that up, there isn't a man of the theater, or any other profession, in his right mind who would not want you to audition on him.

"Yes. I was a patterer."

"A patterer? One of those common street performers shouting the news and hawking wares for tips and drink?" Governor Hutchinson said.

"Once upon a time, yes, on the street," I said. "But later I provided news performances in the taverns, and charged merchants for advertising their wares. It was quite successful. And, with all modesty, I can say I became something of a celebrity news caster—that is what we called ourselves. I was first, but many more patterers followed until London was overrun by news casters overnight. I think I was born to be a news man, but back then I had not the resources to acquire a printing press. So I did it from a stage."

"Why did you stop?" Sally Hughes asked the plate of food before her, avoiding my glance.

"That is a story I may write someday. But it's too complicated, and frankly not the best dinner discussion. I'll save it for another time."

Mistress Hughes raised her eyes then, although she kept her chin lowered. I could not share the lurid details of my retirement from pattering, the backstabbing by an upper-class bitch that led to it, and the death that resulted from it. And yet, her look suggested she could read my mind and knew there was a sad side to my story. "It sounds mysterious," she said. "I would like to hear it someday. When the time is appropriate, that is."

Then I brightened. "It is a story full of murder and mayhem, love and heartbreak. Yes," I said. "For you, I will most definitely write that someday."

"And if you believe him," Jacob jumped in, "I have a camel in Cambridge I could sell you."

More chuckles.

Alicia or Abigail—Cheek Patch Twin—said in full child-like honesty, "I didn't know there are camels in Cambridge. Fascinating."

"There aren't," Miss Hughes said. She tilted her head and gave the twin a bug-eyed look of amusement that would have done some of my more mentally crazed former prison cellmates proud.

"There may not be camels in Cambridge," Mr. Murdoch said. "But I've read there are unicorns in Concord."

"Really?" the twins asked in amazed unison.

"Most definitely. I read it in the *Boston Gazette* just the other day. A miraculous discovery it was. The article was quite specific." He paused and turned his head quickly in my direction, slapping me with a glare like a backhand. "And as we all know, if something is in print, it's sure to be true."

"How delicious," said one twin.

"Who knew?" asked the other.

"Nobody," I said. "Nobody knew until a journalist uncovered it and made it common knowledge in the pages from the press." I raised my glass. "Here's to the Concord Unicorn, and the fine bit of reporting that revealed his existence for us all. Yes, Misses Abigail and Alicia, the world would be a much more uninformed and sadder place without us. The news printers."

"Yes. Without them we would have no political unicorns at all," the Governor said. "For news writers create them in the minds of readers."

Touché.

As tempted as I was to take the governor to task for such a flippant remark, I held my tongue. The smirk on my face would have to suffice, but I made sure he saw it.

"The worst of it in my mind," the governor's man, Mr. Larson, said, "is the masquerade of what really constitutes news these days. Our official government proclamations and positions are rarely reported by half the newspapers in town. Instead, they print a full page of drivel like that absurd theory that made the rounds recently of fathers marrying off their daughters strictly for political reasons."

The governor nodded. "That's not news."

"But it is the truth," Mistress Hughes interjected. "It does happen and no one consults with the daughter about her desires."

The governor and the men on either side of him turned their heads to stare at her as if Mistress Hughes had called King George a gorilla-faced mutant or some other slur that had recently become popular among the colonists. Governor Hutchinson's look was particularly withering. To her credit, the woman only stiffened her spine and refused to retreat back into her social space.

Me? I have a weakness for women with spunk, and the lady definitely tipped the spunk scale in her favor.

"The point *is*..." the governor drew out that word. "The liberal publishers waste all of their paper either criticizing Parliament or printing mindless claptrap and letters that the average citizen doesn't need."

"Not with so much important information being ignored," Mr. Larson said. "Then suddenly it's deemed news because the publishers pass it off as such. It's not. It's counterfeit. It only pretends to be news. It's..."

"Fake?" I offered.

I had first heard the word used among the grifters and confidence men on the streets of London a decade earlier. One of my cell mates during my short stay in the Boston jail after the Reckless Goat affair even used it, and I realized how fairly common it was becoming, even on this side of the pond. Governor Hutchinson chuckled and said that even he was aware of that bit of street slang.

"Does it apply to news?" he mused. "Yes. I like the sound of that. That's what we have these days."

"Fake news," I said.

Lord help us if that ever caught on.

Chapter Eight
An Offer You Can't Refuse

One of Madam Mae Flowers' most enduring qualities, particularly at the height of Boston's social season, was her keen eye for male and female compatibility. Like one of those newfangled tile piece puzzles the jigsaw, where the tab of one piece goes into the slot of another, her prowess as New England's premier matchmaker of human tabs and slots was, to put it mildly, unmatched. Through the course of the meal and our retreat to the library for drinks afterwards I became aware that she had designs to match the governor with Mrs. Abernathy.

On three different occasions, with three different approaches, she questioned Governor Hutchinson about his interest in marriage. His wife had died nearly twenty years earlier.

"It is a shame, Thomas, that you have not found love since we lost Margaret so long ago," she told him. "I miss her as I'm sure you do. But life goes on, does it not?"

"You are not getting younger, and I can tell you from experience, growing old alone is no picnic," she said, noting that he had recently turned sixty-three.

Madam Flowers offered up my favorite exchange when she believed no one was close enough to hear. Maybe it was that her own hearing was failing that she spoke louder than she imagined, but I was perusing the books on a shelf nearby within earshot.

"Take Mrs. Abernathy, for instance," she said. "Clarissa would make a fine first lady of the province. Thomas, we need a first lady. And she is young enough still to satisfy your needs until you are an old, feeble man, as all men become eventually."

"You are amazing, Mrs. Flowers," the governor said in a low voice. "Each time we socialize you have yet another jewel for me to examine. You wish me to attach it to a wedding ring."

As much as I was intrigued by eavesdropping on Madam Flowers' attempts to initiate the courtship of Governor Hutchinson and the widow Abernathy, Madam Flowers had her agenda and I had mine. Mine was to discuss saving the *New England News-Journal.*

A brief but agonizingly tedious amount of time later I had a cigar in one hand and Voltaire in the other. The women had recused themselves to the parlor on the opposite side of the antechamber to do whatever it is that young women do to avoid being bored to tears by cigar-smoking, politics-jawing, business-dealing males.

"*Candide.* I hear it is quite good. I should give it a try someday," Lieutenant Cole said as he tilted up the jacket of the book in my hand.

Voltaire and Swift, Locke, Rousseau, and Plato. All the books required for the well-stocked library of any man of means looked back at me from Murdoch's shelves—mocking me, actually.

My parents meant well giving me an education, but an unfortunate misunderstanding involving my eldest brother's overly playful wife and her moist undergarments on my nose forced me into exile from our family estate at a tender age before I could study those classic works. It was that exodus that led to my career as a patterer on the streets of London.

I returned the book to its original position, careful that its spine lined up perfectly with its shelf mates as I had found it. The whole of the collection was impressive, impeccably arranged and filling one entire wall of the room from the waist to the ceiling. There was not a speck of dust on any one of the volumes that I could tell, nor a crack or crease, suggesting they had never been opened. Murdoch even had a bound copy of Benjamin Franklin's *The Way to Wealth*, which I pulled down and opened just as the governor's aide joined us.

"Ah, Benjamin Franklin," Mr. Larson said. "You could do worse than take advice from him. One of the wealthiest of Americans, and he started with nothing."

"He was the one who inspired me to turn my patter into a business when we spent time together in London. We still correspond," I replied.

Larson took the Franklin book from my hand. "Early to bed and early to rise, makes a man healthy, wealthy and wise," he quoted.

"Get what you can, and what you get hold," I said. While I never read Rousseau, Locke, or the others, I was a frog-flogging Franklinphile and could quote him a length.

For want of a nail...

Never put off until tomorrow...

Keep it simple, stupid.

Just do it.

Larson gave me a respectful nod. "Come join us, Mr. Merriweather."

Governor Hutchinson sat in a stuffed chair angled to take advantage of the fire's warmth while commanding the remainder of the room. Murdoch and his lawyer sat across from him on a sofa while Jacob leaned with an elbow on the fireplace mantel. He waved his glass of brandy to and fro as he prattled on about some horse race he had witnessed, oblivious to the governor's extreme lack of interest. Jacob was in his full rogue mode. I had seen this before when alcohol began to control his senses, and I considered taking our leave for the evening. He would be of no use to me now. He stopped talking when I joined him at the hearth and squeezed his elbow.

"Merriweather," Mr. Murdoch began. "It is not a coincidence that I asked you here today to do a little business in the company of our fine Governor Hutchinson. And it is more so *not* to indulge Madam Flowers' campaign to marry off the governor." Murdoch and the governor raised their glasses with a nod to each other.

"She is a good-hearted woman," the governor laughed. "She means well, and she is as harmless as she is persistent."

Then the governor addressed me. "Merriweather, my advisors have convinced me that I am in need of a loyal partner with a printing press. It is more of a pain each day to find someone competent who hasn't jumped off the liberal cliff following Edes and Gill, Adams, Thomas, and the others. Lemmings. Have you ever looked closely at a lemming, Merriweather?"

"I'm not sure I would know where to look."

"Don't bother. Revolting, no-nose rodents. "

"Sounds like many a tax collector I know," I chuckled.

Mr. Larson picked up the thread of the conversation. "You see, now that Mr. Murdoch owns a controlling stake in your printing business we believe it would be in the best interest for all of us if the *News-Journal* adopted a more friendly position to Governor Hutchinson and matters involving relations between British America and Parliament."

"I see." I nodded.

"I believe you do, Merriweather," Governor Hutchinson said. "You have street credibility in Boston. You have the fourth most popular newspaper in town."

"Third most popular," I corrected him.

"*The News-Journal* is an established, trusted newspaper that has been around for decades," Murdoch said. "And you. Your way with words can be matched only by a few in Boston, and none are friends of ours. Your skill, combined with the proper message, would be a great use for the governor."

Governor Hutchinson leaned back and crossed his legs while handing his glass to his aide Larson. Larson scooted across the room to the liquor table.

"We are at a critical moment," the governor said. "It is incontrovertible to say the majority of citizens in the colonies have not yet taken a firm position for or against the kingdom. Their concerns are of putting food on their table, the health of their children, and the next harvest."

I could see where this was going. "You believe their collective opinion about whether the colonies should bugger the government is still pliable and you want to shape it before the liberal newspapers do," I said.

"Bugger?" Governor Hutchinson smiled. "I do admire your frank talk."

"People simply haven't made up their minds yet," Mr. Larson huffed as he returned with the governor's glass. "And it is up to us to form their opinion for them before things get out of control."

Jacob, who had been standing near the hearth next to me, watched Larson serve the governor and I watched his eyes dart to the liquor table. He took a step but I stayed him, stole his glass, and headed there myself, intent on lingering to keep a refill out of Jacob's hand as long as possible. An empty hand is a sober mind, certainly in Jacob's case. I deliberately paused, passing behind Murdoch as he sat on the sofa.

"And what becomes of my newspaper if I decline this proposition to which you are building?" I asked.

"Then it would be you who is buggered. And trust me, being buggered hurts." This came from the soldier, Lieutenant Cole, who had been standing silently apart from the others around the fire. All the room turned and looked at him silently as if he were an intruder to the conversation. He responded by throwing his shoulders back, removing the slouch that stole respect for his uniform. No retreat there.

He had that right but I wasn't about to surrender, drop my britches, and bend over to let them have their way with me. In fact, I still wasn't sure which way was *their* way. "What do I get out of this?" I asked.

"You get to continue being a printer, and getting paid to do so," Murdoch said. Then he called upon the lawyer, O'Donnell.

"Without going into the details," the lawyer began. "We are restructuring the debt agreement into a new contract, which I will provide for you Monday." And then he launched into a series of details, legalese, hyperbole, explanations, definitions, and various clauses that rule what may or may not be allowed. It would have filled two pages of my newspaper, and he murdered my attention before what would have concluded the end of the first column. I looked at the others and knew I wasn't alone.

"Let me get this straight," I said when O'Donnell paused for a breath. "The gist is that if I agree to avoid criticism of the administration and support loyalist opinions submitted to the newspaper," I said looking directly at the governor. "If I lean

Tory and stay in your good graces, you will allow me to stay in business."

Murdoch shifted his weight forward on the sofa. "And as the administration's preferred publisher, by printing additional broadsides, essays, and advertisements provided by the governor's office, you will gain credits that will have your debt paid in half the amount of time as your current situation allows."

"Possibly sooner," O'Donnell said. "You might well own the printing business free and clear by this time next year."

Whether this was the answer to my prayers or a deal with the devil I couldn't tell, and it wouldn't be clear until after I experienced just how much pressure came with being under the collective thumb of these rascals. But how much harm could there be? I had done exactly that in publicly shaming *The Massachusetts Spy* for derelict reporting of the Reckless Goat affair. And to achieve my goal of owning the shop in a single year more?

"Bring your contract to me on Monday and we'll discuss," I said.

Conversation drifted away from the business of newspapers at that point and turned to politics. It was the cloud over most any social discussion. The ships carrying East India Company tea were due in two weeks, three at the most. What were the colonists going to do about it? Sam Adams printed a number of letters in opposition at *The Gazette*. His cousin John and John Hancock, the local Committee of Correspondence, and most importantly, the mob known as the Sons of Liberty, were all standing up against allowing the tea into Boston. That meant having to pay a tax.

"What the sheep don't understand," Governor Hutchinson said, motioning to his aide. "Larson?" With that, Mr. Larson handed me a written page with the seal of the governor's office at the top. The governor continued. "What the public doesn't understand is that tax or no tax, these shipments will cost them less than the smuggled tea they are buying out of protest. It is all right there in my essay I wish you to print."

Had it been unusual to take submissions from the government in the normal course of publishing a newspaper, I might have been offended because we had yet to seal our deal to become an outlet for the governor's propaganda. But, what's good for the goose is good for the muskrat, I suppose. I would have printed it without a second thought on any other day, but somehow this day it felt prematurely smug.

It got worse when Lieutenant Cole pulled me aside a few minutes later. We paused near a column at the arched entryway to an antechamber that takes one to the remainder of the mansion. "I have an assignment for you," he said.

It was those words, "*I have an assignment for you,*" that rankled me. I did not work for him or even the governor. Not yet, at least. But then he said Governor Hutchinson had been so impressed with my report supporting the soldiers at the Reckless Goat that he—Lieutenant Cole—determined an eyewitness was needed to provide an account of another, more important event.

"I want you to sail on Wednesday with one of our armed coast guard vessels to Newport where our men will board a smuggler's vessel as it leaves with a cargo of contraband on its way to Boston. We will arrest the sloop's owner, a man of notoriety, who will be onboard. It will be quite the coup, and the story would be yours exclusively."

"You are going to arrest John Hancock?" I asked. Call it an educated guess because I was aware of the shipping schedules, and the timing matched the predicted arrival of one of Hancock's ships into Boston Harbor. Cole smiled and would neither confirm nor deny my supposition, which led me to suppose I was correct.

If I had learned anything from being a witness to a crime and reporting the facts that I saw with my own eyes, it was that I may have stumbled upon a previously unheard of form of journalism. Reporter involvement. Until now, newspapers passed along letters, essays, articles from other newspapers, officials documents, and advertisements. Repeating information that was from a two-week-old copy of some other newspaper was considered fresh news. This level of involvement—seeing, hearing, and then reporting—was unheard of. I liked it.

I didn't mind Hancock's politics for they made for good copy. But to describe the scene as one of the richest and most politically active members of Boston was led to jail in irons would be something for which I would sacrifice my left pinky—my right pinky being needed to work the printing press.

"Send the details of where I need to be with Mr. O'Donnell when he comes to see me on Monday," I said.

"Of course this discussion goes nowhere beyond these walls. Nothing gets out until the smuggler is in chains, you understand. Secrecy is paramount. Lack of discretion is, well, it's bad."

I stepped backwards, retreating for a trip to an indoor loo that Murdoch had informed us earlier was available through the antechamber and down the hall. Thank god for the rich and their modern improvements. I felt my expanding bladder would not last for a trip to an outhouse. Not replying directly, but tilting my head while looking away, I wagged my finger at him.

You silly goose. There is no need to say that. Of course I'll keep your secret.

I backed around the column and began turning when I heard a startled gasp and the gathering of gown, a tumble, and a curse.

Thump.

There was a girl on the floor in front of me. I tried to assist her up, but Miss Hughes' slim body, tangled in excessive satin and lace, hip padding that billowed the skirt, petticoat, stays, busk, and god knows what other contraptions beneath her gown, made wrestling her to an upright position clumsy and nigh impossible.

"My apologies, Mistress Hughes."

She flopped about the floor, trying to sit up but impeded by the fashions she wore, which made correcting her fall like trying to get a beached whale to stand on its tail. Without really debating etiquette, without much thought at all frankly, I finally hooked my arms under hers from behind and cupped her small but alluring breasts to get a handle on the situation—so to speak. I lifted her upright, pulling her tight against my own body to achieve a precarious and awkwardly intimate balance.

Success.

Mistress Hughes adjusted her hair, brushed her skirt, turned, and looked up with a smile that was grateful yet impish, and I believed a bit naughty for she lingered a bewitchingly long moment in the close, personal space we shared. Then she thanked me with a vigorous slap across my face and danced away without looking back.

Chapter Nine
Cuttlefish Blues

On the following Friday my eyes jerked open, and after my mind woke up as well, I didn't have the energy to actually lift my head, so I surveyed my situation without moving. The clock on the wall told me I had dozed the morning away. The grit on my tongue, and the foul odor of cuttlefish bone drool I wiped from my lips, told me that I had fallen asleep at my writing desk, snoring sufficiently to inhale the bone powder I had sprinkled on paper to dry the ink. My head rested on the latest attempt at my peacemaking pamphlet. It was apparently so engaging that even I couldn't stay awake reading it.

I looked at the words I had written, with only vague recollection.

It began with gibberish about holding Governor Hutchinson's feet to the fire.

These are the times that try men's soles.

I grabbed the paper and tore it until I had only a pile of scraps. I huffed and I puffed and I blew the pile off my desk and onto the floor. No one would care for that drivel.

I wiped my lips again, sniffed the back of my hand, and cringed. Bugger the badger! Cuttlefish breath is rancid enough when your prose is worthy. I grabbed the first thing I could find suitable for gargling. Fortunately, it was the bottle of Old Bushmills that Jacob had left behind.

I rubbed my tired eyes and cursed Murdoch, that soldier Cole, Larson, and even the governor, who signed off on the attempted bushwhacking of John Hancock. Their blow against smugglers wasn't even a tickle.

On that previous Wednesday I had sailed with an armed British schooner which met Hancock's sloop, *Song of Layla*, as she sailed south from Newport. I joined the boarding party, which was armed with muskets; I was armed with paper and a pencil. No sign of Hancock. I later learned Hancock stayed in Rhode Island after the ship made the stop in Newport. Gosh, could he have been forewarned?

Well, guffaw.

It took no great genius to know Hancock would take pre-cautions to use contacts in Newport to gauge his risk before continuing the trip with a cargo hold full of contraband. Lieu-tenant Cole had revealed that the cargo included illegal Dutch tea and two chests full of Spanish silver. All we found in the hold was a page from a shipping ledger, blank except for a crude scrawl, tacked to a post in the middle.

"Have a nice day," it read.

"No comment, Merriweather," Cole said when I ques-tioned him after returning to the deck. Then he stopped and inspected me as if I had a hand in his failure. Behind him, I could sense the disappointment of a company of soldiers standing at attention a discrete distance away. No foul, no blood. No arrests. No fun.

I did my best to make the story newsworthy without mentioning Hancock or the trap. Governor Hutchinson provided a lengthy statement deploring *SMUGGLERS* creating a *CRISIS* that *MUST BE STOPPED!* All in all, the affair was just one more stare-down between the Tories and the Whigs. A bit of ugliness that, sadly, was becoming too normal.

Morning was breaking when we finished the print run that Friday morning after an all-night work session, and I tasked Bert and Ernie to make delivery rounds as soon as the ink was dry. I chose to keep working, but hardly more than an hour later fatigue got the better of me, and that's how I wound up with a thick head and a snout full of Cuttlefish bone.

"Excuse me, Mr. Printer," a voice from the front of the shop called.

Sally Hughes stood at the counter in a halo of light from the front window. She held a small vase from the Orient that I used as a quill holder, which I now assumed she rapped on the counter to wake me. She wore a straw hat with a broad, round brim. Her dress, simple and straight, was a far cry from the clumsy formal garments that led to our intimate wrestling match a week earlier. I jumped at the sight of her and tried to gather myself, brushing dust from the front of my apron and smearing ink on my face when I wiped remnants of snooze from my eyes.

"Miss Hughes. What a pleasant surprise."

"Mr. Printer. What a pleasant…" She seemed to be search-ing for words while inspecting the pen holder. "No matter."

It was a response flavored with confidence, lightly salted with arrogance, yet tossed in sweet innocence and whimsical self-deprecation for a recipe that suggested she was a unique biscuit. I should have eaten a breakfast that morning for I was very hungry and it invaded my thoughts.

She attempted to return the porcelain to its place on the counter, but miscalculated the exact location while keeping her eyes fixed on me. Instead, she set it on the very edge where it wasted no time heading for the floor.

"Oh my."

The lady bent quickly hoping to catch it but failed, and it shattered into a dozen pieces of china at her feet. Worse, in her rescue attempt Mistress Hughes knocked her hat off and banged her temple on the counter's edge. She quickly stood straight again. Possibly too quickly, for a moment later her eyes glazed. I rushed to the other side of the counter, porcelain crunching beneath my boots, and steadied her with hands on her waist.

It occurred to me I was becoming an expert in having my hands on Sally Hughes' figure, and it was an enviable position to be in, but I wished it had been in less exasperating circum-stances. Still, I could get used to it.

"Come here." I led her to the nearest chair.

"I am soooo sorry, Mr. Printer. Your beautiful pottery is ruined." She held her right hand to the spot on her temple where I suspected a bump was already forming. I went for a cloth and water from the basin at the rear of the office.

"Don't concern yourself, Miss. I am sure I can find another vase like it with ease."

It was a lie, of course. Intricately painted with flowers, dragons, and Asian maidens, it had come with the shop when I purchased it from Mr. Addison. He said it was a very valuable and rare import from China that he had taken in payment for advertisements by the silversmith Paul Revere years ago.

"Are you always this clumsy?" I dabbed at the wound. There was discoloration and a hair-thin scratch with just enough blood to be visible.

She brushed my hand away, grabbed the cloth, and applied it with pressure to her noggin knot. "I'm afraid so."

I stepped back and looked down at her silently. She raised her eyes slowly as if measuring my worth.

"Perhaps…," I began.

"I should apologize," we said in unison, like a two-person choir, the different pitches of our voices working in harmony.

"Apologize?" I asked.

"Please do," she said.

"No. Please. Ladies first."

Mistress Hughes shifted herself from slouching in the chair like someone wounded, to a position proper for a lady. She folded the cloth and placed it in her lap. "I should apologize for not thanking you properly after my embarrassing stumble the other night," she said. "What is your offense you wish to atone for? As if I cannot guess."

Something in her tone struck me as both accusing and playful. Flirting? She batted her eyelashes. What was I to read from that? Before the editor in my brain could take control, I said, "I apologize for thinking less of you for thanking me with the palm of your hand. A simple curtsey would have been nice."

She rose slowly, gracefully. A queen could do no better. Then she tossed the damp cloth in my face and followed that with a royal curtsey. And she laughed. Lord, how she laughed.

I bowed to the best of my ability in return. "Mistress Hughes," I said. "I sincerely apologize if my clumsy attempt created ill will. It was never my intention, and having no significant experience helping a lady in such a horizontal state not of her choosing, I chose an expedient, if indelicate solution to my initial failed attempts."

She nodded. My apology accepted.

"And now, Mistress Hughes, since I do not need to help you up from the floor this time, how may I assist you today?"

She said she had an essay she wished to submit for the *News-Journal.*

Ah, free verse poetry? Recipes, perhaps? Household tips on preparing for the winter?

She fumbled through the gap in her petticoat to access a pocket tied to her waist.

No, perhaps it was something more political, I mused. She seemed the type. Not long ago I printed a similar essay by Mrs. Peters, deploring the large number of feral cats running about Boston willy-nilly and calling on the administration to provide neutering of all the males in town. She assured me she meant that only as it applied to furry critters and not the general male population, though if her husband were to be swept up in the cat crackdown she would not bemoan his fate. Nine children will do that.

"Yes. Here it is." She handed me a sheet, folded, wrinkled, and worn. I opened it to find one side with a few lines written and struck through, not unlike my feeble attempts to write the next Great American Pamphlet. The reverse side was in a decidedly different hand and filled nearly all of the space.

"*Patriotism from a Boston Kitchen*," I read. "Nice title."

"*The time is arrived for women in the Massachusetts Bay Colonies to display the strength of their skirts. Are we no less born for liberty than our husbands? Our sons?*"

I liked the author's words. "Is this your work?"

She shook her head.

"No? Can you read?" I asked.

She scowled and tried to snatch the paper from my hand. I was too quick.

"Did I insult the lady?" I really must stop doing that.

I skipped to the end of the work. "Signed by Mrs. Ima Femme. How clever."

Not.

Give me a possum-poking break. Was there no one with an opinion willing to publish without resorting to some hoity-toity pseudonym? Curse the day Ben Franklin started it with his damned Mrs. Silence Dogood thirty-odd years ago. Doctor

Franklin was a genius who had given our world a great many things, but this whole use of anonymity with a wink and a nudge was becoming tripe. In most cases the true identity was usually a badly kept secret, and the abuse of name-dropping for print's sake had become nothing more than a fashion statement for the printed author.

Well, yes, I confess. I indulged in the practice myself when the occasion warranted it. Rogue Vociferous. Sir Action Jackson. Peter Pickle-Picker was my favorite. I employed it for a scathing smack down of the Seventeenth Regiment of Dragoons. A cavalry unit, the regiment, and its horses commandeered the land of a farmer earlier that spring. They set up camp on and around his crop, fouled the soil in every manner imaginable, and ruined the year's supply of cucumbers. A royal bit of agricultural misconduct there.

I motioned to Mistress Hughes to follow me back to my writing table. The work she offered was eloquent. It was spiteful. It was poetic. It called on the women of the colonies for a formal boycott of the East India Company's tea, starting with the four ships due in Boston any day now. It was not so incendiary as to singe my fingers, but I could feel the heat of the author's passion.

"Do you sincerely recommend that women enlist their husbands to join in this boycott, and to refuse to grant them, uh, certain favors—conjugal—if they refuse?"

"Is that what it says?" Innocent surprise painted her face, set off by large, brown, beautiful eyes. Too innocent and too surprised. The lady was playing me once again.

"I am only the messenger. Though I will admit since no man will allow us to carry a musket, I believe a woman's charms may be the most powerful weapon at our disposal."

Falling prey to a lady's charms had been the primary source of my downfall in England. Actually, it was several ladies aiming their charms at my vulnerabilities at different points in my life that helped me understand just how powerful a weapon that could be. There was no foolproof defense for an honest man to employ. And when it came to charm, I was learning that Sally Hughes had a worthy arsenal.

She tugged the brim of her hat to hide the bruise on her forehead. "So you will print this for us?"

I looked at the page again. Yes, I could see trouble. This would test what amount of freedom Murdoch would allow me under the agreement we had reached. Possibly with some proper editing to soften the rhetoric, I could print it with an acceptable amount of risk and prevent Murdoch from tossing me into the street on my keister.

"Trading marital relations for a political protest is not going to be popular with a large segment of the public," I said. Though I admit it was highly amusing and certainly would grab many a reader's attention. How could I not publish it?

She lingered and we stood there, neither of us wanting the moment to end. "If I may be so bold as to ask, Miss Hughes. Are you a rebel?"

She tapped the paper in my hand. "Are you a coward?" Still smiling, she looked straight at me and drilled my heart with a twinkle in her eye.

Then she gave me a crooked smile and I knew that if the lady's charms were her best weapon, I would soon be a dead man.

Chapter Ten
Finesse Over Fiction

Problem solved.

Or so I thought.

On the following Friday afternoon, the *News-Journal*'s weekly edition included Mrs. Ima Femme's call for a tea boycott and forced celibacy for any man who declined to participate. I placed it in the center column at the bottom of page one, sandwiched between an advertisement for the Milk Street Theater's production of Shakespeare's *Much Ado About Nothing* and a letter from Reverend Virtuous O. extolling the harmony that comes from maintaining marital bliss, especially when it comes to politics. Jacob wrote that for me as a counterpoint to Sally Hughes' call to action. Relying on his past life as a Harvard theology graduate, he included the often-quoted Bible verse from Ephesians instructing wives to submit to their husbands. Old Ephesian obviously never encountered any wives like those I'd known or he would have scratched that line out before it saw the light of day. But I had to admit, it lent rhetorical credibility to the article and the author. More important, it provided a balance of opinions from both sides of the tea tiff. Yes, I was quite pleased.

Clinton Murdoch? Not so much.

The newspaper had only been on the street an hour when Murdoch and his lawyer, Frederick J. O'Donnell, arrived to inform me that Mr. Murdoch found me to be an unreliable partner in this new publishing agreement of ours, whereby he (management) and I (slave) should share the same political tint for the good of the business.

"Isn't that what you agreed to? But first you published such a timid accounting of the government's masterful seizure of Hancock's smuggling ship. Now you are printing this poppycock encouraging women to cut off their husbands'…"

"Poppycock?" I asked innocently.

O'Donnell laughed with me. Murdoch said a publisher loyal to the crown would never do that.

"Ah, well. Mr. Murdoch, I am not loyal to the crown, nor the opposition. I am loyal to the free exchange of ideas, even those you disagree with. Even those I disagree with." I was about to go full Franklin on his oversized derrière and wished Ben were there to rake the two of them across coals of journalistic indignation in person. He would do a better job. The best I could do was a quote from his *Apology for Printers*. Like many in our ink brigade, I had tacked his manifesto of expectations he set for himself as a publisher over my writing desk. I could almost reach out and touch it from where I stood, and I admit I glanced at it in what I might describe as an unconscious effort to draw some strength.

"Ben Franklin would say…"

"What Franklin would say is immaterial," O'Donnell said. Then he grinned with those yellow and crooked teeth. "It's more important to note what Mr. Murdoch would say."

Murdoch coughed up phlegm and paused to swallow it. I had to look away until he was ready to continue. "I would say, 'Do you wish to settle your debt now, or hand over the key to the shop and not let the door hit you on the way to the street?'"

Although it was not an empty threat, I felt no knee-jerking fear either. "You said yourself that I am useful here and you promised you would have no hand running my press. We represented the governor quite well in the newspaper. That is what we agreed to."

O'Donnell lifted his wig and scratched his bald head beneath it. He poked his nose into the pressroom. "We crossed paths with your boy, young Ernest, on the street on our way to this place. He tells us you increased your printing run for this edition and expects to sell every one of them."

Murdoch's face softened. "By god, Merriweather, if that is true I suppose we might overlook your impertinence this time."

"Fair," I replied.

"So Merriweather, perhaps we only need some process to inspect your more controversial items prior to print," O'Donnell said.

"Unfair."

Murdoch leaned against his bent arm on the white frame of the doorway between the front shop and the pressroom. Then, thinking better of it, he pulled back and brushed the grime from his sleeve. "Merriweather, I am not your enemy. In fact, you and I are both decent fellows trying to survive all this nasty hullabaloo infecting the world today. Hullabaloo has become an art form for people like Sam Adams and his rabble. You could be every bit as influential. I have the financial resources to make that happen."

He was selling. I was not buying. And yet I agreed with his premise and found myself saying, "I believe an honest press is needed, indeed. And I believe both sides need to be heard."

Perhaps Jacob was correct. In today's world, the worst ditch was in the middle of the road. Objective journalism may have been a noble ideal, but if it didn't turn a farthing to keep the press pressing, one must concede a bankrupt printer is a silent one. Flog the frog.

Murdoch chuckled, touched the tip of his nose before pointing at me. "I like you, Merriweather. Yes, indeed. You are correct that you have an intrinsic value to us that would not be easy to replace."

That being settled, what was there left to discuss?

O'Donnell said that now that my printing services had been secured, they had created a small group of influentials to advise the governor, with Murdoch being the principal player. "We'd ask that you join our group to advise on ways to shape public opinion surrounding certain issues, as we deem necessary. To use this power of your press along with other loyal printers to ensure that our voice becomes the dominant one in the province."

"We need to not only equal, but surpass the work of the Lib newspapers," Murdoch said.

O'Donnell smiled and nodded. "Naturally." Then he took a small purse from his satchel and tossed it to me. I caught it and it jingled with coin. Not an insignificant amount. Possibly it was worth hearing the man out before slamming the door on his offer.

"Let's call that an advance for services rendered."

Murdoch coughed again to clear his throat. "A salary for your effort."

And allegiance to the Hutchinson administration, I knew. "For turning the *News-Journal* into a propaganda instrument for the government," I said.

"Not exactly," O'Donnell said. "We are only suggesting you pay less attention to, how shall we say, conventional facts."

"Conventional facts?"

"Ones that fog the minds of readers," Murdoch said.

"What other facts are there?" I asked.

"Alternative facts," he replied.

"Alternative facts." I pinched my nostrils, my hand hid my mouth, and I looked at the floor trying not to scoff in their faces. Seriously?

"Your decision on which facts you report, and those you leave by the wayside, is every bit as important in the court of public opinion as the words you use," O'Donnell said. "You made that case more than once yourself."

"Then, Mr. Murdoch, you are advocating I simply need to twist the truth by reporting only the 'alternative facts' you favor?"

"Let's just say the governor has his facts…"

"Alternate or otherwise," I interrupted.

"He wishes them to gain more attention." Murdoch mocked me by twisting a smile onto his face, screwing a finger into his chubby cheek. "Alternative facts. It's all the rage these days."

O'Donnell said, "We don't mean to take space in the newspaper. We are discussing an additional broadside in addition to the newspaper. Something new to be published twice or three times each week letting the governor speak directly to the public."

"He can provide his latest thoughts on every topic," Murdoch said. "A newspaper, no matter how loyal, is a layer that prevents the governor from connecting with his people. No, we want to tear down that wall by creating a method of direct communication. This could be quite effective in winning over the public."

"Short, succinct, and personal," O'Donnell added. He withdrew a piece of paper from his satchel. I recognized the governor's seal at the top of the page and Hutchinson's elegant signature at the bottom, inked with a flourish and twice as large as the uneven scribble of copy above. The message was no more than two hundred-forty words, give or take a revision or two to add a child's worth of coherence and syntax.

"We want this printed and ready to be distributed throughout the town by morning. Can you accomplish that?"

My experience told me it was nearly impossible. "I can do that with my eyes closed," I told him.

"You'd better not attempt it," Murdoch laughed now. He was almost cheery. "We wouldn't want you to misspell and make the governor look less than literate." He lobbed a couple of "tisks" my way.

> Woe is the future of our land when a FAIL-ING ENTERPRISE such as the *Boston Gazette News'* slanderous use of ALTERNATIVE FACTS is allowed to impregnate the minds of noble citizens with FALSE! information, a conspiracy of the rogue Sons of Liberty...

I scanned more than I read. Sam Adams and the *Gazette* were bad. The king and the governor were great. To believe anything else was treason. It was a blatant appeal to readers to trust only his side of the story and reject anything otherwise that you might find in the press. The "ENEMY OF THE PEOPLE," Governor Hutchinson wrote.

"Enemy of the people?" I asked. "Does that include me?"

"Only if the *New England News-Journal* is willing to enable radical women playing fast and loose with their conjugal duties." O'Donnell laughed and patted my shoulder.

"Indeed. I did not care for that at all," Murdoch said. "Merriweather, we are going to pin these broadsides on walls throughout Boston. In the markets, along the wharfs, and next to every church and meeting hall door."

It was a tactic the Sons of Liberty used so effectively to incite resentment among civilians. The governor and Murdoch were fighting back to affect hearts and minds through the sheer volume of their broadsides. A little tit-for-tatism. Write. Print. Post. Repeat. Do it often enough and you create a band of followers who would believe only you and develop a hate for any opposition.

Murdoch pointed to the purse that I realized was locked tightly in my hand and near my heart. "I will send someone around first thing in the morning to collect and distribute the pages. I should have additional work for you tomorrow as well."

What would Ben do? In his *Apology for Printers* he made it clear a printer's job was to provide ink to every voice on every subject, leaving it up to the audience to decide truth. But in the scorching politics of Boston, that may have given the public more credit than it deserved. Bullocks. Anyway, if I reject it, Murdoch would merely bribe one of my competitors into taking on the task, so it would go out into the public square regardless. Why not me? I could spend his money as well as the next man.

"My press is yours, sir," I said, but not without a dash of fatalism.

He nodded. "Yes, it is. Never forget that."

As the men turned to leave, I saw Murdoch nudge the lawyer with his elbow.

"Oh, yes," O'Donnell said. "We have a news item you will want to investigate, something I came across just this very morning. The constable found a body today, beneath Child's Wharf and Still House."

I nodded. Word had traveled from the waterfront to my front door. I expected to spend the weekend collecting more information for our next edition.

"My cousin Constable O'Donnell believes the knife wound in the victim's eye hints of murder."

I had not yet heard that part of the story.

"Bad show," Murdoch said. "Do we know the identity of the victim?"

"It appears to be a fellow named Gunther or Grayson, or something similar. He was a customs agent. Do you recall Lieutenant Cole claimed they had information from a customs agent named Grant? Yes, that was his name. Grant was the source for their plan to seize John Hancock's ship." O'Donnell appeared to be addressing only Murdoch now. "The man disappeared after Cole's search of the vessel turned up nothing but an empty cargo hold, and the lieutenant suspects this fellow had a change of heart and warned Hancock of the raid."

Then Murdoch, staring straight at me, said to his lawyer, "I wonder, Frederick, if this customs chap did indeed have a hand in alerting that bastard. It's clear someone got word to *Layla*'s Captain Clapton to empty the ship before troops arrived."

I did not like the way he looked at me. It was the same cold stare Lieutenant Cole had shot at me on the dock next to the *Layla*'s gangplank. A suspect? Not I. "Do not look at me, sir. You can rest assured; my knowledge of the plan was executed in faithful confidence. If I ever divulge a secret, you'll find it in print, and I will own up to it." And yet the question lingered. Did the customs agent squeal his deal to finger Hancock? And if he did not warn Hancock, who did?

The men gathered themselves, turned toward the door, and engaged in a private conversation, yet perfectly loud enough that there was no mistaking it was meant for my ears as well.

"Actually, Mr. Murdoch," O'Donnell said, "this plays well. Not only will Merriweather have a decent story to investigate over the death of this poor corrupt customs official, but if he did not alert Hancock's ship then we have a spy running loose on the streets of town. Imagine what a coup that would be— to unmask and report the identity of that traitor? This whole affair could end in a public hanging. Good news, that."

Murdoch coughed deeply in response. Another low, wet, phlegm-inducing cough that he refused to spit—and made me sick in the process. "Merriweather, get right on that, will you?"

Chapter Eleven
A Wanker and a Woman

George Herman Grant was a wanker if ever there was one.

He was the victim who did, indeed, wind up on the wrong side of a dagger beneath Child's Wharf and Still House, although my intrepid news investigation and a quick visit to the constable's office determined the blade was found in his throat, not eye. Odd, though. What had taken place that the killer was so distracted or inept that he left the murder weapon behind? Interesting.

A government tidesman, Grant was one of four Boston customs agents tasked with boarding ships and collecting duties on the cargo, accounting for it, and balancing the ledgers before the goods could be off-loaded to the docks, the warehouses, or the pockets of unscrupulous merchants.

Jacob sat on a stool at the corner of my office worktable and held up the latest diatribe from the governor to the lantern's light. Night was falling and Murdoch made it clear we were to work into the Sabbath if necessary to get the post on every church doorstep before the first sermons of the day. He was willing to risk my arrest for Sabbath violation to make a statement. I was reviewing the first pages off the press, searching for errors.

"This Grant fellow was working with the governor's people to catch Hancock silver-handed, so to speak?" Jacob asked.

"They paid him well for his information," I replied. "And, oye boy, was that Lieutenant Cole fellow steamed like a lobster at a summer picnic when it all came to naught. He actually struck one of his command when we returned to the dock here in Boston. And he cursed all kinds of things about being made fools."

The governor's post was a single broadside that filled more than half the page. With four inches given to advertisements in the right-hand column, the rest of the space was a rather unusual letter by Murdoch himself. Though the governor did not mention Hancock by name, his argument flatly declared without evidence that the Sons of Liberty were responsible for the murder. I didn't take my eyes off my work. The sound of Bert and Ernie working the press was nearly drowned out by their sibling bickering.

"Butt head."

"Dung breath."

The top of the governor's letter carried the seal of his office, but Murdoch required a masthead that identified the broadside as a *New England News-Journal* publication. That irked me because I had come to think of myself as the *News-Journal* and yet I had no say in its message.

"So this is what they call their alternative facts?" Jacob suggested.

"That's what Murdoch called them when I protested that there was no hint of evidence to support the governor's position. Nothing."

"I guess each man has his own these days," he said.

I inspected my work. Not a single error there.

The lack of facts, alternative or otherwise, was no barrier to the governor. I had framed with a border one particular section of Governor Hutchinson's screed.

> This **CONSPIRACY** of violence against Mr. Grant, an honorable **CIVIL SERVANT** in His Majesty's employment, and a decent resident of our city, **STABBED, BEATEN AND ROBBED** by none other than that mob which calls itself Sons of Liberty will never be accepted. They will **CHOKE** the liberty of **EVERY CITIZEN**, innocent men and women of Boston, until they control our very lives and the **RULE OF LAW** is their illegal rule by violence only.

In his contribution to the broadside, Murdoch agreed with the governor and then took a direct shot at Boston's newspapers. He suggested a conspiracy by men like Samuel Adams and the liberal press contributed to poor Mr. Grant's murder. He held that Adams and his publishers at the *Gazette* should be held accountable for the assassination, since their words influenced the SOL crowd.

The only attribution Governor Hutchinson and Murdoch wielded in support of their position was one I had come to loath. "They." As in "They" say this. Or "They" say that. And almost always followed up with "As everybody knows..." The problem was that "they" are anybody or nobody, but sounding authoritative as if "they" had sole possession of the truth and their truth was common knowledge. If you can't acknowledge that, it is your fault.

Jacob and I paused staring intently at one another, mirrored stone faces in the looking glass before bursting out with laughter. Rubbish. Pour another whiskey.

Swish. Clack. Creak. Release. Repeat.

An hour later, Bert and Ernie had produced one stack of the post. Thank god it was only one page. I sat at the counter with a reading lamp and inspected the latest pages of the run while Jacob provided moral support, snoring away in my work chair. I had dusted the back of his right wrist with a line of cuttlefish bone powder to tickle his nostrils, punishment for dozing off, and made a mental note to avoid getting within a snake's length of his breath when he awoke.

The bell above the door tinkled. Sally Hughes stood in the doorway.

Stop the presses! This was a pleasant surprise.

I looked past her and she appeared to be unescorted. Unusual considering the sun had set well over three hours past. A woman alone on the street at night carried risks most genteel ladies would avoid. It was unusual but most definitely welcomed in this instance.

"Good evening to you, Mr. Printer." She cocked her head and turned it to follow the sound of the clacking and the squeaking, the rolling, the cursing, and other signals of printing mischief coming from the other room. "It sounds as if I may be a bit late," she said.

"Late?"

"I hope you are close to finishing whatever task your press is engaged in. I have a need of some urgency that I would like you to satisfy."

Though I was British by birth, the red-blooded American male in me took command of my imagination. I immediately conjured up visions of what her her urgent needs might be and ways I would love to satisfy them. As if on cue Jacob snorted, sneezed three times, and came to.

"Hello, m' lady." He pinched his nose and then grimaced after sniffing the back of his hand. "It is good to see you." He sneezed again. His white shirt hung loose at his waist, so he clutched it with both hands and doubled over to use it as a handkerchief to dry a watering eye.

Miss Hughes smiled with tight lips, suppressing a chuckle. No straw day hat this time; she wore an elegant woman's tricorne with a wide ribbon that matched the rose-colored fabric from her gown. And a feather. Her ensemble sang in the kind of harmony that told me she had come from some fancy-schmancy but not quite elegant engagement. My own invitation to the affair must have gotten lost in transit, I bemoaned.

She shifted her eyes from me to Jacob and back as she untied the string holding her deep wine-colored walking cape.

I coughed. "Jacob. Would you go check on the devils to see their mischief isn't causing any issues with this project? Bert should have pressed another sixty by now." I said it without taking my eyes off the lady.

Silence from Jacob at first, and then a knowing sigh. "Pfshhh." Ever the good sport, he left with a bow and shuffled past me with a few grumblings to let me know it was under protest and he expected a full report upon Mistress Hughes' departure.

"Tell me of this urgent need," I said. "How may I serve you?"

She handed me fine, elegantly woven linen-rag stationery, a step up from the discarded scrap she'd delivered previously. There was no letterhead to indicate the source, though from the pattern of the weave and whiteness of the paper I could guess it was purchased from Mr. Darby, the stationer in Haymarket Square. He was the favorite merchant for fine papers and writing ware of Boston's elite from John Hancock on down. I sniffed at it and was disappointed not to find a delicate fragrance, perhaps a trace of the lady's perfume. The handwriting was the same as Mrs. Ima Femme's article.

Mistress Hughes wandered past me as I read the contents of the piece. She appeared perfectly comfortable and welcomed in my writing space behind the customer's counter.

I swallowed hard. "Where did you get this?"

"Are you required to know?"

"Bloody hell, yes. You are accusing thugs of assassinating George Grant at the direction of the governor."

"It does not specifically say the governor," she countered.

Was this a joke? Her airy manner suggested she either didn't understand or was unconcerned about the trouble this could cause. "It only speaks to the conspiracy of those in a broad circle around him to do the deed," she said.

"You have proof of this?"

"I do. A reliable source very close to the governor."

I asked who that may be, but she rebuffed me with a shake of her head. "You, of all people, should know that," she said. "Correct me if my information is wrong, but at our social gathering at Mr. Murdoch's, didn't you allude to having spent time in the London prison for refusing to reveal your source for reporting that something happened to someone for something or other?"

The lady was cagey. And correct, up to a point.

"But it is the publisher's duty to know the source of such alarming information. I would protect the originator, naturally," I said.

She simply shook her head.

"Well, you can forget having this print shop produce this for you," I said. I did not tell her even if we were not already engaged for the evening, Mr. Murdoch would put me out of business before the ink was dry if I dared print this scandalous muck. "How can I tell this is not simply scandalous muck?" I liked that phrase.

"It's not muck. It's true, I tell you. The public needs to know."

"I liked you better when you were merely advocating cutting off husbands' poppycock."

"Excuse me?"

"Madam, I believe it might be best if you take this to Mr. Thomas or Edes & Gill. They will happily publish your opinion."

"They are long closed and tomorrow is the Sabbath. Isn't there something we can do?"

Think. Think quickly. There was a way, but it wasn't a path I would normally choose to take. Her article might yet go public, but Merriweather & Associates could not be accused of being part of the effort.

"Will you swear to me, upon your honor, there is no mistake? That this is all true?" I asked.

"It comes through someone who has firsthand knowledge of the affair, though not directly involved in ordering the poor man's murder."

"Yes, there is a way," I said slowly. "Even still, I can't promise a positive result—the day is late and our options are limited. Come, now. It is dark outside and the streets are full of run-amokers. A gentlewoman should not be alone at this hour."

"Then you will help?" she asked.

"You don't know that which you don't know. It is complicated." And getting more complicated by the moment. "I will explain on the way to your home."

Then she tilted her nose up to the ceiling, blinked, and began to sway as if fainting. I rushed forward as she spun and fell backwards into my arms. I stood there for many seconds, not certain what to do.

She was feather light and as limp as a newly printed broadsheet, still moist from the press bed and hung over the line to dry. Her eyes were closed and her chin tucked against her breast just above while I held her by hooking my arms under hers, careful to avoid repeating the unintentional intimacy of her stumble in Murdoch's antechamber. Then, she patted the back of my hand. I might be mistaken but I was convinced she nudged it closer to her bosom before she said in a strong voice, "You were much better at this the last time."

Flog the frog. I'd been had. "Mistress Hughes, you are playing me for a fool."

She leaned her head back to look up at me without making an effort to stand. "Not a fool, Mr. Printer. But I am playing with you. Tell me," she said sweetly. "Is it working?"

"Not in the least," I lied.

Chapter Twelve
Sticks and Stones Don't Break My Bones

In a small pasture, just beyond the intersection of Sudbury Street where it meets Hanover at the edge of Bling Green, stands a massive white oak tree on a small rise where in the daylight hours you can gaze down on Mill Pond to the north. A lovely spot for a picnic. At night it is as mysterious as a Grimm's Fairytale monster about to clutch you in its branches and devour you. Its mouth is a hole in the trunk, about the size of my head at about the same height.

Sally and I paused to admire the monster. "I see what you mean," she said. She drew closer for the protection of both me and the light from the lantern I had raised above our heads.

"You are such a coward, Mr. Printer. I don't know why I am intrigued with you," she had said as we left the print shop. "Possibly there is something in the water in Boston."

"I have found that copious amounts of wine and rum are much healthier than the water in this town," I answered.

The walk to where she lived in Cambridge District was quicker than I preferred. I had hoped for a more leisurely, time-consuming stroll. It was late enough that you might encounter one or two women on the street returning from shops and homes where they worked. The other women you might find were working the street, if you get my drift. The tree was about halfway between my print shop and where Sally had taken a room with Madam Flowers.

I took her hand and drew her to the base of the big oak. "I must swear you to secrecy. My brethren printers would cut me off at the knees if they knew I revealed this to you."

"Ooh. I love secrets. They are so, so sneaky," she replied.

I placed her letter with the scathing accusation of Governor Hutchinson's role in the murder of George Grant into the tree's yawning cavity and explained, "Only a few know of this. Some anti-British elites who want to be heard but find it critical that they avoid being identified. It is not enough to use a pseudonym or no name at all. Their work tends to be of the most radical nature." Here I wagged a finger at her. "Not unlike a certain person I have come to know."

Sally smiled sweetly but said nothing.

"They do not want to be traced through a partnership with one printer or another," I continued. Caught up in the suspense of my explanation I realized I had dropped the timbre of my voice. I became a patterer again. "Thus, they find their way into mainstream news while keeping their hands clean of ink and any link to their posts."

"Much like my author," she said. "How delightfully deceitful. I love the huggermuggery of it all. It makes me wish I was more than a mere messenger. Oh, but Aunt Mae would send me back home to Maryland straight away if she knew I was here with you and involved in a scheme such as this."

The tree was conveniently located. My shop was in easy walking distance, as was Edes & Gill's *Gazette* as well as *The Spy*. "A few lesser-known publishers who specialize in irregular print runs of sensational tabloid nature are known to stop to see if some anonymous contributor has filled the 'news hole,' as we have come to call it. One fellow in particular, the *Watertown Times-Forger*, is one that comes to mind, and I suspect he'd be most interested in this inflammatory report of yours."

Sally asked why we couldn't just take it directly to the *Forger*.

I said, "Firstly, his identity and his location are a mystery. And given the nature of this…" I pointed to her treatise in the mouth of the tree. "…I strongly advise you to remain a mystery as well."

She was a mystery to me, for certain. I knew precious little about her. I wanted to suggest we remedy that situation beneath the news hole, but common sense got the better of me. We would, I hoped, have sufficient time for chit and chat and things like that in the near future. I took liberty to place my hand upon her arm to emphasize the risk this evening invited. She did not flinch. In fact, she drifted ever so slightly in my direction with the touch.

I lifted the lantern, motioning to different corners of the city before us. "Things are getting dangerous for wordsmiths, my lady," I said. "Last year I aggravated the Sons of Liberty and had a brick shatter my front window with their initials scrawled on it. A few months later they attacked the conservative *Weekly Advertiser*. The publishers gave up and sold the shop to a pair of printers friendly to the governor and they moved out to Castle Island, where they would have protection from the troops stationed there."

"Oh my."

"But it cuts both ways. It has been worse for the liberal newspapers. "The *Boston Post-Examiner* publisher, Graham Snardwod, was accused of a clerical error on a government project and spent three days in jail on trumped-up charges trying to clear his name. When he was released, he found the *Post-Examiner* had been ransacked, his press and cases of type were destroyed, and the gutter outside was a sewer of dried, gummy ink."

"Who did that?" Sally asked.

"I suspect the governor's hand-picked security detail, or perhaps the military wanted to make a lesson of Snardwod. And now he's no longer in business. Additionally, roving squads of soldiers in uniform have lately taken to protesting outside *The Massachusetts Spy*, burning Isaiah Thomas in effigy. Now you have accused the governor or his lieutenants of orchestrating a murder? Murdoch would have my head on a platter if I printed a hint of this, not to mention how much pain the governor might inflict. Especially if this is true."

"I swear to the truth of this document. I will vouch my very virtue upon its truth."

Now that was an interesting proposition. It struck me as odd, but given her earlier deliberate swoon at the print shop, it was not entirely out of harmony with what I perceived was a flirtatious character. A beguiling character. And I believed her right down to my bones.

"You give me little hope," Sally said glumly. "And you scare me more than a bit. But this is important. Please tell me it is worth the risk."

Then she gave me a quizzical look as I set down the lantern. I wobbled, blinked, and laid a fist at my cheek. She stepped forward to steady me as I turned and fell backwards into her arms.

At least I would have, had they been there. Instead, I landed ass-first on the grass and bopped my head on a raised root. I saw stars high in the night sky; they peeked from behind the branches of the oak over Sally. If I had the time, for I certainly had the inclination, I would have invited her to lay beside me and take in the glorious world above. Inverted to my vision, it was hard to see her face clearly, but there was enough light from the lantern to know she was laughing.

"You catch like a girl," I said.

"You swoon like a drunk. I might have hurt myself trying to break your fall. I'm not an idiot," she laughed again. "Mr. Printer, are you playing me?"

"Is it working?"

"No. Not at all," she lied, I knew.

She kept a hand to my elbow as I stood again, a minimal amount of support that was more moral than physical.

"Bollocks," I said.

"Now, now, Mr. Printer. It was more graceful than most, I dare say. Not embarrassing at all."

"No, bollocks in that I forgot the signal."

"Signal?"

I explained that in order for our secret circle of printers to know there was something of value in the oak tree's news hole, the author would dangle a piece of cloth over its lip, something that could be spotted from a discreet distance if one were looking for it. Mistress Hughes thought for a moment and then pulled apart the folds of her cloak. She reached with a certain amount of delicacy under her gown. I would have given my left pinky toe for enough light to see what I believed was a blush in her cheeks. She withdrew a kerchief.

"Will this do?"

I nodded. I stole a moment's pleasure to capture the scent of Miss Hughes as I moved the cloth slowly past my nostrils and smiled at her before putting the kerchief in the tree. She then picked up the lantern at our feet, avoiding my gaze from that moment through the remainder of our walk home.

Chapter Thirteen
WTF?

The *Watertown Times Forger* made a sensational leap into the press pool of news sources in Boston that Monday. It landed with an unwelcome splash in the Clinton Murdoch manor.

"Cesspool, is more like it," Murdoch said. It was Monday afternoon and I had been summoned as part of the governor's newfangled "advisory committee" to share the mayhem that followed WTF's appearance, disputing every one of the governor's broadsheets I had labored to print for Murdoch's men to distribute the previous day.

I wanted very much to sit down, but the head of Governor Hutchinson's security unit, Lieutenant Cole, Lawyer O'Donnell, and the governor's chief of staff, Larson, all stood at attention before Murdoch. Best not to call attention to myself. Even though it was midafternoon, the heavy oak and paneled walls of the study and the dark gray weather beyond the single window left us to survive in the soft light of candles, oil lamps, and the flickering flames from the fireplace that cast wavering shadows on the wall.

Murdoch rapped the head of his cane on the floor of his study so hard that its duck head handle broke off, skittered across the floor, and ricocheted off my shin. "Who is this fucking Philistine who would print such rubbish? Where in the name of Christ did this come from?"

"Watertown?" I offered, pointing to the crude masthead of the *Watertown Times Forger*. The joke was no better received than the broadside itself. I had experienced POMs (people of money) using such gutter language in the past during unguarded moments of stress or debauchery, but any veneer of civility Murdoch might have attempted hit a brick wall that afternoon. What's more, I did not much care. Sleep had been hard to come by since Mistress Hughes visited on the eve of the Sabbath, and I was exhausted.

"We are investigating this and we are tracking down its source," Larson said.

Cole clasped his hands behind him, and his chest and chin jutted forward. Unlike Murdoch, who sputtered profanity while seated near the middle of the room in a chair that might well have served as a throne, the lieutenant seemed amused, if not entirely jolly. He said he would welcome an opportunity to find, engage, and crush the publisher of *WTF*. "Surely this fool cannot feel he is in some way protected by setting up shop a few miles outside of the city. Locating him in a village that small should be easy enough."

"Not to overstate the obvious," I said, overstating the obvious, "but attaching Watertown to the masthead is no guarantee the printing press is located there." I would not have mentioned it if I thought for a moment that fact would go unnoticed more than a moment.

"Lieutenant," Murdoch said. "You are the government's intelligence officer. I asked you here for your intelligence. Surely you can spread your informants out around Boston and uncover the identity of this Forger fellow."

"Merriweather has a point. We don't really know where his printing press is at the moment, although it would be preferable if he were located in Watertown," Lieutenant Cole replied. "The farther he is from the protection of those Sons of Liberty vigilantes, the better for us to control him once we catch him."

I shifted uncomfortably. Perhaps I put Sally Hughes at greater risk than I had forecast. I pondered that. If Cole discovered the *Forger*'s identity, surely his investigation would lead him to Sally faster than a sailor on shore leave could rush down the gangplank and to the nearest tavern. Christ on a cracker, I should have just refused to help for her own good.

Murdoch struggled to stand without the help of his cane, which now lacked its duck handle, to steady himself. Sadly for me he was successful, and he whapped my thigh with his duckless stick.

"All right then, Merriweather," he growled. "It is time to prove your worth. You have your eye on every damned word set in type in this town. Tell us the name of this rogue who is accusing the government of murder and more. Surely you would know."

I shrugged. "If you catch him, I would gladly take a switch to him myself. He has made himself my enemy too. I've taken my share of criticism from Adams on the left, and that Tory John Draper at the *Advertiser* on the right, but whoever is behind the *Watertown Times Forger* crossed a line with what he wrote about me. And it is a sad attempt to dishonor my honor."

WTF was a simple, two-sided sheet with bold, large type in two columns on the front and back. I pointed to the second page and read a section in my best patterer manner.

> As for the government's newly-decreed personal PROPAGANDA publication, the New England News-Journal, its printer Leeds Merriweather was BORN A BRIT and, as such, cannot be considered A TRAITOR to the crown. A bastard, yes, as one might expect in political matters. Therein lies the problem for any AMERICAN who seeks FAIR REPORTING of issues domestic.

The *Forger* went on to suggest that patriotic residents throughout the Massachusetts Bay Colony should buy up copies of *The News-Journal* and keep them in their outhouses—the only good use for the paper. *WTF* called for people to protest by using the newspaper and smear my good name with their excrement. Damning but clever.

"The harm to your precious bit of self-worth is nothing," Murdoch said. "Is this going to happen again? How do we prevent that?"

"There is no way to know," I said. "Unless we can determine his end game. This might be a single publication of something the *Forger* wanted to expose, but found it too ugly and unsubstantiated for even the likes of *The Spy* to print."

"There is nothing that mongrel Thomas won't print if it is aimed at us. Truth be damned," Larson said.

"The governor's response is nearly ready for distribution," I said. At least I hoped so. Mr. Larson had tracked me down at the coffee house within an hour of *WTF*'s appearance at Proprietor Deerfield's place and other public houses that morning. He carried the governor's official rebuttal, hastily scribbled in what appeared to be Larson's own hand, and he demanded that I print it immediately. So summoned here, I had to leave and drag my weary carcass across town, leaving Bert and Ernie to finish pressing copies and bundling for delivery.

Murdoch, Larson, and O'Donnell continued to debate whether the *Forger* presented much of a challenge.

"Perhaps this is just a one-time rant. We may never see *WTF* again," I offered.

They ignored me and speculated on who could be behind this malicious publication. Hancock, Warren, James Otis, Revere. Round up the usual suspects; every man in the room had his favorite cad. Samuel Adams appeared to be the front-runner if this was a horse race of offensive Whigs.

"Enough!" Lieutenant Cole's voice thundered across the room. He had been standing at the window, ignoring yapping dogs behind him, lost in his own thoughts. "Gentlemen, you have missed the most important, and possibly dangerous, revelation in this *Forger*'s document. This mentions the murder weapon, a dagger, had a handle bearing the coat of arms for the 29th Regiment. An officer's weapon."

"Sweet Jesus on cross," Murdoch said. "He is blaming the military. At the very least placed the blame squarely on a member in His Majesty's service."

Cole shook his head as if he couldn't fathom how he wound up in a room full of dolts like us. Like the others, actually, because I knew where he was going with this line of thought. I had seen the original document, and it was the same place that now concerned me about the risk Sally Hughes had taken. For a brief moment my imagination grabbed me by the scruff of my neck and forced upon me visions of Mistress Hughes dangling from the end of a rope in the Fox Hill gallows. What did I do?

"Don't you nitwits understand?" Cole asked. "This Forger fellow has printed information that no one else had access to. Mentioning the dagger gives him away."

"It was a lie, no doubt," someone said, although my mind wasn't in a position to notice who made the comment.

"The murderer obviously had stolen the knife," someone else said.

And yet, it did seem unusual that a military officer would be careless like that. Any seasoned thug from the lowest ranks of society would be ashamed to leave his weapon behind. A trained military man? Not likely.

"The murderer used that dagger and left it behind as evidence, specifically to frame the government. A carefully planned conspiracy, most certainly," Cole said.

"The lieutenant is exactly right. The source of the dagger and its markings was never made public," O'Donnell said. "My cousin the constable kept that a secret." He ran a finger under his wig at the brow and scratched his head.

"Confound it," he said.

I had taken Sally Hughes at her word that her account was true, or true enough at least. Now, O'Donnell confirmed the report. And yet, these fellows tossed the bloody details about in conversation as if it was common occurrence to find a corrupt government lackey left to die under a pier with a military, and likely traceable, knife in his throat.

"Then how did the Forger learn of the dagger's provenance?" O'Donnell asked.

"Merriweather!" Murdoch barked, pulling me back from the beautiful vision of Mistress Hughes as I had last seen her by lantern light. Fantasy interruptus. "Merriweather, you are wasting time here. You need to get this out on the streets as quickly as possible. And you need to add this new angle, a denial by both the governor and Coroner O'Donnell. Both testify to the fact that the weapon in the Forger's account was in no way connected to anyone in uniform. Say there are few clues to the attacker's identity. Everybody loves a good mystery. It's still a mystery."

"But Mr. O'Donnell just now told us his cousin had information known only to him revealed. That would suggest the Forger is telling the truth."

"The *governor* would suggest the Forger is wrong, as you will so report," Murdoch cut me off. "Must I dictate this myself?"

"Let us be clear, Merriweather," O'Donnell said. "My cousin will publicly swear to the fact that there were no markings on the weapon military or otherwise. Do you have evidence to the contrary?"

I shook my head. "Of course not. How could I?"

"It's settled then. The truth is the Forger lied."

I might have been dizzy from the spin they used to obscure the truth. I might have been lightheaded from my recent lack of sleep and sustenance. I most likely was simply exasperated to the point of not caring any longer. Reporting only on what the governor declared, his response, would be the truth whether I believed him or not. Was I being disingenuous? Was that even my call? WWBFD? What would Ben Franklin do? *WTF?*

I bowed slightly to take my exit, thankful to have been dismissed. I left them speculating on the who, what, where, when, why and, most disturbingly, how the Forger had gained access to the information. I knew the answer to all of the five Ws. It was the "how" that caused me heartburn for all the risk involved.

Chapter Fourteen
That Was No Lady...

"Shit!"

"That's what it is. Shit," Jacob deadpanned, though it sounded as insincere as a drunk's pledge to go straight at the end of his next bottle.

We stood on the landing outside my print shop upon my return from the Monday meeting at Murdoch's.

I was not in the mood for this. Jacob, my two young printer devils, and I stared at a most revolting and fetid copy of *The New England News-Journal.*

It seemed someone, or someones, had taken the author of the *Watertown Times Forger* literally when he called for using my newspaper as an outhouse wipe. I hope the person who vandalized this copy at very least read the paper before posting his fecal matter protest. They had tacked it to the front wall of my shop near the corner of the building. The masthead was smeared with his foul-smelling commentary. You would think the author would at least have saved this review for the reverse side, the opinion page, where it belonged. I held my breath and removed it from the wall gingerly, folding it before turning it into a wad that would offend the least, and tossed it into a pile of refuse in the alley between the print shop and Mrs. Strand's wigmaker's establishment.

"I found one just like it on a post at White Street and Hall," Bert said.

"Ooh. Me too. I saw one outside Mr. Cleavers' house," Ernie added. His eyes were large and twinkling beneath the dark hair cut low across his brow, and he tried to cover a smile behind three fingers pressed to his lips. If he had been any more amused by this, the freckles would have danced with glee right off his face.

"You did take it down, didn't you, Ernie?"

"Why should I do that?"

I sighed. How many more newspaper vandals might there be out posting similar protests across Boston?

"I'd say it gives a whole new meaning to desecrate your work," Jacob said. "More like dexcremate. Either way, it's a crappy commentary." He was enjoying this far too much.

Me? I understood the tremendous power of the press. I had used it to move people to do things. Brave things. Cowardly things. Things that defied logic. But this knotted my stomach. It was one more indication that those spoiling for a fight with England could be moved to action so easily because they were looking for only the slightest hint of an excuse to do so. I saw little humor in it. Well, maybe a bit in this particular case.

I said, "If the *Forger* could do so much damage with so little effort using satirical dung, imagine the shit-storm he could cause if he made a serious call for rebellion."

"Ooh. Well played, Leeds," Jacob chuckled. "Almost as if you are accustomed to having someone smear your reputation so distinctly. Smeared your newspaper, your masthead as well. And I believe you missed a spot on the wall there, too."

I shooed the boys back into the shop to start preparing the ink and paper we would need to print the governor's next post. It would be a hard afternoon and I doubted we'd be done by sunset. "And when you make your rounds this afternoon," I told them, "take down and toss any vandalized copies of our newspaper that you come across as well."

Jacob followed me to my composing desk in the back of the office. "Did Murdoch say anything about my offer when you met with them today?"

"You mean other than to call you out for being the sniveling beetle-face lout that you are? Nothing I can remember."

"He did not say that."

"Of course not. But I don't have time to come up with a better insult. Thanks to you, this is not my newspaper any longer. He made that much quite clear again." I sat down and scribbled a few sentences, then stopped to revise them in my head before continuing. Finally, I picked up the composing stick, adjusted the column width, and began transferring letters from my type case to recreate in lead the sentences I had inked on the paper before me.

Resigned to this fickle finger of fate? You bet your badger-bugging bottom. If civil war didn't break out to disrupt life as we knew it, I might pay off my debt and acquire the business from Murdoch before pigs learned to fly.

"I have a plan," Jacob said. I ignored him and kept working while he slipped out the rear door to my office and returned a moment later with the devil's tail to a printing press in his hand and a smile big enough to stretch all the way to Middlesex County. "Come take a look."

At the edge of the courtyard behind the shop, an old work horse hitched to a wagon munched on the tall, neglected grass. Posts of carved wood, slats, discarded copper and steel, disassembled and dead, sat in a pile on the bed of the wagon like a coffin waiting for the final trip to the countryside where it would be buried in its final resting place.

"I traded Mr. Snardwod three new Bibles and a notarized letter of moral dispensation for all sins past and present from the church in exchange for the scraps left behind when he closed the *Post Examiner*. This pile has been sitting on his farm in Cambridge after the Sons of Liberty ran him out of Boston. You remember that, no doubt. Said he decided give it all up and move west after all the damage they did. I got what's left of his printing press."

I told Jacob it was nice to know Snardwod would avoid hell for all the trouble this mob had caused him.

"I don't believe there is an indulgence you can buy for the sin of bad writing," I said. I had said often of how Snardwod was a notoriously poor man of prose if there ever was one and made those of us who took pride in the printed word cringe to be associated with a man grammatically senseless enough to go running about willy-nilly with his participles dangling in public.

Jacob said he knew how I felt about the *Post Examiner.* "There is, though I'm sure, a special place below for bad poets and rotten authors who toss out more gibberish than anyone should have to endure. Indulgence or no, Snardwood will serve his time with the devil in due course." He paused and then blessed me by waving his hand in the form of a cross in front of my nose. "I haven't decided on your future yet. I might have to charge you double and a few years of penitence."

I asked him what we were to do with the corpse from the *Post Examiner*'s business beyond the minimal value of spare parts for my existing printing press.

"We might salvage enough and fashion you a second press? One to which Murdoch has no claim. You have space in the pressroom—we'll store all this for the time being." He handed me the pullman's lever. Someone had tried to break it and succeeded only in creating a slight bend in the iron rod. I held it by one end, letting it dangle like the broken limb it was. I told him to stack the pieces and parts in a corner of the pressroom, out of the way, while I finished composing the governor's post.

Life took a curious turn shortly thereafter. I armed Bert and Ernie with torches after sunset and sent them about town posting the governor's reply to *WTF* and promising anyone who would listen that they would find a full, scandal-mongering report in the next edition of *New England News-Journal.* The streets were still busy enough with men headed home to their wives or to the taverns to avoid them.

Jacob and I had moved the last small odds and ends from the cart to the corner of the print room when the bell over the door in the store summoned me.

"I'm sorry," I called out. "We are closed for the day."

Mistress Hughes entered the shop accompanied by a tall, young woman and an exceedingly handsome, proper gentleman who looked to be not much older than me, and he had Madam Mae Flowers on his arm.

"Mr. Merriweather," the matron said. "I wish to place an announcement in your newspaper. My ward here, Miss Wunderland, is about to marry, and marry well. I believe this calls for special notice and I am going to host a grand event for the occasion." Mrs. Flowers crooked her neck to look up at me as she leaned forward, resembling a wrinkled turtle stretching from the high, stiff collar of her attire that formed the edge of her shell. "It's about time," she whispered.

I couldn't help but wonder exactly how many beautiful young wards like Miss Wunderland for which the tiny matchmaking woman was responsible. Some days it felt as if there was nary an eligible, weddable lady in town to which she had not taken a shine.

The most eligible to my mind was standing there at the door. Mistress Hughes, I nodded silently. She responded with a look that invited all kinds of come hithering.

"Splendid, Madam Flowers," I said. "And this fine gentleman, I assume, is the happy groom?"

Madam Flowers blinked twice at me with those turtle eyes. "Nonsense. Mr. Braddock is my escort." Her response was just

terse enough to convey equal parts amusement and indignation, but carried a hint of possessive jealousy. Braddock simply
smiled and nodded.

"The groom is Mr. Wellington Wellslip," Sally Hughes
said.

Oh? Wellslip was quite a catch. Freemason in good standing. A bit of a fop but a well-connected businessman, member
of the governor's trade council board, and a cradle Tory.

"I told Aunt Mae there could be no better place for the
announcement than your newspaper," Mistress Hughes said.

"Conservative, steady, and stable," Mrs. Flowers said. "And
cheap. I still get compliments on my collection of poetry you
produced for me. Oh yes, those were heady days and I thank
you for it. Thank the Lord I didn't do it for the notoriety."

"There is little of that for most authors," I said. "But I have
two copies on my shelf for sale over there, and I recommend
your chapbooks to everyone looking for fine poetry. I, myself,
was quite taken with your work."

She smiled and nodded gracefully as if she would place my
compliment into a large trunk full of flattery she had acquired
through the years. Madam Flowers handed me a piece of paper
with the announcement written out in a bold hand. She had
even fashioned a headline. "We'd like a prominent placement
on the first page."

"I will place it appropriately and add trim so that it catches
the eye. And for my friends and family? A discount," I added.

I was about to quote a price when she held up her palm.
"Benjamin?"

Mr. Braddock withdrew a note from a pocket within his fine coat and handed it to me. A promissory note signed by Mrs. Mae Flowers. The amount, she informed me, was to be filled in at my discretion upon completion of the task.

"I told Aunt Mae you were most reasonable," Mistress Hughes said.

And most pliable, no doubt. Did she really bat her eyelashes at me?

Madam Flowers exhaled with a smile. "Now that that is settled, come Benjamin, we'd best get along now. Ladies?"

Crash! Rattle and roll from heaven to hell interrupted us. Lumps of lead type skittered across the floor like a small wave on the shore, bounced off my shoes, and ducked under the ladies' skirts. Jacob stood near the door separating us from the pressroom, an overturned bucket at his feet and a dazed look frozen on his face.

"So sorry, ladies," he said. He knelt quickly and began scooping the little blocks of type. "So sorry, sir. Sorry. Yes, I am." He craned his neck to steal glances at us standing over him while he worked and apologized. I escorted Sally Hughes and the others to the door and she thanked me silently, squeezing my elbow.

You wild thing. I winked.

"What in the frog-flipping world has gotten into you?" I raged when they were gone.

Jacob stood now, using the side of his foot like a broom to corral the type into a manageable pile. "Who was that woman?"

"Mrs. Flowers? You know her, doofus."

"No, the other one—not Mistress Hughes."

"Miss Wunderland?" Dorothy, according to this announcement they've asked me to print. "Why? Why should that turn you into a clumsy oaf? And you still have that stupefied look on your silly mug."

He blinked and slapped his forehead. Then he grinned at me. "I know that lady. I mean, well, I don't know her in the Biblical sense, obviously. Well, maybe once. Or twice. I have seen her before. I recognized her, that's all."

He went back to organizing the pieces of lead and placing them in the bucket while I stood there with my arms crossed. He ignored me as long as possible.

"It's just that I am certain I have seen her in Flagg Alley." He said this without looking up, nonchalantly as if he were offering me a spot of sugar for my tea.

WTF? And I wasn't thinking of the *Forger* this time. Several moments passed before his meaning registered. "My god, Jacob."

I really needn't have raced out the door and up the street. I saw the women and Mr. Braddock a short distance ahead under a hanging lamp above the cobbler's shop before I reached Queen Street. If Miss Wunderland was an employee to the mansion on Flagg Alley, and Sally Hughes was connected to Miss Wunderland, then what did that say about Mistress Hughes? Flagg Alley had a certain reputation that would make many a decent person blush. Flog the mother-frigging frog, what was up?

I followed the group, and when they reached the halfway point to Madam Flowers' home they separated, the matron and her boy toy continuing on while Sally and Miss Wunderland turned to the right, back toward the docks. Another right and then a left down a narrow street framed by rowhouses made of brick as it curved past the marketplace. Certainly at night this was a neighborhood for ladies to avoid. I ducked behind a stack of crates at the front of the Gateway Tavern when the women paused before turning up Flagg Alley.

Flagg Alley was twice as long and more broad than most of its kind in Boston and extended beyond the buildings that faced Anne Street. It had once served as the private access to a large house of brown wood and brick that stood at the end of that drive and peeked over a privacy fence. Topped by a crow's nest, a body could sit up there, relax, and enjoy a view of the entire district from the wharves to the Boston Common.

I listened to the voices that floated back to me until I was sure there was sufficient distance before I leaned around the crates only so far as one eye would allow me to spy on the women. I ran forward when they entered a gate through the tall privacy fence in front of the great house. The fence pickets were crooked with age and gapped like a seaman's grin, and I had little trouble following the ladies from my side of the fence as they circled the house to the back where the yard was illuminated by half a dozen torches. Sally and Miss Wunderland hailed two women who had taken up positions near an imposing red door with a large oil lantern swaying on a hook over it. One woman sat on a chair combing her hair and the other stood with one foot on a tree stump drinking from a bottle and smoking a cigar. Both were professionally dressed, which is to say by Flagg Alley standards, not very.

I recognized the woman in the chair. She wielded a hand mirror over her head, patting each side, trying to coerce stray strands back into place. There was no mistaking her deep, dark, mouse fur eyebrows. Mouse brow number one from that evening at Murdoch's mansion. Or maybe number two; who could tell for sure? She threw her head back, laughing at the sky, as the woman with the cigar and booze told what I took to be a bawdy joke. They all laughed, including Sally Hughes.

Sally and Miss Wunderland appeared perfectly comfortable in this place and in the company of these women—prostitutes, for certain. After exchanging a brief hug characteristic of sisters and other kindred spirits, Sally opened the red door and entered the infamous Flagg Alley Bordello.

Chapter Fifteen
...That Was My Strife

WTF? I asked.

"That bastard printing this, this *Watertown Times Forger*, is at it again." Clinton Murdoch spat the words.

Literally. Spittle flew everywhere, and I flinched to duck. I was in a mood to spit back, and I might have done just that if we were not in the company of the ladies assembled in Madam Flowers' parlor. We had reached the end of November, and even though the social season—mating season, as some snide observers like me have demeaned it—Madam Flowers was still planting the seeds of romance with her matchmaking social events. That evening I had met two roosters—fine, young, but unremarkable fellows—and two hens: equally generic but reasonably cultured women who had the men in their sights and matrimony on their minds.

Meanwhile, it appeared Murdoch and Madam Flowers had struck up a flame recently, albeit a faint one that you might find in the final hour of a candle's life, and he had become a frequent visitor to the widow. I was invited to join them and Mr. Larson for a light meal and an evening of backgammon and sociable socializing between the sexes. Murdoch and Madam Flowers were an obvious pair. Mr. Larson had taken quite a liking to another of Mrs. Flowers' protégés, Miss Tooshoes, who was very attentive to him. That left me with the whore.

Sally Hughes.

Not that I was bitter about that.

Severely put out, possibly, given that I had discovered the angel who had stolen my heart was a common strumpet who had tumbled from grace to the gutter. And here she was acting like she was worthy of the pedestal where I had too quickly placed her. My bad. Background check. Very important. I made a mental note to perform a thorough one before allowing myself to be smitten next time. And I *was* smitten with Sally Hughes.

Not that I was bitter about it.

As with most social events, the topics of conversation traveled down different paths, but that evening it returned frequently to tea. Specifically, the cargo of tea aboard a ship that had arrived the Sunday prior, and the imminent arrival of a second one.

"I can attest," Mr. Larson said. "Governor Hutchinson is not going to be swayed no matter how much John Hancock and the others protest."

"Will he have a choice?" Sally Hughes said. Her beautiful lips curled to reveal a kind of smugness that comes with overconfidence. "Now that the *Forger* has revealed the governor's graft, the citizens are likely to be ever more upset."

In a broadside that very day, *WTF* predicted the governor would not turn away the ships and lose an enormous profit. It reported Hutchinson had appointed his two sons, Thomas Junior and Elisha, as designated customs agents specifically to handle the tea shipments. It seems the governor was content with pushing his personal profiting of the office to new levels. In what the *Forger* described as nakedly obscene graft, he detailed the extent of the money the Hutchinson family would reap from its government-sanctioned monopoly to sell the tea once it was warehoused in their facility on Griffin's Wharf.

I could buy a small island on the north bay for that much. "I suppose the larger question is why was the governor hiding the fact that he handed his sons this profitable contract?" I asked Larson.

"He wasn't hiding anything. Yes, it is decided, but it's really nobody's concern. Why should the public care from where they are getting their tea? Even after the Hutchinsons take their reasonable fees, it will still be cheaper for the citizens than any other, illegal, source."

"I believe the larger question is how did he come by this information?" Murdoch asked no one in particular. "It hadn't been officially announced. This blasted Forger appears to have eyes and ears everywhere. How does he do it?"

I strolled to the table where Sally Hughes stood. I handed her my glass, indicated it needed a refill from the punch bowl, and then turned my back to her. "The Forger's source will be revealed sooner or later," I said strictly for her benefit, knowing I stood next to the Forger's source and she was at that moment ladling spiced apple cider and rum into my glass. Are you listening, Miss Hughes? Could my warning be more plain to your senses?

It took no Benjamin Franklin-esque intellect to deduce that if Sally the Strumpet was the conduit of information, then the information itself must be coming from the lips of her clients before, during, or after the peak of their passion in her arms at Flagg Alley.

"Oh God! Oh God! My boss, the governor is—fill in the secret de-jour here—Oh God, that was good, Sally," he would say before rolling off her.

Rolling off her? *What a twit*, I cursed myself. *Get that from your head.*

How many different government toadies, British military officers, or connected men of commerce had she serviced to supply the Forger's press with information? Perhaps they were all in on it? Imagine all of the prostitutes at Flagg Alley sharing the information they gleaned from clients and passed along to the rogue newspaper. That theory had a certain appeal, though I might be overthinking the possibilities. I couldn't know for sure, but as sure as a bear mates in the woods, I planned to confront Sally about it.

I stole a glance at Mistress Hughes and found myself suppressing a grin, for a thought came to me and it tickled my senses. I thought if Sam Adams could get away with using the *Boston Gazette* to not only publish anti-Hutchinson articles in every edition but could also use the rooms in the newspaper's building to organize and direct actions by the Sons of Liberty, why couldn't the Forger have an organization of his own?

Strumpets of Liberty. Catchy, don't you think?

"Well, I, for one, think this Forger is showing courage," Sally said, looking directly at me. It was a withering glare. "It seems other newspapers in Boston, like yours, Mr. Merriweather, either support the administration or underestimate the seriousness of our times. I believe this fellow is doing the public a service."

After a stunned moment of silence, Madam Flowers cackled. "My dear girl, haven't I taught you a thing? You are a lady, as am I. You and I are not entitled to an opinion in political matters. You need to heed your place. Isn't that right, Clinton?"

"Most assuredly," Murdoch said confidently.

A second pause gripped us all as we stared at him.

"What?" he asked in serious confusion.

Mrs. Flowers' comment was so thick with obvious sarcasm, there was no way to avoid recognizing it was a political statement itself. Unless, of course, you were a privileged dolt like Murdoch.

Against my better instincts, I leapt to his rescue by changing the subject. "As far as this tea issue goes, I suppose it will all be resolved one way or another in a fortnight. By law, the governor will have decided the fate of the cargo by then."

"Only if the Sons of Liberty don't take action by then," one of the young roosters piped up. Taylor-Something was his name. Or was it Something-Taylor? I had forgotten he and his pal existed. They had hung back in the corner of the parlor, seemingly caught up in whispering sweet nothings or nothing at all to the pretty young hens there. Now he stepped forward.

"I clerk at a shipping office near Griffin's Wharf. I have seen a number of unfamiliar faces on the dock keeping an eye on the *Dartmouth*," Taylor said. "Yesterday I worked until midnight reconciling our ledgers, and as I left I encountered more than a dozen men as they formed a blockade. One told me the ship's captain hoped to offload the tea under the cover of darkness."

"It didn't work, obviously," I said. I made a mental note to follow up on the story for my next edition.

"It won't last. The governor won't allow it," Mr. Larson said. "I can give you his guarantee to that."

"What if citizens resist? Will he dispatch soldiers?" Sally asked. There was a feisty edge to her question. If it had been stronger I would swear she was challenging the governor's aide to a duel.

"Options are being weighed. We'll find out soon enough," Mr. Larson replied.

"I hope it doesn't involve shooting," I said. I hoped my tone, optimistic, almost hopeful, would mitigate the rising anger I saw reflected in Sally's cheeks.

"If it does, we will be at war," Murdoch said before Madam Flowers rose from her chair and rapped her cane on the floor.

"Enough of politics," she said. "I hereby declare a moratorium on political discussion for the remainder of the evening. Now, let's dine and enjoy our games afterwards. Anyone who speaks of politics, protests, or war will get a rap on their head from me."

To emphasize her point, she slashed the air and lost her balance, only to be rescued by Mr. Larson before she fell. We all laughed, no one more so than Madam Flowers herself.

As we filed two-by-two to the dining room, Sally leaned into me and whispered, "You don't really think it will come to war, do you, Leeds?"

I took her by the arm. "What do you suppose the *Forger* would say?" I meant it in jest but her reply was earnest and stopped me cold.

"We can only hope."

Chapter Sixteen
Dog Balls

Three days later I had a dread that sat like a puddle of bile in the very depth of my compromised soul. It sloshed around my stomach as I returned from a visit to the governor's room at Province House. It was midday and even the pleasant weather couldn't lift my mood. I had met with Governor Hutchinson and his chief of staff, Larson, I was barely inside the door before the governor thrust his latest scribbling at me and ordered me to make it the centerpiece of the next day's newspaper.

"*TREASON IS AFOOT,*" he had written in a bold flourish at the top. "Make sure you use large and bold type for that line so that it makes a statement," he told me.

Splendid. Now the governor was not only mandating my content to the point of near strangulation, but he was editing the look of the newspaper.

"I want no one to mistake our resolve," he continued. "We must dominate the streets with a show of strength at the docks and put these thug protestors in their place."

I skimmed the message, not convinced it would put anyone in any place any time soon even though I was taken aback by the governor's bold threat of military action. The Sons of Liberty's crews had swelled in numbers and continued to prevent the unloading of the tea at Griffin's Wharf. The second of three ships laden with tea cargo had settled in next to the *Dartmouth* that morning, and the protestors increased their patrol of the wharf in response.

In addition to that submission for Friday's newspaper, Mr. Larson handed me pages for three more broadsides, each to be printed and distributed across town, and I was ordered to set all other projects aside if necessary to see that Governor Hutchinson's posts took precedence for the next several days.

I calculated the price for such work and asked for payment. The governor was already several weeks behind, and at that rate I was teetering on the edge of transition from printer to pauper.

"Consult Mr. Murdoch on that matter," Mr. Larson said. "I'm sure he will credit your account with him."

"That doesn't feed the bear. I can scarcely afford ink and paper anymore," I replied. I attempted to control the anger in my voice out of respect for the governor. I was only partially successful.

The governor raised his eyebrows and frowned. "It will all work out, Merriweather," he said. Then he dismissed me with a royal hand.

So my mind was afflicted with funk a short time later when I walked in on Sally Hughes as she was closely inspecting Jacob's balls in the rear of the pressroom.

"Are they really dog skin?" she asked as I reached the doorway.

"There is nothing better," I heard him say. "And they are filled with the best quality horse hair. Here. Grip them like this."

They stood near the rickety frame of the old *Post-Examiner* printing press that Jacob had salvaged. Sally held the handles of two leather pads used for applying ink to the type before it is pressed against paper. The ink balls were among the accessories Jacob acquired in hopes of making the broken press whole again. He may have graduated from Harvard Divinity, a man of the cloth with a firm grasp of Biblical lore, but with one look I could tell the rubble he had to work with provided no chance of achieving a Lazarus-style resurrection, a resurrection that has only been done once to my knowledge, and that was by some fellow with a bit more talent in miracles than my friend.

"Uh, hello, Leeds." Jacob backed a step, putting daylight between himself and Sally.

"Mr. Printer," she said. "See? I am learning your trade." Sally stepped closer and held the ink balls out from her body while turning the blackened pads, stained but long dried from their last assignment, so that they pointed directly at me. Sally rocked her wrists playfully as if inking me like a line of type in the compositing frame. I imagined it was a line of only one word.

You dolt.

Well, two words.

You pathetic dolt.

Make that three words.

At that rate, the number of words I conjured up in self-flag-ellation was growing in my head, and if I did not gain a measure of control, I would soon have sufficient copy to fill an entire page for Sally to slather, beat, and roll with greasy black dye. Pummel me.

"So how did things go at Province House?" Jacob asked. He leaned with one hand on a corner of the Lazarus press. It rocked and wobbled, and I expected it to collapse but it held up. Barely.

"Not well," I said, taking Larson's foolscap from inside my coat. "More work, and no compensation. Again." I had lost several lucrative projects since accepting the arrangement with Murdoch. Being at Murdoch's beck and call to print the governor messages, as well as Murdoch's and Larson's growing number of letters to the paper, meant I could not handle as much work from clients who paid in cash instead of future credits. Truth be told, I was actually slipping deeper into debt with each passing day.

Sally must have read the lines of disappointment in my face like a week-old broadsheet. She held up the pads. "Is there some way I can help?" she asked brightly.

"You would be much better off tending to business at Flagg Alley," I said.

Was that a nor'easter that swept into the room? Sally froze. She stood there and stared at me in a cold and measured way, silently challenging me to continue. I had clearly stepped in a pile of dog dung with that one. So be it. I wasn't in the mood to make nice.

I pulled two pounds in Spanish silver from my purse. Deliberately making a show of it. I held one coin up to the light and not coincidentally in front of Sally's eyes, as if tempting her with payment. Then I handed the money to Jacob. "Be a good fellow and do me a favor. We haven't enough paper. Would you see what you can get from Harker's Mill whilst I compose the story?"

"Certainly," he said, though he did not move.

"Yesterday would not be soon enough. Now, Jacob."

He shuffled to the coat rack. "Left out of all the fun again."

"Trust me, I take no issue with a working girl working," I said to Sally when we were alone. How could I tell her that, in fact, I do have a soft spot in my heart for them? They are a class unto themselves, quite jolly and accommodating in most cases and providing a needed service with more humor and grace than their clients deserve. What made it hard to swallow was the thought that the woman I wanted to adore would be nakedly intimate with another man—no, many different men—night after night. After night after night.

Bloody hell.

"The mistaken idea I had of you as a woman of virtue was formed the evening we met. I cherish the memory of your slap to my face. That was consistent with the character of a lady. I thought you were a lady. My bad."

One moment she appeared to be lost, like a rebuked child, the next moment her eyes flashed in anger. She raised one of the ink pads, to use as a weapon against me I assumed, but she tripped, lost her balance, and fell against the printing press.

This time Jacob's weary old junk of frame collapsed with a mighty crash, its legs buckling and its coil spring bouncing across the floor. She put up a palm to kill any inclination on my part to aid her. Frankly, I felt no sense of urgency this time.

Her recovery was an awkward series of movements. I have seen many a soused man, after drinking himself half blind, stand from a pratfall with more dignity than Mistress Hughes. She finally made it back on her feet and she growled at me. It was one of those long, low rumblings of frustration. Imagine that. A common bordello girl sounding like an angry dog. Naturally. And she cursed in a way more befitting a longshoreman. That was nice as well. Her entire charade as a well-bred lady worthy of Madam Mae Flowers' companionship crumbled before me like the now-deceased printing press lying in a heap on the print shop floor.

"Since you have made your opinion clear, then I will not try to explain," she said. "But I will ask, what about you, Mr. Printer? We are both in the business of providing entertainment. We both take payment for that service. Are we so very different? I think not."

Hold on. The prostitute was calling me...a prostitute? Rubbish. "There is a world of difference in our professions, dear Mistress Hughes."

"Only if you actually share Mr. Murdoch's views and hold them with conviction. I don't believe you do. I really don't. Certainly not with the passion that your printed words suggest. Separating what is true from the propaganda you publish, you are engaged in what we, at Flagg Alley, call E.E."

"E.E.?"

"Exaggerated exuberance. False passion. Moans, and properly timed gasps, and, oh, the breathing. Breathing is very important. We use those to enhance the experience for someone just as you use your skills to support your clients, Mr. Murdoch and the governor. In fact, you incite a certain passion in them that they release between the pages. And you are paid to provide that."

Exaggerated exuberance? I would have protested the comparison more forcefully had I not been struck by her eloquence and the skill with which she made her argument.

Who was this lady?

She spoke in a way that no common pleasure mate I've known would have talked. Not that I had experienced that experience greatly, but sometimes in my loneliness I had taken some comfort there. Her thoughts were refined, her voice was silky, and her eloquence was befitting a woman of more than middling stature. And yet she cursed, and in anger her voice had a tin tone and the sharp edges much like women costermongers and others I'd encountered during my days pattering on the streets of London. A lifetime away from this moment. Odd.

Who the desperate devil was this lady?

Mistress Hughes took my stunned silence for encouragement to continue. I could read that in her crooked smile like a headline spanning two columns. "There is a significant problem here, Mr. Printer," she said. "Think of those poor souls murdered by the soldiers three years ago. Think of that poor fellow murdered by the governor's men most recently. Times are dangerous, and supporting the powers that be have contributed to those deaths. At least no one dies from having their emotions inflamed in Flagg Alley."

"But—"

"Well, except Mr. Briggs. Poor man. Angela says he invoked God's name and then went rigid. Not rigid in a good way. Collapsed right there in her embrace last week. But then, he was more than sixty years of age." She tisked twice. "It took two of us to roll him off her. Though I think he died happy." She paused to consider the irony.

There were worse ways to die, I supposed.

"But the passions you stir up with the governor's or Murdoch's Tory dribble are hardening one side of a debate and making compromise all the more difficult. And isn't that what you have said you really want? Resistance is growing and the governor's agenda is moving us closer to war, not away from it."

I wanted to explain further but she swept past, pulled a dark wool cloak over her figure, adjusted the hood to hide her face, and headed for the door. "If that's the best argument you can make, then all I will say, Mr. Printer, is I may sell my body but I have not sold my soul."

Ouch.

As she reached the door she said, "And to think I came here to warn you."

I had to rush forward and catch her by the cloak. I asked her of what threat she referred.

Mistress Hughes tugged at her cloak but I had a firm grasp on it. She wasn't going anywhere. She pouted. "Oh, I don't remember now." She made no effort to make it sound believable. In short order she explained that the sentiment on the street was that the Sons of Liberty were less than pleased with the Tory turn the *New England News-Journal* had taken, and the rumblings of some form of punishment might be needed to correct the situation.

"What kind of punishment?"

"Well," she said. "I don't think it involves death, though it hasn't been ruled out by at least a few from what I hear. Possibly some mild tar and feathering? I'm not certain. You should expect a visit from someone like Mitchell Curry."

Oh, that would not be a happy thing. Curry was a brute not to be trifled with. He was the reigning bear-wrestling champion in Boston and the next three nearest colonies. That the Sons of Liberty would consider bringing in the leader of the brute squad indicated a serious amount of displeasure on their part. Mistress Hughes put up a little resistance as I pulled her back into the shop. "How certain are you of this information?"

She moved further inside to be near where I had a fire burning in the stove near the corner. "That it has been suggested? Positive. That it will happen? That may depend."

Depended on the tone of my reporting in future issues of the newspaper, I surmised. She appeared to be waiting for a response, but I was measuring the price of my attempts to avoid taking sides. Disappoint Murdoch and I would lose everything I had worked toward. Defy the SOL mob and I would lose everything, and possibly my skin in the process. Flog the friggin' frog. So wrapped up in my own conundrum I barely noticed Mistress Hughes was once again at the door.

I said, "And to think, my primary concern from this afternoon was to warn you as well."

She looked over her shoulder and laughed. Turned to the street and then turned back and asked what I meant. Her eyes, large and inviting on most days, were large but concerned now.

"Treason," I said. "When I met with Governor Hutchinson today he used that word, treason. He referenced the information coming from inside the government and the military that the *Forger* has printed. We both know your role in all this, and he has commissioned Lieutenant Cole to spare nothing to catch the printer's source. You are at serious risk, madam."

Thinking back to our conversation that afternoon, *Treason* had stopped me cold. And the venom with which the governor said it made me lay a hand to my neck at the time. Treason with a capital-T stands for trouble. The hanging kind. Or like too many a prostitute, Sally Hughes might be found mysteriously dead in an alley, victim of a client with too much violence on his mind. A prostitute's death was of no concern to most.

Easy women. Easy come, easy go.

Until you fall in love with one. Damn her.

She moved closer, thinking, and her nose wiggled in a bewitching manner. "It seems, Mr. Printer, that we are both at risk. Is that a sign of our times, or our recklessness? You know not which is a greater risk, caught between Mr. Murdoch who owns you, and now Baby Cakes Curry and the Sons of Liberty."

"Baby Cakes?"

"Oh, yes. He is quite an affectionate child-man when he's not ripping off people's arms and such. Quite a sense of humor and fine looking in an ogre sort of way. And you should see the size of his…"

I stopped her there. "Shut up, woman! Why are you not taking this seriously? They might ruin my life yet I will survive. They will surely snuff out yours like a half-penny candle if given a chance."

She responded by moving closer still. Her shoulders sagged now and I could see worry in her eyes. "I believe in a cause. *The* cause. And furthermore, I am nobody. A common whore, as you suggested. Who would miss me?"

"I would."

Stunned was the word that most came to my mind as the look in her eyes took yet another turn. She placed a tentative hand upon my chest, searching my face for the truth. Then she gave me a beaver smile, tucking her front teeth over her lower lip, and her face was as bright as a lamp at midnight.

Whap!

She slapped my face. "Yes. I believe you would," she said.

That slap carried a message, though I was at a loss to understand it beyond the fact that it hurt not at all. Perhaps that was the point. This was, after all, the second time she thanked me for my concern for her welfare with a slap.

"You know," I said, "you would be much more popular if you used your lips and not the palm of your hand to smack a fellow," I said. That made her giggle as she backed away and adjusted the hood of her cape. Then Sally blew a kiss to me. I called after her as she glided into the dusk.

Be careful out there.

You'll need it.

Chapter Seventeen
Baby Cakes Comes Calling

Brandy never tasted so sweet.

Leeds L. Merriweather. I signed my name on a scrap of paper, crossed it out, and tried again, modifying the cursive in all three uppercase letters. It still wasn't quite right.

L. L. Merriweather. Nope. One more time and, yes, that was right. My autograph. I practiced it several more times and then set aside my favorite. I would take it to Mr. Revere tomorrow, or, if he were not available, Blacksmith Bryan to cut my signature into a wood block that I would add to the cover page below the title of my pamphlet. I was ready to call for peace and compromise; could I convince the rest of the colony to join me? The pamphlet turned out to be a masterpiece, in my humble opinion. I hoped it wasn't too late.

Two ships loaded with tea from the East India Company were stuck at Griffin's Wharf with a third ship off the coast and due in port later that day. It was mid-December and the captains had only two more days to unload their cargo or forfeit it to the customs office now run by the governor's sons. The Sons of Liberty continued to stop them, patrolling the docks day and night with roving gangs. Something had to give because Governor Hutchinson had made it clear the ships wouldn't be allowed to leave port with the tea still on board. What's more, he seemed more unhinged each passing day with the work he foisted upon me, spending more time blaming the liberal media like *The Gazette* and *The Spy* for all that ailed us.

I had finished setting the type for the first two pages that afternoon, and had pressed several in order to proofread an advance copy, while I sat in Proprietor Deerfield's coffee house and celebrated with his best liquor. Tomorrow, I would task Bert and Ernie to begin work on the pamphlet's interior pages while I waited on the cover that would include this beautifully handwritten signature.

"I admit I am impressed, Merriweather," David said after stopping by my table long enough to read the opening pages.

I was pouring more brandy into my glass when I saw Frederick O'Donnell, attorney at law, and the governor's man, Larson, headed my way.

Here comes trouble.

O'Donnell sat down across from me, took my glass, added another splash from the bottle on the table, and leaned back. Larson remained standing, closer to the warmth of the fireplace in order to remedy the December chill. He appeared more interested in the other faces in the room than anything O'Donnell had to discuss with me.

"Mr. Murdoch is very pleased with you," O'Donnell said. "Today…" He reached into his coat and brought out that morning's edition of the *News-Journal.* "…we are finally finding voice in our newspaper."

Our newspaper?

"The governor's words seem to have struck a chord with loyalists from here to Salem. And from Salem all the way south to New York. People want to hear directly from our man in the governor's mansion without the filters that you, and even Tories like Draper and…" He paused, searching for a name.

"Misters Mills and Hicks," Larson said without turning his head in our direction.

"Yes, those fine loyalists who took over *The Post Boy and Advertiser* are now on board with us as well."

Governor Hutchinson had a hand in the sale of *The Post Boy* to a pair of young printers—zealots, actually. He provided funds for the sale after the newspaper was ransacked by a Sons of Liberty mob upset with the previous owners' support of the crown. After that, the governor decided the newspaper could use some protection and he offered the new owners space to set up behind the safe walls and soldiers at Castle Island.

"No matter how loyal you have been lately, Merriweather, you were certainly correct. Nothing is better than having the governor address the public in his own words. And the more presses we have printing our views, the better."

"Strength in numbers, I suppose," I replied. My mood had shifted, and the glow of anticipation over my pamphlet felt like nothing more than the weak wisp of smoke drifting up from an extinguished candle. Murdoch had begun buying up print shops with newspapers in several cities, including New York and Philadelphia. I suppose he had to pay for them because didn't have the time to travel and cheat them out of their businesses the way he had stolen the *New England News Journal* from me over a game of cards. They were small players, mostly, but the combined strength of their subscriptions might pack a significant public influence. It was a network of Tory publishers determined to write history. With each new expansion, my role in Murdoch's burgeoning news empire diminished. How much longer would he even need me?

I took O'Donnell's copy of the *News-Journal* and held it up to the light, not for the first time, looking first to the corner of the reverse side of the front page where I used to print my name as publisher. Proudly, I might add. But I could no longer do that in good conscience. Distancing myself from that newspaper, which I loved dearly, was breaking my heart. And it occurred to me just then that I was not only running out of time to produce the pamphlet that was so badly needed in our divided country, but I was running out of patience. How much longer could I avoid pummeling O.D., Larson, and Murdoch, the whole lot of them, with the dog skin leather of my press's ink balls? Though, the image of Murdoch, eyes blackened with ink from a solid poke, looking like one of those Chinese panda bears, encouraged me enough to steal my brandy glass back from O'Donnell.

It was then that Proprietor Deerfield reentered the room with pomp to rival King George himself.

"Gentlemen. Gentlemen. *WTF.* The *Forger* is here."

Heads turned. *WTF?*

Larson stretched upon his toes, bobbed and weaved, trying to look over and around the heads in front of him. Deerfield raised a dozen broadsides over his white cap. *WTF,* that day's fresh edition. The patrons parted, creating a path like the Red Sea before Moses, and he handed copies to men on first one side and then the other as he crossed the room.

"Just a few shillings while supplies last, fellows," he called out.

When he reached the back wall, reduced to only his last three copies, he handed two to his son to tack upon the wall for the reading pleasure of those who were too poor or too cheap to buy their own.

David reserved the last copy for me. "I am sorry for your loss, Merriweather. You didn't even make the top ten."

Eh?

"The governor's enemy list. According to *The Forger,* Governor Hutchinson has compiled an official list of enemies, people of note he believes ought to be punished at best or controlled at least."

Larson snatched the broadsheet. "Let me see that." He had gone from placid observer to seething faster than a falcon on a field mouse. "Well, I'll be a Mother Flogger."

"What's more, the governor is urging action against them," Deerfield said.

"Mr. Larson, is it legitimate?" O'Donnell asked. "I mean, are the names correct there?"

Larson nodded slowly with his eyes squeezed shut.

"And there is more," O'Donnell continued. "Good God! It says here that Clinton Murdoch is financing rewards to be paid to snitches—as he calls our informants—and not the administration."

"So it's true?" I asked. It did not surprise me.

O'Donnell picked up his hat. "We must get this information to Mr. Murdoch immediately."

"And the governor," I offered.

"Eh? Oh, yes. Him as well."

David dropped into the chair formerly occupied by the lawyer. He took my glass of brandy from in front of me. I had not sipped a bit since stealing it back from the lawyer. At the rate the proprietor Deerfield was going at it, I would have none left to enjoy.

"*WTF* would sell much more if that bloke would print more than the hundred copies or so that I can account for. I could sell subscriptions from here to New Jersey if I could get enough of them. That's what people want around here." He said it loud and proud as if advertising its value as a commodity necessary to one and all. It was all for show.

"Personally, I believe the mystery of the Forger's identity is helping him gain readers that I cannot," I said.

At that moment another body joined us.

"Lord, it is chilly outside. I need brandy to warm me." Jacob Addison slapped David on the back. "Jolly to see you old man."

"I don't think that's any way for a preacher to talk. Even a part-time one," I said.

Jacob feigned hurt. "And thus it was that the prophet Gorb lined his enemies in a row on their knees and baptized each with water from his body's fountain. The book of Joshamia, Chapter seven, verse eleven. Look it up."

David Deerfield raised one eyebrow at me, skeptical but wavering and willing to give the biblical expert his due.

"Look it up, it's true," Jacob repeated.

"Don't bother," I said. I shook my head at the proprietor and grinned. "That is without a doubt from the book of Jacob Addison."

Jacob first clapped his hands and then rubbed them together. His eyes glowed with liquor-induced animation. "Now, which of you will buy the next round? Sirs?"

David reached under the table to his apron's pocket and retrieved a pouch. "I believe, Mr. Merriweather, it is your turn." He pushed the money pouch across the table.

"Oh my. Spanish dollars and coin." I had not expected such a windfall. Flog the frog, this rivaled a slap from Sally Hughes for pleasure. It would be rude to count it at the table, tempted as I was.

"It appears I need to improve my accounting methods," David said. He looked over his shoulder. I'm sure he wanted to confirm O'Donnell was gone. "Loyalists seem to read more, and pay more for their subscriptions. Mr. Murdoch would appreciate that. If he ever finds out. As it is he will get only his fair share."

"I hope he doesn't," Jacob said. I handed him four coins and he left us to fetch drinks from the front of the coffee house.

I gathered my things, tucked them into my shoulder bag, and dressed in my hat and coat for the walk back to the print shop.

"You're not staying for that drink?"

"Jacob will be more than happy to take mine. I am exhausted. Overworked but no longer underpaid, thanks to you." I patted the pocket where I had placed the newspaper profits. "I have my pamphlet to press and Murdoch is sure to have another long day for us tomorrow, responding to the Forger's response to the governor's folly. I need sleep."

"Understood. By the way," David said, "I have some of those new graphite sticks you asked about. You'll have them first thing tomorrow. My cousin brought them with him from his recent trip to Germany."

I nodded. Smuggled them in, no doubt. "Frankly, I've found those pencils useful when ink is inconvenient, rather handy at times, but as for selling them, I doubt they'll ever have widespread popularity. One dozen pencils should be sufficient for now."

"I thought so. I took the liberty of shorting your receipts six shillings, three pence for my troubles."

When I reached the print shop six blocks away I noticed two things immediately.

One: There was lantern light coming from inside the store, crashing through the front window.

Two: Crashing, I say, because there was little left of that window. Only shards clinging to the edges of the frame and threatening to drop onto the walk in front with the others.

I could see a large man—no, a gigantic man—sitting in my desk chair, relaxed and facing the front of the store. He clearly saw me peering through the window but made no movement, only rising with an unexpected lightness but full of purpose after I opened the door and crossed the threshold. He bounced the brick he had used on my front window in the palm of his hand as easily as if it had been a child's ball. Bald head under a knit cap that was tilted far off his forehead, round cheeks with a nose that was three directions crooked, he was even taller and more imposing on his feet.

Not good. No, very bad.

"Evening, sir. Is there some way I can assist you?" Cool and calm, I said it as if staring down a mugger of this magnitude was a common occurrence.

He said, "Ay-lo. My name is Curry. Mitch'l Curry."

Oh, yes, that bear-wrestling, bone-breaking Sons of Liberty Curry of which Sally had warned me.

"Ya' made yourself some powerful enemies. Got 'em all twitched up and grievin' on account of what you be printing. They don't like that none. Insulted, they are. They sent me, you see. That's my job."

He looked at me and waited for a response. I had nothing to offer.

"Did I mention; my name is Mitch'l Curry?" His voice was high-pitched for a killer, coming directly from his throat and not his barrel chest.

"You most certainly did, Mr. Curry." Tremors started somewhere at the back of my spine.

"Good. Good," he said. "I always fancy a proper introduction 'fore I kill a bloke. Seems the only decent thing to do, don'cha agree?"

Curry continued to stand there, giving me time to react. I wasn't certain what I would do if I could figure out what I *should* do, but I feared what I was *about* to do was to baptize my britches like the prophet Gorb did his enemies.

Chapter Eighteen
This Bud's For You

Coming of age on the streets of London, honing my skills as a street corner news performer with the ability to embellish if not improvise stories relying only on my imagination and pluck, I had long accepted the fact that I performed best under duress when I didn't think. "Don't think. Just pitch," I would tell myself. I needed to pitch Baby Cakes Curry that I was not his enemy and he had no need to rip off my arms. Or worse.

"Baby Cakes!" I whooped. I smiled wide. I spread my arms with as much joy as I could feign. "They told me you'd stop round for a visit."

His heavy eyebrows dipped in confusion. Perfect. I approached him like a long-lost brother and wrapped my arms around him, at least as far as they would go with my fingers barely touching at his back. I nuzzled my face against his chest, and the big fellow flinched. He rocked back as if I were a pox-ridden corpse. Eeew! He obviously thought this greeting was most disagreeable. It was certainly not what he expected.

"It is jolly great to see you. My, my, my. Baby Cakes Curry. We meet at last."

I let him slip from my embrace, but not before I took him by the shoulders and met him eye to eye. Yes, there was confusion in there. A child-like mix of befuddlement and wonder. What would happen next? We both wanted to know.

"Go awn, says ya."

I backed away, a bit too cautiously, I'm afraid.

Bad move.

He must have sensed my fear. Maybe I should have curled up on the floor to play dead the way you'd confront a bear in the forest. I searched the room for a weapon as I continued my retreat, backing slowly across the threshold to the print room. He followed, step by step. His eyes had a maniacal, evil glow, and drool trickled down his round chin. I've woken in a panic from nightmares that were more pleasant an image than the looming Mr. Curry. He leapt a step forward. It was a false attack as he held up and laughed when I flinched and backed into the bed of the printing press. Cornered.

Over his shoulder I could see my father's pistol, one of the few items I brought over from England, sitting on the shelf above my writing desk. Even if I could get to it, which I couldn't, I doubt I could get it loaded and fire off a shot before Curry ripped my arms from their sockets. The wood from the dismembered printing press that Jacob had hoped to restore sat in the corner to the left. There might have been a club there. There were other items that I quickly rejected as totally inadequate, so I did the most logical thing. I ran.

Not out of the room, but I skirted around the printing press so that the long bed frame provided a barrier between us. Feint right. Feint left. He was quick, I'd give him that.

"Look here, Baby Cakes," I said. I pulled from the purse in my pocket one of the silver dollars I had collected from Proprietor Deerfield earlier that evening. I held it up, trying to catch the lantern light, and more to the point, my molester's eye. So far so good. "Can I purchase your good will with this? Surely. I will pay you to stop this madness."

"An' maybe I'll just take it all when I'm done." He stepped to the opposite side of the bed, only two feet distance and a wooden frame between us. As I anticipated, he tried to snatch the coin from me, and what followed was a dizzying thrust and parry of hand movements before I dropped the coin and it skittered down the press's frame onto the stone coffin.

Come get me.

And so he did. Curry reached for the silver dollar beneath the wooden plate in the press's belly.

Most definitely a bad move, big fellow.

With a lightning move born from years of backbreaking experience, I grabbed the devil's tail, the lever just over his hunched shoulders, and pulled, sending the plate down and pinning Curry's hand in the press. Try as he might, there was no escape. The more he struggled, the more pressure I applied.

"Say you're *soooooory.*" I mocked him and squeezed a bit more.

He resisted before finally surrendering. "I'm *soooooory.*"

"Really?" I pulled the devil's tail.

"Yeeow! Yes, really. Really sorry." He grimaced and grunted, unable to pull free, and his face was turning fifty shades of red with the effort. I knew I only had to pull with a bit more strength to break his hand. It would be a simple matter, but what was the use in that? I could kill him and the Sons of Liberty would only send another mug or five to finish me off.

"Promise me you'll not do anything rash until you hear me out. If what I have to offer isn't acceptable, then you can resume your duties."

He gasped with agreement. I released the bar and he slumped to the floor. A quick look at his hand convinced me he was going to be sore in more ways than one, but nothing broken, something gained.

"Let me put on a spot of tea and we'll have a chat," I said. I told him I had a proposition for him. What I left unsaid was that I was knitting various scraps of its elements, inventing that proposition as I moved to the stove. The tea kettle was still full of water, and there was a reasonable hint of dying fire left in the stove to rekindle. I looked up and Curry was standing between me and the threshold to the print room with a pained look and his right hand tucked beneath his left arm.

"You called me Baby Cakes," he said. "Why?"

"Oh, that's something I picked up from a mutual friend of ours." I winked at him. "I think you know several ladies, in fact, of whom I speak."

He looked down at his boots, not embarrassed, but not willing to admit patronizing Flagg Alley. Amusement dressed his face as he removed his cap and twisted it in his huge, uninjured hand at his waist.

Cheerily, I said, "All the strumpets speak very highly of you, I must say."

Wink. Wink.

Curry looked up and, by god, the boy was blushing. "D' they really talk me up?"

"Quite. Baby Cakes they call you because you have such a kind heart. A big heart, they say. Oh, and a big.... Well, 'nuff said." I had him distracted, if not entirely detoured from his task. He was basking in implied admiration of a fellow fellow. Man-to-man compliments carried their weight in gold.

"Well, I do take care. To be gentle with them ladies, that is."

"They appreciate it, too. Come now," I said as if we were the greatest of pals. "Take off your coat. Put your feet up. Let me fix you some tea. I mean, if you are going to kill me this evening—and it's unavoidable, as you have a job to perform—there is no earthly reason we can't part as friends, mates, chums, best buds, in fact." Then I grinned at him like a partner in a confidence trick underway. "A better thought, my friend. You don't seem to be a tea man—I think I have just the thing."

By the time we had downed half the remaining Bushmill's Whiskey that Jacob had gifted me, I had learned several facts about my good friend Mitchell Baby Cakes Curry. And the facts were these:

First, despite all the glamour, notoriety, and celebrity status that came with it, being a champion bear wrestler didn't pay as well as you might think.

Second, Baby Cakes had been forced to make ends meet by taking on the odd job like manhandling unruly patrons in taverns where brawls were considered a source of entertainment, and breaking an arm here or a nose there on debtors who were delinquent too often on loans acquired from disreputable sharks on the street. Also, menacing shopkeepers to pay a monthly stipend to the Sons of Liberty to protect them from unruly mobs (like the Sons of Liberty) and brute collectors (like Baby Cakes Curry.)

Third, he didn't like this job.

"I don't favor having to rough up nobody," he said, waving his whiskey glass for a refill. "Actually, I hate that part of it. See, people take a gander at me and right away, ptooy!" He turned his head and spat. "They're scared off right away."

"You do your job very well," I said.

"That's cheese, nothin' to it. If I put on my angry face, like this…" He gave me a sample and it was intimidating. "And if I drool a little, like this, well, most are beggin' for mercy before they know what I'm after."

"But you're certainly not above breaking a nose, or a knee? Maybe slice an ear off?"

I poured more whiskey. I didn't believe I had enough to make him forget entirely why he had come to the *News-Journal* office, but his story was fascinating.

"Yer a right decent fellow. Shame to be bustin' ya up and all. But Rudolph G., he's captain in the Sons' O' Liberty crowd. He says to me it's gotta be dun, offers me good money, and says if it's dun good, it'll be more work for me." Then he put a finger to his lips, shooshing me, and said murder was not officially on that night's agenda. He had just wanted to begin with that threat so that I would feel satisfied with the eventual pain he intended to inflict. "As long as ya don't give me too much trouble."

What a relief. It appeared I was only to be maimed, not executed.

Then Curry leaned his large frame forward and to his right, putting weight on the wooden arm of my editor's chair. "I'll be jake with ya. I only took on this nasty business on account of I need the loot. I won't enjoy it. Nope, strictly business if that squares things even a bit with ya."

It did nothing of the sort.

The thought of buying my way out of trouble returned. I asked Baby Cakes Curry what drove his urgent need for capital at that moment. "I would feel significantly more at ease about this affair if I knew it was to finance a worthy cause."

He stood, unaffected by the whiskey, towered over me, and reached for my throat, I thought. Instead he took the bottle from my hand and held it up to the flickering light from the oil lamp, inspecting it, admiring it actually. It had no more than a few swallows left, which Baby Cakes dispatched in one.

"Rita," he said. "Ya mentioned the girls at the house," he said, relaxing his tone a bit.

I swallowed hard. Rita must have been one of the working gals of Flagg Alley, and this sap was in love with her. The irony of it goosed my gullet. Sally, my own Flagg Ally Floozy, had cast her own spell on me.

"Rita's the most choice," Curry said. "I'm gonna marry her as soon as I works up a decent stash. Fellow can't marry a girl that fine without somethin' more than whats he got in his pocket."

"Absolutely," I agreed. I was moved. I took from my pocket the silver dollar I had used to trap Curry in my press. I placed it in the palm of his hand. "Friend," I said. "I can't fathom a more beautiful reason to suffer whatever pain and humiliation may come of your task tonight than to give my all for true love."

Then I spread my arms and let out the long sigh of a man resigned to his fate. "Well, I suppose you have other important assignments. Time's a-wasting. We might as well finish this. Let them all know I took it well."

His eyes turned misty. Was he about to blubber? "Mr. Merriweather, I don't do words good, but if I could, why, I'd thank ya like a proper gentleman, I would." He asked me why I was so nice to him, after he had come to do me harm and all that rot.

I reached for the bottle that now hung spent and moping from Curry's huge hand. "Sally," I said. Then I looked at him with a resigned grin. "Miss Hughes, a working girl at Flagg Alley just like your Rita. You see, we are brothers where love is concerned, both smitten by the charms of those lovely women of that unique service profession."

"Sally? Sally the abbess?" He blinked and smiled. "Oh, she's first-rate, Madam Hughes is. Runs the girls fair and square, though me thinks she could do well for herself if she'd turn a trick or two. I know plenty of blokes who'd pay twice to plug her." Then he slapped his face hard enough that I flinched. "Sorry, Mister. I didn't mean nothin' by that. It's just that she runs the joint but don't turn no tricks. Wouldn't hear it."

My Sally. My, my. I wondered if Jacob Addison still sold indulgences, for realizing how I had so easily assumed things that no decent fellow should assume without more than circumstantial evidence. She wasn't Flagg Alley Sally the common whore after all. As if the clouds before my eyes parted, the troubling visions that had plagued me of men putting their groping hands and throbbing extensions of their bodies on the woman I loved evaporated.

I needed time to devise some penance for myself and set things right with Sally. I had no time to deal with the foolish vandalism that Baby Cakes Curry had in mind just then, so I pleaded with him. If he would just hold off for a day or two, I would be happy to schedule a date and time for him to return and complete his assignment.

"Could you come back and we can finish this transaction on Thursday?"

"No, sir. That won't do at all, at all." He told me he and his Sons of Liberty friends were employed for the day. Dock duty. He said they would be patrolling the warehouses around the tea ships docked at Griffin's Wharf. And after that...

"After that, what?" I asked.

"Me and the boys. We've been told we're going to take down those ships on Thursday 'less they sail outta here before we get to it. But that ain't gonna happen."

"No, it ain't," I said without sharing his enthusiasm.

I looked at my empty hands, my soul felt just as vacant. If what Mitchell Curry said was true and the governor followed through on his threats, we would be at war by Friday. "Well, we have no more whiskey," I told him. "Let me put on that pot of tea. Sit a spell more, and I'll explain a proposition I have for you."

I opened the stove. There was still a glow in the embers from that afternoon's fire; a few sticks of kindling and some paper would have us cooking in no time. The kindling was handy, next to the stove, and a small stack of excess newspaper misprints sat next to my writing desk. I had one hand on the top sheet when I looked at the proofreading sample of my pamphlet sitting there as if mocking me.

See? If you hadn't dawdled so long, we might have had some use. We might have made a difference. We might have stopped this war.

"Shut your trap," I said.

"What?" Mitchell asked, confused.

I just shook my head, separated several sheets of the pamphlet, and laid them in the belly of the stove. I watched it until the flames flickered and grew, inward from the edges and toward the top of the first page.

When in the course of human events some truths become self-evident, foremost among them is that we all are created equal.

Well, it wasn't very good anyway. Just more of my claptrap, words that would never stand the test of time. When the flames were sufficient I added a few sticks of wood on top and closed the door.

Chapter Nineteen
A Wench with an Axe to Grind

Thursday evening, a little more than an hour after sunset, I stood at the rail of the *Dartmouth* docked on the north side of Griffin's Wharf with a belly full of tea crates. Its sister ship, the *Eleanor*, docked on the south side of the wharf and slightly behind while a third ship, the *Beaver*, only yesterday joined them and rested at anchor a short distance into the harbor. All three ships were under the watchful eye of a British man-o-war in the deeper waters of the port. Make no mistake, the warship was there as much to keep them from slipping out of port in the dark of night as it was to protect them from vandals.

I shifted and took weight off my left arm, as I had rested both elbows on the rail while looking down at the dock where the number of voyeurs was growing in number. Anticipation was the mood of the night. I needed to be circumspect and not lean on my arm in its sling. It was merely a prop, and I had forgotten the injury was as fake as any streetwise grifter's counterfeit scheme. I had summoned the constable as soon as

Baby Cakes Curry left my shop two nights previous and filed a complaint against an unknown assailant. A busted window and the brick used to smite it told him the shop had been broken into. Jacob's pile of timbers, which had been a working printing press in a previous life, was now as useless as a pig in a snowdrift, and lead type scattered willy-nilly about the print room told the constable that vandals had done a decent job. And my damaged shoulder and arm in a sling? That told Constable Fife that I had also been molested. I told him I had arrived at the office that night to find it ransacked, and upon taking issue with the ransacker, found myself to be a ransackee.

Constable Bernard Fife dutifully noted my story and said it would be investigated. He predicted it would be hard to solve the case since the whole affair had happened so quickly and I couldn't provide a description of the assailant. The possibility of the matter getting much investigative effort from the sheriff's office was highly suspect, but that gave me comfort. By the time I found myself on the ship on Thursday, good ol' Baby Cakes had already collected his reward from the Sons of Liberty for a menacing well done, and I was committed to keeping my arm in a sling for a few more days at least to complete the charade.

On the other hand, I was greatly agitated by Sally Hughes. I wanted badly to correct whatever trouble my misunderstanding over her employment at Flagg Alley had caused, not giving her a whit of credit for entrepreneurial spirit, by lumping her amongst the common worker bees at the bordello. The fact that she earned her keep not on her back but with her head caused me to reassess and put her back upon the pedestal I had once placed her. I had gone in search of Sally first thing Wednesday morning, but no one seemed to know where Mistress Hughes was. She had been missing for several days, actually, and neither the girls at Flagg Alley, nor her aunt, Madam Flowers, had seen her.

I was fearful, and wondered if Lieutenant Cole's efforts to find the source of the Forger's most scandalous scoops had finally been successful and led him to her. The longer Sally remained missing, the greater my anxiety, and the more my imagination invented all manner of assaults to which she would fall victim. Nervous and waiting at the rail of the *Dartmouth* for the pending assault on the tea ship only served to make my state of mind worse. Let us get this over with so I can get back to worrying about things that mattered.

"You are hardly the boarding party we've been told to expect," Captain Hall said as he greeted me on deck. He did not smile.

"They are on their way. Did you hear the bell in the South Church tower? That was the signal." I assured the captain that I was an objective observer only, a newspaper man who wanted to witness whatever commotion was about to take place. "I mean to capture the true nature of the event."

Captain Hall looked at me as if he had never heard of such a ridiculous idea. But I had learned from witnessing the assault behind the Reckless Goat Tavern that there is tremendous power to support the truth when one reports what he has seen with his own eyes as the representative of a newspaper. It had never been a part of a reporter's duty before, but I felt it might become the new normal for future publishers. And at any rate, I felt compelled to be an eyewitness to this moment.

"Trust me," I said. After we stood listening to a distant swell of a mob like a giant breaker about to hit the Boston Sound, I said, "I would never fault you for assuming I have an agenda to promote one side or the other based on politics, but I will only report what I see with mine own eyes."

Captain Hall was in all respects a decent and admired sailor. Tall, rail thin, and bony in a very American way. His accent betrayed his New England upbringing, and I asked him what he thought of being raided by fellow Americans.

"Just to tweak lawmakers in England an ocean away?" He did not answer directly, instead studying me before planting a hand on my shoulder.

"I have only two concerns in this evening's dance," he continued. "First, and most important, that there be no harm done to my vessel." As if to emphasize the point, he drew back the long tail of his coat to reveal a pistol at his hip. "The second demand I make is that there be no harm done to my good name. That is all."

"Done." I told that *my* demand was to be allowed to print the truth. And I said we should start, for the record, with his full name.

"Davy Jones," he said after a short thought. "Captain Davy Jones." He had a distinctly American sense of humor. I made a show of noting it on the paper I had pulled from my coat pocket along with one of those graphite sticks Proprietor Deerfield had smuggled for me. "You are stand-ing remarkably tall for a dead man," I said. I had acquired Captain James Hall's name long before asking permission to come aboard, and even addressed him as such at my boarding.

He laughed. "If the rest of this evening is this cordial, I shall be quite a happy sailor."

We chitted and chatted a few minutes more while my nerves felt ever more raw. There was a strong wind high above us, pushing patches of clouds across the sky, playing peek-a-boo with the moon. Yet it was a mild December night. It would have been more pleasant if it was not for a fishing trawler in the slip at a warehouse upwind whose crew had left it unwashed after dispensing its cargo with the rotting portion of its catch, a mound of unwanted fish rejected by the wholesaler, heaped on the waterside of the warehouse,

Was it my hearing or my anticipation that had me attuned to the sound of an approaching mob?

"Cap'n Hall!" A crew member called him to the port gangplank. While the mob grew on the dock, three civilized Mohawk savages asked for permission to come aboard. How polite. Their Indian disguises fooled no one, though I gave them a nod of approval for ingenuity. After a brief negotiation Captain Hall ordered his men to stand down.

"No interference," he commanded.

More than two dozen grown men, nearly grown men, and even a couple of lads dressed in buckskin and blankets, faces smeared with lamp black and wielding hatchets, filed up the gangplank and set to work. It was far from the raucous, out-of-control affair I'd expected. They were chattering amongst themselves, laughing nervously and quite cheerful, but dedicated to the task and fixated on that to the extent it kept them from getting rowdy. After half an hour of hauling crates from the cargo hold, devising a methodical system of transfer, gutting the wooden crates with their weapons and dumping the tea into the water below, a fiddler joined them and set up in the stern of the *Dartmouth*. They were getting the hang on it and the fiddler played music to make their sweat and strain merrier. The chore must have been exhausting, but it had become entertaining now that the threat of violence was slight, and the overall mood of all aboard improved.

"This is going well enough, I suppose," Captain Hall sighed. I stood next to him in the raised bow of the ship along with his first mate, Mr. Ward.

"You should be quite happy, I should say," I told him. "Can I quote for my report that you are satisfied that there was a measure of respect and decency if one overlooks the criminality of this evening?" That had a nice ring to it. I held a scrap of paper in my sling-hindered left hand, making notes with my pencil under a lantern hanging from the rigging to the mast.

"I don't like this at all," Mr. Ward said. "I'm thinkin' these Mohawk thugs have not given a rodent's ass worth of time considerin' the consequences."

"Oh, they know they'll pay heavily," Captain Hall said. "And therein lies the point of all this."

I agreed. "They are baiting the government."

At that moment there was a flash and a crash from a short distance in the harbor. A cheer and then panicked shouts rose from the third tea ship anchored there. "Ward, I'm worried about the *Beaver*," Captain Hall said.

"Leave it to them to create a ruckus."

It only lasted a few moments and then the captain of the *Beaver* signaled that all was well. I could almost feel a collective exhale from all aboard the *Dartmouth*. I know I had been holding my breath while activity on our ship paused to take stock of the situation in the bay. One misstep might lead to one shot fired, which might lead to a rush by a company of soldiers that I knew were formed just out of sight behind the brick row houses on Battery Lane. And if that happened, would the man-o-war send a cannonball in our direction?

Despite all his bluster and threats of military conquest over any protest in the papers, my meeting with the governor on Thursday morning left the impression that the brass balls he claimed to possess were no more solid than the ink pads Sally had teased me with back in my print shop. Later I heard the governor had convinced the army's acting commander to hold back unless violence was unavoidable. He was going to let the protestors have their way and make them pay for it later.

Oh, Sally. That little vixen. Where was she?

I left the captain, with his permission, to inspect the process in a more personal manner. Two men on a winch raised crate after crate from the cargo hold. Teams of rogue Indians carried them to the rail, smashed the lids open with their tomahawk and axe blades, and balanced each wooden chest on the rail, first pouring a good measure of tea overboard before tossing the chest in after it. Two vandals swore at me when I stepped between them and the rail. One added a sharp elbow to my arm in its sling to make his point. I made a few notes capturing details, everything from the weather to the sound the tea made as it splashed in the harbor's water. I peered over the starboard rail and observed how the light from the torches and the half moon in a sky that was only partly clouded reflected on the muck along the ship's hull, making the bay look more like a marsh, so thick was the mess. My paper was nearly full, and I experimented with phrases and sentences I intended to compose in full later. I leaned against the main mast, safely out of the line of activity.

Pity those boys, I thought. Two young lads captured my attention. They were the most earnest but least effective of the vandals. Admire their spunk, if you will. They carried their tea chests to the rail nearest the hatch, using two hands on a small axe to split it open. It took them several whacks to accomplish that part of the task. It was comical. One lad was swimming in a buckskin shirt big enough for a man three times his size; the other had cut a hole in a blanket for his head and draped it over his shoulders. Both had applied too much lamp black around their eyes. Buckskin Boy wore a beaver hat that kept slipping down his brow. Lifting the chest to the rail was a strain because the boys' height put the rail just above their bellies. Not to be outfoxed, they had set one crate on the deck as a step to get the leverage needed to finish the task. Smart boys, I thought, until the taller of the two, who had a hand gripping the shirt of the other to steady his partner on the step box as he pitched a crate overboard, dropped his axe on the other's foot.

Oh, the string of crude profanity the crate-pitcher let loose. I will say, as far as his vocabulary was concerned, the lad had a terrific future in the navy. But I knew that voice.

I rushed forward and grabbed the little painted Mohawk by the shoulders and spun him to face me.

"Sally Hughes. You little shipwrecker."

Her scowl almost outperformed her profanity. "Sez you!" Her eyes were wide and cold, accentuated by the black grease beneath her eyes and covering her cheeks and along each side of her face to her chin. I looked at her cohort, now standing timidly a step away.

"Mouse Brow. Uh, I mean Miss Abigail. Or is it Alicia?"

"Shhhhhh! You twit."

Sally shoved me away, quite hard, and I stepped back. Oh, yes, I was a fool—sorry about that. But as I fell back, so did Sally, first planting her bottom on the rail and then tumbling overboard like a sack of tea.

"Whore overboard!" I shouted.

Sally struggled in the muck of tea leaves, and her heavy, wet buckskin shirt hampered any swimming motion she attempted. She tried to grab one of the floating tea crates, but that was just as futile and she couldn't keep her head above water and gobs of tea out of her mouth and nose.

I dove into the water. A moment later I found her and pulled her close, kicking through the muck along the ship's hull to the rear, where I knew there was a dinghy platform and stairs to the dock. I looked up to see faces lined along the rail of the *Dartmouth*, and there were concerned shouts until I signaled we would survive without help. A mild cheer reached us from above, and then murmurs—the sounds of men returning to work. Back to it. No drowning to see here.

"Relax, I've got you. Stop struggling, will you?"

"You loon."

Although she attempted to kick and take control of her fate, it only made my job more difficult, and her wet disguise was billowing with air and water.

"Pardon me, my lady," I said. "But I am going to save your life whether you like it or not."

We were not making much progress so I adjusted my hold on her as I twisted to a side stroke and pulled her onto my hip at the surface. It helped. Her blouse billowed with air like a pufferfish, and the fabric floated to the surface about her neck. I had no choice but to cling to her body under it, which had no shift to cover her naked skin. Yet my touch seemed to calm her desire to fight and she surrendered. I kicked my legs and pulled with my free hand to maneuver around the stern of the ship.

And then, just as a slight wave lifted us toward the dock, filling my eyes and nose with tea sludge, Sally slipped her hand beneath her buckskin blouse. She placed her arm alongside mine to tighten my hold on her body, nudging me closer to her bosom in the process. We would be safe.

We were almost to the ladder and coasting slowly to the pier when she said, "Thank you. For saving me, that is."

"My pleasure," I coughed.

With her right hand she traced the length of my arm and let it rest upon my hand beneath her shirt, her fingers separating mine so that we were interlocked, aiding rather than resisting the rescue effort. "Rest assured, I will slap your face for it later." But her squeeze was affectionate in nature, encouragingly so.

"That too, madam, will be my pleasure."

Chapter Twenty
The Child Bride and the Forger

Sally's naked body was everything and more I had imagined it to be during some long and recently restless nights, more of them than I care to admit. She revealed it as we warmed ourselves next to the stove back at the *New England News-Journal.* And to think all it took was my asking what in the world made her such a feisty little rebel.

I was jesting.

She was deadly serious.

We were wet, giddy, and breathing heavily by the time we reached the print shop. Some anonymous donor had handed us blankets after we climbed the stairs to the pier, before we dashed up Queen Street. Thank god the weather was mild enough not to kill us with cold between the *Dartmouth* and home. I fetched a muslin work shirt from my apartment on the second floor above the shop and gave that to Sally to cover her top, along with a large shop towel that was passably clean to wrap around her waist. Then I set about lighting the stove's fire, stringing a line over it to dry her Indian disguise, and keeping my eyes averted as she turned her back to me and changed into my dry clothes. For my part, with no clean, dry shirt left, I covered my chest as best I could with an apron, leaving my shoulders bare and chilled. I tried to compensate by stoking the fire higher than I might otherwise.

After we settled in with cups of tea, the graveness of that night settled over us and that's when I asked her, in an effort to lighten the mood, where her liberal sympathies had come from. I didn't expect a true answer, and she had a more difficult time with the question than I'd anticipated.

Finally, she rose from her chair and came to me until her thighs brushed my knees. Slowly she untied the strings of the neckline and lowered the blouse over her shoulders and down to her waist. Then she took my hand and pulled it to her body. Drawing one finger from the others, Sally traced a long, unsightly scar in her perfect skin above her left breast. Someone had defiled one of God's most blessed works of human creation, and it sickened me to my core. Stick a knife into the *Mona Lisa* and I could have cared less. This was horrible. I withdrew my hand, kissed my fingers, and laid them again on her scar there. A sad smile came to her slowly, and then she turned her back to me as she pulled my printer's shirt back over her shoulders.

"I was barely fifteen years," she said. "My father, a very rigid Loyalist, married me to a business associate of his. Ian Hughes was nearly twice my age. Father confessed later that he feared losing his estate to some future American suitor. He never admitted, though, that he sacrificed me, his only daughter and her dowry, in order to control who would have his legacy."

The fire in the stove crackled and popped in reaction to this news when she paused. To my eyes the room grew darker, though I knew the oil lamps were not losing a whit of light. The sadness that descended on us just made it seem so.

Sally spoke in measured tones. Her new husband was also a leading government counselor in their town and had served on the royal governor's committee of advisors. Some had said that Ian might one day be the next royal governor of Maryland. She was with child two months after the marriage, but the little one was lost before birth. Sally was still in bedrest when her husband battered her in a drunken rage.

"He shamed me for not providing an heir. My father had little sympathy at the time and advised me to mind my place and accept it. He promised it would resolve itself and pains were taken to hide my bruises until I recovered. It would have been a public scandal because Ian was such a force in the community and on a path to the appointment as governor."

She nearly died giving birth to a son a few months into the following year. She survived but the child did not. She was not yet eighteen.

"Shortly after, one night he took me to his bed. When he was finished, he took a knife and left me with this scar. He threatened he would do worse if I failed again to produce an heir. He wanted not one, but many children and said I was wasting my youth and his time."

She said she had stopped bleeding by morning but didn't stop crying for another day. When he had finished with her again the next night, while he was spent and sleeping, she took money from the household budget that Ian had thought he had hidden from her and walked out of the house. She relied on those funds as well as loans from friends and distant relations to make her way to Boston, where she was taken in by her Aunt Mae.

"Aunt Mae placed me in a convent near Philadelphia, where I did scullery work and many other chores in exchange for room, board, and private tutoring to give me an education. I was there nearly a year before I finally realized that in order to help finance the abbey, a number of the sisters entertained Catholic priests and Protestant preachers for money. They were men who couldn't dare be seen near a brothel."

Sally poured tea for the two of us, and she joked there was no rum or other alcoholic juice to flavor our cups. "A stiff drink would be most appropriate for this woeful tale of mine." I was thinking how easily she shifted her manner, her speech, even her posture between the lady I had met at Murdoch Mansion and the Flagg Alley madam. She snapped her fingers twice to pull me back to the present and quickly added that before I began to entertain any ideas of her stay in the convent, that at no time did she service any visitor to the Sisters of St. Mary Magdalene. She said it sharply. I deserved it.

And while the ludicrous irony of the service the sisters performed in the name of the prostitute saint had me twisting with fun inside, I kept as straight a face as possible when I replied simply, "Why in the world would I think that?"

Sally simply gave me an evil eye before looking at the floor and offering something of a confession. "I have been tarnished through association. I can see it in your eyes, and you have already indicated you believe as much. And yet I can say truthfully I have been with no man but my husband, Ian. Never."

How does one respond to that? Especially a man who is drawn to this woman more with each passing moment? I fumbled and mumbled apologies and then asked what had become of the husband. Had she heard from him since she left the Maryland colony?

Sally lifted her head and jutted that cute bulb of a chin while the sadness and despair in her eyes faded away. She replaced it with a glimmer that bordered between triumph and amusement. She told me no one seemed to know what became of Ian.

"I received a letter after moving from the convent to live with my Aunt Mae. It was my father asking forgiveness, and he made a plea for me to return to the family home. He said I would be safe because Ian was no longer a threat."

That created another concern in my mind. "Perhaps Ian is still tracking you at this very moment. Might he appear on your doorstep any day?"

Sally shook her head. "Father wrote he had last seen my husband when the two of them spent a day hunting boars in the woods miles from town. They became separated during the hunt and at sundown only my father returned. His letter was a bit cryptic, but he suggested that Ian would never be found."

I could not be more shocked, but Sally was not finished.

"I waited several months before writing to Father; my anger was still that deep. I told him that I would return if for no other reason than to finalize our permanent estrangement in person." Her father never got Sally's letter; he had been hanged for Ian Hughes' murder.

Now it was my turn to attend to the teapot. I took it from the stovetop, bent over her as I poured a bit into her cup. I lingered for a moment. I stroked her dry cheek with my finger. There were no tears. Something in her eyes convinced me she wouldn't allow tears, and yet, she looked up at me with gratitude that I felt came from my merely being there to hear her story. Then, in a hoarse whisper, said she had never shared the full story with anyone before.

"Even Aunt Mae doesn't know all. But you asked," she said after a long pause. "I think if anyone has justification for despising a way of life where a woman can be bartered for land and cattle, treated as nothing more than just another form of livestock for breeding while being subjected to violence at the whim of a man she doesn't love, and shamed for not wanting to accept it, then there is no hope for a civilized society." Her anger returned. "Do you?"

It was clear any answer I would give would be immaterial. She sipped her tea as melancholy slowly returned, and we sat in silence for what felt like an eternity.

I am not one for useless platitudes at moments like this. "Oh, I am so sorry to hear of your loss." Or, "I know how badly you must feel." Well-intentioned rubbish, but rubbish just the same.

I stood and circled her chair. *Dare I?* I wondered.

"I, too have secrets," I said. I went to the shelf near my writing desk. "This pistol? It was my father's. This book? It belonged to a woman, my sister-in-law, actually, who altered the course of my life. They are the only valuable things I brought from England with me."

As important as those mementos were, nothing could match the letter I withdrew from a small drawer tucked under one shelf.

"When I was a patterer in London, I achieved a certain level of notoriety and a bit of wealth by commercializing the news performance. At the urging of a woman I thought I loved, I pushed boundaries in my choice of items we chose to patter from a tavern's stage."

The idea for the effort came from my friend Benjamin Franklin, and it was so popular that other taverns across London began scheduling competing news performances.

"And then, eager to feed the beast, as we called it, I told the true tale of a distant royal relative, the Duke of Earl, who had a peculiar and illegal affinity for young men. I received this letter from Doctor Franklin informing me that shortly after I sailed for America, a mob for the reformation of London morals formed and killed the duke."

Guilt threw its heavy arm around me at that moment, like the juvenile delinquent schoolmate whose antics you followed too frequently, usually all the way to detention hall. Franklin's letter had informed me that the mob burned down the Molly house he was known to frequent. Three others died in the violence. Was the earl's sexual preferences news? I doubt it. Did it incite others to act? Most definitely.

"And so, those who wonder why I am loath to support any movement on either side of the relationship between those of us living in the colonies and Mother England, I carry a measure of grief for having killed a man through my reporting news."

"But now you are taking sides with the governor and Murdoch, and that is inciting more hatred. Look at what took place tonight," Sally said.

"Things will only get worse," I said. "Jacob has indicated my personal day of reckoning is coming. I believe this may be it. Print for them or perish."

Print or perish. In spite of the doldrums that threatened to choke the evening, it did have a nice ring to it. Perhaps I should use it on the masthead of the paper that was now only mine in name.

Sally set aside her teacup. She stood in front of me and once again climbed out of the shirt I had given her, this time discarding it entirely on the floor. She took my hands and pulled me to her naked body, wrapping her arms around me and burying her head in my chest. Once again I stroked her cheek gently and this time found tears.

"I need you to hold me tonight."

I did. For the longest time. Until she said the most amazing thing.

"Thank you, Mr. Printer. Thank you for rescuing me. Thank you for searching for me with such intensity these past days and for being so concerned. Oh, yes, they told me you had come to find me. Most of all, thank you for this moment. I have never felt this before." She sighed like a contented lover. And then she said, "But, too, thank you for being my knight in shining armor. Thank you for being my Forger. "

WTF?

Sally did not lift her head. Instead she nuzzled more deeply into my chest. "I may be a woman," she said. "But I'm not stupid. Anyone would have seen it in this story of ours long ago. You left a trail of signs only a blind man would miss. You are the Forger. You are that rascal publisher, writer, and scandalmonger alive and in person, and I love you for it. But I am no fool."

No, that would have been me.

Chapter Twenty-one
Tempest in a Tea Spat

"I suppose this means I will have to make an honest woman of you now."

"Not if I make an honest man of you first, Mr. Forger."

Sally tugged at the collar of the coat she wore to ward off the next morning's chill. The coat was from my limited wardrobe. And the cap she wore? That was a nice touch, replacing the too-large beaver fur she wore the night before, which must have been floating among the clots of tea in the harbor. The lady did disguise well, I say. We walked with a determined pace to her Aunt Mae's home in Cambridge District.

"At what point did you come to realize that it was I who took your information and put them into print as the Forger? Was it immediately obvious?"

"I was suspicious that when you offered to merely pass along the information I provided to this anonymous printer, it was not unreasonable to assume the ruse. Any reader of this unfolding story of ours would have deduced as much."

"And when the Forger suddenly appeared from nowhere at exactly that moment, it would be hard to think otherwise," I said.

"After I left a second message in the tree more than a week later, I returned to watch you at your printing press in the middle of the night. That was the essay on Governor Hutchinson calling a meeting of colonial officials to be held at the inn he owned on the road to Milton. And requiring each committee member to spend a night, and their money there.

"*Graft to the Rafters of the Colony Inn.* Nice headline," I said. "And a decent editorial, except that it isn't illegal to pay the governor to attend a meeting he required. That is one of his lesser bits of graft. Practically normal now."

"Well, it is still foul. He is rich enough already," Sally said. "Bloody hell."

"My, such language for a lady."

Sally put a hand to her cheek, feigning embarrassment. "Sometimes the Flagg Alley Sally escapes and runs amok. It's getting harder to restrain her every day. Aunt Mae is beginning to worry."

I was learning how she attempted a delicate balancing act of dual personalities. And yet it was arousing in a way that needed a bit of restraint on my part. I took her hand.

"I waited and watched you that night. It was two hours past midnight. I nearly froze to death."

"Woman. Did you give absolutely no thought to the danger of a lady on the street, unaccompanied, at that hour?"

"It's not so dangerous if you're dressed like a man. You can get away with all kinds of mischief."

Imagine that. "Be that as it may, I never imagined after the first publication of the *WTF* there would be a second," I said. "And now we've done four publications. I only took such a circuitous route that first time because I wanted a cushion of deniability, hiding your connection to the *Forger* and the other way around. That was much easier to believe when it was to be only one scandalous broadside, at which point we might have left it to Sam Adams and the other liberals to investigate and carry the story further."

As I anticipated, they had been eager to reprint *WTF* in the pages of their own newspapers. They added editorials with strong opinions further attacking the government, and the *Forger*'s words reached all of their subscribers, taverns, and coffee houses up and down the American seaboard. The *Forger* had become a notable voice overnight. As more citizens beyond Massachusetts looked toward Philadelphia and Boston for leadership, anyone of note in those cities could hardly sneeze a political position without having it spread like a virus in newspapers and pamphlets.

"Aunt Mae had a visitor from Virginia recently," Sally said. "And she brought with her a copy of *WTF* she had found in Richmond. How did you manage that?"

I raised a finger to my lips, a sign of caution. Two soldiers were strolling in the opposite direction on the street. They seemed to be inspecting the faces of each pedestrian.

"Searching for suspects, no doubt," I whispered when they had passed us with more than a once-over. Sally kept her cap low on her brow and her nose pointed at the ground.

"As to your question," I said after creating a safe distance between us and the redcoats, "it helps to have connections." I explained that dozens of copies of *WTF* mysteriously appeared at David Deerfield's backdoor. He was one of three postmasters in Boston, after all. "Ask him. He will swear he knows not who put them on his door," I said.

"You mean he'd lie," Sally replied.

"Lie?" I staggered comically as if wounded myself. "I would not challenge his honesty, miss. Either way he would swear ignorance."

From there, the papers found their way into the saddlebags of riders he hired to distribute mail and the other Boston newspapers across the province and throughout the colonies. Some of his best customers were the thirty-odd printers with newspapers of their own. "And like Edes & Gill, and Thomas at *The Spy*, those fellows are hungry for the latest information on the doings and the misdeeds of our governor and his friends," I said.

The light of day was dull with dark clouds threatening rain, and foot traffic along Sudbury Street moved swiftly. Everyone was intent on getting back indoors before the storm hit. I laughed at that thought because, as I pointed out to Sally, the real storm had hit the night before and rained tea leaves from three ships in the harbor. Ha!

Sally squeezed my hand as we safely reached the low stoop on the east side of her aunt's home in front of the door to the kitchen. I could hear the housekeeper stirring inside, rattling pots and pans and implements of breakfast construction, but Sally didn't seem to care. "What ever am I to do with you now, Mr. Forger?"

"Whatever are you to do with*out* me?"

Her scowl was playful. "Now that I think of it, I still owe you a slap on the face for taking advantage of me last night." Then she smiled. "While swimming in the water, I mean. Not that other thing later."

"Perhaps I should run up a tab as I have in Mr. Deerfield's tavern, and you can give those spanks to me all at once sometime."

She leaned back against the door with her hands buried deep in the pockets of my coat. She shivered slightly.

I said, "You are cold. You should get inside now. And I? I have work to do today that should already be underway. We must get the word out about last night's protest."

"As Merriweather the reputable Mr. Printer, or as the rogue publisher of that scurrilous scandal sheet *The Forger*?"

"I believe it might be best if the Forger takes a holiday. It's only a matter of time before he is traced back to us. And I could use the rest. You, as well." I reached out and tapped the tip of her nose. "Though to mine eyes, I see no ill effects. Even after the soaking you took in your dive off the ship."

Sally hesitated, looking down as one might consider her first step toward navigating a perilous slope. "Before you ask and I will be required to refuse, let me say that yes, while much of the information I have shared with you comes from the bedrooms at Flagg Alley, there is also another, more valuable source which I will never reveal. Not ever. Just trust me; it is someone who needs protecting, and that person's information is as good as gold. We've shared a good many secrets since last night. This is one I must keep to myself."

"Then I do not want to know. 'Tis better that way. But I have great fear that you, my lady, will be caught between this person and the gallows."

"But there will be more information to come out. Important things, I'm sure. Whatever shall we do?"

"Bring them discretely to me. I will know what to do then."

I left Sally with a soft peck and a promise that I would soon see her again.

"I will ask Aunt Mae to allow you a social visit if I am here," she said. "If it is to be at Flagg Alley, be sure to bring a purse full of coin. I wouldn't want the girls to get the wrong idea."

My two print devils, Bert and Ernie, were tossing a ball on the street when I reached the print shop.

"Why are you misfits out here when there is work to be done?" I scolded them. "Big news last night. We have a newspaper to publish."

"Visitors, Mr. Merriweather. They told us to wait outside." Bert indicated the figures on the other side of the patched-up front window with a jerk of his head and an anxious look on his face.

Clinton Murdoch, his lawyer O'Donnell, and a man I had not seen before were waiting inside.

"My oh my," I said and went straight to the coat stand. "Isn't life exciting these days? What a night that was. All the town is abuzz. We will sell stacks of broadsheets, for sure." I strutted past them and plopped down at my writing desk with my elbows firmly planted atop scraps of paper. I palmed my right fist with my left hand and held them to my chin. I would have liked to say it was prescient, a move to prevent my jaw from hitting the floor, but that would have given my initial wariness too much credit. "To what do I owe this unexpected pleasure?" I asked.

O'Donnell gestured to the stranger. He was likely in his early twenties with a high forehead and receding hairline, suggesting he might be bald before sundown. His spectacles made him look like a learned man, and he had broad shoulders above a narrow waist. A printer's build, I thought.

"This gentleman is Roscoe Sweed," O'Donnell said. "He is to be your new assistant printer."

"Odd. I don't recall hiring an assistant."

"I hired him," Murdoch said. "And I have tasked him to relieve you of the heavy workload we have heaped upon you. He will take over some responsibilities starting with the *New England News-Journal.*"

Chapter Twenty-two
The Price of Doing Business

I had been on borrowed time as well as money from the start. This moment had been coming, inevitable actually, and I was prepared for it only in my mind, though not my heart. My head was full of plans, some of my favorites involving all manner of minor violence against Murdoch and his followers. Other schemes seemed quite practical, possible, and even preferable, but of course I had acted on none of them. I took a moment to stick my head into the press room and gauge how far Bert and Ernie had gotten to prepare for a day's print run. Not far at all. I also took a strong sniff of the air, which was heavy with the scent of oil, turpentine, and damp rag paper, like a gentleman snorts a pinch of snuff to sharpen his wits.

O'Donnell grinned with his yellow teeth and swung his sharp nose like a pointer toward Mr. Sweed, who had taken up a position behind the lawyer, and then to Clinton Murdoch. "I've already made the case to Mr. Murdoch that you need an assistant. How many times have you whined that the amount of work the governor is giving us is costing us valuable civilian clients? We hired Mr. Sweed yesterday and he will solve the problem for us."

"Except that Mr. Sweed no longer works here," I replied. Then I barked, "Sweed, you are fired. Sacked. Collect your personal items, and leave us now."

Sweed looked far too confident for a mere assistant. "But I haven't even started yet." Then he looked at Murdoch. "Can he sack me?"

"Most certainly," I said before Murdoch could offer his two pence worth. "It is still my name on the business license and atop the letter of incorporation. So this is still my print shop unless you intend to buy me out."

"Then, Mr. Merriweather," Murdoch laughed. "I wish to make you an offer for your share of the business—a minority stake, I might add."

"Not. For. Sale," I responded.

If my maths were any good—which actually were lackluster back in my days at King Edward Grammar School, and that is probably why I gravitated to the creative life of words and speaking—I had ledgered enough numbers to know I had been making headway against the debt I owed Murdoch thanks to the governor. For while I was deeply cash poor from losing business that paid in silver, the credits they gave me under our agreement for printing Governor H's posts had pushed down that debt faster than I'd anticipated. Surely Murdoch could see that I would be in a position of a controlling share by summer, and then I would have the upper hand.

He turned to Sweed and told him to go off and settle into the apartment Murdoch had arranged for him. We would have details agreed upon in no time.

"Roscoe is a good man," Murdoch told me. "He has been working under Mr. Rivington at the *Gazetteer* in New York. Damned fine Loyalists there."

I nodded. "Rivington has quite the conservative following and he's only been publishing the *Gazetteer* since spring."

Like me, James Rivington was born on the other side of the pond. Unlike me, he was a king's man through and through, and that cut straight to the pages of *The Gazetteer*. Rivington beat me to America by some five years or so, but until launching his news sheet, he was best known for owning *Rivington's Bookshops*, a string of outlets printing pamphlets and books in large cities, including one that had been on King Street in Boston for several years.

"So you see, Merriweather, Mr. Sweed has a grand pedigree in proper publishing with conservative, loyal values," Murdoch said.

"What's more," O'Donnell added, "we have just recently acquired a newspaper in Maryland. That gives us presence in four colonies. Mr. Sweed will not only help you with the *News-Journal*, he will be our man to coordinate a consistent message between all of our newspapers from this shop. We'll have a network of broadsheets to reprint and carry Governor Hutchinson's writings to the rest of America."

You mother flogging lobcocks! I choked on the words I wanted to spit at them, then stopped to take a slow breath. They exchanged a glance, tight-lipped with the corner of their mouths curled in a tiny triumphant smirk as if my initial silence convinced both they had pulled a fast one over on me. That was their initial step to wrestle the newspaper away from me.

"If you men have any honor," I said, and I was convinced they had none, "let us drop the pretense, shall we? We know there will be no work for me if our only press is fully engaged under Sweed. And that is clearly your intent." I had no doubt Sweed, acting on Murdoch's orders, would be running the shop and dictating my duties in no time at all.

"There is where you'll be wrong, Merriweather. We need your services greatly," Murdoch lied. He shook the head of his cane at me like a schoolmaster. "We have ordered a new printing press, an impressive model of the most current fashion. Expensive, but I think you will be pleased. We have ordered it under the company's credit and so you will own a portion of it as well."

The hit of print room snuff must have worked, for my mind was clear and I immediately recognized a trap. Murdoch had used the print shop's license to buy an expensive press without my permission and put me deeper in debt.

"It seems to me all I will own is the bill."

"Nonsense," O'Donnell scoffed. He said the new printing press would arrive from England a month or two into the new year, and that Sweed would be busy arranging a system of information exchange amongst the Murdoch newspapers until that time. "So your continued employment here is needed. And once our second press is working at full capacity, you should be able to increase the workload and the revenues they will provide to have it paid for soon enough."

Did the bastard say *my employment*? I owned the business, at least until bankrupted by their play. O'Donnell handed me a contract for the purchase of the press. I gagged at the price and quickly calculated it would add at least a year to repay my debt to Murdoch even in the best of times. But after the previous night's assault on the tea ships it was clear we faced what was possibly the worst of times.

And I was shagged.

I tried to protest but Murdoch would have none of it, although he did flinch and take a step back, raising his cane like a wizard trying to ward off some approaching devil, when I moved closer.

Back and forth we argued. I said he had no right to make a purchase that would add to my debt. He said, by holding the majority interest in the business, he had every right to do so.

I cursed. He cursed back. I was angry enough that I ignored the arrival of the governor's man, Larson, and the soldier Lieutenant Cole. When I did take notice, I set aside my feud with Murdoch. My anger, on the other hand, was a boulder-sized chip that stayed camped out on my shoulder. I took a breath and considered that he had given me until early spring before Sweed took over and I would be tossed with little dignity into the street gutter with the rest of the waste.

"This is our official response to the hooligans who did such damage last night at Griffin's Wharf," Larson said. He handed me three full pages of ugly scrawl, enough to fill a two-sided newspaper. "Your task is to print it under the governor's name. This will ensure that the public hears from Governor Hutchinson directly, as well as make it abundantly clear to the vandals and their instigators—Adams and Hamilton, Warren and the like—that this behavior is greatly frowned upon."

"Condemned," Cole said. "And the governor is offering rewards to informants that lead to arrests. We'd like to distribute it no later than tomorrow morning."

I scanned the governor's message quickly. One capitalized word jumped out from the paper. "A curfew?" I asked.

"Certainly is the proper thing," Lieutenant Cole answered. "Wouldn't want the rabble to spend time relishing the affair. Quick action is strong action."

"Mr. Larson, you understand that to produce a double-page broadside such as this on such short notice will stretch the limits of our abilities here," I said. Fueled by my dispute with Murdoch, I was determined to show some backbone. I tossed in a lie as well. "I have today's edition of the *News-Journal* set in place and we are about to go to press. This would be extremely difficult. A backbreaker, actually. As such, I must insist on a surcharge for this service."

This was worthy of what we in the printing business refer to as the "AA." Aggravation Adjustment. It was reserved for

special clients who deserve mild retribution for their unreasonable demands. Or their behavior. Or their bloody attitude.
Occasionally because of their politics, and this occasion seemed
to fit all of those. Maybe I should double it.

Larson and the others cased the scene with skepticism. The
stillness in the press room was a giveaway.

"Even better," Larson said. "You can simply replace whatever you had planned to publish about last night with the governor's report."

"But I was on the *Dartmouth* last night as an observer.
I had planned to write a firsthand account of the affair," I
said. Then I had a flash of inspiration. "It is very much the
manner in which you asked me to witness and report the
capture of Hancock's smuggling sloop."

"We know how *that* turned out," Lieutenant Cole
grumbled.

I couldn't help a triumphant grunt myself. Cole was still
resentful at how he had been outfoxed by Hancock. Yes, the
truth hurts. And I aimed to print the truth of the Boston
Tea Affair. I had already given a grand, iconic name to the
protest. One that I suspected would go down in history if I
could stay strong and keep from having my editorial control
usurped by the governor's message.

"Merriweather, you will be more than adequately compen-
sated for today's task," Larson said. "Yes, a few pence to your
surcharge for rushing this job through. I'm sure the governor
will approve. You can add it to the credits against your debt to
Mr. Murdoch here."

Murdoch and O'Donnell both coughed, cleared their throats, and turned as if searching for someplace they would rather be.

"The governor's generosity knows no bounds," I said. "At this rate of return, I will be bankrupt in no time at all."

That settled that as far as everyone in the room not named Merriweather cared. Lieutenant Cole stayed behind. "Shame about that nasty business Tuesday, and your confrontation with those militants," Cole said. "Knocked asunder in your encounter with the Sons of Liberty and all that rot. Though it seems to me your shoulder has healed quite nicely. You *will* be able to handle today's assignment, no?"

Did he suspect there never had been an injury at all? It sounded so. Then I realized I had been wringing my hands. I wasn't wearing my arm sling and I hadn't given a thought to my false injury since falling into bed with Sally somewhere between midnight and our pleasant bit of snookery. I let my left arm drop limp to my side. I used my right hand to raise it like a week-old, tired stalk of celery. "I heal quickly," I said.

"Of course. It is clear you are not a happy chum, having gone so far as to attend last night's ruckus with no place to report it, given the governor's priorities and all that. You will be happy to know I have some news which you will have the opportunity to publish."

And then Lieutenant Cole said what I feared most. That stopped my heart.

"We may not yet know the Forger's identity. But soon. We *have* uncovered the identity of the person who has been his source of information. That devil fooled us for much too long, but got careless and was recognized by one of our men on the tea ship last night."

Cole speculated the informant had hidden out overnight to avoid trouble until returning home late this morning. Then Cole took a few steps to the window—judging the time of day, no doubt.

"Someone you know. That is why I came here. Our men are making an arrest as we speak."

Chapter Twenty-three
A Snitch in Time

I hadn't given a thought to Francis Akeley in years.

"Tell me what you know of him," Lieutenant Cole demanded.

"I haven't given a thought to Francis Akeley in years," I responded. How was that for an answer? Simple. Direct and to the point.

"We are arresting him for taking part in the assault on the ships last night. But there is more to it than that."

"Is he the lone arrest from all this?" I asked. "Is there anyone else?"

Lieutenant Cole shook his head and cursed the limp-spined superiors who appeared to be opposed to a massive sweep to arrest the usual suspects.

Thankfully my brain was ahead of my mouth for a change, exactly opposite of my normal way of communicating. A good thing because it was less likely to cause me trouble. Lieutenant Cole's suspicion of Francis remedied the panic attack that was clutching my windpipe. Sally Hughes was not the *WTF*'s snitch most certainly on her way to the Boston jail at that moment. Piss on a penguin. I had been rattled for a moment.

Jacob Addison's cousin Francis was the target of their investigation. "A fine young lad, as I remember him," I told the soldier. "Francis was working here in the print shop when I was hired by Mr. Addison. Of course that was long before I acquired the shop."

After I arrived in Boston and hired on at the *News-Journal*, Father Addison sent Francis to Harvard to acquire some education and polish in hopes of bringing him back to the family business.

The young man finished two years at Harvard and then found employment in the Hutchinson administration as a clerk. "From there, I don't know what happened to him," I said. "I suppose he's still a practicing bureaucrat, isn't he? Smart enough that he should be in charge of some minor government agency by now."

"Actually, you'd be surprised," Lieutenant Cole said. He dropped into a chair near the retail counter and leaned back. Cole withdrew a dagger from a sheath on his belt. He used the tip to pick at imaginary dirt beneath his fingernails. Cole explained Francis had become one of Clinton Murdoch's two personal secretaries. "I haven't mentioned this to Mr. Murdoch yet, tempting though it was as he was so full of himself in front of you this morning. We know that as the man's secretary, Mr. Akeley had access to much of the information passing between the governor, the governor's aides like Larson, and Mr. Murdoch. We haven't yet discovered how he conveyed information to that word shit who publishes *WTF*, but we will find out. And he will tell us the identity of the publisher, I am sure of that."

I had never been so happy to see a dog barking up the wrong tree in my life. And yet, I was concerned for Francis. I had fond memories of the young man. "What will happen to him?" I asked.

"I'm torn between hanging him for treason or assigning him to await a trial in the brig on the HMS *Louis*, where he might be drowned while trying to escape."

Apparently innocence and acquittal were not on the official docket if Cole got his way. Then the soldier stopped picking at his fingernails and looked at me hard. "And what concern is it of yours? You only need to report it."

I shrugged and effected my best dog face. I told Cole that I had been fond of Francis and that it pained me to see him in trouble like that. "Although, being part of the Mohawk Mob doesn't tie him to the *Forger* now does it? Certainly you have more than that. And probably more than simply being one of Murdoch's employees whilst being a tea-tampering Mohawk."

"We do." Cole refused to say what more led them to suspect Francis Akeley. He was, in fact, snippy in his response. "That is information reserved on a 'need to know' basis, and there is no need for you to know."

"Lieutenant, I am hurt, and more than a bit put out. It pains me that you treat me as if I were under suspicion as well.

I don't like the tone of your voice. I don't like the look in your eye. I don't like…well, I don't like much about you at all." So there, you moldy bit of accusing cheese.

The lieutenant took his dagger by the tip and feigned chucking it at me, then drove it into the wooden display table at his elbow. I refused to flinch. Much.

WTF?

I stared at the handle. It was naturally a military issue. What gripped my attention was a family crest on the hilt near the cross guard and fancy script with the owner's initials. *DIC.*

"At what are you staring?" Cole demanded.

I stammered. "Oh, a fine weapon you have." I swallowed hard. The dagger bore the personal markings of the knife that had killed Customs Agent George Grant. That was one bit of detail Sally had provided after we published our first *WTF* report. Later when I went back to the coroner against Murdoch's directive to see the weapon with my own eyes, Coroner O'Donnell reported that the murder weapon had mysteriously gone missing.

Now the knife stood like a guilty exclamation point in the table between me and Cole. Sally was right about the markings. Now they pointed to Cole as the killer.

Cole struggled to remove the dagger for it resisted his tug at first. He resorted to using both hands and a rotating movement that served to deface the table more. He said his search of Watertown and other possible locations turned up no hint of *WTF.*

"That narrows down our list of potential traitors to you and four others with access to a printing press. And I won't eliminate any of you at this point."

Not only did I know that, I had been expecting the logic of it to smack Cole and his investigation long ago. That it had taken this long was the only real surprise. I had invented several excuses and potential rabbit holes in my mind to distract Cole and was prepared to pull one out at any moment. And yet, to hear him outline it in such a straightforward and, yes, menacing manner, scared the bloody snot out of me. It didn't help that he was so cavalier about what fate might be in store for Francis Akeley. My first impulse was to try to keep Francis' neck out of the noose, but how to do that without tightening the noose around my own? Or, more importantly, Sally's? And then I realized that Francis must have been the source of information outside Flagg Alley that Sally was protecting.

I faced Lieutenant Cole with both palms out. "My hands are clean in this matter," I said. Then stealing a glance at them I noted they were stained with long-dried ink, lead grease from the type case, even a bit of the lamp black I had wiped from Sally's disguised face in our post-coital snuggles. I dropped my hands guiltily, and then with a shrug and a smile placed them behind my back.

"I believe you," Cole said.

"You do?" Bugger the badger, I couldn't keep the surprise from my voice.

"No. Not really," he replied. "But then I only said that because we seem to be engaged in a game. I don't think you are as stupid and pliable as either the governor or Mr. Murdoch believe, but I don't have enough evidence to the contrary. You don't like me, and I am suspicious of you for reasons I just can't quite comprehend. But I will find out."

With that, Cole rose to leave, only to be blocked by the arrival of Jacob Addison.

"Merriweather! Leeds Merriweather, you miserable gob of badger snot. Did you know there are a couple of lobsterbacks out front?" Jacob burst through the door. He pulled up. "Oh. Good afternoon, Lieutenant. I should have guessed your sentries weren't here looking for reading material. Though I doubt they can read, and from the looks of it, I doubt you are here to buy a book."

"Jacob, you just missed the governor's man Larson," I said. I showed him the governor's work. "Larson brought a submission and an order to print about last night, though he didn't think it was necessary to pay for it."

"I told you owning a printing business is the quickest road to the poorhouse. Praise the Lord that's Murdoch's problem now. I am thankful he cheated me out of any financial obligation to this failing news operation."

He turned to Lieutenant Cole. "To what do we owe this visit, Lieutenant? I am naturally curious, though I suspect it has something to do with the vandalism at the wharf. All the town's talking about it."

"You'd be correct, Mr. Addison. In fact, I was on my way to see you today."

"Me?"

"You."

"It seems Francis Akeley is in a spot of trouble over it," I said.

"Our little Frankie?" Nobody did mock incredulousness like my friend Jacob.

"The lieutenant stopped by today to ask after Francis. It seems Francis may have some involvement in that scum Forger's efforts to embarrass the administration," I said. "Putting two and two together with our print shop, he came up with six and assumed collusion with the *News-Journal,* I'm afraid."

"Not just your newspaper, more than that," Cole said. "But yes, I'd like to have a word or two with you, Mr. Addison, since you are familiar with this Akeley fellow. As I hear it, you were the one who trained him in the craft of news."

"Francis has been working as Mr. Murdoch's secretary lately, it seems," I interjected.

"So I had heard. Poor fellow," Jacob replied. "Yes, Lieutenant, I'd be happy to share with you what I know. He's hardly a rogue, and possibly I can put your suspicions to rest. My office is closed for the day but I hear Proprietor Deerfield has received a shipment of an intriguing claret. French, yes, but I don't hold that against him. Join me for a drink and we'll say grace and discuss this nasty business."

Lieutenant Cole noted that it was barely noon. "Your office is closed for the day?"

"Well certainly. This matter pertains to action against the crown, does it not? And by my calculation it is five o'clock in London. Closing time and time for a drink. If you'd prefer to schedule an appointment for a later date, contact my man, Sidney; otherwise I will be at the Star Coffee House for the remainder of the afternoon."

And most likely well into the evening, I suspected.

Jacob tipped his cap to the soldier and turned for the door. Cole looked at me, straightened his shoulders, made the best of it, and followed Jacob. They were standing just outside the open door when Jacob paused.

"Oh my, nearly forgot why I came. I will catch up with you momentarily, Lieutenant." He pulled a thick bundle of foolscap from inside his coat and patted Cole on the arm with it in a most friendly manner before stepping back into the print shop.

"Here is the contract," he said in a hushed tone. "I had Mr. Hartford insert the clause you requested and he notarized it for me. All it needs is your signature. And you owe me two quid."

"I will add it to the debt on the shop that I owe you. Wait. That would have to go to Murdoch now, wouldn't it? You can collect it from him."

Jacob said, "That debt will be worthless if what you fear happens."

"I truly hope it does not." I took the contract from him. It was for property insurance, something relatively new for businesses beyond maritime ventures. Mr. Hartford had long been an agent for Lloyds of London in the shipping trade. He began selling property insurance when prominent businessmen in Boston created the Fire Contributionship Board to protect their holdings as well as profit from the sale of insurance to nonmembers.

"After my brush with death or dismemberment at the hands of Baby Cakes Curry, I think this is the right time to take precautions," I whispered. "I will take care of it quickly since I have a decree from the governor about last night to print. I fear this one might really push the Sons of Liberty to take action against the newspaper. If not now, soon."

"For what it's worth, I believe this deal with Mr. Hartford is a very smart thing. Something bad is going to happen, whether it's a good kind of bad or a disaster, I hope you keep your limbs in the process."

Chapter Twenty-four
Words Matter

Boston, January 3 in the year of OUR LORD 1774
Sirs;

> A farce, reports of **SPIES** running **AMOK**
> within the Hutchinson Administration, have
> captured the **RECKLESS IMAGINATION**
> of his **INCOMPETENT CADRE** of advisors
> to such a degree that they are now considering
> **A MOST GRIEVOUS ACT** against **EVERY**
> informed member of our community.

The Forger was on a roll. Samuel Adams leaned over the letter I had delivered. I leaned over his shoulder as he read it, and Isaiah Thomas stood opposite of us at the desk leaning over to read it up so down. Throats cleared. Hems became haws with a few knowing "He's got that right" chuckles thrown in for good measure.

We were in Samuel Adams' receiving room, the room that served as his workspace. I thought the *News-Journal* print shop was a cluttered mess, but Adams' personal lair matched his unkempt appearance. He cared about neither. Only words eloquently making a point mattered to Sam. He read more.

> Unofficial communications of Corruption and Incompetence inside the Governor's House have now brought us to the BRINK OF SUPPRESSION. Those imaginary SPIES do not exist, and yet the administration is about to use that absurdity to force the CLOSURE AND BANKRUPTCY OF ALL NEWSPAPERS not printing the propaganda of our MOST DISHONORABLE GOVERNOR HUTCHINSON even if such OPPRESSION requires MILITARY PROSECUTION.

"A pretty fine bit of writing," I said with a mental pat on my back. "Has the Forger been proven wrong yet?"

Adams was supporting himself with his elbows on a flat-top desk littered with pamphlets, pages, discarded feather quills, blackened and bent nibs, and ink bottles, some that had been knocked over recklessly and left to lay there like dead soldiers on a ravaged battlefield. Black spots stained several places on the desk, evidence of dried ink that had once upon a time spilled and flowed over the edge and down the side like a waterfall into a puddle on the floor.

"But why bring this to me?" Adams asked. "The Forger has never been shy about using his own press."

"It certainly appears to be authentic," Isaiah Thomas said. "That is his signature for sure. But I agree, Samuel. Why didn't he just print it himself?"

The answer was a simple one. Unfortunately, not one I could reveal in full without implicating Sally as well as my creation of *WTF* as a way to assist her in publicly shaming the governor. So I offered an edited version.

"The Forger has encountered issues, I am told," I said. "When this letter came to me, it needed to be made public, but Murdoch has me on such a short leash, and he is looking for any excuse to yank it, that I felt it was safer, and would have more impact, if I brought it to you fellows. You can plainly see the bind I'm in. As long as Clinton Murdoch has his grip on the *News-Journal* I would be committing publishing suicide were I to print this."

Possibly actual suicide. Death by Lieutenant Cole, I feared.

"Thank God Edes & Gill are as radical as my reputation," Adams chuckled. "I would revolt if I were in your position."

"It has been on my mind of late. Murdoch is trying to monopolize the news. And he's asked the governor to crack down on everyone else," I said. "What he can't steal, he buys. What he can't buy, he's trying to convince the governor to shut down. That means you."

"Hmmm. The Forger argues that Murdoch was very much an instigator of a plot to shut us all down. Right there," Adams said, stabbing the page near the middle with enough force that he poked the page out of his left hand. "Murdoch orchestrated a meeting with the governor's office to work out the details of a new treason law in what is certain to be an unpopular, most likely illegal effort."

I nodded. "They'll be after you with an impossible curfew, and soldiers with warrants of treason for inciting every manner of protest now in the wake of the tea assault. But make no mistake, fellows, Murdoch is as much behind this as the governor."

"At least you would be free to go on publishing, Merriweather," Adams said. "Mr. Murdoch will make sure of that."

True words and words matter. "And that is why I brought this to you." It was clear the Forger needn't publish that particular story independently, for I knew Adams and Thomas would take it on. This was an assault on all of us. This was about our freedom to print. Nothing was more important than that.

I didn't want to know how Sally discovered that news before passing it along to me, though I suspected one of her Strumpets of Liberty had turned the trick and learned of the governor's plan in the act of servicing one of his men, or perhaps the governor himself. Who knew for certain?

"I like this line from the Forger mocking the issue as FECKLESS FOLLY by those BUNGLING FOOZLERS," Thomas said.

I was at the top of my form when I wrote that. I had shared thoughts about taking the Forger to *The Gazette* and *The Spy* with Jacob. And while he agreed it was a sensible course, he took note of my anger and suggested the quickest and best path to put the fear of god into Murdoch would be to ransack his home or one of his other buildings, posting the Forger's commentary there.

"A thought," I said. "I could gather the entire mob necessary for the price of a three-night stay at Flagg Alley." As delicious as that sounded, my cash flow was insufficient and I couldn't ask Sally for her girls' favors gratis.

"Ah, the spirit is willing, but the purse is weak. Matthew: twenty-six-er-something," Jacob preached. Once again he proved that the Bible was a place where all my best ideas went to die.

Adams said, "As I see it, we have so much less risk by printing this letter than you, Merriweather, and everything to lose if we do not."

"Agreed," Isaiah said. "It's imperative that if we value a free and open press we must stand together on this matter. Sign me up. I will address the issue as well, in a fashion that will be a call to indignation for my subscribers beyond the province."

"I will send a note along with the Forger's piece to the Hall brothers in Salem," I said. "I know Ebenezer as a good fellow and he will put it in their *Essex Gazette*. And, hey. Mr. Green at the *Courant* down in Hartford? Murdoch purchased one of his competitors to grow his little empire."

"Takes no brains to determine which way his frisket will swing on this issue," Thomas laughed.

Enemy of the people, are we? Flog the frog. We smiled at each other.

"Gentlemen, we have just begun to fight," I said.

Adams and Thomas shared contorted, if not confused, faces before turning and mocking me. They did not say a word. Their look was comical and I'd rate it somewhere between a quizzical "What did you do with the real Merriweather?" and a condescending "It's about time you deduced the right side. What took you so long?"

"Politics make strange bedfellows," I paraphrased Shake-speare with a shrug. I was not fully convinced at that moment that I had skipped across the partisan river to join them on the other side. This fight was too personal for that. I lost my battle in early March.

By February, Murdoch had invaded my print shop and set up an occupation force of three led by one Mr. Roscoe J. Sweed along with two assistants. Their weapon was a new Jenson Blaew model printing press that stood like royalty across from my rundown but reliable Gutenberger. I would give a pinky toe for a Jenson Blaew.

Sweed turned out to be a humorless man with arrogance that comes with having been able to learn skills easily at too young an age, and we did not get along at all. He believed the printing press was just a piece of equipment to perform a job. I still believed that each printing press had its own soul and its own destiny to touch lives.

WTF went missing in action through the winter while I, the rascal Forger, was a thorn in the governor's side as I got information from Sally and turned it into stories other newspapers carried. The Sons of Liberty performed a decent dismantling of the tax collector's office after the *Massachusetts Spy* published an exposé I had written in the name of the Forger. Governor Hutchinson, his sons, and entourage ran up an outrageous bill using taxpayers' money for two weeks of a government retreat that included officials from throughout the province. They held it at an exclusive property in Charles-town favored by the attendees, many of whom just happened to be wealthy Tories while the property just happened to be owned by Hutchinson's family. From the taxpayer's pocket to the governor's purse. It was another Flagg Alley exclusive provided by the strumpet spies.

And spies? Not long after that report by the Forger I noticed a disturbing pattern at Proprietor Deerfield's coffee house and other taverns where politics were discussed and thoughts of what actions could or would be taken were whispered. Strangers—quiet, serious-looking men in the upstairs subscription room—began drinking there more frequently. One or two looked familiar; I thought I had seen them with the governor's security officer Lieutenant Cole. Now they were men out of uniform, which was unusual in and of itself, and I began to believe there were others roaming the streets in search of information on troublesome citizens the way women, not in the employment of Flagg Alley, roamed the street in search of men with hard cash in their pockets.

My battle with Murdoch escalated through winter. He had become the tyrant-in-chief in my mind. Sweed had adopted the role of propagandist as the *New England News-Journal* moved more solidly into the Loyalist lane with each passing day. We slithered into spring and I had the most advantageous position to observe the claptrap Sweed printed on the government's behest and compare it to information obtained from Sally's ring of prostitutes that the Forger distributed to other newspapers. At times their stories were so opposite that someone had to be lying. And as far as I could tell, the only sort of lying the strumpets did was on their backs for a few coins and a wealth of scandalous intelligence.

I greeted sunrise on the first Sabbath in March from Hanover Knoll near the western tributary of the Charles River, looking down across Beacon Hill, across the city to the bay. Two things were obvious. First, despite the fact that no one was harmed in the tea ship protest, war was inevitable. There were still deniers out there, but I was no longer one of them. Parliament closed the port of Boston in response to the tea affair and the citizens were in an economic stranglehold of lost jobs, spreading poverty and random acts of violence in retaliation. Mother England was choking us, and how much longer could it be before shots would be fired and men would die on a battlefield?

Second, the print shop and the newspaper were no longer mine, and pretending otherwise only brought more heartache. Though it was not official, Sweed had absorbed more control with Murdoch's blessing, and my role diminished. The straw that broke the llama's back occurred that previous day when Sweed directed me to deliver the latest edition of the paper to postmasters in Salem and Concord for subscribers north of town. And he instructed me to continue my ride to Portsmouth where I could deliver it to the Murdoch owned newspaper there. I had gone from publisher to delivery boy so quickly I was surprised the fall didn't kill me. I walked out and up to Beacon Hill, where I waited more than two hours in Murdoch's parlor as night fell to see the old foozler. He was first occupied at tea with Sally's aunt, Mrs. Mae Flowers. Then had some urgent business requiring his attention. Then it was his afternoon bath and toilet. Finally, there was me.

"It seems Mr. Sweed is doing an admirable job," Murdoch told me after I had launched into a series of grievances. He gave no quarter and was too enthusiastic in the solutions he offered. Each one resulted in having to surrender my percentage of ownership to him. As for being reduced to the role of delivery boy?

"I've heard you are a competent horse rider," Murdoch joked. Then he poured himself a drink but offered me none. "Thirty days. I will have O'Donnell draw up the papers. You can sign over your share to me for which I will reduce your debt to only the remaining amount."

"That's not buying my shares. That's stealing them," I said.

"Nonsense. The alternative is foreclosure, bankruptcy, and debtors' prison. Now *that* would be rude."

I went to his liquor cabinet, grabbed the bottle, and poured my own drink under his disapproving eyes. "I surrender," I said. "I will give you my answer soon enough. But I feel it is my duty to warn you of the whispers."

"Whispers?"

"Yes. I have heard several hints on the street that Mr. Sweed's conservative articles are starting to rankle a good many people, and after that band of soldiers and Tories threatened Isaiah Thomas in front of *The Spy*, burning him in effigy and all that rot, I fear an attack of retaliation on the *Journal* might be under consideration by the Sons of Liberty."

I can't swear to any one reason why I bothered to tell him; I suppose it seemed fair. What I did not reveal was that I was prepared for just such an event. My contract with Mr. Hartford, at the Fire Contributionship Board, was insurance for that. Murdoch had made it clear the future of the print shop would be none of my concern within the month. I raised the fine, crystal shot glass etched with Murdoch's initials that I had filled with his scotch. I savored the liquor to the last swallow before raising it, empty, in toast to him. I kept the glass and pinched his bottle of scotch as well when I left the house. The weather was not unbearably cold, and the stars were like a siren's song overhead, so I carried the bottle to Hanover Knoll where we, like intimate friends, spent the night by campfire until sunrise. And like intimate friends, the scotch comforted me as I brooded.

Two days later a judicial server from the magistrate's office delivered notice that I had thirty days to make good on my debt or lose my rights to the print shop. It included an inflated bill for the acquisition of the new printing press and charges related to its installation that would not only have left me penniless, but with a debt that was sure to land me in prison.

Two more days later, well after midnight on the eve of the *News-Journal*'s scheduled deliveries at the end of the week, Jacob and I stole into the print shop. Sweed and his assistants had already printed three hundred copies and stacked them on the bench, bundled and ready to go out first thing in the morning. The front page still sat composed in its galley and ready to be squeezed to life one more time. After reading it, I made revisions to a few lines of type that elevated the nastiness of Hutchinson's Tory blather. Like his administration, he succumbed to weak verbs and adverbs.

I fixed that.

"Did the governor really use that phrase '*FAKE NEWS*' to take a shot at Edes and Adams and the other newspapers?" Jacob asked. He was reading the galleys over my shoulder. "What in sweet Jesus' name does that even mean?"

"It doesn't mean anything. He just thinks it makes him look clever."

"Lord help us," Jacob chuckled.

I was particularly proud of adding an inspiring bit about how the *SONS OF LIBERTY* protests showed nothing more than the *IMPOTENCE* OF THEIR LEADERS. Challenge a man's manhood and you are assured to get a response. I could honestly say I wasn't positive it would incite a reaction, and I couldn't predict when it might, but any decent journalist with half a nostril for news knew the who, what, and where part of the story. The "how" was still to be determined.

Farther into the piece I found a nice space, offset in the body, for one more attack on their honor and challenged them to prove me wrong. That was the key, I thought. Then I spent the next few hours pulling on the devil's tail while Jacob Addison assisted me, pounding ink with glee onto the type before it slid into place under the press.

It felt as if my every pull of the lever was full of anger and squeezed another tear from my eye. We finished in plenty of time to replace the previously printed bundles with our revised edition that I expected would spark a major fit of hissyness.

Two hours later Jacob and I were lounging on a corner at Dock Square, not long after sunrise, when my little apprentice Ernie and his comrades passed by, distributing the newspaper across Boston and spreading the news at three pence a throw.

On Sunday, we stood on a corner of Treamount Street in the dark of night and watched the print shop burn.

Chapter Twenty-five
For Whom the Bells Toll

We stood there, stiff-backed and staring forward like soldiers lined up for inspection with buckets instead of muskets in our hands. Jacob, Baby Cakes Curry, and I watched as the volunteers from the civil brigade pumped water from two fire engines working on opposite sides of the building. Each fire engine had a team of six strong backs, three men to a side, pumping in unison the levers that fed the hose on top. The engine commander steered its spray on what was left of the walls while a line of men passed buckets of water from the nearest well to keep the fire engine's belly full.

"I have to hand it to you, Leeds, you know how to antagonize," Jacob stated without taking his eyes off the scene across the street. "Those Sons of Liberty are not happy."

"Pissed us off royally, you did," Baby Cakes Curry said.

"Yes, I suppose I did," I said.

We continued to watch in silence. A light mix of snow and drizzle had been falling since before the mob reached the print shop that night, and it had helped contain the blaze that broke out in the midst of their task of destroying the shop. I couldn't know from this distance which had been more destructive, the mob or the flames, because those same men who had vandalized the building were still on the scene and immediately joined the volunteers who had fought to get the fire under control. Now I stood in cold, wet slush across the street while the sweat I had worked up in my attempts to help soaked my nightshirt under my jacket and chilled me to the bone.

"Nothing much more we can do here, now," I said. "Jacob, it might be best if you move along. It will be daylight soon."

He refused to turn away, still staring at the chaos in front of us. "I'm going to miss her. She was a grand old gal."

"Well, she went out in style." Only then did we look each other in the eye. That corner of the street was well lit with lanterns from every house up and down Treamount and its arteries. Clusters of neighbors stood on either side of us with lanterns and torches, and I could clearly see my comment had tickled him. He nodded ever so slightly.

"Mitchell," I said to Baby Cakes Curry. "Maybe it would do well for you to ride along in the cart with Mr. Addison in case he crosses paths with any straggler hooligans."

"If it's hooligans that worry you, thems are the blokes what are pumping the fire engines o're there. Ain't gonna bother nobody none now. Too busy. And b'sides, their work's done."

I sighed. "Yes, it is. But I'd feel better if Jacob had your company. I thank you for your help this evening. Please, come see me tomorrow for a pound, if you'd like."

"Oh, no sir. I couldn't do that none. Uh-uh. I'll keep an eye out for Mr. Addison all right. Maybe I'll get to punch a soldier or two if they tries to stop us. That's more likely to be happening."

Jacob, who had climbed onto the driver's bench of his cart, barked, "And that's all the more likely to happen if we keep yapping the night away. Get up here, boy." The cart contained a few items we salvaged from the site. He promised to return in a day or two and hunt for anything we might have overlooked.

The fire was down to a few flames licking the roof that had collapsed into the building. I circled the property in quiet reflection, resigned and depressed but not ready to leave. I stopped to brush from my hat flakes from the light snow that had been falling earlier, only to find that it was ash. Fire takes on the smell of its victim. A forest fire smells different than a burning house, which is different than logs on the hearth, which is different than trash at the dumping ground. I was breathing the worst kind as I wandered out back where a slight breeze pushed it into my face and up my nostrils. This had been my life.

A young man approached me as I turned to Treamount Street. He sidled up next to me when I stopped to pat the backs of the volunteers. Some of them were Sons of Liberty vandals who were pleased with the statement their protest had made and proud of their quick work to limit the damage. I ignored the first and thanked them for saving what they could. The young man said his name was Arthur. His face was familiar and he reminded me that we had crossed paths before. He fancied himself a news man with several submissions printed in the *Boston Gazette* and wished to interview me about the fire.

"I was with friends at the tavern when we heard the first alarm of the fire bell," I began. I told him that hints of political retribution against the newspaper had surfaced and that the tolling of the bell stabbed at my heart and brought panic. "Although I had no immediate evidence, I heard the bell and knew it tolled for me."

"Do you believe this was a deliberate attempt to silence you? Are you confounded by the destruction? Do you know who is responsible? How much damage was done? What will you do now?

His questions came quick and we spoke casually and comfortably as I headed toward King Street. From there I would walk down to Flagg Alley where I knew the ladies would provide a bed for the night. An empty bed, mind you.

At first, I liked Arthur's understated enthusiasm for the story. Always happy to help out a budding journalist. But as we walked and talked, his questions became more partisan with an edge that I recognized were meant to build a story he had already written in his mind. News people do that. I had employed it myself occasionally but tonight I became more annoyed as we talked. More so by Arthur's tone as he apparently wanted to blame me for being on the wrong side of his politics. To Arthur, my Loyalist articles were reason to fault me for inciting a riot, which came back to bite me on my cheek. And not the one near my nose.

His questions turned: Are you surprised by this, given that your newspaper last week revealed the names of two men familiar to many, exposing them as leaders of the Sons of Liberty movement?"

That question was loaded, and I thought it was such a pip that I laughed. But it was his final question that elicited a response for which I will be forever equally ashamed and proud.

"So, I have to ask, Mr. Merriweather, how does it feel…?" he asked as we stopped at the corner of King Street. I placed my hand on his shoulder and faced him, for it had become certain earlier that it was only a matter of time before he asked that trope of a question.

How does it feel?

A swift kick to a man's testicles was painful to the point of making him unaware of anything else. It usually faded, though never quickly enough, and it hampered your every little movement for some time. He fell in a heap onto the cobblestone from one well-placed admonishment from my right knee. I helped Arthur back to his feet after he collapsed, and I coached him through the process to begin breathing again properly if not without some difficulty.

"It feels quite like that," I said before strolling off to Flagg Alley.

Chapter Twenty-six
God and a Little Help from His Friends

To tell you Murdoch was fit to be tied would be an understatement of major proportions, larger than his prodigious derrière.

"What do you mean I owe you for this, this disaster?" he asked.

Mr. Hartford, the Marine Insurance and Fire Contributionship for Protection of Homes director, was a short but solid man. One who did not scare easily because of his single-minded attention to rules and details of contracts. He was a man who believed he was never wrong. And I counted upon that.

"Mr. Murdoch, the irony here is quite amusing," Hartford said with as much mirth as a funeral director. "As chairman of the Fire Contributionship board and one of its principal investors, you will be responsible for sixty-four-point-three percent of the business's value, compensation for the loss of property. It's payable to Mr. Merriweather under the terms of our insurance contract with him."

"Not to worry, Clinton," I said with as straight a face as I could muster. "I will turn that over to you to clear my debt."

It had now been more than a week since the fire that destroyed the print shop. Murdoch paced, stomped, and threw a fit while Hartford and I watched him rage in, around, and through small piles of snow on what had once been the print floor. A storm blew through Boston with significant snowfall that prevented us from inspecting the site sooner. Baby Cakes Curry, his father, and younger brother worked at clearing the site of the Sons of Liberty wreckage. The Currys had shoveled and shoved much of the snow into those piles and now attacked with axes the roof that had collapsed into the building, trying to remove it to allow our inspection for what remained beneath.

"Will you cease that infernal racket?" Murdoch erupted.

I tisked at him, suggesting that was no way to treat his employees, considering the insurance claim for which he was the principal underwriter would be paying for their work. He looked at Mr. Hartford and demanded to know which director of the Contributionship had authorized the contract since at least one member of the managing partners was needed to approve it.

"It was Mr. Addison," Hartford said. "As one of the legacy members of the board through his father's holdings, I could see no reason to question his direction in this matter. And as the stakeholder who had paid premiums on this property for many years, it seemed quite natural."

"Then let him pay the claim."

Hartford coughed and looked at me. I feared a retreat but he held firm. A contract was a contract, after all. "Well, it seems Mr. Addison is no longer a member. He canceled his stake and sold his position in group last month."

"What idiot..." Murdoch paused. "To whom did he surrender his share?"

It was difficult not to laugh. Even the stoic Mr. Hartford labored to stifle one.

"Governor Hutchinson. Well, the governor's son purchased it for him."

And that was how Murdoch and the governor wound up paying me for the privilege of having my print shop destroyed. Of course, Mr. Hartford went on to explain that I had requested to amend the terms of the insurance payment so that the money would go directly to Murdoch to retire the debt I owed him. Murdoch was, in effect, paying himself for the death of my newspaper. No, *our* newspaper, as he had taken to assert since stealing it.

Sir Francis Bacon may have said revenge was a dish best served cold, but I say torching Murdoch in this manner like a pig on a spit was significantly more satisfying.

I knew what he was thinking so I said, "I had no advance knowledge of this travesty—I swear to it, Clinton." I loved the freedom of using his given name, as one would address an equal. "Honestly. But didn't I warn you? With so much Loyalist copy, only a fool would leave himself vulnerable." I waved at the piles of debris. "I thought it proper to protect our investment against exactly this sort of thing."

Mr. Hartford handed us each a page of paper. One was a bill to Murdoch for his portion of the payment that would come from the Fire Contributionship. The other was a bill of credit to me for the amount the business was covered above and beyond what I owed Murdoch. I would give that note to Jacob, and with the money he made selling his stake in the mutual insurance cooperative, he would be paid in full for the print shop business and I would be a man free of debt but of dubious future. Broke, actually.

Freedom. What a lovely word, but it was just another word when you had nothing left to lose. A good friend, Robert McGee, had written that long ago. Perhaps I had saved it for just such a moment as this. Regardless, it made me feel good and that was good enough for me.

Later that afternoon, almost as the sun was setting behind Wachusett Mountain, I thought Jacob might kiss me when I handed him the script for payment from Mr. Hartford. At first, he resisted.

"I can't accept it. I was the one who lost the print shop. You had no need to make things right with me, Leeds."

"Now we are square."

We were once again working up a sweat together. The weather had warmed considerably after the last snow and I removed my winter topcoat as we dragged a large potbellied stove into the outbuilding behind the Congregationalist Church. The shed was enclosed, with four paddocks of a stable on one side that horses and their owners had abandoned after Jacob preached an incredibly effective sermon one Sunday on the lessons of St. Francis of Assisi. It was about treating animals with more respect, and heathens with less. His congregants set about setting free their dogs and chickens, goats, rabbits, and horses. Some gave up hunting game. Jacob was that persuasive. The man had a gift as a preacher, but his love for hedonistic and, frankly, unrepentant satisfaction created a hypocritical conundrum that Jacob was the first to recognize. He still owned the land on which the church had been built. This would be my home until better circumstances presented themselves.

"Frankly, I would rather keep a bed at the whorehouse," he said. We were moving an overused bed mattress on loan from Flagg Alley. We put it on the floor next to the wall dividing the enclosure from the horse pens. We placed the stove in the corner to the left of my mattress and pushed my worktable to the opposite wall between the stove and the door at the entrance.

"You must be joking," I said. "Permanent residence at Flagg Alley? Do you know how hard it is to be forced to listen to the sounds that seep through the walls of those rooms at all hours of the night? A man can't get a decent night's sleep there."

"Not if he's alone, for certain." Jacob nudged me with his elbow. "Or with company, and there is plenty to be had there."

After a moment he asked, "Are you really going to be the best man at Baby Cake Curry's wedding?"

I smiled. "You don't refuse a man like him. He worked hard to convince lovely Rita to marry him. What's more, she has been saving for this, stepped up her production if you will, in order to provide a small but not insignificant dowry for the marriage."

"Grand. He's such a keen fellow for a marauder. The damage he and his fellows did to the print shop was a work of vandalistic art, if you ask me."

I told Jacob we'd best hurry if we were to get the rest from his wagon into the building. I nearly choked when he pulled back the canvas covering the neatly arranged wood there.

"Christ on a biscuit," I said.

"It's all here."

Jacob's cart held a dismantled printing press—every bit of it preserved and spirited away from the print shop the morning of the fire.

I looked at him, stunned. "Jacob, I had no idea. You rascal. You saved our press."

He shook his head. "No. This is that new Jenson Blaew model. Didn't Murdoch saddle you with its debt before the fire? It seemed that if I only had time to salvage one, I might take the best."

"Well this will make starting over easier. Good god, look at all this," I said. Jacob had filled the cart with barrels of ink, type cases, and other accessories needed to print. I had known I would work my way back to building my own publishing business again once I could free myself of Murdoch's leash. I thought it would take years but I hadn't planned on this.

As a news man it might be my nature to ask, but I avoided trying to find out how Jacob knew the attack would take place that particular night.

"You stole Murdoch's printing press?"

"Technically, I rescued it. Murdoch is being paid for it through the insurance. And a printing press is a terrible thing to waste. There are so few good ones to be had."

"How do we explain it missing? Mr. Hartford will certainly take note of that and tell Murdoch."

"It's amazing how similar your bed frame from upstairs, a brass bed warmer, a few china plates, a spring from a broken down funeral carriage—and that, I thought was poetic brilliance on my part—along with assorted junk lumber can be creatively piled to resemble a printing press when it is left in a heap on the floor."

"Why didn't you warn me?" I asked. "I would have helped."

"When I heard of the plot I negotiated with a person of influence amongst the Sons, forestalling the worst of the ugliness with a small bribe." He shrugged. "Besides, I was busy. First I had to dismantle and cart away the Jenson press. Then I had to construct a decent facsimile that wouldn't be recognizable once I set fire to it."

"Are you saying you were the one who started the fire?"

Jacob nodded. "Those Sons of Liberty didn't mind it—they cheered, even. Until that point they were content to leave it at crippling the newspaper. No, the blaze was my doing because fire was part of the insurance contract."

I was speechless, and for a man who makes his living with words, that was quite an accomplishment.

Jacob reached past me and plucked a leg of the press frame from his cart as one might take a rutabaga from the grocer's stall. He held it up in the fading light and brushed at some imaginary soil on its skin. He admired it, round and nubby and solid.

"My grandfather and my father created the *New England News-Journal.* Maybe I didn't have their passion for the print and the work it required, but I'll be a badger's mother-flogging mistress before I let Murdoch have her. He stole her once from me and that was my fault. He was going to steal her from you, and that is his crime."

Jacob threw his shoulders back, and pointed at the sky while holding the leg of the printing press like some ancient warrior's spear. You could almost imagine him at his preacher in the pulpit best when he thundered, "Vengeance is mine, sayeth the Lord—Romans 12:19. And whiskey for all who do the Lord's work." He took a few more pieces from the wagon and headed inside with a laugh. "But I think He was preoccupied today so I was really just doing the Lord's work for him. No sin in that, right?"

I laughed and pulled a bucket of type over the rail of Jacob's cart. "I will assist you in the Lord's work, oh Prophet Jacob. What's more, I am His thirsty servant. I only hope we don't have to wait until we get to heaven for that drink."

Chapter Twenty-seven
Hot Is Better Than Not

Once upon a time, so the words of a fairy tale begin. Back when I earned my keep as a patterer reciting the news on street corners across London, I was part of the world of street merchants who sold everything from fruits and pastries to lace and weapons. I sold information without the advantage of having a printing press.

Once upon a time.

The weather in Boston that March of 1774 reminded me of the sleight-of-hand grifters who would set up their own table near me in London when I drew a crowd. They played a shell game and took money from gullible passers-by. In Boston that month, each day kept us guessing and wrongly predicting sunshine or snow. Pleasant days turned freezing overnight and then back to tease us with sunshine again. Eventually it all gave way to the bitter cold that could tempt even the most righteous to commit some heinous crime hoping God in his mercy would send them straight to hell. At least it was warm there.

Sally Hughes came to me in Jacob's church stable where I had taken up residence on one such frozen night and led me back to her Aunt Mae Flowers' home. It was late and the madam had retired. Safely warm in a place altogether more appealing than hell, we talked quietly in front of a fire in the parlor while she rested her head in my lap. Eventually we found our way to her bedroom upstairs.

What now?

Yes, that indeed was the question.

"I will resume printing once enough time has elapsed," I said with confidence. "I hope no later than fall." We were lying close, both on our backs but with our arms linked and our bodies touching as if we were one beneath the heavy blankets and nothing more than noses exposed to the night air. Candles on either side cast soft dancing patterns of light on the bed's canopy draped above us. I watched the reflected light with a sleepy, contented gaze.

"You absolutely must return to publish again. It makes you who you are, and that is someone special, Mr. Printer," she said.

"I might stick to publishing books, pamphlets, and the like. They pay better than newspapers, and are much less likely to incite riot. I have little appetite for riot right now."

"We need riot," she said, staring up at the canopy above. Then Sally rolled on her side and placed a hand on my chest. "But more than ever we need your voice. The colony, the Americas need you. You have a gift, Leeds. Don't let Murdoch destroy it."

"You, my lovely little radical, have Adams and Thomas to do just that. And they will be remembered long after we are all dust. Every scrap of the *New England News-Journal* that I had saved for posterity went up in flames. But…"

"But what?"

I pinched her cheek. "But we had a frog-flogging grand time while it lasted."

She raked my chest with her nails in response. Then she laughed, tilted her head, and though I could not taste her lips, I heard the sound of a kiss directed at me. "Then you *are* going to publish a newspaper again and I will help." Simply stated, had there really been any doubt? She rolled over on her back and snuggled the blanket under her chin as if our future was sealed and she was comfortable with it.

Sally Hughes snores. Not that I object, mind you. As I drifted between light sleep and minimal wakefulness through the remainder of the night, the lady beside me sank deeply into slumber and sounded as if she were sawing lumber. But floating between dreams and reality, I overstayed my welcome and only realized it at the first sound of stirring in the house. I dressed quickly. Sally had woken when I left her bed and sat there rubbing her eyes while I gathered myself. One last kiss and I would be gone.

"The back stairs to the kitchen are that way." She pointed over her shoulder in the direction that I assumed led to the rear of the house. "They are dark at this hour, but a better way to leave before Auntie Mae is awake. Let me guide you." She had not yet tied the sash to her robe when we were startled by a knock at the door. It opened slightly, only enough that I could see a candle in somebody's hand through the sliver between the door and its frame.

"Sally, my dear. I have so much to do today I am up early." It was Madam Flowers. Her tone was lilting like a lullaby song, but her voice was aged and as coarse as a raven's caw. She cleared her throat. "Please don't be rude. Invite your gentleman caller to stay for breakfast. No one should send her paramour away on an empty stomach."

"Yes, Auntie."

"Well, this is awkward," I said.

A short time later, Aunt Mae and I sat at a table in a smallish drawing room adjoining the kitchen. Hazel the housekeeper had set it with dining ware, a large pot of tea, biscuits, and fruit before disappearing behind a swinging door. A fire crackled in a utility stove by the outer wall that had a window high above it. I looked at the window and it was dark outside; daylight was still more than an hour away. The nook was more of a walnut-paneled cubby hole, most likely reserved for the servants in a more extravagant time.

"I'm glad you intend to recover from this horrible mischief of the other night," Madam Flowers said. "You see, I have the need of your services."

Small talk? She gave no hint of her thoughts about having found me in bed with her niece. Was that a topic to be discretely ignored for the moment or ammunition for a broadside later? I couldn't tell. Madam Flowers appeared comfortable to share her table with me. Sally was due to join us as soon as she dressed and coiffed for the day.

"I must say, Clinton Murdoch is quite ill-tempered right now. Not that I should find fault with his anger. But I had warned him that your newspaper was playing with fire. Yes, the pun was intended." A smile creased her face. "And now fire has gotten the best of him. Oh, yes, he is not a happy customer."

The grande dame had a sense of humor, and I admired the way she kept it close to her heart until she was damned good and ready to release it. We sat and measured each other, performing our own kind of shell game, substituting our thoughts for the tiny ball under the shell.

She said, "Tell me, Mr. Merriweather, what do you think of all these political shenanigans going on now? Your most recent burn notwithstanding."

"The print shop meant everything to me. So I am no friend of anyone who would destroy it. I have every reason to detest them."

"But you surely understand their motivation. Am I wrong in thinking you were prepared for it?"

"I was. I confess. As you said, we were playing with fire." I stared the old lady down. "They assaulted my business, but pardon me for saying this, Madam Flowers, we can't ignore the fact that your companion Mr. Murdoch destroyed it in a different way by assaulting the truth, and I am ashamed at having a hand in that. In a way, all three of us—the vandals, Mr. Murdoch, and myself—we are all guilty to some degree."

"And your political views? Where do you stand?"

At this I went into retreat. A minor one, but a step back just the same. "I don't know what to think anymore."

"You are a liar, young man." She waggled a bony finger at me when I tried to protest. "Oh yes. You may think you are caught in the middle, but you took sides when you decided to ignore the obvious warnings that some kind of violence was going to take place. You were complicit.

"And, let me be clear, young man, you took sides when you decided to aid my niece by printing the information she provided to you. Oh, yes. Mr. Forger, I know about that, too. It was as obvious a canard as believing you came here last night with not a thought of spending the night in my niece's bed." Her face drew inward as she pursed her lips, and the creases in her cheeks became more pronounced with the stern look she gave me.

"Would you believe me if I said I escorted her upstairs only to prevent her from catching cold?" I asked. "We stayed close to one another under the blankets of her bed, and I embraced her in order to ward off frostbite?" Humor is the weakest defense when you are caught with your pants down, but there was no sense in fighting back; it was all I had.

"Well, don't expect a snuggle from me to prevent *your* catching cold," she sniffed. She drew a napkin to her lips as she said it. For the love of God, the lady was suppressing a grin and used the cloth to hide it. I pretended not to notice as I offered to pour her another cup, though in a relaxed manner that passed for understanding betwixt us.

"Ah, there she is," Madam Flowers said in her frog voice. Sally swished into the kitchen nook. "Our little rebel. Hazel has warmed tea for us, dear, and will have breakfast soon. Sit down. I was just about to offer Mr. Merriweather a proposition."

A proposition? The words barely registered as I watched Sally take a seat at the table. She was only modestly reticent, hardly obedient, and if I hoped to gain some direction on how to handle this affair with her auntie, dash the thought.

"Yes, a proposition," the older woman said. "One that will be beneficial to everyone. Well, everyone except Mr. Murdoch, I believe. Though Clinton is a valuable companion and quite useful in his own way." I thought that an odd comment, the kind that could be ripe with meaning or mean nothing at all.

"I don't advocate that mob violence of the other night, but Clinton is in need of a good tweaking now and again. What I have to offer might nick him more so."

She went on to explain that as Loyalists who kept their heads down but refused to renounce their ties to the crown grew more concerned for their safety, the number of merchants moving to the protection of British forces at Castle William left Madam Flowers' family holdings in a bind. "There are a number of properties we have acquired over the years that sit empty these days. Taxes don't stop when a tenant moves on," she said.

At the urging of a letter by Mr. Murdoch in the *News-Journal*, Governor Hutchinson implemented an additional vacancy tax on properties within the city's mercantile district. All business owners could apply for a hardship exemption, yet only Tory merchants received a break.

"I'd like you to consider calling upon my properties man-ager, Mr. Reemax. He will find suitable space for a printing business. That tiny, rundown shed Sally tells me you are occu-pying is no home for a respectable business. As I told you, I have need for a printer and it can be arranged when you feel you are up to the task."

I wanted to kiss the old gal. Despite her earlier jest about not snuggling me to save me from the cold, I felt a warm bliss that rivaled a night of getting cozy under the blankets with Sally.

Well, almost. Nothing could ever be that satisfying. We might have to try it again someday.

Chapter Twenty-eight
Not My Type

"Don't you just want to kiss her?"

Sally said it quickly before blushing. Her aunt wasted no time when Sally had joined us to reveal the offer she had made to me minutes earlier. "I think that is a wonderful idea. And I know just the place, Auntie."

"I think we should leave that up to Mr. Merriweather," Mrs. Flowers said.

"As of this morning, my primary concern is that I cannot afford to pay for any space until I establish a bit of working capital. After what I have been through, I want no part of a large debt. So, if you are willing to hold that offer until I am no longer the penniless rogue printer, I would happily be your tenant."

"Nonsense," Madam Flowers replied. "I said I have a project for you. I am willing to barter my space for your talents."

I pressed Madam Flowers to tell me about her project. Her answer was vague and less than satisfying. A pamphlet? A book? A series of essays? All of the above? Or, God help us, a newspaper? She only said it would require a good deal of effort on my part but it was something near to her heart.

In due course I could no longer justify my continued presence and I bid my farewell. Sally offered to accompany me out the kitchen door, but Madam Mae would not let that happen. It was her house; the rear of the house was for servants and deliveries. Social callers deserved the privilege of using the front door of the home. "It is proper manners," she said. And she practically commanded Sally to remain and finish her porridge and tea while she, Madam Flowers, escorted me out. We paused in the entry all as I struggled to wrap the wool scarf around my neck and tucked its tails into my winter coat.

I said, "You, Madam Flowers, are a woman of the world. Let us be straight with one another. What is it you wish to accomplish by helping me regain my business? Am I being bribed in some fashion?"

The lady cackled like a witch, except that her face was soft without a trace of menace. Mae Flowers had been leaning on the walking stick she used for support. Small and stooped though she may be, she lifted it and poked me in the chest with its handle quite solidly for an old woman. Enough to make me step back and suck in a quick breath. Maybe she was a witch after all.

"Once you are in a good place with the print shop I would like you to consider employing that lovely young woman in there of whom you seem so fond."

"So that is the project you wish me to take on?" I asked. "You want me to employ Sally? In the print shop?"

"She is a woman of letters and equally proficient with numbers. You could do much worse and you would be doing me a great favor." Madam Flowers explained that Sally was too headstrong to let her aunt support her until such time as a husband was found. "But I want her to leave that home for wayward girls they call Flagg Alley."

Wayward girls? She made it sound as if she did not fully comprehend what went on behind the Flagg Alley doors, but I was certain the old woman knew about Sally's career choice.

She said, "Don't get me wrong. She is providing commendable benefit for those young ladies. Hazel, my housekeeper, for instance. I would never have thought to employ her without Sally's urging. Now Hazel is married with two children and comes here three days a week to help out. And there have been several others who have married and married well, or have found employment."

"You make Flagg Alley sound like an orphanage for grown women," I said in jest.

"Why, yes. That is a good way to put it."

Of course I kept a straight face. It wasn't easy.

"And Mr. Merriweather. It is quite apparent that Sally is smitten with you. I do hope you keep any future rendezvous more discreet. But more importantly, I am fond of her. If you so much as cause a tear in her eye, or a disgrace to her reputation, I will ensure that you suffer in ways that will make the destruction of your beloved newspaper feel like nothing more than a flea bite by comparison."

And then to my great surprise, she stepped through the door, reached up, and kissed me on the cheek. She shivered and retreated to the warmth of the house, closing the door.

Later that afternoon, as the weather blessed us with blue skies and moderate temperatures, Jacob and I rummaged through the wrecked shop that Baby Cakes Curry and his mates had cleared.

"I don't see much worth keeping here," Jacob said. He stood over a pile of books that were water sogged and blackened but too thick to have been incinerated.

I squatted under a wooden slab of roof, where it was held up by a scorched work bench that had some legs to it. "We only have the type from one of the presses. Where is the rest?"

He wasn't listening.

"I said it's too bad you couldn't have saved the type blocks from the second press."

"I heard you," Jacob snapped. He said it with enough force that I jerked my head backwards as if he had thrown a punch.

"All right. What happened to it?"

"Uh, well, I… I told you I had to bribe the gang to buy enough time to rescue the press before they took action. I offered money but they would have none of that."

"You don't mean to say they took the type case?"

"In a bucket. That was the deal. No lead type, no forestalling them. They made that very clear to me. And, actually, they could have gone in and stolen it all if they had chosen to do so."

That was confounding. "What in the world would they want with a bucket full of letter blocks? Most of those fellows can't read, let alone compose a print." I was lost, looking around the bench where the lead type would have been and then over to Jacob. Slowly I came to the only sane conclusion.

"So the boys are going to melt the lead for musket balls to arm their militia," I said. He didn't respond but looked truly contrite.

"Like it or not, welcome to the fight," he said.

I thrust my hands deep into the pockets of my coat and turned my back on him. I made my way out to the street where I paused, not really knowing which direction to take. America was my home now and had my heart. My sympathies lay with her and I would easily choose America over the place of my birth if my contribution only meant using my press in support of the cause.

But flog the friggin' frog. When shots were fired, maybe not that month or next, but eventually, someone would die. He would be a British soldier felled by a bullet that had once been an innocent vowel or an elaborate curly uppercase consonant melted down for ammunition. An ampersand. How dangerous could an ampersand be? Fatal, I suppose. Yes, eventually someone will die from a musket ball that once had been a chunk of type from my printing press at Merriweather and Associates.

Chapter Twenty-nine
Starting All Over Again

The *Boston Free Dispatch* made its debut in May of 1774 on the day that the commander-in-chief of British forces in America, Major General Thomas Gage, returned from England to resume his duties as North American military commander. It was a Friday the 13th, as if that were a warning of things to come.

I felt the determination and pride one gets when climbing back into the saddle after being tossed by an ill-tempered horse. We had set up shop on a good corner location, long vacant, owned by a company affiliated with a larger collection of businesses run by an anonymous board of directors. It was a tangled web of corporate connections, and only we knew Madam Flowers was the spider at its center. The shop sat at the edge of a row of businesses along Ann Street near the marketplace where there was no shortage of taverns and no shortage of foot traffic to and from them. That created a stream of passers-by who might be lured into catching up on the latest news by purchasing the *BFD*.

Our initial edition drew much more attention than the arrival of General Gage. No, his landfall at Castle William away from the main port had lacked any official hullabaloo, but the latest offering from the Forger caught everyone's eye and waxed sales of the newspaper. I felt safe enough to print it given that the Forger had been contributing to the liberal newspapers ever since what I, he, we, now called the "Boston Tea Spree." Catchy title, I thought. I was certain that would catch on as a defining description of that night's affair, possibly go down in history as the de facto name for the protest in the way Samuel Adams had turned the Boston Massacre into something iconic.

The Forger provided information no one else had. In addition to resuming his role as the military commander of the American colonies, General Gage would assume the additional duties of governor of the Province of Massachusetts. Hutchinson was suddenly old news and was being replaced. He had been criticized in England as feckless and too weak in his response to the tea protest. Gage came in and immediately declared himself the "law and order" governor with a mandate to use whatever means necessary to keep protests in line. By now I had seen enough of the feisty Americans to know that was tantamount to putting wings on a warthog and expecting it to fly. Ain't gonna happen.

But what really shat on any warm and fuzzy feelings that surfaced from Hutchinson getting the old heave-ho was that the general brought an additional company of foot soldiers to enforce the rule of law in Massachusetts. It was a clear show of force that was meant to make a statement. That statement being "Hutchinson-the-wimp is history; I am in charge so don't even *think* of resisting."

"No one liked Governor Hutchinson anyway," Sally said to me as I was setting the type for that edition. "Not even you Brits."

"Well, he is an American like you. We're not supposed to like him," I replied. "But then, he's not as pretty as you. And not as smart. And not so, well, everything." I paused with my hand over the type case, obsessed with getting the words just right. Sally was not helping precisely because she was trying to be helpful. She was leaning over my shoulder and the fragrance of her perfume and the nearness of her body made being obsessed with words nearly impossible. She had every right to watch the story's creation. I was working from her scribbles and she was the one who wrote the story for our newspaper.

"We can thank Gloria for this," Sally had said at the time.

"The girl with the chipmunk cheeks?"

"Don't be like that. She is a sweetie and popular for her full figure. I should be so lucky."

"Mistress Hughes, you are perfectly popular with me. I have no quarrel with your diminutive figure. You may be diminutive but you are petite."

"Those are one in the same," she laughed. And she promised that when my hands were less occupied she might favor me with a kiss.

Two weeks earlier it seemed that the governor was in an awful state. He sent someone to fetch Gloria from Flagg Alley and escort her to the Boston Social Club in Beacon Hill, a discreet private house where manly camaraderie and games of chance could be found, business deals could be conducted, politics discussed, and plots hatched. When requested, young women could visit for singular companionship, and thus notable gentlemen could avoid being discovered on the scene of Flagg Alley or the other two bordellos of Boston. Gloria had become a familiar, if not frequent, visitor to the governor at the club whenever he was feeling blue.

"The governor was in the snittiest of snits and the evening did not go well," Sally said.

"He didn't abuse her in any way, I hope."

"No, he had some functional issues."

"Ah, unable to perform." I smirked.

According to Gloria, the governor sat on the edge of the bed after several failed attempts at horizontal intimacy, and silently pondered for what seemed like an eternity the sad state of affairs in which he found himself. He pondered so long that Gloria simply wrapped her arms around the governor to comfort him, and then she lay back and napped on the bed. The night was paid for; he might rise to it yet. Instead, the governor woke her later and instructed her to leave, but not before Hutchinson handed her a gift. It was a broach of significant worth. A parting gift, he said, for staying with him as well as all the previous evenings they shared.

"It was then that the governor confessed he had learned that very day he was out of favor with the king and his replacement had set sail. General Gage had orders to take over and was already en route to Boston."

"I could see how that would crush a man of his ilk," I said. "A lifelong loyal administrator who learned a very hard lesson about how expendable civil servants are to this king. It would crush his soul. It would crush his, well, everything." Catchy. I had no inkpot near so I took one of those new pencils, licked the graphite tip, and added the expendable line to Sally's notes to be set in type.

"Ewe. I hope you don't expect me to kiss you after that, Mr. Printer," Sally fussed.

And that was how the *Boston Free Dispatch* had an exclusive account of the coming transition of administration. One that the Forger warned would come with a vindictive, heavy hand.

The second edition of the *Free Dispatch* was full of letters to the editor with opinions over the change of administration and what it would mean to the citizens but lacking the eyeball grabbing impact of our first print run.

Third edition? Boring, despite my best attempts to elevate it.

But then, our edition the first week of June... Now that was a righteous jollystomp, one that bagged Clinton Murdoch. Not that I would take satisfaction in that any more than I would wish a bad case of scurvy upon him. Which I would.

According to the Forger, Murdoch had recently acquired two inns, one in Salem and the other on the highway to

Cambridge, that were previously owned by Governor Hutchinson's sons. He purchased them at a price so low that even I could have afforded the investment. It was a parting gift from the governor, and no real loss for them because as it turns out, the Hutchinson sons had acquired those properties when the governor used eminent domain to confiscate the hotels in the name of the colonial authority. The original owners cried fraud but had no success getting the governor's hand-picked prosecutor to prosecute. And the timing was so suspect, coming a week after Hutchinson's exit from power, that there was little doubt Murdoch was part of the original confiscation.

I met Murdoch's former secretary Francis Akeley at the Green Dragon Tavern that evening. I offered him a job as my assistant printer. Madam Flowers insisted the amount of work we would soon have required it, and she advanced me money for one salary, supplies of ink and paper, and everything else needed to publish our first edition in May.

Francis and I made a deal and then did our best to endure a bottle of low-quality Vermont wine to celebrate that day's scandalous report. "I'll wager Murdoch is twisting in a fit of his elephantine blubber tonight," I said.

"Let him." Francis laughed.

I sniffed the wine in my glass. "Good god, I hope General Gage realizes the damage that has been done by closing the port. Not a single shipment of French wine or a decent Spanish Madeira since." That didn't stop me from pouring another glass.

By and by, a half dozen redcoats from the 34th Cavalry taking up several tables in the corner were joined by comrades from a different company. That stopped me. One of the new arrivals was Lieutenant Cole, the former governor's military intelligence officer. We exchanged glances throughout the time it took to finish the bottle. Then he and a soldier of lower rank but significantly higher bulk approached us.

"The lieutenant wants you to know that he's not pleased with you. Not at all, sir," the hulk in the red coat said.

"*Moi?*" What a shock.

Not really surprising since the second part of the Forger's report I had written revealed that Governor Hutchinson had been using a military liaison account to pay his personal security detail, soldiers who were already receiving wages for that assignment from the army. I did not mention Cole by name in the piece, but any reader with more than a brick's worth of intelligence would recognize him. More importantly, it was clear he and the others were double dipping into government funds. The Forger gleefully suggested that would be one more vice that would become passé with the corrupt governor's departure. The military had its own system of graft; stealing from itself was not on the approved list.

"That was some scandalous lie you published this morning," Cole said. "And I don't appreciate the Forger's attempt to tar me with such trash. I'd love to say that to this fellow in person. Perhaps you could finally arrange an introduction since he's found a new home in your newspaper. Quite a coincidence."

Lieutenant Cole cocked his head as if he noticed Francis for the first time. "Oh, you're that fellow arrested for that dirty business down at the docks. Didn't know they'd let scum like you out of jail."

Francis was not a large fellow. And the mild temperament one gains growing up with education and spending much of your adult life among books could, at moments like that, handicap a fellow. I knew well enough because I also grew up in a house where I was educated extensively, though my parents meant no harm. Still, the lingering effects left me with a minor scar on my ego that caused me to overthink sleights when immediate action was important. As for Francis, spending time in the Boston jail appeared to have hardened the edges of the man.

He rose and stood and shook his fist at the soldiers. "You bull's pizzle."

That response confounded Cole and the ensign so that all they could do was stare back at Francis. Give him credit, *Henry IV* was always good for a classic insult borrowed from Shakespeare and one that I wish I called up more often. I tried not to laugh as they all stood toe to toe to toe, and given their furrowed brows, I doubted either soldier had ever heard of the Bard. Superior intellect and determination might not have won this battle of wills, but it was enjoyable to watch.

The tavern itself did not stop to notice this confrontation, but several civilians on either side of us did. And they leaned closer as if they had a personal stake in its outcome.

"Bull's pizzle?" I heard someone murmur.

The ensign blinked first, tired of the game, and turned away with a dismissive wave of his hand. Unfortunately, his fingers raked the brim of Francis' hat and knocked it to the floor.

Francis then made an error in judgment by placing a hand on the fellow's elbow as he turned, which is a serious breach of order when addressing a soldier. In Boston, at least. A bloke from the next table retrieved Francis' hat and took up his own position facing the ensign and Lieutenant Cole. He thrust the hat into Francis' chest, pushing him aside and shifting to confront the soldiers himself. This would not end well if someone didn't appeal to cooler heads, I thought. I rose quickly and knocked over my wine glass in the process. What happened as I turned to catch it from rolling off the table I will never, know but in that moment shoves were exchanged and curses uttered. Bodies joined the fray, and the soldiers from the 34th, taking notice of the fledgling riot, dashed over to provide backup to their comrades in uniform.

Of all the brawls in all the taverns in all the world, this rose up as one that deserved a place in history. Certainly in the top five. It took only moments before the sum of tavern patrons were exchanging punches either with the soldiers or with each other. Blows landed while bodies crashed about overturning chairs and tables. I never saw the punch that sent me back into a seat at the table. My jaw aches just thinking of it. I jumped back into the fray and shoved the nearest redcoat from behind into a pair of waiting American fists.

Suddenly a single pistol shot called an end to it all.

I rocked back on weak knees and struggled to keep some kind of balance. Pain. Mother flogging severe pain. Some good neighbor caught me as I wobbled but refused to go down. The crowd parted like the Red Sea before Moses, and across from me Lieutenant Cole held a smoking pistol.

Chapter Thirty
Not Quite Dead Yet

I didn't recall much after that. In fact, I didn't recall much of anything that took place for well over a month until I woke in a bedroom that was strange to me with more clarity than usual. I did have vague memory of unfamiliar faces, coming and going often, faces full of concern floating before my eyes and so near that we may have been sharing the same breath. They faded away as gently as they had come, almost with a rhythm like waves. I also saw some familiar faces—Sally was one, Jacob another—drifting through at a distance, distorted as if I could see them in the panes of a cracked mirror, along with whispers and mumbles that for some unknown reason filled my very soul with dread. Hush.

Mostly I had the recurring vision of Lieutenant Cole standing barely to one side and behind the protection of his ensign. The vision was veiled. Over and over I saw Cole raising his pistol and pointing it in my direction in a motion that was slow and dreamlike through the narrow alley between soldiers jostling with tavern patrons.

Now the mist was clearing, and I judged from the slim bit of light between curtains that the sun was high but the room was otherwise dark and now empty of those ghosts. It smelled of medicine and alcohol cleanser. I tenderly explored the moist cloth wrapped around my left shoulder, under my arm and across my neck and chest. Pain be damned, I finally managed to raise myself to a sitting position. The room looked familiar in style but foreign to my memory.

A woman slept in a chair in the dark corner near a dresser with a book splayed on her lap and her chin on her chest. She wore a white cap and white apron. I cleared my throat. It was dry and rough as hickory bark.

"Excuse me," I croaked.

The woman's head jerked and then she bolted to her feet. "Well, well, well. Mr. Merriweather. How are we?"

"I don't know. More importantly, *who* are we?"

She laughed. "Oh, they did tell me you're a clever crumpet. That is an excellent sign. I'm Nurse Ratched." She came to the bed and laid a hand on my forehead, considered my temperature, and then took a wet hand towel from a basin nearby. She dabbed my cheeks and eyes and wiped along my jaw from ear to ear. "Mistress Hughes will be so happy to see you are with us again. It was nip and tuck there for a while. 'Course, being ever optimistic, I was rooting for nip and it looks like I was right."

She replaced the towel and washed her hands in the air. "There," she said. "Let me fetch the mistress. Don't go away." She chuckled her way from the room.

Sally entered a few minutes later along with a maid who carried rice cakes, soup, and water on a tray.

"Good day, Mr. Printer." Her eyes opened wide. "Ah." She exhaled the word like a long sigh of joy and relief. The maid placed the tray on a table near the bed, while Sally kissed me on the forehead and then the lips, and then she said, "Doctor Warren tells me he has treated worse cases, though not many. You had us all frightened since they brought you here. Even the doctor was growing concerned because you lost so much blood. Then the infection set in and we feared the worst."

"Was anyone else hurt?" I asked.

Sally inspected my wounded shoulder, took the bowl of soup from the tray, and sat close to my right hip. "Nothing severe. Nothing more than you'd expect from an average public house brawl. Cuts and a broken bone or two. Left a few knife scars, naturally."

I tilted my head forward when she spooned a thick broth of onions, egg, and beef stock through my lips and then I leaned back again to swallow. Repeat.

"And what of Lieutenant Cole?"

She gnashed a corner of her lower lip. "No word."

I stopped her hand on its next spooning. "Sally, there is no secret in this town to which you are not privy. He didn't just disappear."

"Actually he may have, in a sense."

She set the bowl on the tray and leaned to pick up a copy of the *Boston Free Dispatch*. She placed it in my lap. "Francis' account of the incident is there for you."

"You published? Without me?"

"Well, you were a bit under the weather and quite useless to us." She smiled and tried to place a rice cake in my mouth, but I took it from her with my good hand in order to feed myself.

"You were delirious for most of the time," she said. "Kept making the cutest little chipmunk noises."

"Chipmunk, huh?"

"Oh, don't take that the wrong way. You were weak and near death. In fact, it's that same squeak you do when we make love." Sally licked a dribble of soup from the tip of her finger and stroked my lips.

"Jacob helped quite a bit in your absence," she said. "Francis was arrested with several others that night at the tavern, but they were all released after enough citizens protested that no action was taken against the soldiers. Francis returned in time to give us his testimony. Wrote it himself and the *BFD* survived without you."

It was gratifying to know that I had created something that could continue without my oversight, though that knowledge was also a cuff to my ego. I was not as crucial to the *Dispatch* as I would like to think. With or without me, ink happens.

"And back to Lieutenant Cole. Disappeared, you say?"

"He's on his way back to England."

Sally said Military Governor Gage had rounded up all the soldiers involved in the brawl, put them on a ship, and sent them back to England, where they would stand trial. "I can assume Lieutenant Cole must be among them. General Gage posted a public notice that he had ordered it under the new law giving him authority to remove trials from the colony. He claims that the soldiers wouldn't get a fair trial here."

"It's an excuse," I said. Disappointed and angry, I shook my rice cake at Sally. She ducked as it flew past her. In my weakened condition I didn't realize how feeble my grip was. "Sorry about that." I asked her for a second biscuit. "What a farce. There will be no justice, and no trial in England."

Cole would get away with trying to kill me. Damn him.

I nudged my body deeper into the blanket. The pain was not as bad as I feared. Fatigue crept over me now and I was too sleepy to talk politics and the injustice of it all, and so I feigned an overly long yawn as I settled in. "I hope casting my lot with you radicals isn't going to be the ruin of me."

Sally inspected the bandages and kissed my forehead one last time. She nodded. "Judging from the wound here, I believe we've done as much damage to you as we can. If you survived this, we both will survive whatever is to come."

She left me to nap, but my mind refused to cooperate. Mulling over the whole affair with nothing to do but stew, I could see how everything had led me to this moment of introspection. I had escaped an unfair government in England, only to make my way to America, where I had to endure it again at the hands of the same monarchy a million miles away. Murdoch, an ardent Loyalist, stole my newspaper and left me bankrupt if it were not for the American friends I had found. The king and his military governor now wanted to thump the back of our britches with martial law that would affect everyone I know. My personal ledger was heavy with reasons to stand with Sally, Madam Flowers, even Jacob, and take the Whig position. The whispers of rebellion sounded more reasonable every day. And getting shot didn't hurt.

Well, except physically, of course. That hurt a lot.

Yes, Madam Flowers had predicted this. When push came to shove, I Whigged out.

Summer set upon Boston, and British warships had taken up positions to enforce the Port Act by the time I ventured out of Madam Flowers' home without any assistance for the first time a month later. The threat of infection had passed. My legs, though still weak, were strong enough but I had not recovered full use of my left arm. Jacob chided me that it was the same shoulder and not too dissimilar from the injury I had feigned after winning over Baby Cakes Curry in order to save the *News-Journal* the first go 'round.

"I don't believe I should believe you were hurt," he said.

Jacob had assisted me on two short trips to visit the *Boston Free Dispatch* office after I was strong enough to leave my bed. But the freedom of making the trip on my own was something that felt like a rebirth. More joyful than even pulling the first edition of our newspaper from the press.

"Grand to be seein' ya, Mr. Printer, sir," Baby Cakes Curry greeted me before I reached the door to the print shop.

"Grand to be seen, Mitchell." I smiled and took his hand. "'Mr. Printer?' It appears you have been talking with Mistress Hughes again."

He nodded. "She runs a tight ship. Runs us right, she does."

"How is business at the coffee house, Mitchell?"

"Right swell."

I gazed up at a sign over the store next door to the print shop. During my convalescence, Madam Flowers opened a coffee house and hired Mitchell and his wife, Rita, to run it.

To my mind, however, Baby Cakes Curry had a more important job. Before opening the print shop, I hired him and his father to provide security for us. Mitchell's father was a trapper and guide in the Quebec territories during the winter, and carried even more bulk than his son. With his wild beard and perpetual crazed look in his eyes he was an imposing figure. Mr. Curry was best known for hunting with nothing more than a rope and an Indian arrow. He didn't need a bow. He preferred killing his prey with his bare hands. "Ya gotta give them critters a fightin' chance," he liked to say.

"Quite noble of you."

He bragged that at age sixty-something he could still take down a bull moose three times his weight in hand-to-hoof combat, and I vowed never to get on his bad side.

I was secure that the money I paid them for protection was worth it, and it proved so during my convalescence. These two were Sons of Liberty down to the marrow in their bones. It was the military that concerned me. After our incident at the Green Dragon, General Gage instructed his troops to take no guff. Too many soldiers took that to mean they were at liberty to pick fights, detain citizens on the flimsiest of excuses until those men paid a fine to the soldiers, and randomly inspect merchant shops for contraband, usually causing damage to those businesses they felt were not sufficiently loyal to the new military governor.

"Had a squad of Lobsterbacks come by a few times, Mr. Printer, sir," Mitchell said. "Giving us the stink eye and threatening all sorts of twaddle."

Daddy Curry spat. "Damned good thing they stayed on their side of the street. Oth'r wise I'd of skinned them like a skunk."

And women dare not venture out in public unless in the company of an escort. Rumors spread of assaults. Some were exaggerated but they were not entirely without merit. Sally had been confronted on the street at dusk two blocks to the north by three soldiers. She brushed away their hands as she passed but they followed her down Union to Ann Street. When she increased her pace to get away, they chased her with whistles and catcalls down the empty alley around the corner and right through the door of the print shop. When Old Man Curry appeared out of nowhere with arrow in hand and his deranged appearance, the soldiers quickly, and quite meekly according to Mr. Curry, staged a quiet retreat.

By the end of August, I still had not yet regained the dexterity in the fingers of my left hand enough to set type with enough speed to be of good use. I was beginning to worry the damage was permanent. Sally proved to be a quick study, and by then she could set an entire page as quickly as Jacob on one of his sober days. I was quite pleased with the sales and growing subscription rate of the *BFD*. There was much to report, and I thought we might realize a profit soon.

"So much news," Francis said one morning. "It's difficult to keep up." He sat at the composing table, transferring type to the galley for a new page of the paper. Francis slapped my hand away when I tried to assist and suggested that I should sit down and write the next article. I still had one arm in a sling but I could write copy like nobody's business.

So much news. Americans responded to the port blockade by driving cattle and carting necessities up through the narrow strip of land at the Boston Neck. Then Gage declared martial law and dissolved the colony's charter that allowed legislative elections. Towns across New England had been electing their own for only the past hundred years, and so it was not surprising that act went over like a lead barrel of goat bladders. One letter to the *BFD* suggested it created more hatred of the military governor than if he had been convicted of being a serial kitten kicker. And nobody likes a kitten kicker.

Boston and several other cities ignored the new law banning meetings while their leaders took at great risk of being arrested for doing so. We printed the fiery and most eloquent speeches from those meetings when we could get them. One of those took place in Salem. On a stove-hot Wednesday, Francis and I were taking a tea break in the shade of the building and looking for excuses to procrastinate at any meaningful work when Sally swept past and into the office.

"Leeds, I just got word the army is mustering soldiers to march on the Salem Town House to stop tonight's correspondence committee meeting and arrest the leaders." Sally was breathless. "The Salem militia is mustering and getting volunteers from miles around. They will surely put up a fight."

Mayhem was in the making; could war be far behind? I grabbed my hat and bolted out the door.

Chapter Thirty-one
Three Thousand Guns Can't Be Wrong

I did not make the trip as quickly as I would have liked, but even with my left arm still in its sling, I managed to reach the Salem town square before sundown. If this was to be the beginning of a civil war, I had to witness and report it. The feud between England and its American stepchild had been simmering for a decade and accelerated with the tea affair. This could make the future of the colonies. Bugger the badger, it could change the mother floggin' world. I had to be there.

Nervous anticipation grew as I borrowed an old horse that Jacob kept at a boarding stable on the north side. Its name was Nag, a horse not particularly spirited so it prevented me from jostling my wounded shoulder too much. Mounting her was a bit of a bother, though.

There was a rise in the highway just south of town, and as Nag and I reached that point I could see the hustle at a British encampment between me and the bay. I paused to watch reinforcements from Boston disembarking from a navy ship and organizing with the regulars. One hundred? It was hard to tell. How many of those foot soldiers would be sent into town?

The colonists who patrolled, if you could call their aimless movement on the streets surrounding the Town House a patrol, had an air of anxious calm about them. No one seemed to be in charge and no one seemed to give a badger's bottom about it. They were armed and ready to fight and that was enough.

I headed directly to the one place where I could find out what was happening. The newspaper shop for the *Essex Gazette* was two doors up from the town house that served as the governor's new residence. Ebenezer Hall, who published the newspaper with his older brother Samuel, sat outside straddling a tree trunk that had been turned into a bench. He was on the end facing the square with his elbows on his knees and he sucked on a pipe, blowing long streams of smoke while he soaked up the moment.

"Mr. Merriweather," he said as I gingerly dismounted and tied Nag to a post. "So good to see you."

He didn't turn his head until I sat next to him. Then he twisted, smiled, and shook my hand. "It has been too long and Samuel will be happy you are here." He offered his sympathies for my wounded shoulder and tugged gently at the cloth of my sling. "I can't say how pleased I am at your recovery."

"I saw the mention you gave my attack in the *Gazette*," I said. "Two inches worth on the back page. Seriously, my friend? That is all I am worth to you?"

"You should have avoided getting shot on a day when General Gage made news with his latest duty tax increase. Sincerely poor planning on your part."

"I will make a note to check the good governor-general's agenda next time."

Ebenezer slapped his knee. "How about some beer? Wine? Got some very decent local applejack."

"Perhaps later," I said. I waved my good arm at the armed bodies roaming in front of Town House.

"Come to see for yourself what history we are making?"

Ebenezer pointed the stem of his pipe at a group of men clustered just beyond the door of the meeting hall. "This morning there were twenty or so militiamen in town when the correspondence committee meeting was delayed. Now it's more than two hundred. If we avoid bloodshed, then all this will be forgotten. If not, well, we'll be reporting on the start of a war."

And so we waited. And we waited into the night. Several times men darted into the print shop to see Ebenezer's brother, Samuel. Ebenezer said they were leaders of the Correspondence Committee. They rushed out again and disappeared into the crowd, ignoring the questions I threw at them. The number of musket-packing Americans grew and grew. There must have been a thousand by then.

Eventually Samuel Hall emerged from the print shop and marched to the top step of the Town House where he read a statement. The colonists' leaders had decreed the military governor had no authority over them to restrict meetings, and they elected representatives to a county convention that would convene in due course.

"Tweaking the governor's nose," Ebenezer said.

"It's more than a tweak. It's a bloody bear poke," I replied.

Hall also reported two of the committee's leaders had been arrested and others would be taken by force if necessary.

"We must take measures to protect our rights. Resist peacefully if possible," Samuel Hall cried out. "But fight if you must!"

His words brought a rousing cheer from the crowd. It carried like a wave down side streets away from the square, and it was obvious that I had underestimated the size of the militia now assembled. One thousand? Pffsh. It had to have been more and appeared to be growing still. How many I could not venture to guess, but they now outnumbered the soldiers considerably.

The Salemites and the thousands of men from the outlying towns built campfires on the streets and made it plain they were not going anywhere. The campfires served as meeting stations where gun-toting militiamen could gather for a nip of beer or something stronger. Their women provided coffee, tea, and cakes.

If gunfire erupted it would do so under a glorious, starry summer night. Across Mill Pond we could see the redcoats distributing torches to keep their ranks well-lit and ensure their presence and their threat couldn't be ignored.

I do not wait well and became restless. Even if the army backed down under what had become an overwhelming number of colonists, I decided I couldn't leave Salem without a story.

News happened fast those days. I anticipated I could return to Boston and get something in print by Monday, four days away. It all depended on what would happen over the early morning hours. What was happening at the moment was...

Nothing.

So I swam into the ocean of bodies, looking for interesting characters to stop and ask what, specifically, had lured them to come into town armed as they were. I stopped at various camp-fires to seek answers. We printers, like Adams, Thomas, and the Hall brothers here in Salem, were all eloquent people, not only informing but shaping opinions. I had my share of readers whom I believed looked to me to validate their preconceived notion of the world around us. But what were these common folk thinking? Nobody had asked them.

The vast number of men who took up arms in Salem, many of whom had traveled significant distances to do so, confirmed in my heart that the message of resistance was taking root. And not by a small measure. Three thousand at a moment's notice? I didn't impress easily, but this was frog-flogging amazing and I needed to know why.

I thought I might ignite strained conversations since these people were not of a sort to voluntarily submit their opinion to the newspapers. It turned out to be easier than I'd imagined. My experience on board the *Dartmouth* in the midst of the Boston Tea Spree gave me a taste for it, but as a rule we newsmen rarely did mingle with participants in the course of human events. I found myself craving a mingle. So mingle I did.

"Taxes," said Ray, a twenty-three-year-old pig farmer from three miles west of Salem. Yes, follow the money. "That's why I'm here. I don't want to pay for a bunch of politicians to decide what I got to do to survive if they are so far away they don't know us from Adam."

"I can't sell my beans no more. Not since that fartleberry gov'ner shut up the port there in Boston there," according to fifty-one-year-old Edward, who had come down with two dozen members of the Danvers militia. Yes, personal suffering by a heartless government.

"No taxation without representation." That was from Roscoe Prine, a thirty-four-year-old mechanic in Salem. "Read that in the newspaper and that says it all," he told me when I asked how he'd formed the opinion. The newspaper reported it; they believed it; that settled it.

I spotted a lad no taller than the musket he carried. His name was Tom, a sixteen-year-old from a village near Swampscott. I asked him why he came to Salem. "I dunno. My pa says grab my gun we's goin' on a turkey hunt. I like shootin' turkeys." He stroked the long barrel of his gun and gave it a wistful look. I could see the dejection in his face. "No turkeys here."

They came from Havenhill and Cambridge, from as far away as Bedford and as near as Peabody, as well as Lynnfield, Wakefield, Strawberryfields, and Sallyfields. You really, really had to like that. And Boston. Of course, Boston.

Midnight came and went. Salem women went up and down the streets armed with blankets on which the out-oftowners could sleep. Me? Sleep was the furthest thing from my mind. I longed to talk and listen, and then talk and listen some more. I experienced rage against the government's abuse of power, real and imagined. Conspiracy theories abounded about farms being confiscated on a widespread basis in colonies far away, and a theory of a government plan to turn everyone Catholic. Some feared Parliament's passing the last of the Intolerable Acts, one that would consolidate all that land up in French Quebec and make Catholicism the official religion of the region. "They'll force that on us next, by God."

I also experienced confusion and fear.

"Why are you doing this?" I asked the town blacksmith who was wielding an axe.

"Because everyone is doing it. It's the right thing to do. We must stick together."

For what? I asked that often.

Amid much hemming and hawing and vague answers, one stood out. "So no body who don't live here can tell me what I can and can't do on my land. On *our* land."

There you had it. No matter how you sliced and diced and carved this turkey, the one common beat that I heard from deep in their hearts was that it was all about having a say in their lives. Control of their laws and their land and their future. As I meandered away from the crowd I felt a new kinship. Their call to arms and willingness to take action, while much more important in the grand scheme of things, was no different than setting fire to the *New England News-Journal.* Something good might…no, *must* rise from the ashes.

My energy faded as the sky welcomed its first bit of light, though the stars were still visible above. Someone pointed me down Essex Street, where I found the town's water pump and fountain about two blocks from the Town House. I drank and I washed my face and neck, and then curled up against the trunk of an elm. I was exhausted and couldn't keep my eyes open any longer, so I drifted into a shallow sleep with visions of letter blocks leaping at me from the type case and then falling into the compositing frame, perfect sentences perfectly arranged for the press and a pamphlet I would publish. At last I knew with the kind of clarity you find only in the fog of dream the essence of which we were about to fight. I knew what I saw, what I had heard, and what it told me.

It was the have-nots and the want-to-bes pitted against those in power who would do anything to keep them in their place.

And at the dawn of a new day, wasn't that really what every revolution is about?

Chapter Thirty-two
Who Was That Man?

In a word or four, there was no shooting. I was relieved, I suppose. Yes, I was, but I had to admit with some small measure of shame that the journalist in me was disappointed at the loss of opportunity to report on what would have been the biggest event of our lives.

Thursday came and the militia refused to leave, as did the company of British soldiers. Who would blink first?

General Gage ordered the county sheriff to arrest the committee members for holding an illegal public meeting, but that proved useless because the sheriff couldn't find any civilian deputies to do the work. Someone buried an axe in the front door and posted a threatening letter at the Tory home where Gage had spent the night. An informal squad of militia volunteers patrolled that area, with a large group maintaining a presence at the gate to quiz anyone wishing to visit the home's owner or the military governor. By the afternoon, that patrol got into a fight with a crew of volunteers who had begun drinking too early in the day and wanted action. Irony of all ironies, it was the Americans who provided protection for Gage against an increasingly restless and unruly mob when they used their fists and bats and musket stocks to chase them away.

"Is that all the bloodshed we're going to see after two days of this?" Ebenezer Hall asked. I supposed not every news printer can control his bloodlust for a good story.

General Gage didn't need an axe in his door to see the writing on the wall. With as little fanfare as the colonists would allow, he rode off to a safe location. Drumbeats and bugles soon followed, and the troops withdrew as well. A cheer swept across the town, and it must have been like nails in the boots of the soldiers with every step of their march out of Salem. With luck and a cooperative horse, I could be back in Boston shortly after sunset, work through the night to write and set the front page, and get two hundred issues of the newspaper printed by noon tomorrow. I nudged Nag to keep up a steady gait on the highway back to town and ignored everything else while I wrote in my mind the words I would use to tell this story.

I was still a good distance from Cambridge and the Charles River crossing when the sound of hoof beats pulled me away from my muse. Wordplay interruptus. I hate that.

"Whoa, there."

Two soldiers galloped up from behind and forced me to stop. They dismounted with rifles in hand and blocked me from continuing.

They demanded answers. Who are you? Why are you here? Where are you coming from? Where are you going? Were you part of that mob in Salem? And most importantly, are you armed?

"Only with my rapier wit," I responded to their last question.

The soldiers looked at one another with faces as blank as a granite wall and twice as cold. What a waste of jest.

They ordered me to dismount and asked why I had one arm in a sling. The shorter of the two, a no-nonsense-looking sergeant, took pains to inspect my arm beneath the sling.

"Nothing up my sleeve," I said. Not so much as an intolerant grin. Apparently I was shooting blanks that day.

"Clear," Sergeant Poker Face said to his companion, who stood in front of Nag with one hand on her bridle and the other clutching his rifle against his chest, finger ready at the trigger.

"May I go now?" I asked when it seemed we had exhausted every reason for them to hold me up.

No.

They used their muskets to force me and Nag well off the highway a few minutes later when we heard more horses approaching. Quite a few. A military company approached from the north. Two, four, six soldiers in an advance guard. Two noticeably high-ranking officers rode behind them as they passed us. I recognized the giraffe-necked Major Marcus Henry as one. He had been in charge of the military command until General Gage returned from England. And there was General

Gage himself, who rode an appropriate two paces ahead of Henry. Four more soldiers formed the rear guard, followed by several more riders in civilian dress.

The two soldiers on each side of me stood at attention as they passed. The riders never looked our way, ignoring us like clumps of horse droppings on the side of the highway. It was only after they had passed that one of the civilians in the rear pulled up where the road curved a short distance from us. He turned enough to shoot a hard stare in our direction. He wore a dark riding coat and a hat low across his brow. He had a dark face to match his clothes, a mustache, and a trimmed goatee.

"Oye," I shouted. I took a quick step toward him but was felled by the butt of one soldier's rifle to the back of my head. From my knees I got my last glimpse of the rider as he disappeared around the bend. Who was that man? Was I seeing things? Dealing with the pain of a noggin conking I was a bit dizzy, but if he wasn't that low-down Lieutenant Cole, he looked so similar he could have been my would-be assassin's brother. But then, don't all snakes look alike?

On Saturday evening all of us at the *BFD* were feeling good about being first in Boston to publish our account of the Salem Affair when General Gage once again made news. He surprised everyone by sending over two hundred soldiers across the river to confiscate gunpowder from the Massachusetts Bay Provincial armory in Charlestown and move the powder back to Boston, where the army could make sure it didn't fall into the hands of cranky Americans.

After midnight, Sally and I were snuggled in the bed of the madam's suite on the ground floor of Flagg Alley when an urgent knock roused us. It was one of the mouse brow twins. Beyond that, I was too deep into the comfortable drowsiness that descends just before sleep to see clearly and identify which of Sally's Strumpet of Liberty spies had interrupted the rest I needed so badly.

"Abigail?" Sally said as she opened the door. Abigail, yes, that was it. It seems she had just collected from a client, a soldier who'd revealed the general's plan as he was undressing for a quick shag. He was in a hurry beyond the norm, came and went more quickly than usual. Apparently he had slipped away while the troops slipped into Charlestown and was expected to be at his post when they returned.

"Do something, Leeds," Sally said to me.

"What would that be?"

"Anything. We must stop them."

I thought it must have been too late for that, but once again the possibility of war begged for a true reporting from the scene if possible.

Unlike Salem, Gates had surprised the militias and there was no resistance, no bloodshed. Only more bad blood. Daybreak was nearing when I finally arrived in time to cross paths with the soldiers who were returning to Boston with wagon loads of munitions while a few dozen Americans could only lob insults at the soldiers.

General Gates had evened the score.

Chapter Thirty-three
A Game of Cat and Mouse Fur

If losing so much musket ammunition to General Gage's troops was a beat down for the local militia, do not cry over your spilt gunpowder. Gage had done nothing wrong, at least according to a letter he had provided to all the newspapers in Boston after the ammunition was safely stored in town under military protection. Legally speaking, I suppose he had a point. Gage was appointed to run all of the military functions of the New England province; therefore, he could do as he damned well pleased.

He did not put it in those exact words, but his argument was clear that anyone who objected could go bugger a badger for all he cared. Unlike Governor Hutchinson, who would have gloated in poetic terms and tossed in a few juvenile but well-aimed barbs at the intelligence and impotency of his political adversaries, Gage was much more direct.

"Get over it."

And worse, "Get used to it."

The Tory-tongue kissing *Boston Weekly News-Letter* printed the general's submission in full.

Likewise, the *Post-Boy and Advertiser* printed it twice on consecutive Tuesdays, in the event any of its meager number of subscribers missed it the first go-around along with publisher John Hick's bootlicking piece in support of the raid. I called the raid "The Gage Outrage" in the *Boston Free Dispatch* article. It was another of my clever epithets that, for some reason, failed to catch on.

Hicks, the Loyalist, on the other hand, wrote:

"You GO, General," along with an additional call for further action against the *HUMAN SCUM of LIBERALISM.*

On the flip side of that doubloon, Benjamin Edes at the *Boston Gazette* only made passing reference to Gage's letter as a ludicrous justification offered by the *MILITARY TYRANT,* at British command headquarters.

And Isaiah Thomas—oh, young Thomas—ignored the letter entirely but set out his partisan views in terms that caused even me to blush at the thought of putting those words into print. Thomas discovered how incredibly easy it was to get under the skin of a thin-skinned leader. Since that most scathing issue, British soldiers started sending a patrol to march past the *Massachusetts Spy* on a daily basis. So much so, that in a quiet moment over tea at the coffee house next door to our print shop, Isaiah confessed to me he was beginning to worry.

"Merriweather," he said. "I'm no coward, but I am seriously considering a move. Just pick up the damned press and relocate to a safer place out of Gage's reach." He sipped his tea and winked at me. "You had it easy fooling everyone that the Forger was publishing *WTF* in Watertown. Strong militia there. You can expect more problems like mine now that you've brought the Forger home under your own roof."

It seems I'd fooled only the foolish. "Was the Forger's identity that obvious to you as well?"

He nodded. "Not immediately, of course. But you have a rogue streak I admire. I would wish to be you when I grow up. *If* I ever grow up. I would have gladly posted the Forger's exclusive reports if you had asked."

"What? And let you have the credit? Pa-SHAW!"

We had the latest edition of *BFD* on the table. The Forger was quite a draw and I used those articles to call attention to the straightforward stories printed under my own name, no name at all, or of my recent favorite pseudonyms like Dragnetus. Just the facts.

I provided Gage some voice by printing selected portions of his letter. And then, in a companion piece filling a column to the right, the Forger took both the general and the partisan lickspittle Tory press to task in words that would make Shakespeare himself weep with jealousy. The writing was that fine.

But the most gratifying part of the Forger's work I had written for that day's newspaper was information I'd received through Sally that the governor had ordered troops to stage a similar raid on munitions stored in Worcester. From some soldier's lips to a strumpet's ear to Sally's attention to the pages of the *Dispatch*, secrets came in spurts at the bordello.

Some came during casual conversation fueled by alcohol in the parlor, and others in bedroom braggadocio by soldiers, clerks, and associates of the local military units who felt the need to stroke their self-worth before the women there. Big secrets were often a measurement of status for weak men. The women, on the other hand, never mentioned that where rank was concerned, size didn't matter when money was exchanged.

Isaiah and I sat in the coffee house and speculated on what might happen next. One of his sources had brought word that morning that Gage reversed himself and called off the mission to Worcester after the *Dispatch* hit the streets. Militiamen were already taking up positions around the armory while a new system of express riders had been formed to summon others from outlying towns.

I told Isaiah, "The combination of plots revealed and the prospect of facing a force potentially larger than Gage could muster did the trick, I'd say."

"We are having an impact, old man. If we can affect Gage's military strategy like this, we can effect a larger goal. Our newspapers prove it." Then he leaned forward and pounded a fist on the table. "Power to the people, Merriweather. Nothing short of independence will do. If we are to be oppressed by a monarch, let him be one of our choosing."

"Better a king we elect than one determined by lineage?"

Isaiah was almost salivating at the prospect. Then he stiffened, sitting straight, and took stock of the coffee house with wary eyes. We were alone save for Mr. Harrison, the haberdasher from down the street, and a companion. Their conversation seemed relaxed and mingled with the distant, constant clank of the press from beyond the door separating us from the *BFD* printing office.

"That sort of talk, especially when you put it into print, is going to get you into deeper trouble, Isaiah."

"Not going to back down. Wouldn't be prudent," he said.

One week later Gage sent troops to Cambridge, where the militia had stored three canons with barrels of powder. But express riders reached town well ahead of the soldiers and the ammunition mysteriously disappeared. If insults were musket balls, it would have been a bloody massacre of redcoats. A small army of armed colonists greeted the soldiers, but cheerfully stood by while a search of the armory and nearby buildings yielded nothing, and the soldiers executed a hasty return to Boston.

I was there to see it play out. Having received the same tip as the alarm network, I stood ready with pencil and paper to record the event. Aside from the taunts coming from the citizens along the road, it was all quite cordial in my mind. But as the crowd dispersed in the predawn cold, the clouds decided there was no reason to hold back and a light snow began to fall. I had taken shelter beneath an overhang of a blacksmith's shop to collect some information from the captain of the militia before my own retreat to Boston to write up the account. His answers varied from easy confidence to halting loss of thought. His eyes darted over my shoulder, forcing me to turn several times. There was a motion-less figure, barely visible, blending into the dark brick wall of the armory across the way. I stopped the militiaman in mid-thought and headed that direction. Who was this fellow? A spy? He seemed much too interested in my activities. I hadn't gotten far when he moved off and I lost him amid the stragglers, who refused to take victory for an answer and were still spoiling for a fight.

Then two days later I saw the man again. I was unloading bundles of supplies from the O'Malley Paper Mill in front of the *Dispatch* office with Mitchell Curry. Bollocks if he didn't look even more familiar in a sincerely creepy way.

He had long, unkempt hair that spilled out from under a brown wool-felt hat. It was a broad-brimmed mechanic's winter hat that cast a shadow over his face. He wore a mustache that rounded his mouth and dripped from the cheeks on either side, falling to his chin. Spaniard? Pirate? Quite difficult to tell. What did he think was so frog-flogging fascinating on my side of the street?

I went inside the print shop and turned to the front window before the door even had time to close behind me. The stranger paced a block, moving first closer to the shop and then away again. Sally joined me at the window from the desk, where she had been engrossed in balancing the month's ledger.

"I think we have a spy," I said. I pointed to the stranger. "The one in the long riding coat over there."

"What will you do?"

I put an arm around her and gave her a squeeze. "Keep an eye on him. I'm going out the back. With luck I can circle around and confront him before he disappears."

I was only a few steps into the back alley when the coffee house door banged shut again. Sally had donned a bonnet and heavy coat. She came running up.

"What are you doing?" I asked.

"Someone has to keep you out of trouble. The last time you did this you were shot."

I tried to move off as quickly as possible, leaving her behind while explaining there was too much risk. She would have none of it and ran to keep up with me. We merged on to Anne Street in time to see the mystery fellow walking south. I followed him while Sally tagged a few steps behind me.

"Have you no sense, woman? Please return to the shop."

Sally lifted her skirt an inch and splashed through a street puddle without even flinching. "If I had known I would be following a spy across town today, I might have borrowed more sturdy shoes. Well, so be it."

We followed the mysterious stranger into the crowd in Marketplace Square. At one point he paused near a tree and glanced in every direction. I steered Sally in an angle where I could keep my face away from the stranger while moving close enough to get a better look at his. I saw enough to know he must have been the same civilian rider at the rear of General Gage's escape from Salem.

"He's headed to the military camps on the Commons," I told Sally as the spy picked up his pace away from the square. Then he took an unexpected turn down a street across from the green and ducked into an alley between two rows of brick buildings. He removed his coat as he approached a door that I suspected led into a basement of the building to the left. He didn't seem to notice us peeking around the corner at the mouth to the alley when he looked back from the landing above steps down to the door. He took a kerchief and wiped his face before he ducked through the door, but not before shooting a last look in our direction. At last, I had a moment to see him clearly. The mustache was gone and his face was a whiter shade of pale. What the bloody hell was that assassin Cole doing roaming free on the streets of Boston? I ran forward. Sally followed much more cautiously. The door was unlocked.

"Leeds, don't go in there."

"Don't fret, Angel. A quick peek is all I need. If I am not back in a few moments, fetch Baby Cakes and his friends."

"No, sincerely, Leeds. You don't know what you'll find there."

Sally was right about that. I stumbled down a short series of steps inside the door before I found myself on a landing at the edge of a very large parlor. It was as if the world had suddenly stopped spinning. Nobody moved and everyone held a breath. The place was hazy with smoke. More than a dozen men, many of them British soldiers who had shed their uniform jackets, sat at tables littered with bottles of wine, glasses, mugs of ale, or whatever they had chosen to imbibe. Money, silver and paper script, cards, dice, and dominoes topped the tables like trash strewn on a sidewalk. And skirts. Several women attended to the soldiers, running pitchers from a bar at the back wall.

The chatter returned and the gambling and carousing picked up anew as two soldiers at the nearest table stood and reached for muskets leaning against the wall. It seemed the crowd was content that the matter was being addressed and no longer required their attention.

"Sorry. So sorry. Wrong address," I said. I bounded back up the stairs and took Sally by the elbow once outside. We hurried back to the main street. No one followed.

"That was awkward," I said.

"No doubt. Gambling and women and wine, oh my!" she said. "How indecent. Perhaps we should report them to the authorities."

"Madam, you are teasing me."

"Absolutely." Sally explained that soldiers camped on the greens of the Commons had established a parlor for recreation away from their officers' watchful eyes. "I arranged for a couple of our girls who wanted some additional work to come here when they had time away from Flagg Alley."

"But what was Cole doing in civilian clothes? What is his game?"

Sally reached up, cupped my chin, and pressed her fingers under my nose, leaving a string of hair pasted above my lip and curling down over the left corner of my mouth. "You were right. He was spying on us. He must have dropped this on the steps."

I pulled the hair from my lip and it left a sticky residue that I rubbed several times.

"What is this?"

"It is a false mustache, silly. Part of his disguise."

"That much is obvious," I replied. "But I mean, what *is* this?"

"Mouse fur. Apparently it's not just for ladies anymore," she said with a smile.

He must have thought spying on me would lead him to the Forger.

We resumed walking in silence for several long blocks.

"I don't believe he was spying on you," Sally said after we entered the Marketplace on our way back to Anne Street. "He was spying on me."

"You?"

Then it hit me. Oh. My. Mother-flogging god! "He was down the street on the corner. The corner of…"

"Flagg Alley," Sally said.

Chapter Thirty-four
The Winter of Our Discontent

Just because you are delusional doesn't mean someone isn't out to shag you.

Or so Jacob told me in an attempt to justify the steps I took through the cold winter months where nary a cheerful face could be found in Boston. The fuse had been lit and was slowly making its way to the powder keg. No one was happy. It was only a matter of time before things exploded. I was convinced.

Now that I knew Lieutenant Cole was still in Boston, and therefore still a menace, I took to carrying my father's pistol, one of the few items I had salvaged from my youth and exported with me when I escaped from England. I also spent the majority of every walk looking over my shoulder for Cole and assassins, or anyone who bore any resemblance to Cole and assassins. One could not be too careful.

While Jacob agreed with me on that point, he began to think I was obsessed with spies. Maybe he wasn't too daft after all. It seems I kept seeing Cole's face everywhere I went for weeks, always with enough distance to slip away before I could confront him. At the tavern, the market square, strolling past the *Dispatch*, the corner near Flagg Alley, on the street to Madam Flower's house in the Cambridge district, and any street near the military camps on the Commons. Real or imagined, mysterious figures haunted me.

I met with the new constable, the new justice of the peace, and the new magistrate, all appointed by General Gage after he sacked the duly elected authorities. With the lawyer Robert Treat Paine at my side, we accused the military of harboring an assassin. Mr. Paine had recently returned from the continental convention in Philadelphia and he was spoiling for a fight. He accepted my case without asking compensation as a way to prove one of the colonists' grievances adopted there. In the end, however, Gage's handpicked judge insisted we were mistaken and that Cole had returned to England and was awaiting a military hearing there for his "errant shot that inadvertently wounded."

"I wish to give testimony to the contrary." I wasn't confident the court would hear me out but it was necessary to put up a fight.

The magistrate assured me that would be perfectly fine, and would be my right, if I chose to sail back to London and wait for the trial to begin at some unspecified date in the coming months. Case dismissed, stymied, and unconvinced, I continued to conjure up Cole sightings for weeks to come.

One night in December near the first anniversary of the Tea Spree at Griffin's Wharf, Jacob and I were approaching a tavern not far from the docks, which had been left virtually desolate since the British navy began enforcing the port closure, when Lieutenant Cole stepped out of a dark alley and accosted us. He was disguised as a pauper in a heavy, hooded winter cloak, hunched over and wielding a saber. He stepped from the alley and stood before us, blocking our path to the tavern door, and laughed—squawked, actually—like a raven with a throat full of broken glass. His threatening motions with his sword, his open palm that he pushed at my face, and his defiance to give way told me this was no pauper interested only in the contents of my purse. So I pointed over his shoulder.

"Would you look at that?" When he turned his head, I leapt upon the villain, tossing him to the ground while ripping off the hood of his cloak to reveal his face.

Jacob hung back and laughed. "Leeds, you bloody dim-witted fool. You narcissistic nincompoop." He bent over and pulled us both to our feet. "Are you all right, Miss Tilly?"

Now, in the light from the tavern, I could clearly see our assailant wasn't Lieutenant Cole at all, but Tilly Ipswich, a hag of the streets older than dirt and twice as filthy. She had lost her mental faculties somewhere in the previous century, I suspect, and was not a stranger to anyone in Boston who had a kind heart and a few pence to spare. I had, myself, contributed to her meager upkeep once or twice. How in the world could I have not recognized her?

"Because you are searching for ghosts where none exist," Jacob admonished me.

Miss Tilly squawked again and batted me with her cane that I had mistaken for a sword. I apologized and dug into my purse.

"Bloody badger-bugging bollocks," I murmured before handing her my entire purse. "I am an idiot, madam. Forgive me." She patted my cheek and I could see pity in her eyes before she turned and cackled her way back into the black of night.

"It was her mustache that fooled me," I said. "And the cigar."

"I could see that," Jacob replied, stone-faced.

Despite the Miss Tilly muddle and other moments of jitters, throughout those winter months I was less concerned for my own safety than the safety of Sally and the women at Flagg Alley. I insisted that she have Mitchell Curry or his beaver-trapping, arrow-wielding father escort her anywhere she might travel when I could not be there myself. Of course she resisted.

"I am far from being the helpless little woman you think," she said.

We were making our way one morning through the rain-slick streets from Madam Flower's mansion to Flagg Alley. Sally would conduct her weekly reading and charm lessons for the girls before joining me at the print office that afternoon. For her, the morning was also a chance to exchange the latest gossip and tidbits of information any of the women might have acquired from the girls' clients.

There was no shortage of news over the winter months. Star Coffee House proprietor David Deerfield had added several additional express riders to his stable of couriers to import newspapers from Philadelphia, where colonial leaders met. At the top of their agenda was to be a unified response of nearly all the colonies to the British punishment of Boston. A long list of other grievances followed, so every report and rumor generated in Philadelphia captured eyeballs far and wide.

It was an incredible time to be a journalist. Our world was changing and news spread at a previously unheard-of speed. It was of an immediacy both challenging to maintain and exhilarating to execute. For the first time in history, we were as close to reporting events as they happened as man will ever get. It only took two days now from proclamation in Philadelphia to print in Boston.

I did not frequent boxing matches but experienced enough of them to understand the subtle strategy of getting into an advantageous position before launching into an attack to pummel the puss out of an opponent. The mild winter months into 1775 had me feeling that was happening before our eyes, with the two sides circling each other, looking for an opening. And it felt as if all of New England and parts beyond were watching and waiting through the initial sparring before someone landed the punch that would draw blood.

With the arrival of another four hundred marines in Boston, loyalists were more emboldened to come out of their closets, be more vocal, and even stage demonstrations in support of the crown. When a gaggle of Tories with a detachment of redcoats at their side marched down Anne Street and stopped in front of the *Dispatch* office, staring down me and my two-man squadron of Curry and Curry Senior, it was time to take action. The miniature mob hoisted a straw image tagged with my name and burned me in effigy before moving on. I only caught a quick glimpse of it before the flames overwhelmed the little figure. I think I was more offended by the fact that the effigy looked nothing like me at all. Quite homely.

A group performed the same trick on the street in front of Isaiah Thomas' newspaper the following week, and two bystanders who took issue with the protest tried to stop them but were beaten by the mob and arrested by the soldiers. Two days later the *Spy*'s office was ransacked. The vandals might have done worse but for the timely arrival of the Sons of Liberty, who "arrested" one of them. The man was turned over to the constable with broken ribs and a face that was unlikely to look the same again, and not too unlike my own effigy. Quite homely, I say.

Isaiah surrendered.

"This is too much, gentlemen," he said. "I have some connections in Worcester and I will move my printing press there. The Sons of Lib are strong there and the distance from Boston should be safe but not unmanageable for continuing our work. We must not be silenced. Not now."

I had a dalliance with similar fears of violence. Only Baby Cakes, his old man, and a couple of Sons of Liberty mates provided a bit of relief. They had taken to keeping an eye on the print shop around the clock. Though Isaiah may have invited trouble, he developed a habit in that no article in the *Spy* about Gage was complete without the use of two or even three nicknames, like *TYRANT, SCOUNDREL*, and, my personal favorite, *CHAMBER POT TOSSING AUTHORITARIAN*.

And so, with Isaiah gone from the public square while in the process of moving to Worcester, in Boston it was left to Edes' *Gazette* and my *BFD* to battle for readers with the two Tory newspapers, using opinion pieces and news that was slanted left and right. I was convinced my version of events was the most correct, while the Tories proclaimed they were true historians of the moment and that their facts—no matter how tainted we knew them to be—would prevail. Many times our newspapers and pamphlets were written as much to inflame passions as to inform, and Boston had become a town where one was defined less for who they were, but rather who they read and who they hated.

The violence finally became too much and drove Madam Flowers away. She decided to wait out the storm at her family estate in Lexington. She was not alone. Boston's well-to-do packed up and relocated where they hoped to be out of harm's way. I convinced Sally to join her aunt in Lexington as well.

The afternoon she left she rebuffed my proposal for marriage for what had by then been at least the hundredth time. I offered the hundredth and first with no better luck. We stood near Jacob's wagon, weighed down with Sally's belongings, at the corner of Flagg Alley.

She held me tight and then gave me the most luscious, lingering kiss. I said, "I want to marry you. Will you favor me to say yes?"

"Of course, Leeds. I have been wanting this since, well, since the very first time I slapped your silly face." She kissed me again. "But I wish to ask one small favor before we wed.

A small thing, actually. Just a little matter I would like you to handle."

"Ask me. I will do anything you desire."

"Would you please boot the bloody Brits out of our land before I marry you? Be my hero. Do that and I will be with you 'til death do us part."

She laughed, reached up, and gently tugged my earlobe.

"Is there some wiggle room for negotiating? Possibly a wedding before war? I may need a bit of time to complete this 'minor task,' as you call it."

Sally took my hand as I helped her into the wagon. "Leeds, the times are so uncertain and we have so much more work to do. We must consider that above all else. I do love you, but your timing is atrocious."

"Just consider it while you are in Lexington. I will ask again. And again and again until you say yes." I squeezed her hand one last time. "Stay safe, my little rebel."

I stood at that corner and watched as Jacob steered them up the street and turned to the road north to Lexington.

Then from behind me came the sounds of scuffle, cursing, clattering, and commotion of brawling. I turned to find the assassin Cole pinned against the wall of the millinery shop with his feet dangling inches off the ground.

Mitchell Curry held him there by the throat.

Chapter Thirty-five
Catch Me If You Can

I nearly danced to Baby Cakes' side. Cole struggled to turn his head to me, but was reduced to staring me down with only his wide eyes pressing to the edges of his sockets. "Well," I said. "Are you happy to see me or is that a dagger in your pocket?" Actually, he had dropped the knife to the ground; it just sounded funnier the way I said it with a voice full of saucy innuendo.

Cole tried to respond, but Baby Cakes' chokehold prevented anything more than a raspy cough. I picked up Cole's blade and replicated the threatening move he made in the print shop what seemed a lifetime ago. Now the boot was on the other foot.

"Tell me something," I said. I used the point of his dagger to separate the folds of his long jacket. A longshoreman's disguise today, he dressed in dungarees and a knit cap. "Tell me why you seem to have taken a singular—how shall I say this?—interest toward me. There are far more valuable targets for you to harass across the city. You could better spend your time on the trail of Hancock, Adams…you know, the usual suspects." I suspected he had men doing exactly that. He wasn't stupid enough not to.

"Okay, Mitchell, you can relax, but only a little. Kill him if he makes a move." Baby Cakes lowered Cole until he could stand on his own. He gave Cole's head a final nudge before letting go, whacking it into the brick. When Cole had taken a breath and collected himself, I asked again, "Why me?" The dread that Cole might seek revenge for having failed to kill me in the tavern, a concern that jabbed me every time I tried to lift my wounded arm, returned.

"Because that's what we do." The voice didn't come from Cole, but rather behind me. Cole's accomplice from the night at the tavern stood a few short feet away with his pistol aimed at Baby Cakes' head.

"Good job, Hogan," Cole said in a voice that was still too weak to be authoritative. He reached for the dagger, gripping at my wrist, but I twisted it enough to draw blood on the back of his hand before dropping the blade again. In what was quite a show of strength, I could see in Cole's face the struggle to mask his pain. His eyes watered and he blinked them away.

"It is one thing that we have to deal with these stupid, rebellious colonists," Cole said. "We will crush them in due time. But you, Merriweather, you are Warwickshire by birth, as am I. You have spat upon every fine thing it means to be British by consorting with these Yankee Doodlers and have a higher duty to Crown and Country."

"A traitor. You should be hanged for treason," Hogan said.

"I would advise against that," came an old man's croak from behind him. From out of nowhere, Papa Curry had materialized and now stood with his loaded crossbow and pressed the tip of his hunting arrow to the back of Hogan's skull.

The line forms to the right, I surmised. No one was quite sure who was scripted to make the next move, and the standoff might have lasted deep into the night but a shout from down near the boot shop distracted us all. Three or four roughnecks had taken notice of our dance line, each of us with weapons drawn. One of them roared an angry command to the others and raised a club. The men began marching at us with the quick step of a gang spoiling for a fight. Then they turned it into a dash with a war whoop. The distraction was enough that Cole and Hogan lashed out and threw us off balance. They ran. And like hounds after a fox, the pack of roughnecks raced in pursuit.

"Well, that was interesting," I said.

"Would of been funner if I could of knocked him about the noggin a bit more," Baby Cakes replied.

"Could of, should of, would of," Old Man Curry sighed, disappointed.

I bent and picked up Cole's dagger sitting at my feet, abandoned in his retreat. Isn't it curious the way life hands one variations on the same situation, so similar that they would chill the spine? Reminiscent of the night I pulled a knife from a soldier's back behind the Reckless Goat Tavern, I held Cole's dagger and looked for something to wipe away his blood on the edge of its blade.

A squad of British soldiers splintered at the crossroads where the spies had turned to escape. Some took off after the hounds and the rest ran toward us.

Possibly someday someone more brilliant than me will codify the notion that insanity is being confronted with a situation and doing the same thing over and over again while foolishly expecting different results. A true genius wouldn't have wasted time pondering; he would get the bloody hell away from there. While I wouldn't claim to be a genius, I did not hesitate to ponder or welcome the British soldiers' arrival as I had on that night at the tavern. I skedaddled without a second thought. We all did, separating in different directions into the maze of backstreets and alleys that defined the neighborhoods around the docks and cover was plentiful.

Escaping the redcoats was easy; outrunning the apprehension of what Cole may have had in store next was an entirely 'nother kettle of carp. What if he had been standing nearby long before we knew? I wondered what he heard. Had he overheard Sally say she would continue the work of her strumpet spy network? Lounging on the street near Flagg Alley in disguise worried me that he had, indeed, tracked the source information that had ended up in the pages of my newspaper under the Forger's name. Did he think she was responsible for passing along military intelligence that helped the colonies stymie General Gage and his troops from impounding arms and gunpowder? The knot in my stomach made me glad Sally had gotten out of Boston none too soon.

With the port closed, there was no shortage of young men out of work. After I pressed her to pay more attention to her safety, she began paying several blokes to protect Flagg Alley. A few gladly undertook a long shift, providing security downstairs in exchange for a few minutes of pleasure upstairs. But work for the Flagg Alley women was slow and getting worse. Several of the most popular girls were forced to find a position with brothels in New York, Baltimore, or other cities where trade was still bustling and not every pence needed to be preserved for the next meal.

HARD TIMES for certain industries, I wrote in *The Dispatch*, using my Forger persona. We railed against Parliament's port closure act and how it forced poverty upon the longshoremen, the warehouses, and merchants. And by way of introducing readers to the plight of the poor, forgotten workers, I announced the bankruptcy and closure of the Whipp Inn Fellowship League. A rival bordello to Flagg Alley.

> Further, this DASTARDLY STRIKE by a HEARTLESS PARLIAMENT against the economy of Boston is now CRIPPLING the most INNOCENT OF CITIZENS. The recent bankruptcy of one of our PREMIER CHARITABLE FRATERNITIES for the middling class men about town has forced a fair number of SWEET, VIRTUOUS MAIDENS employed there into a life of ILL REPUTE, trading their intimate favors on the streets in order to STAY ALIVE.

While prostitution was illegal and most definitely frowned upon, and bordellos paid significant bribes to officials that ensured they would deny such establishments even existed, there was a naiveté among the public that astonished me. I ignored the fact that most if not all of these *VIRTUOUS MAIDENS* were trading their favors in a formal setting long before the Boston Port Act, as did every other newspaper along the seaboard that reprinted my article. My account spread far and wide. Portraying sadly single, hard-working young ladies as innocent victims of cruel government policies inflamed the public spectacularly. For many a reader, victimizing struggling young women might be only a step less severe than choking chipmunks on the empathy scale.

Flagg Alley had not yet succumbed to the downturn in business, but Sally was concerned. "What will we do? Where will the girls go if there is no work to be had?"

We were together, once again sharing our warmth under heavy covers in her bedroom at her aunt's townhouse after exchanging our own intimate favors. It was the middle of the night early in April and sleep was impossible. Sally had returned to town for a few days to attend to the bordello's business, as well as to provide a bit of editing and polish to the latest sermon from the clergyman Doctor Robert Patterson before we printed his next pamphlet.

Yes, the clergyman with a wife and six children was among Flagg Alley's clients, and he had introduced God into the lives of several girls there. He had apparently made it his mission to personally convert as many of them as he could lay his hands on. In the process he developed an intellectual admiration for Sally and trusted no one else to approve of his brand of fire and brimstone before going to press.

And so it was that Sally was in town the afternoon of April 17th when we learned the news. That morning Clinton Murdoch woke up dead. The despicable pirate who had stolen and looted my *News-Journal* had been found stone cold in bed. Common wisdom held that his advancing age, health, and girth had done him in. Some speculated it was heartache that came with his diminished influence since the Hutchinson administration folded. Sally suggested something more sinister.

"Why?" I asked. "I'm hearing nothing to suggest foul play."

"Perhaps it's my woman's intuition. Perhaps all your talk of Cole running loose has me fearing the worst." She slowly locked the galley of type into its frame, containing page four of Doctor Patterson's pamphlet. Her mind was elsewhere, and I carried the finished galley to the printing press and set it in place with one eye on Sally, who sat at the composing desk with her forehead wrinkled with worry.

I admit there were times when I didn't know what was going on in my own mind, but it did not require a gypsy's talents to suspect what had hunkered down in Sally's head. I asked anyway.

"I assume there is some connection there. Murdoch and Cole?" For why else would she associate the assassin with a dead man?

"It began when I brought you the information about the customs agent's murder. You remember George Grant? Well, it was Clinton Murdoch who let it slip that the governor had ordered it."

Ah, yes. "Poor George. What a way to die. I suppose a public hanging wouldn't have been nearly as satisfying." At the time, Sally claimed the source of her information was close to the governor but evaded all my attempts to draw more from her. Back then seemed like a lifetime ago.

She nodded. "Since then, Mr. Murdoch has revealed a number of things. He was actually quite loose with information in private. And quite useful to us, to you, and to the Forger."

"You believe Cole found out and decided to exact his revenge on Murdoch?" Suddenly it became clear why Cole had arrested Francis Akeley for passing information out of Murdoch Mansion to the Forger.

"So Cole was correct. Francis, as Murdoch's secretary, really was guilty of spying on the old man."

Sally looked dejected. "I wish it were that simple. No, it was someone else. Utterly trustworthy."

"I've always said strumpets make the best spies," I attempted to jest.

Again Sally shook her head, but as before, she evaded my efforts to learn who had acted as the bridge from Murdoch to her and from her to my press. As it turned out, it did not take much longer for it to reveal itself in a most odd, almost amusing manner.

Rita burst the print shop door open and stuck her head inside.

"Madam, you best come now to the house. We's got trouble brewing and ya need to see this. Oh, dear. Oh, dear."

Dash. Across the street and up to the house.

Sprint. Through the parlor, where girls mingled with patrons and watchmen.

Rush. Up the stairs to the largest of the bedrooms at the end of the second floor.

Tumble. Over each other with the harsh, sudden stop after bursting through the door.

Whoa.

Freeze. At the sight of two girls on the bed protecting their modesty in flimsy robes while one pointed a pistol at a client, naked save for his stocking feet.

He was clamped into a chair by the heavy hands of a house watchman. Meanwhile, Baby Cakes Curry held one end of a rope that ran out the window, where the opposite end was tied to the feet of another naked gent dangling in the cold air like a Christmas turkey strung up in a butcher shop display.

Chapter Thirty-six
Soldiers and Strumpets and Spies, Oh My

"Ha-lo, Mr. Printer. Evening, lady," Baby Cakes said. "Seems I hooked me a big'n." He pulled on the rope, raising his catch to where we could see the feet just beyond the windowsill. "How ya doing out there, Bradley?"

He got a muted roar and several curses in return so he relaxed his grip on the line, letting it plunge a foot or two before he jerked it tight again to stop the fall. This time he got an anguished howl. That must have hurt.

"Jezebel, what is going on?" Sally asked the strumpet with a gun.

"These two freebooters came in for a quick foursome. And when they wanted a few extra things that aren't on the menu, they refused to pay the boost."

"On top of that," the other girl said, "it was rush, rush, rush. Like they had someplace else to be. Makes a girl feel cheap."

"And this one," Jezebel said. "When I squawked about not paying fair price, he cut me with his ring. See?" Jezebel turned her cheek. I could see a red scratch and a dribble of blood from her temple to just below her left eye. "So Lazy Lucy and I played along."

"Strung them along," Lazy Lucy nodded. "I did them a number eight, you know, so to keep them occupied while Jezzy poached his pistol from his things over there and called for help."

I looked sideways at Sally. "Number eight?"

"Don't ask."

I went to a cane chair in the corner where the men had thrown off British uniforms with little concern for where they landed. A belt with a scabbard and empty holster dangled preciously from a peg on the coat stand over discarded undergarments. I picked up one of the soldiers' red coats with a lieutenant's insignia no less. Yet it had no regimental patch. Curious. I looked at the soldier fidgeting in the chair, and I would have sworn his lower lip trembled as he kept his chin tucked to his chest. No, he was not officer grade material.

"What's the rush, fellows? Came for a little nookie before heading out? Is tonight the night?"

The chair-bound soldier sniveled.

"Oh, we already know," Sally said.

Plans for a march on one of the arsenals beyond Boston had already reached the ears of, well, nearly everyone who was listening. The militias had been warned, and the chance of a surprise was minimal. All that was missing were the marching orders.

On your mark. Get set… All that rot.

Adams, Hancock, Paine, and a few other resistance leaders had headed north to the safety of a Hancock cousin's home in Lexington, fearing that if they lingered in Boston arrest was inevitable.

I stuck my head out the window and stared down at the officer's feet. It was an odd sensation to be talking to his toes in the dwindling light of the day and the shadows on the ground one floor below us melting away. "What say you, Lieutenant Bradley? What are you fellows up to?"

"Go to bloody hell." Yes, that's more like it. He was the senior officer of the two.

It was then that I noticed the lapel of his jacket I held had a small silver pin. I knew it too well and my throat clutched. Lieutenant Cole had worn an identical insignia of the special forces for intelligence and security.

"Haul him up, Mitchell."

Bradley was actually a bit more contrite, still naked but standing on his own feet beside the open window. Brrr. I thrust the lapel pin under his nose. "Are you boys here for work or pleasure?" I told him I was aware of the significance.

Bradley was young, not more than twenty by my estimate, and probably teetering between a military career and deciding he had no stomach for being an officer. I believed he knew what he should do—refuse to cooperate—but he had little to hide literally or figuratively. There was little dignity for a soldier stripped of his uniform.

"We had an assignment," he said in a voice that carried an Irish lilt. "To arrest the madam of this house and hold her 'til commander returns. When we learnt of her being not on these premises, I decided we should wait and see what we could find out. Well, biding our time and such…"

I glanced at Sally and asked the soldier, "Where is Lieutenant Cole now?"

Bradley shook his head. He said he had already given up enough information. "If you would just return us our clothes, we'll just chalk this 'ere adventure as a jolly failure of unfortunate timing, and we'll be on our way. No arrests to be had, I'll report." He attempted to smile.

"Mitchell, toss his ass out the window again." And toss him Baby Cakes did. Bradley refused at first to answer my questions even as he hung again by the rope; blood must have been rushing to his head. Baby Cakes jiggled the line for good measure so that the soldier's body would bang against the wooden wall.

"That'll put a splinter in your bum," Baby Cakes called out to him.

Eventually the lieutenant relented and admitted that he was, indeed, in Lieutenant Cole's intelligence unit. Just following orders. That's all. He pleaded for Baby Cakes to release the line and let him go now. The fall would only do so much damage from one story.

"Where is your lieutenant now?" I had to ask him three times.

"On the road. The road north. Concord. Lexington. I dunt know for certain."

I told Baby Cakes to haul him up. "Quickly."

When he was once again in the room, Sally took the pistol from Jezebel and placed the barrel beneath the soldier's chin. The poor lad shivered more from the cold than fear, but his body was scraped in several places and shriveled significantly in one.

"What is he up to? And don't stall. I don't have as much patience as my husband."

Husband?

"I dunt know. Truly I dunt. All I know is we'r supposed to come here for the arrest while he rode north to attend to some witch."

"Which witch?"

The younger soldier in the chair finally spoke up. He almost looked hopeful with his eyes wide and darting to his discarded uniform on the floor at the foot of the bed. "I heard," he began. "I heard the witch owns this place. I heard Lieutenant cursing himself into a blue streak just before he left us our orders."

My reaction? Huh.

Sally's reaction? Oh. My. God.

She had a hand to her mouth as she grabbed my elbow and dragged me from the room, slamming the door behind us in the process. "Leeds. Cole's gone after Aunt Mae. He's probably on his way to Lexington right now to harm her."

Wait. "You are saying Aunt Mae owns Flagg Alley?"

Sally looked exasperated. I was wasting time. She bounced nervously on the balls of her feet. "And the Red Bear and the Whipp Inn. She owns every one of them in Boston. With Aunt

Mae's money and social position, who would ever challenge her even if they were to suspect such a thing?"

It was clear now. "And yet, of all the secrets your little nest of strumpets uncovered, the secrets that crimp Cole's knickers the most came from Murdoch," I said. "So *she* was the one who gave you all that information. Of course. And you think he took his revenge on Murdoch…that's what upset you so."

Sally nodded. "Shut up and let's hurry. We've got to get to her before Lieutenant Cole does."

Back in the master bedroom I told Baby Cakes, and the other fellow guarding the little soldier, to lock them in the basement or one of the rooms. "Turn them over to the Sons of Liberty, for all I care," I said. "Just make sure they stay out of sight until we get back."

"What about you?" Jezebel asked. "Where are you going?"

"To warn the, uh witch," I stammered. "Or catch up with Lieutenant Cole. Whichever comes first."

"Ha. Good chance of that. You won't get far," the younger soldier scoffed. "Our boys are out full tonight. You won't get past them patrols, and then you'll be sorry, mate. You'll be sorry." He seemed to have regained his nerve, but his revelation showed his intelligence was still at muskrat rate. Mine, on the other hand, kicked into a higher plane. I grabbed the soldiers' uniform from the floor and ordered Sally to do the same. She wasn't much smaller than the little one. This might work. Belts? Hats? Right.

"You don't mean…?" Jezebel started. I shrugged as if to suggest it was the best I could do on short notice.

"It will never work," Lazy Lucy said. She sat up from where she had been lounging on the pillows of the bed, content to be a spectator for all that was playing out in the room. I looked at her and then at Sally. Even Sally looked uncertain though not unwilling. Then I stepped over to Lazy Lucy and patted her cheek and told her to close her eyes. "Don't fret," I said before quickly, and as painlessly as possible, ripping her mouse fur eyebrow from her painted face. I turned and planted it beneath Sally's nose. Instant mustache.

She touched the fur, pressing it more firm to her face while she grinned. "This had better work, Leeds, or I will never marry you."

"If this doesn't work, it's unlikely we will live long enough to reach the altar. Now quit dawdling."

Chapter Thirty-seven
The Midnight Ride

But a dawdle was frustratingly unavoidable. Or so it felt. We returned to the *BFD*, where Francis was cleaning up and preparing for a full day at the press's devil's tail tomorrow. Doctor Patterson's sermon pamphlet awaited. But wait it must. We startled Francis by arriving in uniform after soldiering up at Flagg Alley. Of the clothes we poached, mine were only a tad tight while the other jacket hung on Sally like a blanket on a rag doll. But miracles happened in the most unusual places. The military garments Sally had to wear were no match for a house full of women with an arsenal of pins and stays, clamps and ties at their disposal. They tailored the new "Ensign Hughes" to look most proper and set to ride out in no time at all.

"What the...?"

"Francis, straighten up, man, and prepare to print on the shortest of notice," I said.

I explained we were off to Lexington, a trip that I prayed would be one of warning and not rescue. Sally explained the who, what, where, and when of our mission.

"But how will we get there?" she asked of me. "How will we find Cole and how will we stop him?"

"*How* always resolves itself last." I pocketed several blank pages and a couple of sharpened graphite sticks from the top of my writing desk. From the bookcase next to it I pulled the pistol my father had bequeathed me so long ago. We had left Lieutenant Bradley's piece with Jezebel, and I wasn't about to traverse the post road unarmed. I warned Sally that if we were arrested, wearing those red coats as a disguise was the quickest way to finish our trip at the end of a hangman's rope.

She twiddled one end of the mouse fur on her upper lip. "Bloody hell it will," she said in a voice as deep as she could affect. And her attempt at a British accent was just as laughable, though neither of us had a disposition for jest at that moment.

"Best leave the talking to me," I said.

We tracked down Jacob at the Green Dragon and Sally waited outside in the shadows, watching for anyone who might raise a suspicion while I circled the taproom floor until catching Jacob's attention. It wasn't until I doffed my hat that Jacob recognized me and joined me at a table near the entrance.

"I need to steal your two horses for the evening," I told him. I explained the reason for my costume and that Sally was waiting outside similarly dressed.

"Good play," he responded. Though he was skeptical about her ability to be a convincing pipsqueak of a soldier, there could have been no quarrel over her right to make the ride. "Your dress may come in handy. Word tonight? They have increased patrols on the post road, and speculation is spreading like wildfire that the redcoats are up to something huge. I mean mother-flogging huge."

Jacob went on to say they had arrested the tanner, Mr. Taws, on the road between Boston and Medford. "They let him go after an hour or so and he came back here." Jacob pointed out the fellow who had been sitting at the table with Jacob when I arrived. "Poor slob hasn't been sober since. Our fellows say a march on Concord is everyone's best guess. But they will be greatly disappointed."

Jacob and I saddled up his two horses and convinced Blacksmith Avis Hurts to loan us a third horse for "Ensign Hughes."

"This fellow is one of Hancock's lot," Hurts said. He looked at our uniforms, wary if not downright revolted, until Jacob assured him we were good fellows doing good work. "If what you're telling me is true, Hancock won't mind. Worthy cause and all that."

We rode to the Charles River crossing where we were stalled at the ferry master's cottage. His wife said her husband had gone to convey someone to the north shore.

"A soldier, he be. Like you. Came a thunderin' in here like the whole world was endin' if'n he don't get across to Charlestown, making like yesterday would not be soon 'nuff. But me husband should've been back by now. Gots me a bit worried. Didn' like the looks of that man nohow."

By that point Sally was ready to swim across if necessary, so anxious that each delay brought out the common side of her personality. If nothing else, however, it gave her time to adjust her riding habits.

She was no stranger to the topside of a horse, but had never straddled it in britches before. "I don't understand how you men do this. It is quite uncomfortable and must be even more so for you, what with excess baggage in your pants." She swayed in the saddle, jiggled the reins to practice, and lost her balance when Nag the horse, possibly sensing her rider's insecurity, lurched in protest. Once more I found myself helping Sally to her feet from a fall to the floor.

"We have to stop meeting like this," I said.

She mounted again and paced the shoreline near the landing. Then we heard a timid bell ring in the darkness from out in the river. I responded with a bell hanging from the pylon at the landing's edge, helping guide the ferry home. Then I noticed a tall stranger coming from the cottage. He paused halfway between us and where Mrs. Rowan stood in the open doorway. The man was caught up in a moment of indecisiveness and, I believed, caution. He was silhouetted in the light from the tiny house, but seemed familiar enough that I chanced calling out to him.

"Mr. Revere?" I jogged up the slope to him and put out my hand. "Mr. Revere. It's Merriweather. Leeds Merriweather."

Then he smiled. "Of course," he said. "The newspaper man. You had me confounded for a moment there. Nice uniform. When did you enlist, Mr. Merriweather?" He asked it with good humor and I explained our mission.

"I thought this disguise might help us get past the patrols quickly, less resistance," I said, attempting to keep my growing concern at bay.

"An assassin, you say? My God. I hope you reach your destination in time. Oh! There is Mr. Rowan now. Let's be off. We both have pressing missions, I'm afraid."

Ferryman Rowan apologized for delaying us. "Bloody redcoat bastard hauled me up to the first patrol he found and left me with them soldiers. Snuck off the moment they thought I'd just sit and wait and that's how I got away."

Once we were underway, Revere explained that he, too, was on a mission to prevent mayhem. "The troops are on the move, and we now know they are preparing to take this route. We must get the word out."

We crossed as quietly as possible. A British warship was anchored downstream. Sally climbed onto Nag—a horse with not much giddy up in her gallop—when we reached the other side, and Nag made it difficult to ride with the urgency we wanted. I decided a moderate but steady pace would prevent us from wearing out the poor animal. I wish we had considered trading her for a newer edition before leaving the stable.

We were not much more than a mile out of Cambridge when we were blocked by two soldiers in the middle of the road. The next thing I knew six more redcoats had emerged from the trees to surround us. I surveyed their faces by the light of a torch one uniformed lad held, while the officer on horseback who appeared to be in charge of the patrol studied me in return. I stiffened my back and shoulders.

"Well done, gentlemen. It seems all is under control." I nodded. I disguised any hint of Americanism I may have acquired in the six years since landing in Boston, replacing it with a bit of Cockney from back in my days on the streets of London. The patrol leader was a lieutenant who, after finishing his assessment of us, relaxed and settled back into his saddle. I was thankful he did not outrank me.

"And what is your purpose?" he asked. Not threatening, not wary, he was going through the motions of being in charge. His name was Smith.

"The British are coming," I laughed. And then I explained troops were gathering on the edge of Boston as we spoke. They would be marching within the hour to deal with those damn bloody colonists in Concord. This lifted the spirits of the soldiers and they greeted this information with murmurs of approval.

"Great news."

"'Bout time."

I said we had been sent out in advance to apprise the patrols along the route to be vigilant for spies who might ride to warn the militia. "Have you seen any suspicious characters? Unusual movement?"

The patrol leader said that they had, in fact, detained a few civilians at one point or another. "We had no way to secure them for long."

"Yes, this fellow here is a spy," I said. "For us, that is. He will be useful to identify our ultimate quarry at the end of the road."

He told me there were two more units along the highway to Lexington and another one on the road west of town leading to Concord. I then knew what lay ahead. It was not comforting but didn't seem insurmountable either. Take the risk.

"Carry on," I said to the patrol.

We set out at a pace as quick as Nag the Horse would allow until we stopped at a small bridge crossing the upper Essex River. Three soldiers were squatting around a campfire near the foot of the bridge. They jumped to attention and grabbed their muskets as we approached.

I was leading Jacob with Sally as our rear guard. When the patrol saw my uniform they assembled themselves, saluting. For most of the ride since leaving Lieutenant Smith and his men outside of Cambridge, I had been formulating a response to encountering the next patrol. I had a troubling question. A sincerely necessary question, though I was not optimistic the patrol could provide an answer that would improve my mood. I made it brief.

"At ease, men," I said. There was no officer here and I took advantage of that, sitting tall above the nearest soldier. He was a chubby fellow who seemed unfit for a combat unit, and he reeked of alcohol. They all seemed a bit unsteady. This man's britches were stained, and his cap with a sergeant's hat was skewed to one side like a sloth on a tree stump. Good Lord, they will take just about anybody into the ranks these days. Almost made one ashamed to be British.

"Soldier!" I barked to pull his attention away from Jacob.

"Hadley, Sir. Sergeant Hadley."

"Yes, Hadley. Our troops are on the move and will be arriving in due time. Stay vigilant and don't let us down. We're going to handle those swines in Concord. We believe this gentleman here has some important intelligence we urgently need to convey to Lieutenant Cole. Has he been this way?"

"Yes, sir. At least I think, sir. There was a Captain..."

"Lieutenant, Sergeant," corrected one of the other grunts.

"An officer who rode through earlier," the sergeant resumed. "He stopped but didn't offer his name. We was patrolling on the other side of this bridge and he ordered us here and told us to stop anyone from crossing." He looked uneasy as if contemplating whether Cole's orders included two lesser officers and a civilian.

"Medium height, dark fellow, hair and eyes?"

"That would be him. Yes, sir."

"Yes, he is our commander," I said. As I interrogated the sergeant, one of the foot soldiers broke ranks with two timid steps forward. He looked up at Sally, studying her. She glanced down with disdain and then returned her attention straight ahead.

"Get back in formation, soldier," I barked, and the private jumped back in place. "You are standing at attention."

"Sorry, sir. The ensign's face seems familiar. I thought..."

"You thought nothing. You will think nothing," I said. He stared straight ahead but continued to dart his eyes at Sally. I was convinced that given enough time he would recall where he had seen her. *Let us speed things up, shall we?*

I could see the glow from Lexington in the distance. We were close. I prayed we were not too late. The private who had been captivated by Sally sucked in a breath. His eyes opened wide. His jaw dropped. Recognition had slapped him in the face. But before he could say anything, Jacob spurred his horse and galloped off across the bridge.

"Ensign, after him! Don't let him escape!"

It was an awkward scene, comical in most instances, as Sally and Nag the Horse were both unsteady and slow in their launch. She finally managed to coerce her mount into a lumbering, quick trot in pursuit of Jacob. I reined in my horse and then used my Voice of God that I had frequently employed on the stage in London to say, "It would be wise to sober up, Sergeant, by the time Major Colonel General Skittlepants arrives with the advance guard."

Skittlepants? Sometimes I was tickled by my creativity on the fly, but then this fool probably would not have recalled the name of his own unit's commander, so there you go.

"And I advise you to tell no one of our mission here. It is quite sensitive, and the possibility of war rests in your hands tonight, Hadley. You don't want to find them shooting at you tomorrow."

Chapter Thirty-eight
A Musket, a Madam, and Mayhem

I reached Sally and Jacob after they had paused on the lane leading to the Flowers' property, a fine two-story country house and several outbuildings. Light from the downstairs windows suggested activity, confirmed by smoke from the chimney on the parlor side even though midnight was approaching. Sally pressed us to move forward immediately, but I held back to watch. Wary.

"I just saw some movement near the door," Jacob whispered.

Wait. Yes, there it was.

"A soldier," I said. "Standing guard. Sergeant Hadley mentioned Cole had purloined a member of their patrol."

The moon was more than half full and had struggled throughout the evening to pierce the clouds that had filled the sky most of our ride. But the clouds decided to grant us favor at that moment and parted like theater curtains for an appreciative audience.

Yes, one redcoat paced near the home's entrance with rigid regimental steps. He seemed a fine, upstanding representative of his majesty's military compared to his inebriated comrades at the bridge. There might be hope for the British rank and file yet, and that scared me right down to the fungus in my toenails.

"Stay close to me, Sally," I said. "Jacob, you circle around and position yourself at that corner of the house. Now let's go be heroes."

I waited until I believed Jacob had enough time to be nearing his position, then Sally and I approached the house with quick gait. The soldier stopped pacing and raised his musket.

"Halt!"

"At ease, Private. We have an urgent message for Lieutenant Cole." I dismounted and tied my horse to the rail in front of the window. Curtains. Damned curtains prevented a view of anything inside, not even a shadow there. Sally climbed down from Nag the Horse while I stepped forward and saluted the soldier in return. "Sergeant Hadley suggested we would find you here. Lieutenant is inside, is he?"

"Yes, sir."

"Fetch him for me. Tell him that Lieutenant, uh, Smith is here with critical information about our advancing troops and urgently needs to speak with him."

"Advancing troops, sir?" Oh, how he smirked at that. Well smirk this! As Isaiah might say.

"Get to it, man," I barked and then took his musket from him. He put up a half-hearted struggle, confused and resisting at first, but then resigned to the wishes of a superior. He left the door ajar when he entered the house. Jacob used that moment to join me.

If every confrontation could have been that easy, we might have taught the world to sing in perfect harmony. No fights, no wars, less news on which to report. That might possibly create a more boring world, but I didn't have time to consider it further because the soldier returned, opening the door wide. I grabbed him by his uniform sash and tossed him to Jacob, who spun him to the ground beside a row of iris and gorse, where Sally put a foot on his chest and pointed her gun at his skull. One down.

When Cole stepped into the open doorway, I planted the butt of the musket between his eyes and sent him skidding backwards on the wooden floor of the foyer. "Nasty wound, Cole. I hope there is no infection. Take it from me. That is very likely to kill you. Or perhaps you will be one of the lucky ones and survive."

"I hope not," Sally said. She had entered behind me and Jacob pushed the private to his knees next to Cole. He tried to wipe the blood from his gash away, but I fenced with his hand using the muzzle of the rifle, and kept him from accomplishing anything.

"Merriweather," he said. A simple statement, strong but neutral. This time I allowed him to press the crook of his arm across his eyes and nose, soaking up blood as he lay prone on the floor.

Someone called out from the parlor. Jacob stood guard over the soldiers. Sally and I rushed into the salon.

"Oh!" Sally uttered.

"My!" I added.

"God!" we said in unison.

Madam Mae Flowers, her son Harold, and his wife were trussed and the room ravaged. At least Cole had the good manners to bind the old woman upright in a straight-backed chair. Harold and Maude were bound hand and foot. They were left to roll about on a floor of debris consisting of books and papers yanked from the bookcase across on the wall opposite the fireplace as well as a couple of broken shelves broken into rough shards, shredded fabrics, and kindling from the hearth, some of it in little piles.

My god, Cole had intended to torch the place.

"Oh dear. Oh dear. Oh dear. Thank god. And thank you, my good fellow," Madam Flowers cawed in her aged raven's voice. She stopped and blinked several times after Sally ran to her, gently cupped her face, and kissed her forehead. "Young man, if not for your silly mustache, you bear a striking resemblance to my niece. And your touch is as delicate as hers. No offense, sir, but you should be more manly." And then she exclaimed, "Oh. Dear, it *is* Sally. Splendid."

Setting the captives free was not as easy as knocking Cole on his keister. I was unfamiliar with the knots, most likely military in origin, and resorted to using my knife. Sally cried. Aunt Mae soothed. Harold and Maude bitched and offered to solve our problem of what to do with Cole by taking him out back, whipping him, tying him to one of the horses, and dragging him by his feet back to Boston.

"I like that plan," Jacob said.

"It sounds all very reasonable," I said. "Except that British regulars are marching toward us, most certainly up the post road."

Cole perked up. He lifted his head and looked at me from the floor of the entryway. "Are they?" He dropped his noggin with a thump and slapped the floor with one hand. "At last." He was grinning. I was tempted to kick him. We dragged him and the soldier into the parlor and settled them onto the floor against a fancy French sofa. Despite having the situation well in hand, I was anxious. Skittish. Mother-flogging buggered. What to do with our prisoners?

Sally pulled the mouse fur from her lip and twitched her nose and mouth to each side several times like someone bewitched. She coaxed Madam Flowers into retiring upstairs for the remainder of what was now the morning. Maude offered to make tea to calm everyone's nerves.

"Add some chamomile, dear," Madam said. "I need as much help as feasible to sleep after all this excitement."

We watched Sally escort her aunt up the stairs one slow step at a time while tugging at her own britches in every which manner.

"Well, Leeds. I guess we know who *won't* be wearing the pants in your house." Jacob laughed.

By the time Maude came in with a tray of tea and biscuits, I had made a decision. I didn't want to give up the numerical advantage of three against two and gave the woman an errand. "Maude, I need you to find whoever is in charge of the militia. Ask at Buckman Tavern. Just find someone, whoever can get a message to him, and describe our situation. Tell him we are sitting on a spy, and request some advice on what to do with the man. Wait until you get a reply."

It was not a large parlor, and I paced behind Jacob and Harold as they faced Cole. Behind Cole, a window—and only darkness beyond that. "What in blazes are you smiling about, you toad?"

Cole dabbed at the gash on the bridge of his nose with a kerchief. The blood had stopped oozing from the wound and Cole had a lovely trail of it drying along the left side of his nose. It disappeared in a smear around the corner of his mouth and across the bottom of his chin. He attempted to clean it away.

"You farmers are in for it now. I have been waiting for this day. If left up to me, I would start this war myself."

"It seems you will likely miss it," Jacob said, and he nudged Cole's upraised knee with his boot.

Cole shook his head. "No, I will be there. It's not a matter of whether I will escape, but how." He paused. "Of course, you could make things easier by releasing me now. Surrender. Save us all some time and effort."

"Surrender? You don't seem to grasp we have the upper hand here."

He shrugged. "It only appears so. I've been in worse situations."

"How did you manage to become such a ratbag? An officer should have some measure of principle." I posed this to Cole, though he took no offense.

He shrugged. "My nature." He had the matter-of-fact passion I had seen in the men as they waited to confront the soldiers in Salem. The passion that I had written about. And all the while, Cole glanced about measuring our resolve, measuring the distance to the window or door as if calculating an escape. Was he distracting us while he plotted?

Cole said he regretted he had not killed me in the tavern. "Missed it, by *that* much," he said as he pinched his thumb and finger together. "But I will."

Then he bragged about two express riders from Boston whom he caught carrying information to militias. I remembered the man. He had died in what we thought was a fall from his horse returning from Medford after townsfolk successfully removed supplies from the arsenal there just before British soldiers arrived.

"That was not an accident."

The other local rider simply disappeared in mid-summer. There were others.

"Like Grant, the customs agent." I stated it as fact.

"Hardly the first. Won't be the last." He sighed. "Work. Work. Work. It seems every day now there is some rogue or spy in need of being dispatched, and networks like your house of whores to be revealed. I should have burned it down months ago."

His cavalier attitude was troublesome. "And what of Clinton Murdoch?" I asked. That suspicion had stuck with me ever since Sally revealed her "woman's intuition."

He shook his head with disgust. "A fool. Sadly, too well connected to do much about it, and too close to those with information. He became expendable once General Gage arrived."

"So you….?" Jacob said.

Cole nodded. "And of course, which leads me to Mrs. Flowers, and well, that is why we are all gathered here this morning, isn't it?"

I paced between the hearth and the doorway, thinking. "You seem to have no problem revealing so much. Why?"

He said it was quite simple. "You do not have grit to kill me. You will hang. So I have done you a favor in that you will not die ignorant."

The arrogant bastard.

"Jacob, slash his throat," I said. Jacob looked at me with hopeful anticipation, hopeful that I was not joking. "Seriously?" his look said. But I shook my head. If only, I wished.

Maude returned with word that Colonel Parker had ordered us to hold the prisoners through the morning. He would decide a course of action once the British marched back to Boston.

Jacob grumbled. "I do hope they don't linger. Nothing to see here, folks. Move along."

"Mark my words. That army will be chapped to the hilt when it comes up empty in Concord," Harold said. And then he feigned hitting Cole with his poker again. For all his bravado, Cole flinched.

So we settled down for what was undoubtedly going to be a long, nervous siege in the parlor. I changed clothes, discarding the uniform disguise for my own garments left behind on my previous trip to Madam Flowers' country house.

Shortly before dawn the bell in the old belfry across the road and on the south side of the green rang out with insane urgency. British soldiers must have been within sight. I went out to the stoop at the front door while voices, some shouting and others anxious with fear, carried in the stillness of the night's last hour. They came to me across the small pasture separating us from the village green as bodies bustled in that direction. Some were running. Others, spectators or witnesses or those just curious, took a more cautious approach. Among them were women and children whose men had gone to answer the alarm. I returned to the parlor.

Everyone was standing except the private. Jacob and Harold flanked Cole, who stretched to the ceiling and rolled his neck. Getting loose. "Well, must get at it. Time to get to work."

"Sit down. Don't be insolent."

He looked at me, Jacob, and Harold. But mostly at me. "You'll have to prove first you have enough soldier in you to stop me. I don't believe you have. Trust me, this will not end here."

Cole tried to force his way past Jacob but I stopped him with a palm to his chest, hard and determined. Parker had ordered us to keep him here and I would do just that. Jacob threatened him with the bayonet, but I knew the good Christian former pastor would rather kill his inner demon than another human.

Cole and I measured each other, wondering who would strike first, and we were frozen like that when Sally stopped halfway down the stairs, leaning over the rail to speak to us through the doorway.

"What is going on? I heard alarm bells."

No one answered. And then with a yelp Sally lost her footing on the next step and tumbled down to the base of the stairway. Badda-boom. She landed with a thud and groan. I went and knelt next to her. "My dear, clumsy wench."

The next thing I knew a melee erupted behind me. Jacob's body sailed across my line of sight from behind one side of the door to the other like a wounded bird in flight. Harold cried out. And then there was Cole. Cole stepped quickly through the doorway, stopping to snatch an oil lamp from a table near the entrance. He hurled it across the room at the base of the wall, where it shattered and ignited the floor-length window dressings.

He was out the door before I could rise from my knees. Flames climbed the curtains and the oil, spilt from the lamp base, snaked with fire across the floor, across the wood chips and paper he had scattered about. Smoke filled the room.

The house was going to burn.

Chapter Thirty-nine
How to Start a War Without Really Trying (Or...Oops!)

Quick. Quick. Quick!

Jacob jumped up and tore at the curtains as the flames crawled up the fabric toward the ceiling. "Holy Lucifer in hell, that is hot." He beat the curtains against the wall and the floor, and wrestled them in a ball to extinguish the flames.

Harold took a bucket of sand from near the fireplace and doused the fire that licked the base of one wall, while Sally rushed in from the kitchen with another to snuff the flames that were spreading from a pile of debris on the floor.

I took the soldier's jacket from the uniform I had left on a chair near the entrance, chased flames across the room that jumped from pile to pile, and beat back the remainder of the fire.

Frankly I doubted the citizens' protection committee could have done as fine a job of handling this emergency. If the *Boston Free Dispatch* failed, we might have had a future in firefighting.

We all collapsed in our own way when the threat was gone, each of us wiping away smudges of ash and soot, coughing and wheezing.

"Now what?" Sally asked.

"Oh, I suppose we shall all be hanged," Jacob said. "Lieutenant Cole will insist once he gets back to his command."

"There you go," I said. "All I've ever wanted was a good story to tell and a newspaper to print it. This is a hell of a story. Maybe Francis will pen a wonderful obituary for us in the final *Dispatch* edition."

Yet, one did not get to be an astute journalist without being a good judge of character. Cole had the arrogance and lust for vengeance that kept me thinking he would not let this drop without putting his personal stamp on the end of our story. No, he would be waiting in the shadows for closure. I was willing to bet my life on it. And I did.

"Do you hear that?" A roar came from the village green. Mixed sounds punctuated by breaks of silence.

"I am out of here," I said.

I took my pistol, checked the powder and ball, hoping I would not need it, and left without another word. I looked in the barn behind the house, and the surrounding grounds facing the green a short distance down a slope, and beyond small homes on the frontage road. I looked into the sheds and behind the bushes. Maybe Cole had made a full escape. In that case, returning to Boston was not going to happen.

I stopped at the edge of one house along the frontage road. Good god. The village stable and Buckman tavern stood on the road to my left. Across the road soldiers had formed three lines in attack formation on the east side of the green. To my right, fifty or so American militia held their ground, although with less precision and I suspect a wavering heart.

"Don't do this," I whispered to the tension that permeated the situation.

The two sides exchanged taunts and whoops. Spectators stood in small clusters at various points, most in front of the tavern, while others took up positions at the corners of the triangular village commons. Dangerously close but not any direct line of fire. Idiots. Fearful for the lives of their loved ones and willing to risk their own safety. Pleading for peace. *Don't do this.*

Just then Cole appeared from the opposite side of the house and approached until he was in the middle of the yard between the house and the green twenty yards or so from me. His face, and particularly his uniform, were nearly unrecognizable, muddied as if he had stumbled through a deep horse-dung puddle. But he tugged at the skirt of his jacket and marched at me like a man who would take no prisoners. A low hedge along the edge of the road stood between us and the armed militia, the British Army, and chaos in the making.

"So, Merriweather, is it to end here? He raised a pistol and aimed at me. I raised mine. I had been here before but my hand quivered slightly nonetheless. Visions. Visions of facing an expert marksman in a duel in a countryside clearing outside of London. I survived. He did not. Though it was not my hand that pulled the trigger leading to his death and my flight from the law. It brought me to America and this moment. Just as my nemesis that day so long ago had been supremely confident, so too was Cole. He must have been convinced that I would not initiate an exchange of gunfire. He glanced over his shoulder at the militiamen.

"Fucking cowards!" he shouted.

Indeed, it seemed Colonel Parker had relented and ordered the Americans to stand down. Some remained there defiant while others lowered their muskets, dragging them as they walked into the arms of their sobbing wives, mothers, and fathers, even a few children who were too young to understand the importance of the moment.

"You see?" Cole returned his attention to me. "You have no spine amongst you." The battle on the green was over before it began. The only battle that remained was between Cole and myself. This time it was Cole who chose to stand down and lower his weapon.

"So is this where it ends?" I mocked him with his own question. I did not lower my gun but kept it trained on his chest, though I knew there was no heart inside. He pointed to his troops in formation.

"Perhaps we live today to fight another day. Though the sooner the better." With that he turned, stepping toward soldiers that had formed a line in the road along the green. Although his retreat closed the distance slightly between us at an angle, I relaxed. Now I lowered my weapon, whereby Cole turned swiftly and fired. To this day I swear I heard the shot as it whizzed past.

Cole stood there, seemingly amazed that he had missed his mark again, and now stared down the muzzle of my weapon. I had no time to fire because suddenly the air cracked and filled with the sound of gunfire. Volleys of musket shots and volleys of screams added to the pandemonium. Smoke became a fog over the grounds. Commanders rode their stallions around and between lines of the formation shouting at their troops, with contradicting orders countermanding each other.

"Shoot, goddamn it!"

"Hold your fire! Stop. Stop firing!"

"Second line, ready up. Fire at will!"

Some Americans returned fire as they disbanded. Some ran. The first line of grenadiers attacked with bayonets and pounced upon the undermanned militia. Many of them who had defiantly dawdled instead of leaving the area peacefully now fell to the ground, splattered with blood and mud.

I stood mesmerized by the sights and sounds that began so quickly and so forcefully while Cole seized the opportunity of my confusion. He turned and ran down the road to his mates. The sun had not yet reached the sky. The air was thick with smoke from musket fire and visibility was poor, but I could see him shouting and pointing as he raced toward them, and he raised his hand, waving his pistol in the process. The soldiers finally ceased their fire but not before one final shot from the right flank of the regiment dropped Lieutenant Cole in his tracks as a hunter might kill a charging elk.

Oops.

Even so, it took the bloody bastard three more days to die.

Chapter Forty
'Til Death Do Us Part

In the year that followed, both sides denied firing the first shot. The newspapers accused the opposition of instigating the conflict with that shot based only on where their own sympathies lay. Whigs blamed the army. Tories blamed rebels. I avoided the subject in my reporting for *The Dispatch*. I had no desire at the time to publicize my part in starting the long conflict, the death, the misery, even the eventual vindication that followed from the exchange of gunfire that morning in Lexington.

Some might argue all war is personal on some level. This was a personal vendetta gone terribly wrong, and I knew the first shot was one fired in anger and that I was its target. It had nothing to do with rebellion, but it changed the world. I could see that now.

Soldiers carried Cole to Buckman Tavern when they realized his identity and set up a cot in the ell of the building. A company of grenadiers surrounded the tavern while the commander of that unit issued orders while hunkered inside. The army waited for a wave of reinforcement before heading out to Concord, leaving the colonists to drag their dead and wounded husbands and brothers to the nearest homes. Eight American colonists died that morning. The army positioned soldiers on the main roads east to protect its rear and prevent Lexington's militia and this reporter from following them to Concord. Sally joined the women who tended to the wounded, getting them into the nearest homes and inns. Jacob tended to their spiritual needs, blessed the bodies of those who had died, and comforted the grieving families.

Me? As black a day as any I had experienced, and yet I had to record what I had seen. I couldn't stop myself if I had wanted. This was a day that would live in infamy. I scribbled notes on scraps of paper that I stuffed into my pockets once they were filled. I questioned those who had witnessed the affair. I questioned those who had survived the gunfire. I tried to interview John Muzzey, who had been standing next to his brother when Isaac Muzzey was killed by musket fire.

"You lost your brother this morning. I am sorry for your loss. Can I ask you some questions?"

He answered me with his fist, punching me so hard I fell backwards and bashed my head against a stone. It drew blood. I deserved that. I lay on the ground and watched the gray clouds swirl across the sky as if they were frowning down upon me. Frowning on us all. The universe was not happy and I wondered if I would ever learn how to avoid crossing that fine line between seeking what the reading public needs to know and stomping on their grief for no other purpose than to satisfy the public's morbid curiosity. Would any journalist? I hoped perhaps someday. I suspected not.

Certainly not that day. I had a war to cover.

Perhaps I might one day create a word to capture the chaos beyond chaos that followed the lull through the noon hour and morning became afternoon. The lull was like a tide that pulls back from the shore innocently enough only to gather all its strength just beyond sight to come crashing back with a vengeance only nature can muster.

I sat on a rock near the triangle of roads west of town. The hill provided a decent view while I sharpened the tip of a graphite stick. What should I write next? I could see the road on the opposite side that spilled into town behind the meeting hall; more soldiers were arriving. Why so many? There must have been a thousand in addition to the troops that had marched on Concord. It wasn't long before a rider galloped down the highway from the opposite direction. Citizens began reemerging from their homes. And then I heard the drums from where the rider had come.

Rat-ta-tat and a rumble tat. It was the beat I'd heard in Salem when the army had confronted an overwhelming show of force from colonists.

Retreat.

A column appeared from behind the rise in the road moving quickly. Officers on horseback led other officers on foot who were leading soldiers quickstepping in a formation that was far from the disciplined procession and superior attitude with which they left Lexington. This was a ragtag group. They had their rifles raised, looking for targets on the higher ground to their left and right. Then came soldiers limping and hurt with soldiers propping up their mates as they struggled to keep pace with the advance company. Then came open wagons. Several passed within a stone's throw below me, and I could see bodies, five or six soldiers writhing in pain or lifeless in the carts. I was watching death in that retreat.

"Son of a mother flogging wretch."

Whatever had taken place in Concord diminished the holy mess we had endured that morning in Lexington. The Americans had fought back. They had drawn blood. The company of soldiers retreating from Concord flooded into the village green and joined up with the reinforcements. It was a confused mass of redcoats. Who was in charge? What were the orders? What to do now?

And then the worst thing happened. It started slowly at the house nearest Buckman Tavern and then spread, consuming each house within easy reach, circling the green. The soldiers began plundering the homes and lighting fires. Most residents in the homes nearest the fighting had evacuated to a safer distance when the bell in the old Belfry warned of the approach of the reinforcements.

There was no discipline. Soldiers kicked down doors and fired shots indiscriminately into the homes. Fire shattered the windows of one home, and the flames consumed its walls in little time at all.

I raced back to Madam Flowers' estate, circling behind the rampage and nearly taking a musket ball from a filthy wretch of a soldier I had interrupted slaughtering pigs in a pen behind the Harrington house.

"Thank god, Leeds," Harold said when I reached the gate to the property. Harold and his son had taken up rifles and positioned themselves along the fence, staring down the slope to the town center.

"Is everyone all right?"

"Inside. Sally has returned. Mother, Maude, and the maid are prepared to flee in case those bastards head up the road. Our stable hand is rigging a wagon out back."

"Sing out if you spot movement in our direction," I said.

Sally leapt into my arms, her eyes aglow. "Leeds, oh my Leeds." She kissed me and then gave me a playful slap. Even the gravity of the day could not quash her spirit, though I suspect her lightness of being was not entirely honest. She said, "I was so worried when you disappeared. I shall never forgive you if you get yourself killed."

"It would ruin my day as well."

She explained that Aunt Mae had supervised the collection of everything of value. They were finishing the last trunk and placing it in a wagon behind the house. I pulled her to the front window, where we could watch the disorder unfolding below.

"We will pay mightily for this," she said.

Jacob joined us within the hour as it appeared the army had done its damage and started back to Boston.

"Concord was a rout if you can believe some of the reports," he said. "One rider tells of hundreds of soldiers killed against a handful of casualties on our side. I'm not saying I believe it

fully, but make no mistake—we fought and we won the day."
He had heard militias from as far away as Woburn took on
the British regulars near a bridge on the edge of town. "And
they hounded them with shot for most of the march back here,
killing more."

We crowded at the window, shoulder to shoulder, and I
tapped on the glass. "They are trying to hold their heads up,
but look, it isn't easy for them. They are an army on the run."

I waited for a pound, an ounce, or even a dash of guilt,
guilt for rooting against the army of my birth.

Nothing. I was spot-on American now with no hint of
reluctance.

I hustled to the kitchen looking to fill a pack with food. I
had no time for a meal. Maybe some rags in the unlikely event
I needed to patch a wound or two. A canteen of water.

"Maude, have your man get my horse ready."

"But Leeds…," Sally said.

"Only a fool would think Captain Parker and whoever com-
mands the other units would let the army escape unmolested. If
I hurry, I can skirt around them. I want to be in Boston when
they arrive. Where did you put that other pistol?"

"*If* they arrive," Jacob said.

Sally shook her head. "It's too dangerous. They'll see
you coming and I don't think they are in any mood to take
prisoners."

"I will take care. But we will never see a moment like this
again." I took a moment to gather my words and looked deep
into her eyes. "Some are born to make history. I was born to

record it." I tickled the tip of her nose. "Holy putrid prose. That is some serious kind of trite, don't you think? Write it down and stash it away somewhere. Some historian someday will find it and think me an eloquent genius like Adams or that fellow from Virginia—Jefferson Somebody is his name, if I recall."

"Promise me," she said. "Promise me you will not attempt to make history. Watch it and write about it, but do it from a safe distance. Please?"

"I will if you do me one tiny favor in exchange. A small thing, really."

Sally looked at me with a twinkle in her eye. Lord, the woman could read me like a book. A children's primer at that. I looked at Jacob and he simply said, "Awwwww."

No more than ten minutes later Sally and I stood at the foot of the staircase where it curved back into the foyer facing the parlor. Aunt Mae and her son Harold flanked us. Jacob stood on the first step with a Bible in his hand. The Good Book was only to make the marriage official. He stumbled through the vows.

He looked at me. "Do you…?"

"Yes. Yes. Of course. Love and honor. Let's speed this along, shall we?"

Jacob shrugged. All right, then. He turned to Sally.

She nodded. "'Till do us part."

Jacob plowed ahead. "With this ring as a symbol of ever-lasting union…"

Ring? Wait. We'd skipped the ring thing.

"Oh. We can't have a marriage without a ring," Jacob said.

Aunt Mae to the rescue. She produced an elegant and a bit overstated ring that she had been clutching in her folded hands. She smiled broadly. "I had been saving this for my next marriage. I hope it brings you good fortune and happiness."

"By the power vested in me by George, His Royal Highness, King of England and the Massachusetts Bay Colony America, I pronounce you man and wife."

We kissed with tenderness that is of such sweet devotion that it, too, should have a place in history.

"I love you, Mister Printer." She exhaled.

"I love you, Missus Printer."

"Okay. Love is all around us," Jacob said. "Vows exchanged? Check. Ring? Check. Kissing of the bride? Tying of the knot? Check like no other. Now, husband, I suggest you put your ass in the saddle and ride."

Without another word, I scooped up my hat and left them with a smile. I put two pistols into the holsters on my saddle and rode hard to the village. With a hard ride and good fortune, I could catch up to the army in Cambridge before it finished crossing the Charles River.

But first I had one more stop to make.

Chapter Forty-one
Life, Liberty, and Pursuit of a Honeymoon

The soldiers had cleared out. There was no one to stop me at the door of Buckman Tavern. Cole lay on a cot in the corner behind several other men who were being nursed by their women and a Doctor Prescott. Two men lifted from a table one of the wounded the doctor had patched. Lucky to be alive. They put him on a stretcher and carried him home. I made my way to the corner.

"He isn't going to make it," Prescott said when he joined me. I could see in his face it was no great loss to his way of thinking. "An army doctor dressed his wound before the retreat. That is as much as we can do."

"Merriweather," Cole coughed. I had thought him unconscious but he cocked his head and looked up at us. He grimaced but did not groan. "Come to see me off?"

I really wasn't sure why I felt compelled to see him. Perhaps a need to settle in my own mind all that had happened between us.

"Have you heard the news? Oh, but of course you have. That is your stock in trade, isn't it? The war has finally begun."

The emptiness of my heart prevented me from offering a response. I wished I could pity the fellow, but neither could I find anger. This man had tried to kill me. I stood silent.

"So now we know. This is how it ends," he said. It was obvious that pained him greatly. I turned to go.

"Merriweather. Print my obituary. Let it be said I was loyal. That is enough."

I searched out tavern owner John Buckman and gave him the entire contents of my purse. "See that the soldier gets a proper burial in the cemetery. Headstone and all."

"Why would I do that?"

Because this death was personal? It had a face. It breathed the same air as I. It could well have been me. Because… "So that no one will forget they are human too," was all I said.

The Boston Road was a trail of evidence, signs of battle. The ride was slower than I had anticipated because I could not ignore the details I witnessed. Twice I happened upon wounded militiamen who were returning to Lexington, having given up the chase for want of strength and gunpowder. They described how they used the woods and rock walls, or an occasional building, to harass the British when the terrain was favorable for ambush. They were full of pride and no small amount of confidence. I made more notes on the remaining scraps of paper I carried.

"I jes knew we'd show those johnnies," one told me. He described the battle from whence he came. "Gave 'em what for. Now they got dead bodies out in the trees they ain't comin' back for. We let 'em have it full, we did."

"Sent 'em runnin'," a man named Corday bragged two bends and a bridge farther down the road after I had asked him of his experience.

Regardless of the amount of joy—yes, that was the word for it—in the mood of those I came across on the road, it was a victory for the farmers and small-town mechanics who had dared take on the greatest military in the world. It was infectious even if I suspected it might be fleeting. I was still talking with Corday when Sally and Jacob galloped up. We stayed to let the horses drink from the stream.

"No use in riding hard now," I told them. "We will never beat them across the river."

"It will be dark soon," Sally said.

"I have a wife to see," Jacob added.

"I doubt she missed you, Jacob my fellow. You are so seldom at home in the best of times."

"Yes, well, as nauseating as it has been, watching the two of you has me thinking I might amend my social habits. A small amount, certainly, but change starts somewhere."

For the next two miles I talked of Cole, his impending burial, and the stories I had collected on the ride, and I mused on the various approaches I might use to inform the public. After that?

"I don't know, exactly."

We rode through Cambridge, where people scurried and mucked about with all the excitement and none of the purpose one might experience after having an army march through your town twice in so many days. Two armies, actually. One going out confident and organized, and one coming in dragging and humiliated. Rumors flew about on every street corner. Victory. There was no mourning to be found. Cheering and song surged in waves from an inn where two main roads intersected.

Jacob said he knew of an excellent vantage point just outside of town, and we followed him along a gently sloping trail to a peak overlooking miles to either side of us and the spread of Boston ahead with more lights twinkling, more torches flickering, than stars above us. A dozen or so armed Americans had also taken up position on the hill under torchlight to watch as the last of the troops boarded longboats leaving Charlestown to our left. Was it truly a mere twenty-four hours ago that we had ferried across that point in this direction under the cover of disguise and darkness? It had been a full day of rescuing a household, capturing assassins, and starting a war. I was exhausted.

We settled down on a small, flat patch, using my coat as a picnic blanket on which we sat and ate the rations I had carried from Aunt Mae's kitchen. We talked softly, contemplating the future.

"Now what?" Sally asked.

"Well, this will be the start of something exceptional," I replied. "That much is assured."

"It will either end well or be a complete cluster-flog," Jacob said.

One thing was certain. Unless the gods above stepped in soon to make peace, the thing I feared most a year earlier was now our future. It would disrupt everything. Oh, not for just me, of course. War is a brutal sentence of turmoil for everyone. I had wanted peace, but now that the hope was gone I squeezed Sally's hand. "Looks like we'll have to take on those bastards together."

"This is the right thing for us all. I'm convinced of that."

"It won't be even a smidge easy," Jacob said. "There are going to be a few idiots who look at what happened today, like those fellows you talked to back there, who'll say otherwise."

After another long break of silence, I said, "Then we have a job to do. Possibly more important than ever." I smiled. As best as I could read their faces, they didn't quite follow my logic. "I am having a moment of clarity. Not really extraordinary yet, but I think front page worthy. If we truly are to go to war then our newspaper, our pamphlets, our words will be critical to buck up morale when things do turn dark."

"To rally support," Sally said.

"To justify sacrifice. To convince anyone who will read our words that what we have to lose together is much more than any individual hardship to be endured. I once expected to write the ultimate pamphlet calling for peace. Not going to happen. There is no middle ground in the middle of a war, not even in print."

Jacob stood. "I need a drink." He went to his horse and came back with a bottle of wine. "You're not alone in bringing provisions," he chuckled. "Sorry, I didn't have room for glasses. Have a slug."

"Ladies first," I said.

Sally took a swig.

"Stolen from Aunt Mae's. I don't think she'll mind."

We passed the bottle. Then Sally shocked us. "Not as much as she would have minded losing all that gunpowder and ball she paid for."

"Aunt Mae financed the militia's armory in Concord?"

"Aunt Mae has been buying and storing supplies for them for several years now. She predicted this. Oh, and you can't imagine what a cannon cost. Oh my. She would have been royally displeased if the Redcoats had gotten their hands on that."

Flog the frog, you could have knocked me over with a toad-stool. I had stumbled into a nest of rebellious women masquerading as prim and proper socialites. Who would have thought that possible?

"I never realized owning a bordello in Boston could be so lucrative." I laughed. Sally took another sip from the bottle and then held up seven fingers.

"Seven? Seven houses?"

She nodded. "All three in Boston. One in New Haven, one in Philadelphia. Two in New York where the Tories like to play."

Jacob grabbed the bottle from her and took a long, hard draw. He shook his head, mostly to clear the thoughts that had gathered there. "Isn't that a kick in the head?"

A cheer arose from the riverbank below and from volunteers behind us on the peak of our hill. We could see that the last of the British longboats had begun its journey across the river under the watchful eye of a warship at anchor near the mouth of the bay. All I could do was shake my head, amazed. From the frightful calamity of the morning to the revelations Sally had shared, what could possibly eclipse this day?

"So, Leeds," Jacob said. "It sounds as if you have given up completely on that majestic pamphlet to bring about peace you had your heart set on."

"And it would have made him famous, too," Sally added. "Don't fret, Mr. Printer. There are millions of words out there at your disposal. Maybe if you pick the right ones you could publish something inspirational for the cause instead. I'm sure something will catch your fancy."

Let them laugh!

Jacob tossed the empty wine bottle aside. "Adventure. Love. That's what it's all about. You certainly have had more than your share if you ask me. If not that, then for what did you come all this way to America?"

I thought about it. "I came for the opportunity to have a nice, normal, stable life. One with the freedom to come and go as I please, create my dream publishing business. To be happy. That's what I came for."

"Isn't that what we all want?"

"Truth, for certain. I'd say it's pretty evident God wants that for us."

Sally said, "I think that is our right. Maybe that's what we're fighting for, wouldn't you agree?"

And then she rolled over and wrestled me flat, tickling and kissing me.

"Well, Mrs. Printer, you picked an awkward time to get frisky."

She sat up again, this time on her knees. She handed me the graphite stick she had stolen from my pocket. "You should write that down. It may be useful someday."

It wasn't half bad as it emerged from the word salad in my noggin. "Sally, you amaze me. A strumpet, a spy, and now a pickpocket. Is there no end to your talents?"

"You haven't seen the best of me yet. This is our wedding night, is it not?"

"Whoa. I believe that is my cue to leave you two alone," Jacob said. Near the point we had left the horses, he crossed paths with one of the volunteers as they began drifting away. Jacob borrowed a small torch the man had been carrying and brought it to us. He handed it to Sally.

She held the torch over us while I sat and mused over a blank scrap on my knee. Let's see, what were we saying? Oh, yes. Our rights. I wrote them down as I remembered.

"This, I know, is self-evident," I said as I wrote. "We are all created equal and God has given us unalienable rights to...uhm, what? To Life. Liberty... And to every opportunity to chase that which would make us happy," I finished with a flourish.

I glanced at Sally, seeking approval. That's not what I got.

I crumpled the paper into a small ball and tossed it out into the darkness toward town.

"All right, then. It needs work. Just not tonight."

If you enjoyed *The Printer and The Strumpet* and wonder how we got here, read on. Here is a sample from the start of *The Patterer,* the first book of the Misadventures of Leeds Merriweather Trilogy:

Chapter One

London-1765.

Blood and lust make the world go 'round, I say. You may argue that it is money—the pound or the pence, the farthing, the shilling, the crown, gold or silver—that makes it spin. God knows money is good. I will tell you straight away, I have personally found it quite handy when bartering for a wench or wine in those rare exquisite moments of self-indulgence. But if you believe that, you'd be as wrong as tits on a bull.

Ladies, forgive me. A crude turn of phrase, that. Men, you expect it. But I will, for the ladies' sake, attempt to rein in the crudeosity of my tale. It won't be easy what with britches dropping nearly as often as your jaw. What I offer is a tawdry tale of bullets flying and death-defying antics—but also a tale of love. Man on woman. Man on man. Camel on...well, let's have none of that here, shall we?

Mostly, this is a story about oral stimulation.

Wait! Don't run. No need to even blush. It's not at all what you imagine. Although your imagination did just have a go with you, now didn't it? Cheeky devils. Yes, you are my kind of crowd, and you have proven my point. Blood and lust make the world go 'round. Repeat it with me. That, in fact, is my world. And I offer it for sale to you. Got two pence and a halfpenny? Then step up even closer, and let's have at it. You see, I am a patterer. At your service.

That is my exceptional skill. It is also my curse, as you will surely see.

Now the first rule of a good patterer is to begin with the most titillating, scandalous or horrific story you can find. Flesh it out whenever possible with references to bodily fluids, and never, *never* let facts get in the way.

Actually, I have a saying, which I made up, entirely original, though you may steal it if you wish: "If it bleeds, it..."

"Leeds!"

That's me. Leeds Merriweather. The roar of my name as it rolled like thunder through the printer's shop yanked me rudely from a deep and dreamless sleep. A bellow this loud and spitting anger could have awakened Shakespeare himself. And this just in: Shakespeare is still dead.

"Leeds Merriweather, you lazy son of a raging git! The ink's dry an'a day's a-wasting."

Charles McNabb owned the dusty print shop where this story begins. He added an exclamation point to his roar with a kick to my ribs. I squinted up at him from the corner of the pressroom where

I had curled up for the night with a soft pillow and a hard floor. It seemed as if I had only just closed my eyes before being subjected to the indignity of McNabb's boot. I know for a fact that it was nearly dawn when, like a weary tomcat, I padded in and settled down with a snout full of gin and a head full of stories I had collected from a long night patronizing the public houses along lower Fleet Street.

"If'n you're not going to sell for me today, it'd be certain I have plenty like you who will," McNabb said. He carried a bundle of the day's edition of his broadsheet, the *London Tattler-Tribune*.

"Aw. Go easy if you please, sir," I said. My ribs where McNabb's boot struck ached, but, oh, how my head throbbed even more. February had just given way to March, and the light from the window danced with particles of dust creating a veil of sorts before my eyes. I sniffed. Oil and ink, parchment and stain. The aroma of the printing press, of literature freshly baked. And turpentine. I love the smell of turpentine in the morning.

McNabb slapped the back of his hand on the broadsheets. "Cannibalism," he cried. "Adultery and ravishing of maidens."

I love the ravishing of maidens. It sells newspapers.

The publisher was a short Scot with a gunpowder temperament, and that morning something put a spark to his britches. "'Tis death on the high seas. By God, I am good."

I asked, "Good for what?"

He aimed his next kick at my privates; I raised a knee just in time. "Don't you be insolent, y'ragged lump of gutter waste. If this story d'nnot draw a decent income today then we have no business doing business in this business."

I used the brick wall behind me as a brace for my back as I inched up—slowly, very, *very* slowly—to a standing position. War drums were beating in my noggin, and the battle for a clear head was most definitely in doubt. Too much gin last night, for certain. I took the broadsheet McNabb forced upon me and glanced over the all-important lead story beneath the *Tattler-Tribune* banner.

Spank me senseless! "Lord Thurston's shipwreck? What the bloody hell is this?" I demanded.

"A fine bit of writing, if I say so myself."

"A fine bit thievery, I say." That weasel McNabb had attached his name to the story—*my story!* I was the one who mined the details of the shipwreck over a bottle of rum from a Portuguese captain whose ship happened upon an uncharted island. The crew was taking on fresh water when they discovered what was left of a tourist yacht in the lagoon and the remains of the rich nobleman, his wife, and the others who perished with him.

"What is this dung you've printed here? What happened to what I wrote?" I wanted to rip that newspaper and wave the tatters in McNabb's ferret face. I had only turned the details over to McNabb on the promise that I could print and sell the story under my name. All I had to do was raise a couple of quid to cover the cost of printing. All the right elements of a great story were there, not the least of which was potential for profit. McNabb understood that. He held out his palm, and the way he rubbed two fingers against this thumb said it all: Show me the money.

I shook my head. "Soon."

"And what of yesterday's sales? D'ya drink it all away as usual last night?"

"'Course not," I lied. Yes, I was penniless again. Even McNabb could read that much in my bloodshot eyes.

"It is a fine story, lad, and I couldn't let it waste away a-waiting for you." That bugger, McNabb, knew a golden story when he saw one.

All they found were the bones of the good Lord Thurston and those six who were shipwrecked with him. The evidence of the extreme hedonistic life they lived and left behind created a tale so repulsive and so enchanting in one, that it was sure to shock and awe and produce profits. More important, this was a story to be told and re-told and remembered for generations. And it was mine to tell first.

"Lad, 'tis a sin to give stock to such profound pride. Be prudent," McNabb said. "You're a better man for surrendering it to me, and the story is better for it; that is my duty as editor. Now run. Run and patter. Patter and run, whichever it is that you do." He waved me off, dismissing me as one might shoo a cat from the supper table.

"Leave the wordsmithing to McNabb," he said. "You have every chance to patter your version on the street. You have a handsome face, a strong voice and straight teeth. You were made to patter, not to publish. That is your proper lot in life. Accept it."

I looked down at McNabb. He was barely as tall as my shoulder. My left hand clenched, balling up a corner of the *Tattler-Tribune* I held. I snapped at him. "This was mine. You said it was a story beneath you."

"She rose to the occasion," he said with a smirk. McNabb handed the broadsheets to me. "Do you want them or shall I find another patterer today?"

I moved to the window and bent at the waist enough to peek at the sky above the roofs of Fleet Street. The clouds were grey but not dismal. More distressing was the odor of the fish market carried on the wind. Whitefish today, and not a fresh catch apparently. Strong enough and blowing up from Billingsgate Wharf, the wind would invariably carry my voice away from the crowds I hoped to capture. Bloody hell it was, this would be a difficult day.

I turned to face McNabb, took one of the broadsheets from the bundle and waved the front page at him, not ready to back down from this duel. "You agreed I could rent your press to print my own."

He laughed, "What? You have no money and c'nnot afford it, you foul-breath alley dog. Be intelligent for once. Why should I allow you to compete with me? 'Twould be like lettin' you shag me wife and offer you me own bed for the purpose. I may be a Scot, but I'm not insane, man."

I took a step toward him, and then sharply veered right, to the large typesetting table in the pressroom. To my left, near the front door, a wall of books, pamphlets and assorted printed pages for sale stood behind the counter where McNabb serviced his customers. Everything for the literate gentleman, from pens and ink to writing paper and wax seals, sat on display across the counter itself. At the back of the pressroom, McNabb's assistants, Simon and Garfinkle, were preparing the printing press for another go and pretending to ignore our battle of wills and ink-stained egos.

Pacing back to McNabb, I considered my limited options. No respect, I say. Some day, I knew, I would have my own press and see my words, my ideas in print instead of being cast on the wind as they were now. Even on a calm day words disappeared within the moment at each street corner where I stopped. No one respects the patterer, but put your story in print? That, my friends, is a whole 'nother kettle of carp.

Change would come, of that I was certain. But until then there were meals to be purchased and rent money to be paid. Both, sadly, had been hard to acquire of late, and dodging my landlord who selfishly insisted on being paid for overdue rent had become a daily game.

"How is your head this morning?" McNabb asked, as if the matter was settled and forgotten. "And your rhyme? How will you pitch this?"

"My head? As right as ever. My rhyme? Far too splendid for the drivel you have written here," I said.

"Leeds, 'tis that attitude that makes you so difficult. If I want a bit of criticism I have only to spend more time with my wife. Show some conviction, man. And be positively positive in your expression. Be cheerful, even. Fer no mon wants to buy death from a grump."

He was right, of course. In pattering, proper disposition is nearly as important as a winning smile and the tale's details. I admitted to McNabb as much, and it placated him. So, I handed him the one copy I had waved in his face a moment earlier and stepped next to the window. I counted only those papers in my hand. "Three and twenty papers," I said. "That is two pence, half-penny short of three shilling in total."

He shook his head. "No, lad, the count is twenty-four."

"But Mr. McNabb, see for yourself."

I handed him the bundle of papers in my hand and, in return, took the single broadsheet he was holding. I rolled it cylindrical and tapped it like a baton on the palm of my left hand while McNabb counted the papers.

"I am sure I printed out exactly four over twenty," he said. He looked at the table in the center of the room. He looked to his left and to his right, clearly confused. He counted again as if he could perform the Lord's own fish-and-loaves miracle to increase it by at least one, but the stack in his hand had not changed.

Then I pointed my rolled newspaper to the printing press. McNabb's eyes followed the sweeping motion of my paper pointer. "Is it possible you left the final print on the press?" I asked. I took the bundle of broadsheets from him, and while he stumped to the press in the back of his shop I unfurled and added the sheet in my hand to the others.

"No, 'tis not here."

With a shrug I placed the newspapers in my satchel where I still had six as-yet unsold copies of *The London Gentleman's Magazine* and three books I had purchased at discount from Mr. Hawke, the bookseller six doors down. I slung the satchel's long leather strap over my head, collected my hat and turned for the door. "Well," I said, "If by chance the missing copy appears, do send it my way. I should have made three; maybe four stops by then, and will most certainly reach the Monument within three hours. I'm certain that with a story so compelling and cleverly written as this, I should be sold out in no time at all. Possibly before I reach London Bridge."

Mr. McNabb accepted that as certain fact and grinned. "Do your job, and my words will do theirs." Then he demanded payment for the twenty-three *Tattler-Tribunes* he could account for. I sheepishly shook my head.

"I c'nnot go on giving you papers on credit, lad. Why can't you pay on the front end like the other patterers? 'Tis no way to run a business."

"You tell me; you're the Scot. And don't I always make good? I am the best patterer you've had, Mr. McNabb. No one sells your trash like me."

"I'm not so very certain of that, me boy. On the soul of my sainted muther I say n'more credit. This is the last time."

"That is precisely what you said last time." I smiled. I was starting out my day with a one-paper profit. And with that extra two pence I could afford a full meal that evening. It would be my first of the week.

With a gulp of the thick London air and a sip of thin potato gin from the flask in my pocket to steady myself, I began my march across uneven cobblestones toward my first stop, a busy corner at Cheapside.

"Hummm." I drew out the sound like a monk's chant to test my vocals. I would need them proper today. The tone sounded strong enough; it carried a depth, timbre, and a bear-like resonance that comes only after a fair night of drinking. Some say London gin will put hair on your chest. I say it'll put baritone balls in your voice. At least for me, more than three nips and I sound like God on high, Himself. With what I could remember of the previous evening's rounds, I was bound to be thrice as strong that day.

I will tell you, I do not fancy the overuse of rhyme in pattering as so many of my compatriots do these days. But this was a story so full of twists, and characters uncommon in London, that it demanded just such a fine, Merriweather touch. A wretchedly wealthy, shipwrecked aristocrat, his wife and his five fellow castaways, ("fellows" being a relative description; two were lusty females—harlots, I was happy to note), left to fend for themselves on an island.

I began shouting more than twenty paces before reaching the corner. Drama on the high seas! Cannibalism! Lust on the high seas! Lusty cannibalism! Come hear me out, I have details!

A crowd formed around me like the first innocent swell of high tide when I stopped across from Cheapside. I stepped on a small platform I built there and paused. I looked over the faces before me and let tension and their expectations of entertainment build. I held up a copy of the *Tattler-Tribune* and directed their attention to first the masthead, and then the story of Lord Thurston and the plight of all those aboard his yacht the *Minnow*.

"Step right up, and come hear a tale.

"A tale of a fateful trip." My voice was strong. More passers-by paused to listen.

"It started in a distant port—aboard a tiny ship."

I told them of the first mate and the captain who was brave.

"And sure, they set sail that day for what was to be a three-hour tour."

"A three-hour tour?" a woman asked, wide-eyed.

Indeed. "A three-hour tour."

Keep up to date with the latest fiction from the Brill Creative Industrial Complex with our newsletter full of fun musings, excerpts of coming attractions, and freebies.

http://larrybrill.com

And if you want to support this funny, feel-good fiction, you can purchase any of our novels at Amazon, Barnes & Noble, IndieBound, and Bookshop

About the author

Larry Brill grew up with three life goals in mind. First, to have a career as a journalist. Second, to write an award-winning novel. And last, to pitch for the San Francisco Giants. He never got past little league due to trouble mastering the curveball, but two out of three ain't bad. 25 years as a TV news anchor and four novels later, Larry is the author of funny, feel-good fiction. His novel Déjà vu All Over Again won a 2019 Independent Book Publishers Association Award for fiction. He lives and writes at the Brill Creative Industrial Complex in Austin, Texas.

www.ingramcontent.com/pod-product-compliance
Lightning Source LLC
Chambersburg PA
CBHW030550260626
47157CB00006B/2252